Praise for Th

'It's dark and violent, a gc
Thrones *and* X-M

'Astonishingly good. ★★★★★' Sun

'T.K. Hall has produced an original, savage, powerful and
incredibly moving story. He captures the harshness and
darkness of the ancient woodland so vividly; it is like the
author himself has slid back in time. Robin and Marian are
like you have never seen, and I am sure this novel will grip
anyone who reads it, as it thoroughly gripped me'
Jilly Cooper, Mail on Sunday

'*A bold interpretation that's weird, wild and
wonderful*. . . Game of Thrones-*style*'
SFX Magazine

'Magic. If you love Alan Garner, Mythico Wood, wild
gods and wild places then read Shadow of the Wolf.
Reading this book takes me back to that place in my teens
where a book carried me away from all the worries of the
world and the chaos in my head to another place. Breathless.
Haunting. Wild. Magic' Jackie Morris, co-creator of
The Lost Words *and* The Lost Spells

WILD WOOD RISING

T. K. HALL

David Fickling Books

Wildwood Rising
The Blind Bowman: Book 3
is a
DAVID FICKLING BOOK

First published in Great Britain in 2025 by
David Fickling Books,
31 Beaumont Street,
Oxford, OX1 2NP
EU Rep: Authorised Rep Compliance Ltd., Ground Floor,
71 Lower Baggot Street, Dublin, D02 P593,
Ireland.
www.arccompliance.com

www.davidficklingbooks.com

Text © T. K. Hall, 2025

Cover by Leo Nickolls

978-1-78845-331-8

1 3 5 7 9 10 8 6 4 2

Papers used by David Fickling Books are from
well-managed forests and other responsible sources.

MIX
Paper | Supporting
responsible forestry
FSC® C018072

DAVID FICKLING BOOKS Reg. No. 8340307

A CIP catalogue record for this book is available from the British Library.

Typeset in 10/13.25 pt Baskerville by Falcon Oast Graphic Art Ltd.
Printed and bound in Great Britain by Clays, Ltd, Elcograf S.p.A.

For Lizzie, Beatrix and Matilda

How long must you wander this wasted world?
How much time has already passed? A day – a month – a year?
Impossible to tell. The seasons ended when the great forest burned.
All time since has been but a single midwinter's night.

Why, then, won't you lie down to die?
This body is ravaged – as blackened as the ground on which it walks.
Every breath is torture to your lungs. Every footfall hot needles in
your bones. Your mind screams to perceive what the Earth has become.

Yet still you drag this walking corpse across this lifeless land. Perhaps
death simply does not want you. Not after all you did – all you failed
to do.

Or is there some yearning, even now, drawing you onwards? Some
promise of . . . what? Redemption? Vengeance? No – these are mere
phantoms – more so than they ever were.
What then . . . ? Refuge?

Yes. That is what you seek.

Even now, when all else is lost, you cling to that final hope. That you
might find a place to welcome you home. Where you may lay down this
hollow flesh, this burden of guilt and grief, and allow the dust and the
years to blow over you.

Where at last you may cease all your struggles . . .

And sleep your final, never-ending sleep . . .

Prologue

'The wind's rising,' Lucas called out to his sister as dust eddied around his feet. 'Time to find shelter.'

'Just a little further,' Arora called back. 'We're on track today. I can feel it.'

'That's what you said yesterday, and the day before that. And what have we found? A few clipped shillings. Some arrowheads.'

'Which were the surest sign of all,' Arora said, her head low to the ground, like a hound following a scent. 'I'm telling you, little brother, our luck's on the turn.'

One of these days you're going to push our luck too far, Lucas thought to himself. He paused to peer back the way they had come, then swept his gaze across this whole blasted landscape. It was always a dismal place, the bare ground grey and eroded, layered with dust and sand. From horizon to horizon it was featureless, save for the occasional naked hillock or stone-dry riverbed or shadowy ravine. But today, to Lucas's eyes, the Lost Lands appeared more wretched than ever. Not so much as a lone buzzard broke that hard white sky. No sign of even a sand serpent or a lizard.

He turned and hurried after his sister. At first, with a spike of fear, he failed to see her. Like him, she was dressed head-to-toe in sand-coloured rags. They kept scarves wrapped around their mouths and noses to keep out the cloying dust, and their hoods raised against the punishing sun. To soften the glare of white light that blazed off the leafless ground, they wore bone blinders with narrow slits.

Dressed like this, Arora blended with the landscape, especially now she had stopped and dropped to one knee. As Lucas fixed his gaze on her at last, something else caught the top edge of his vision. It was a hulking white outline.

'Sis, up that way – a fallen tree,' he said, hurrying to her side. 'We can take cover there.'

'All right. We'll go as soon as I've got this.'

She was using her knife to chisel away at the sun-baked soil. As she dug around the object, one edge of it gleamed. Despite his eagerness to get on their way, Lucas watched, intrigued. And when she finally stood with the find, brushing it clean of dry soil, he stared, spellbound. The object was made of copper. It was dented and discoloured. But there was no doubting what it had once been. It was a goblet.

'It really belonged to them?' he said in hushed tones, as she offered it to him. 'To the outlaws of Sherwood?'

'Who else?' She smiled. 'Whose lips do you think it touched? Will Scarlett? Blodwyn Kage?'

'What do you think it's worth?'

Arora shrugged. 'These things are trinkets. Father always said so. One day we'll be standing in Robin Hood's Cave. Then you'll see what treasure means!'

She was moving off again, but Lucas remained where he was, cradling the goblet in both palms, his mind full of wonders. The twins were twelve years old – too young to have ever known the fabled forest, Sherwood, that they say once carpeted this land. Growing up, their father had told them endless stories of it. How the wildwood was so saturated with life that you could not set your foot upon the ground without creatures scurrying

4

from your path. How when you needed to eat you had only to reach up and pluck fruit from a tree. When thirsty, you merely knelt at a spring or a stream.

Wandering the wastes, treading this cursed earth, Lucas often found these stories hard to believe. Except at moments like this. Standing here, holding this relic from that mythical past. From that golden age of heroes and gods, when forest fighters lived in the treetops and waged war against the enemies of the wild!

From the west came a hollow howl. In the distance, a column of dust spiralled skywards. Hurriedly stowing the goblet in his backpack, he hastened after his sister.

Ahead of him, she had dwindled to almost nothing. She appeared to be moving to lower ground. And as he gained on her, he saw that, yes, she had entered a wide depression – like a bowl scooped out of the earth.

He moved down the slope after her. The ground down here was different: it was dotted with smooth, round pebbles, and with tiny bones fused into rock.

'There was water here,' Arora said as he joined her. She was kneeling once more, digging again with her blade. 'I think it was a lake.'

A lake.

Lucas stared around him, trying to make it real – to envisage this great expanse filled with sparkling water and swimming with life. The effort was beyond him. Look at it now. As the sun lowered, becoming red and angry, it bathed the whole bowl in a crimson hue. It made the land look raw, like flesh peeled of skin.

Again the plain howled, heavier and more tormented than before, and the wind reached Lucas with enough force to pelt him with grit.

'Whatever that is, sis, leave it. There's a dust storm brewing. We need to go.'

'I've almost got it,' she said, through gritted teeth, twisting her blade. 'It was buried deep, but I think . . . Ah ha, yes, here it is!'

She stood with the object resting in her palm. It was made of greenish rock, like jade. It was in the shape of a teardrop . . . or a heart.

'What is it?'

'An amulet,' she said, delighted. 'Or . . . a love charm! Yes – look – this fissure down the middle – I think it was in two halves! The heat of the Great Fire must have fused them together!' She grinned as she pocketed the charm. 'I told you our luck had turned. What will we find next?'

They headed towards the fallen tree they could see on the far side of the old lake, the wind swirling around them as they went, stirring dust and dead flies.

Climbing up out of the bowl, they came in clear sight of the tree. Fire had stripped it to a bare skeleton. The sun had bleached it white as bone. At close quarters, it was enormous. Even lying on its side, its trunk towered over the twins.

And now they could see it was not alone. Beyond the first tree, they found the scattered remains of another two, and a fourth – and more. There must have been dozens of these trees in all. They arched up from ground like colossal ribcages and backbones.

'It's a giants' graveyard,' Arora said, her voice hushed as they moved deeper amid the remains.

Lucas wrapped his robes close, feeling chilled. The sun was setting and the temperature was falling fast. Night-mist, green and sickly, was seeping up through the cracked soil and snaking through the twisted skeletons of the trees.

'Look!' Arora whispered. 'Do you see it? Is it a mirage, or . . .'

Both of them stopped dead and stared. The mist had swirled aside to unveil a phenomenal sight.

It was another ancient, broken tree. Except this one had not been uprooted. Instead, the trunk had snapped, leaving behind a hulking stump. But what amazed the twins – what held them here, awestruck – was the fact that this stump appeared to still be *living*. Green shoots grew up out of its exposed roots. Its top was bushy with shrubs, like the hair on an old man's head. All around its base sprouted wildflowers and ferns and even small saplings.

In all their journeying across these wastes, the twins had only ever seen scraps of vegetation: the occasional corpse flower, or clump of burn weed. And now, here in the middle of these ash-white bonelands, there blazed this beacon of green.

'Here's our refuge,' Arora whispered, as wind moaned outside the Giants' Graveyard. 'See – the stump is hollow. There's our way in.'

As she moved towards the green oasis, Lucas stayed put, suddenly on full alert. He drew his slingshot and knelt to pick up a rock. A flash of something had crossed his path. There – he saw it again. The blur of reddish fur, the flash of golden eyes.

Whirring his slingshot, he stared into the shadows beneath the twisted trees. He saw nothing more, yet had the intense impression he was being watched. There was *something* there, studying him, he was sure there was . . .

'Sis, wait,' he called, going after Arora. 'This place . . . Something's wrong.'

'It keeps out the wind, doesn't it? What more do you want? Are you going to let me do all the work, as usual?'

She had collected a pile of firewood, and was now dragging it towards the ancient tree stump. On this side of the stump was a triangular fissure, like the jagged entrance to a cave. Arora was now edging backwards into it, disappearing into the blackness.

Scurrying to pick up sticks she had dropped, then pausing to sweep one last look around the Giants' Graveyard, Lucas ducked in after her.

7

Inside was a world of its own. The walls of this tree-cave must have been as solid as stone, because every last murmur from outside now died away. The aroma in here was fresh and green, albeit with a hint of decay. The ground was soft with mulch, which emitted a slight warmth, putting Lucas in mind of a creature's burrow.

'See,' Arora whispered. 'The perfect place to overnight.'

It was almost pitch-black in there, though. Working by touch, in tandem, the twins built a small pyramid of kindling. Lucas added a spark from his strike-a-light, and then they carefully fed the flames with sticks. The fire ate greedily, the fuel bone-dry, the hollow tree stump acting as a natural chimney.

From his backpack, Lucas took a large sand-rat he had trapped that morning. He quickly skinned it with his hunting knife, then started skewering it onto a sharpened stick.

But then he paused. He put down the stick and the rat. He picked up his knife.

Then he became very still. Arora was already motionless. The noise of her breathing. The faintest moan of the wind outside, and the pop-crackle of the fire.

Finally, Lucas said: 'We're not alone, are we? There's something in here with us.'

Arora gave a slight nod. 'What do you think it is?'

He went on staring. The twisting light of the flames. The blackness at the rear of the tree-cave.

'It looks . . . man-shaped,' he said.

'Does it?' Arora murmured. 'I thought I saw fur.'

'It hasn't moved. Maybe it's dead.'

Arora lifted a burning brand from the fire.

'What are you doing?' he hissed.

'We need to look closer.'

'What? . . . No!'

But she was already on her feet, and was moving towards the

back of the chamber. Lucas went after her, his eyes fixed on the menacing silhouette. That black shape in the deeper blackness.

As they edged closer, and the shape resolved itself, Lucas took hold of Arora, hissed in alarm.

'Sis . . . Don't!'

'It's all right,' she murmured. 'He can't hurt us.'

'H-how do you know?'

'You were right,' she said. 'He's dead.' Freeing herself from her brother's grip, she edged forward. 'After all this time . . . how could he not be?'

'H-he?' Lucas stammered. 'It's . . . human?'

Arora crouched in front of the dark figure, lifted her light, illuminating a deathly face. 'Don't you know who this is?' she murmured. 'What we've found?'

'You don't think . . . It's not actually . . .'

'Who else could it be? Just look. Exactly the way Father described – just like in all the stories.' She turned with the torch, and she was smiling, and her eyes were wide. 'I told you we were in luck's way, didn't I? Trust me, little brother, this is worth more than a treasure hoard. This will change *everything*. Me and you . . . We just found Robin Hood.'

Part One

Buried Seeds

I. Bloodlines

'On your guard!'

At the clipped command of his swordmaster, Rex set his fighting stance. Gripping his ironwood blade, he met the eyes of his opponent. He was a tough ranger named Neville. He was twice Rex's age and built like a bull. But he would not get the better of Rex – not today. Not with his father watching.

Rex raised his eyes, briefly. There, on the viewing platform, was his swordmaster, Alpha Johns. And standing next to him was Rex's father. He held himself as still as stone and might almost be a statue, except for those eyes of his which blazed ice-blue and missed nothing. Rex's grip tightened on his sword, and he stood ready.

The sun was low, its red glow touching the battlements. But even at this hour it was sweltering in the combat yard, Rex already sweating beneath the padding of his sparring suit. A hot wind was blowing too. It came from the west, howling out of the wastes, roaring up through the city streets before reaching the castle. The wind carried with it grit and dust, a fresh flurry of which now found its way over the ramparts and down into the yard, where it swirled across the cobbles.

His every nerve braced for battle, Rex ignored the howling

wind, refused to acknowledge the dry taste of it in his mouth or the itch at the back of his throat.

Finally, Alpha gave the command.

'Begin!'

Neville came heavily forward, hefting his weighty training sword. Rex circled, giving his bigger opponent space. Rex feinted left, spun right – just in time to avoid Neville's blade as it swept down in an overhead strike.

Rex counterattacked with two quick hits aimed at the midriff, which Neville turned with a backhand defence. Neville attacked once more – a vicious reverse that would have floored Rex had he not ducked away a moment before.

For all Neville's size, he was quick on his feet, and in these opening exchanges Rex found himself on the retreat, meeting his opponent's barrage with soft blocks and snatched counter-attacks. As he was driven back across the yard, and the dust swirled around his feet, he felt his courage slip. A small voice whispered that his confidence had been misplaced – that he would leave here in disgrace.

The wind strengthened, howling around the ramparts so heavily that a pennant was torn from its pole and flapped away towards the Keep. With each breath, Rex felt the hot dust tightening in his chest, and for a moment he feared it would be this that defeated him.

No – not today – I won't allow it, he told himself, while his father looked on. *This fight is mine!*

With a quick flick of his blade and a feint, Rex spun away from Neville, leaving him thrashing at thin air. Rex attacked from Neville's blindside, forcing his opponent into a desperate improvised defence. While he was off balance, Rex struck again and again, darting around his adversary, slashing at his legs, his chest, his midriff.

'Hit!' Alpha called out from the viewing platform as Rex's

blade stuck his opponent on the knee. The impact was cushioned by his padded leather greave, but even so the blow made Neville groan and stumble, and before he could properly regain his feet, Alpha was calling, 'Hit!' once more as Rex's sword caught him square on the shoulder.

Neville was on the back foot now, flailing, all precision gone from his parries, no proper form in his stance. Rex, in contrast, had found perfect poise and rhythm, his years of practice condensed down into this moment – this flick of the sword – his blade in fact now operating of its own accord as it swept left and right, probing for openings, narrowly missing Neville's padded helm and the decisive strike that would end this contest.

His eyes, of their own volition, darted once more to his father, his cold gaze as inscrutable as ever. Was he impressed by what he saw? Proud of his son for so easily besting a veteran of the Guard?

These thoughts came and went, Rex's full focus locked once more on his opponent. Building on his dominance, he increased the intensity of his attacks, which kept Neville flailing like a baited bear. It would not be long now. Soon, one of these strikes would land and Rex would be crowned victorious.

Another surge of wind, even heavier than the last, howled over the battlements and down into the yard. It lifted grit and sand from the cobbles and hurled it at the swordsmen.

The bombardment hit Rex in the back. It caught Neville full in the face. The ranger cried out in pain as he lifted his free hand to his eyes.

To Rex, everything became slow and clear. His opponent's sword waved uselessly before him. His head was fully exposed. Strike now, and Rex would win this contest.

Yet his own blade remained still. He just watched Neville trying to force open his eyes, tears streaming down his cheeks.

Afterwards, Rex could not have said how long he hesitated.

But in that space of time, the world spun on its head. In pain, enraged, Neville roared and lashed out blindly. The blow was so unexpected that Rex failed to raise his guard. It caught him full in the chest and sent him sprawling.

Perhaps this surprised Neville as much as it did Rex, because the ranger made no move to build on his advantage but merely stood there, blinking, his eyes red and streaming. Rex tried to stand, but failed. The blow had left him breathless. And now, as he had feared, his lungs betrayed him. Succumbing to the hot dust, he began to cough and cough, curling into a ball as he wheezed and gasped for air.

Through blurred eyes, as he fought for breath, he watched Neville just standing there, looking pained and uncertain. Then the big ranger dropped to one knee, bowed his head.

Rex saw why. His father had left the viewing platform and was coming down the steps into the combat yard. He made his slow way towards the swordsmen, his black robes billowing in the wind.

The Sheriff stopped and looked down at Rex. The ruined side of his face, puckered like melted wax, was livid in the last light of day. But his expression remained neutral, his cold blue eyes giving nothing away. Finally, without moving his gaze from Rex, he addressed Neville.

'Who ordered you to halt the contest?'

The ranger raised his head. 'Sire? I . . .' He glanced towards Rex's sword, which lay out of arm's reach. 'My . . . my opponent is defenceless, sire.'

'As were you, when you were blinded by the grit. You were at my son's mercy. Yet he hesitated. I trust you will not make the same mistake.'

With both hands, Neville gripped his ironwood sword. 'You mean, you wish me to . . .?'

'I wish you to finish the contest. Nothing more, nothing less.

You know the rules. Three clean strikes to the body, or one to the head.'

'Wait,' Rex said, fighting for breath, struggling to stand. 'I can continue.'

'Certainly – should your opponent allow you the chance.' The Sheriff looked fully at Neville. 'Of course, if he should lose this fight, from such a position of advantage, he will have proved himself unworthy to be a ranger of the Guard.'

Rex made a lunge for his sword. This galvanized Neville into action, and he brought his own blade thumping down onto Rex's back. The blow flattened Rex, drove the air once more from his lungs. He broke into another coughing fit. Above the noise of his own rasping, he heard his father say: 'Hit. Continue . . . Ranger, I said continue.'

After a pause, the heavy, blunt-edged sword thundered down once more. Even through the padding of his sparring suit the blow was jarring, pain shooting through Rex's ribs. Already rasping for air, he now endured nightmare moments were he was entirely unable to breathe.

'You pulled your strike. No hit,' he heard his father say to the big guard. 'Continue.'

The ironwood sword slammed down once more, heavier than before. And it crashed down a third time, and a fourth, while the Sheriff berated the soldier for his poor form.

'No hit. Again.'

Thrice more the blade came down, while Rex shuddered and shook and coughed, while his breath rasped in his lungs and black spots swam before his eyes.

There was a pause. He braced himself for the next strike. It never came. He went on coughing, until finally the fit subsided and he became still. Tears pricked behind his eyes. He bit his lip hard and focused on the pain.

Finally, he rolled onto his back and looked up, the world

blurred. Neville was nowhere to be seen. But his father was still here, his hands behind his back, watching him. He looked pale faced now, and his chest heaved visibly as though he was struggling to draw his own breath.

'You are aware,' the Sheriff said at last, speaking slowly, 'what age I was when I became the Sheriff of Nottingham? I was fifteen years old. The age you are now. I did not have the luxury of sparring swords. Of second chances. At my word, fighting men lived and died. Stand up, son. Look at me.'

His lungs on fire, every inch of him throbbing with pain, Rex rose as steadily as he was able, forced himself to hold his father's gaze.

'I see defiance in your eyes,' the Sheriff said. 'Perhaps even a shard of hatred. Do you suppose I am wounded by it? Let me assure you of one thing. My role, as your father, is not to be loved. Nor even to be liked. It is a father's role to shape his son for purpose. To forge him into the man he must become. Make no mistake, I will play my role, no matter what it may take.'

With that, sweeping his black cloak around him, his father turned and strode away, until he was swallowed into the shadows beneath the Keep.

Hanging his head, Rex listened to the howling of the wind. The swordmaster came to stand at his side.

'You know,' Alpha said, 'not every father cares enough to teach their son a lesson.'

Rex ground his teeth. 'I should count myself lucky.'

'He sees greatness in you. We all do. But this path of yours won't get any easier. So yes, perhaps in time you'll be grateful for his methods.' He put a big hand on Rex's shoulder. 'But you've had enough for one day. Come on, let's get out of this wind. I'll help you stow your equipment, then we'll raid the kitchens, what do you say?'

*

It was fully dark by the time Rex walked back through the castle, past the bustle of the scullery, through the Inner Ward. Watchfires now blazed atop the ramparts, the flames frenzied in the wind. Sentries were calling watchwords from one tower to another. From the direction of the stables came the whinnying of horses, and the stamp of hooves. This wind was spreading agitation throughout the whole castle. Scullions and apprentices dashed here and there, while their masters shouted and doors slammed.

For Rex's part, he was too sore and exhausted to care about anything other than reaching his bed. Now that his blood had cooled, the pain in his ribs was sharper than ever, and he felt unsteady on his feet.

When he reached the White Tower, two sentries snapped to attention. A third man rapped on the iron-studded door with the butt of his spear, before a porter heaved it open. None of these people looked Rex in the eye, only stared dead ahead as he went inside and started up the spiral staircase.

He passed the small dining hall and the receiving rooms, and continued to the top floor chambers – the so-called Queen's Apartments.

As he walked along the corridor towards the Solar, he became aware of a disturbance. From the other side of the double doors came a crash, followed by a yell.

'I said, get out! All of you! Now!'

There was a heavy thump and something smashed, before the doors burst open and three body-servants came rushing out. They almost ran straight into Rex, then stopped, wringing their hands.

'B-begging your pardon, my lord,' one of the young women stammered, looking fearfully back towards the Solar at the sound of another crash. 'We only went to light the lamps and to help her try on her new garments.'

There came an almighty thump, and the sound of something breaking, at which the servants jumped, and one began to cry.

'It's all right,' Rex told them. 'I'll talk to her.'

'B-but your father,' the first maid stammered. 'His orders were—'

'It can't be helped,' Rex said. 'If anyone asks, I told you to leave.'

The young women glanced at one another, looked at Rex with a mixture of fear and relief, then stepped around him and fled.

Rex continued to the double doors. As he entered the Solar, something sailed towards his head. He ducked away and the flask exploded against the wall, splattering it with red liquid.

'I said, leave me be!' his mother shouted, preparing to hurl another missile before blinking and fixing her gaze on him. 'Oh, it's you. Where have you been?'

Rex took in the scene. The usual opulence of the Solar had given way to ruin and disarray. Heirloom furniture had been tipped over; the big gilt-edged mirror had been smashed to smithereens. Garments lay strewn everywhere.

His mother's appearance echoed the chaos. She was half dressed in kirtle and tunic. Her hair was knotted and dishevelled. Dark lines of face-kohl ran down her cheeks like black tears. At her feet was a large flask, its stopper removed, dribbling the last of its contents.

'Yes, I've had some wine,' she said, fixing him with an unfocused glare. 'Why shouldn't I? You leave me here with these parasites. These sycophants.'

'You frightened the maids. You could have just asked them to leave.'

'You've been running around playing toy soldiers, I suppose. Acting the little prince. You know what I've been doing? Listening to dukes and lordlings singing my praises – smiling while they bring me gifts. Look at all this – look at it!'

She kicked at the garments on the ground, and stamped on them. 'They all want to see me wearing their dresses – like I'm their private doll to be prettied!' She scooped up a brocaded gown, then began hunting the room, flinging open cabinets, sweeping objects off tables. 'I need a knife! Why can I never find a knife when I need one! He tells them to hide them, I swear! Nothing sharp – nothing real!'

Giving up the search, she attempted to destroy the gown with her bare hands, tearing at its sleeves. 'Do you have any idea what it's like for me, sitting there nodding my head, admiring their wit, when I want to slit every one of their throats! All his flatterers and lapdogs!'

'Mother – calm yourself. What's happened?'

'Nothing's *happened*. Nothing ever happens! We sit in this gilded cage, waiting for the world to end. Except it already has! He ended it! And what do these fools do? They bring him gifts – and me – his queen! They honour the man who killed the world! We're already in hell – where else could we be?'

'Mother, please, you're delirious. I don't know what you're talking about.'

'No – you don't, poor boy.' She laughed – a mean sound, and desperate. 'Oh, there are things I could tell you, little prince, that would spin your head. You better leave me – go on – before I gabble it all and be damned.'

Rex set himself. 'I won't leave you like this. You need—'

'I said go! I – I want to be alone.' She gave up trying to destroy the gown, dropped it to the ground. As she did so, all the fury abruptly went out of her and she slumped back onto a padded bench. 'Please,' she said softly, without looking at him. 'I . . . think . . . I need some time to myself.'

Rex looked at her, weathering a storm of resentment and regret, wanting to go to his mother, to help her, but something holding him back. Knowing in any case that it would be futile.

Now that the fire had burned out of her, there was barely anything left. She looked pitiful, sitting there with those slug-trails of kohl on her cheeks. She looked . . . old. Her skin wan and her shoulders slumped. Even her eyes – those vital, varicoloured eyes of grey and green – had suddenly lost their lustre, and had become watery and vacant.

Rex had seen his mother like this before, of course, on many occasions. Often after one of her outbursts she would retreat into the opposite state. She would sit motionless, unblinking, as though staring into the deep past. These melancholies could last for hours, or days, or even weeks. How long would she remain buried in this one? Was there anything he might do to pull her out of it?

He shook his head. He knew from experience that nothing and no one could reach her when she was like this. Only time could bring her back to him.

So thinking, with sorrow and exhaustion pressing upon him like a dead weight, he slouched away to his bedchamber, desperate to lose himself in the oblivion of sleep.

II. Captive Queen

Locked in her stupor – in this hateful state between wakefulness and sleep – Marian was unable to say what had actually occurred and what she might have dreamed. She had a memory of fat men with red bulbous faces – and they were showering her with gifts.

And afterwards . . . she had talked to Rex, hadn't she? Had they argued? She had the vaguest recollection of lashing out with her tongue – of wanting to hurt him with her words. Why? What had he done? What might she have said to him? Not knowing sent a jolt of fear down her spine, sufficient to shake her from her trance.

She blinked around her, as if waking, taking in the disorder of the Solar. The remains of amphorae. The smashed statuettes. She barely remembered doing any of this. Her head throbbed and her vision was fuzzy. How long had she been lost in her blank melancholy? The moon was full and high, casting its bluish light through the large oval embrasure. She judged it was a little after midnight.

Unsteadily, she stood, her head pounding, and she went down the corridor to Rex's bedchamber. The door was ajar. She stood looking in. Rex lay sprawled on his back, bare-chested, half-covered by a sheet.

She crept inside and knelt at his bedside and watched him sleeping. As she did so, she suffered a wave of emotion for which she had no name. Sadness and dread and regret all rolled into one. Gods alive, look at him! He was a man already.

Yes, that formed the core of this heart-wrenching emotion: a sudden jolting fear at the passing of time; as if she had blinked and years had slipped by. How had her baby boy become this? Those broad muscles of his chest. That untamed, shoulder-length hair. That dark, flawless skin, just like hers when she was his age. Those strong lines of his jaw and cheekbones, so much like his –

She severed this thought at the root. Over the years she had trained herself to push such ideas from her mind, as if even to think them would be too dangerous . . .

As she watched him, and the wind howled against the tower, Rex became restless. His breathing became more rapid and uneven. He tossed his head from side to side, his eyes visibly darting beneath the lids.

'No, you can't . . .' he murmured. 'You mustn't. It must live . . .'

She stroked his hair. 'Shh, it's all right. You're having a bad dream. You're safe. You're here with me.'

He began thrashing his limbs, as though trying to wake himself, and he gabbled more fearful words. It wrenched Marian's heart to see him like this. All his life he had been visited by night terrors. She examined one of his bare arms, and she saw, as she suspected, that the skin there was chapped and raw. This was another of his afflictions: vulcanism of the skin. It often erupted when he was most agitated.

'It's just a dream,' she whispered, shaking him gently. 'Whatever it is you're seeing, it can't hurt you. It doesn't exist.'

Abruptly, Rex awoke, startling her as he sat bolt upright, wildness in his eyes and his bared teeth. He took hold of her, one hand closing around her throat.

'Rex, it's me,' she gasped, catching her breath. 'You're safe. You were having a nightmare.'

He stared at her. Slowly the savage look left him and he lowered his arms.

'Wherever it is you go, I wish I could come with you,' she told him. 'I'd face it for you in a heartbeat, you know that.'

He lay back down, turned his face away.

'You don't need to be ashamed,' she said.

'I'm not.'

'Your arms look sore. I'll fetch something for it.'

She went out and returned with her apothecary casket. She took out a balm made from willow bark and primrose and field mallow, and she began applying it to his arm.

'There's no need,' he said blankly. 'It's fine.'

'Your skin is on fire. I can see it is. This will douse the flames.'

He shrugged her off. 'I said stop.'

As he rolled away from her, he winced. He tried to wrap himself in the covers, but not before she had caught sight of his ribs.

'Those bruises – how did this happen?' she demanded. 'Now what's he been making you do?' She lifted the bedclothes and hissed between her teeth. His whole back was shades of black and yellow and blue. 'Rex – you need to tell me – what happened? He might have killed you!'

He pulled the bedclothes away from her. 'As if you'd care,' he mumbled. 'I doubt you'd even notice.'

This sat Marian back on her heels. She took a long breath, watching Rex, not knowing whether she wanted to yell at him or sob or scream. Finally, she closed her eyes, laid a hand on the back of his neck.

'It's happened a lot recently, hasn't it?' she said quietly. 'I've been . . . absent.' She stroked his hair. 'But I'm here now. And I'm staying, I promise.' As the wind moaned, ghostly against the tower, and moonlight bathed the chamber, she leaned towards him. 'What's more . . . I'll prove it. What would you say to an adventure?'

Finally he half-turned and opened one eye.

'What kind of an adventure?'

She smiled. 'As a matter of fact, I've had something in mind for some time.' Her smile widened, a hint of madness in her grey-green eyes. 'It's not for the fainthearted. Do you think you're up to it with those bruises? Of course you are. All right then. Get dressed, quick as you can. With this moon, and this wind – yes – tonight's the night we've been waiting for!'

What lunacy was this? What had possessed Rex to follow his mother out into this wild night? Just what did she have in mind?

To avoid the sentries at the foot of the tower, they had climbed out of the big oval embrasure, then clambered down using the ivy that grew all across the stonework. From there, wearing their dark cloaks and hoods, they had crept across the Great Ward and the inner cloisters, then used more vines to climb up the side of the Scullery, and were now scampering across its tiled roof.

The wind tore at Rex and forced him to stay low and fight for his footing. Ahead of him his mother leaped across the gap that led onto the roofs of the kitchens. To his brief alarm, it was not a clean jump, leaving her sprawled on the far side. But quick enough she was up and running on once more. Rex made the leap, landing with a jolt of pain in his ribs, then scampered after her.

In spite of himself, he found he was grinning. So many times, when he was younger, he and his mother had run reckless adventures like this. In his mind, *this* was his mother, and always would be – this figure ahead of him, bursting with life, full of surprises and schemes.

She was crouched now, one hand raised. Rex knelt at her side. 'Bandogs down below,' she whispered.

'They won't catch our scent – not with this wind.'

She smiled at him. 'What about those sentries in the barbican tower?'

'They're too close to their watchfire. It'll make them blind.'

Her smile widened, and she nodded. 'So then, our path is clear. You take the lead from here. We're heading for the Menagerie.'

'We are? Why?'

'You'll see. Trust me, it'll be worth it. Go on – get going.'

Rex went onwards, using creepers to rappel to the ground, before flitting past the Guards' Barracks and the Arsenal, sticking close to the buildings, his dark form and that of his mother's blending with the moon-shadows.

They crept together past the aviaries: row after row of goshawks and gyrfalcons sitting on their perches, their eyes stitched shut to blunt their hunting instincts. Then they were stopping again on the edge of the Menagerie. It was a menacing looking place in the moonlight, with its heavy cages and the shadowy, half-seen shapes within.

'What are we—' Rex began, before his mother cut him short.

'There's someone coming,' she whispered. 'Out of sight!'

They hid behind a shed used for storing carcasses for animal feed, the stench of old meat thick in Rex's throat as he held still and watched. Two figures were now clearly visible, moving amid the cages, the light of their storm-lamps gleaming off the iron bars and sometimes catching too the gleam of dark fur, the glint of yellow eyes.

The older, hunched figure was the beastmaster. Rex recognized him by his limp. The young man at his side must be his apprentice. The pair of them moved slowly down the line, lifting their lamps to peer into cages, eliciting here and there a growl or a hiss from the creatures within.

'You're always hearing phantoms,' Rex heard the old man

grumble. 'This wind stirs them up, that's all it is. Let's get back indoors.'

The glow of their lamps turned and dwindled and was gone.

'Path clear,' Rex's mother whispered, excited. 'Here – take these. You remember how, don't you? I'll start that side, you start this. And be quick!'

To Rex's astonishment, she had pushed a set of metal rods into his hand. They were curved at each end. Lockpicks. Did she really mean to . . .? Yes – she did – and she was already doing it! Going to the first of the big cages, she was working at the lock.

'Mother – what are you doing?' he hissed, going to her side. His heart was thundering, and he didn't know if he was exhilarated or horrified. 'This is . . . it's . . .'

'It's long overdue,' his mother whispered, her eyes gleaming wild. 'You know where these creatures come from? They say there are mountains in the east that pierce the heavens. Forests as old as time. And now they live like this!'

Her voice, beneath the wind, did not sound like her own. Was she still wine-addled? Or had her sanity cracked?

He stared into the big cage. In the deepest shadows he could just make out a black sinuous shape. And a pair of piercing yellow eyes.

'Won't they attack us?' Rex murmured.

'What with? You think he'd keep them here if they were dangerous? He has their claws removed. Their teeth filed to stumps.'

As she said this, there was a metallic clunk and the lock released. Rex's disbelief spiked as his mother hauled the door open. Rex sprang away, expecting the creature to make a lunge for freedom. Instead, it remained huddled at the back of the cage.

'It's all right,' Marian whispered to it, standing there unafraid. 'You can go.'

Then she was on to the next cage, her fingers working the lockpicks. 'Come on,' she laughed to Rex. 'Get on with it. Free them all!'

Perhaps her madness was contagious – or was it this wild, moon-bright night making him lunatic – or just the untamed joy of seeing his mother once more full of fire and mischief? Whatever the reason, Rex found himself hurrying to help, going to the cage opposite hers and working its lock. As he did so, he sensed the creature within watching him. What was it thinking?

This beast was even larger than the last, and its fur was striped orange and black, like fire. It remained utterly motionless and silent as it watched him with amber eyes. Its smell washed out to him – a savage aroma of damp fur and old blood – and this made his heart thunder. It had been a long time since he had picked a lock but his mother had taught him well, and soon the mechanism clunked and the door fell open. Rex heaved it wide, and without daring to glance back he was onto the next cage.

'That's it, almost there,' his mother whispered. 'Three more to go.'

The next lock took Rex longer, his fingers starting to shake. He closed his eyes. One of the beasts was here – right at his back. He could smell its breath, feel the heat of it on his neck. But then, when he steeled his heart to turn, there was nothing there. He returned to his work, and soon the last cage yawned open.

'Come on, quick,' his mother whispered. 'We need a vantage point.'

Not far from the Menagerie was the soldiers' barracks. Climbing onto a loaded wagon, Marian led the way onto its roof. There they sat, in the shadow of the old watchtower, their hoods raised, and they watched.

The Menagerie now made a bizarre sight to Rex, all the cages standing wide open, and suddenly it seemed unreal that this was their doing. His heart lurched afresh as the first of the beasts padded out. It was the one with orange and black stripes. It moved with a power and grace that Rex found mesmerizing. It flowed like fire. It merged with deep shadow and disappeared.

As if this first was a signal to the others, all the other creatures began to emerge. Another big cat, this one as black as the night, sinuous as water. A bear, scarred all over, limping and growling and finally bellowing as it lumbered free. Other creatures hissing and snarling and prowling and darting away, some of them so quick that Rex barely caught a glimpse.

And now came the screams. From somewhere over by the barbican tower came a wail of terror, and Rex's mother smiled. Shouts and gargled yells filled the night air, and doors slammed, and people were running, and then all across the castle there was pandemonium.

'The beast – the beast has come!'

'Lord save us!'

'Guards! To arms!'

The wind howled, carrying sounds of fear – shouts for help and calls of alarm and horrified cries, mixed with the terrified whinnying of horses.

'You're sure they won't hurt anyone?'

His mother shook her head. 'These predators are for show only. Mind you,' she added, as more screams filled the air, 'not everybody knows that. And the fear is real enough.' She smiled. 'This castle has slept long enough. It's time to wake up!'

By now the barracks had burst open and soldiers were pouring out, half dressed, gripping spears and crossbows. From somewhere unseen, Rex heard the hiss-thwack of quarrels letting loose, followed by a howl of animal pain.

'They'll kill them,' Rex said, the realization only now hitting him. 'They can't get out of the castle grounds. They'll corner them and kill them all.'

'They were already dead,' his mother said. 'Worse than dead, caged like that. This . . . will be a mercy.'

As she said this, her tone changed. Turning to her, he saw that her wild jubilation had given way to a pensive expression. Her eyes were glazed, as if looking at something far away, or long ago. Rex suffered a pang of loss. Was it finished, then? Was his mother once more sinking into herself, leaving him here alone on the surface?

Rex hugged his knees, listening to the grunts and growls and howls of pain. A heavy creature slumped to the ground with a last bellow, and people were shouting, barking orders.

At some point, Rex realized that all these sounds were dying down. And so was the wind. On the battlements, flags and pennants barely fluttered. The moon had taken on a ghostly glow. In an hour or so it would be dawn.

'So then, that's done,' his mother said in a dead tone. 'For better or worse. For what it was worth.'

Something told Rex these were the last words he would hear from her for some time, and indeed she raised her hood and held her silence as they stood and returned the way they had come, sneaking like phantoms back towards the safety and seclusion of the tower.

III. Lost Company

Kit and his warriors crouched out of sight amid a thicket of bramble and briar. A bowshot behind them lay the wastes. Ahead of them, the land dropped away towards an old riverbed. The slopes were covered with scrub and mean farmland. Down there, too, nestled in the lee of the hillside, was a village. An unremarkable scattering of longhouses and crofts, with only one droving route in or out, it was the kind of place that the rest of the world might have entirely forgotten.

Except they hadn't. Because today twelve strong horses stood tethered in the nearby orchard, and red-cloaked soldiers were stomping into the village. They had with them a captive: a boy of around ten years old, whom they shoved and kicked ahead of them. His hands were tied behind his back, one of his eyes was swollen shut and there was blood around his nose and mouth.

'We couldn't have timed it better,' whispered Ira Starr, her green eyes glinting in the shadows of the briar. 'Looks like they're planning a show trial.'

Midge Millerson grinned, his cleft cheek turning it into a hideous leer. 'Ha – we'll give them a little show of our own.'

There were seven outlaws in total, every one of them as scarred and gnarled as the wastelands, each of them gripping a trusted, much-bloodied blade. Every set of eyes remained locked on the village as the soldiers herded the peasants onto the common green.

At the centre of the green, where the Trystel Tree once stood, towered a stone statue. It was identical to those scattered all through the shires, in all the larger villages and the market towns and at every crossroads. It depicted the Sheriff of Nottingham, his musculature exaggerated, his face unblemished. In one hand he held a spear, which he was thrusting into the heart of a forest serpent, the creature writhing in its death throes at his feet. In the shadow of this statue, all the peasants were now gathered.

One of villagers stepped forward. He was presumably the hetman. He was thin but tough-looking, his skin weather-beaten and leathery. He stood silent, defiant, while the lead soldier ranted at him and at the other villagers, occasionally gesturing to his captive or slapping him round the face with the back of his hand.

At that moment, Eric O'Lincoln returned, snake-crawling through the leaves to join the others among the brambles.

'What's it all about?' whispered Sonskya Luz. 'Did you get close enough to hear?'

Eric nodded. 'The boy is the hetman's son. They're accusing him of poaching. Caught him trapping rabbits in the warrens – on the edge of the Lost Lands. They say the warrens belong to the Sheriff.'

Much Millerson shifted heavily, gave a grunt of disgust. 'The Sheriff lays waste their world, then denies them the right even to scavenge in the ashes.'

'The boy's to be punished by the loss of a hand,' Eric continued. 'And they say the hetman himself must wield the axe.'

'Sadistic ones, eh?' said Jack Champion, hefting his twin scimitars. 'This will be my pleasure.'

'What concerns me is what they're doing here in the first

place,' said Ira, fitting a fresh string to her bow. 'They didn't ride out to the edge of the wastes just to bully peasants.'

'Wait – look – what's happening there?' Midge was pointing to the threshing barn. From behind it, four, five, six more peasants came into view. Each of them gripped a hayfork or a maul or a mattock.

'Seems these sheep have teeth,' said Jack.

Kit sighed. This was supposed to have been a routine patrol of the Lost Lands and a check on the boundaries; he had not anticipated running into any soldiers. If they had to fight, he wanted it to be a clean ambush. Moments ago, it would have been just that, the Sheriff's men at ease and complacent, too intent on menacing peasants to be on their guard. But now they were on full alert, drawing swords or winding crossbows. The captain of the squad was hollering orders at his followers and threats at the armed villagers.

'These swineherds have less sense than their pigs,' Midge sneered. 'They want to fight, we should leave them to it.'

'There's a lot of open ground between us and them,' said Ira. 'This could cost us.'

Kit watched the captain of the guard brandishing his bludgeon, threatening to kill the hetman unless the rebels lay down their arms. All this sent Kit spiralling back to the dark events of his childhood. Suddenly, that village down there might be Tyrwell, where he grew up. That hetman might be Leonhard Franks, a man who raised Kit like his own son. A man who was murdered, along with the rest of the villagers, in the name of the Sheriff.

Kit rose to his feet. 'We won't just stand aside,' he told the others. 'Ready yourselves.'

As he spoke, a powerful gust of wind suddenly arose at his back, lifting his cloak. With uncanny speed the wind intensified, hurling stalks of grass and sticks and grit. Still it blew heavier, bringing with it a cloud of dust, which rolled out of the wastes and enveloped them before continuing down towards the village.

The outlaws were looking at Kit as if this was his doing. It wasn't, but they didn't need to know that. As the wind strengthened further, and the veil of dust swirled, Kit gripped his bow and looked each one of them in the eye.

'There's our cover,' he told them. 'Strike hard and fast and they'll be dead before they know we're here.'

So saying, he broke from cover and led his marauders in a direct run for the village. With their heads lowered, their dark cloaks billowing in the wind, they were demons risen from the pit, murder blazing in their bloodshot eyes. They took the wind with them, wrapping them in a shroud of dust.

Even so, as always in the moments before battle, Kit suffered a stab of doubt. Was this the day his luck finally ran dry? Would it be here, in this nondescript place, that the last of Sherwood's rebels would lie down to die?

And then there was no more space for doubt, nor thought of any kind. Because the outlaws had slipped past the boundary stone and the first of the houses, and they were stalking across the green towards the statue of the Sheriff.

And now, directly ahead of Kit, a shape and colour had emerged from the dust. The figure of a man. The crimson colour of a cloak. And Kit's hands were drawing his bowstring, and his arm was coming up and taking aim of its own accord, and quicker than he could blink his arrow was gone and his foe was falling in a spray of blood.

All became a dream state then. The world slowed and speeded up in the same timeless instant. It fractured, becoming a scattershot of hard, hateful sounds and images. Like summer lightning in the blackest of skies.

To his right, a soldier was falling, a rock from Midge's slingshot removing his skull-helm and half of his skull with it.

Simultaneously, his father, Much, was staving in a ranger's head with his mighty quarterstaff. Another soldier raised his blade, but Kit's second arrow flashed and the man's severed hand dropped to the grass.

There were screams of shock and fear and fury, and there were fountains of blood, and Ira had trapped a ranger in a net and was skewering him with her dirks, Sonskya was slaying another man with her hatchets, and Kit's bow was singing a third time and a fourth, and Jack was slashing his bloody swords, and there were more screams and flashes of crimson amid the dust, and as quick as that it was done.

Kit spun in place, an arrow nocked, looking for his next mark, his heart beating hard and the killing fury still on him, unable or unwilling to believe there was no enemy left to slay. The bodkin of his arrow passed across peasants, all of whom stood frozen, staring at him, awestruck and terrified.

Finally, the wind abated, dropping as suddenly as it arose. As it did so, Kit's killing rage drained away and he stared around him at the sprawled soldiers, and finally he allowed himself to believe that the fight was won.

'Ha!' Midge leered madly, kicking at the corpse of the lead soldier. 'One minute they were bullying swineherds. The next that dust blew over them – and there were devils in it!'

While the villagers gathered, holding one another, some of them weeping, and the hetman embraced his son, Kit stepped through the battleground. He looked over to where the soldiers' horses were tethered. They were heavily laden, as if for a long expedition.

'Kit – there's a live one over here,' Eric O'Lincoln called from near the wellhead.

Kit joined him and the pair of them stood looking down at a soldier whose eyes were open. He was sweating and shaking and grimacing, while his blue innards glistened.

'You caught that boy by chance,' Kit said to him. 'You were stopping here to steal provisions. Why? Where are you headed?'

The man showed bloody teeth as he stared up at Kit with hatred and defiance. 'Wh-where else?' he spat through the pain. 'We were coming for you.'

'Congratulations. You found me.'

'H-he won't ever stop, you know that? He'll hunt you down like the dogs you are!'

'I thought he'd given up sending men to die in the wastes. Why now? Why is he sending scouts again?'

The man barked a desperate laugh. 'You're doomed, all of you! So is your godforsaken forest – what's left of it. He'll raze it to the ground, do you hear me?' He laughed again, delirious. 'Seven of you! Y-you think seven of you are going to stop us?'

Kit discharged an arrow into the soldier's heart, ending his hateful babble.

'We need to leave,' he told Eric. 'If he sent one squad, he'll have sent others. They might be closing in on Gaia as we speak. Finish searching the bodies, take anything we need, then we'll get underway.'

When he went back to the green, he found the villagers awaiting him expectantly. The hetman stepped forward, together with six or seven others. Among these were the rebels who had armed themselves against the rangers. One figure in particular drew Kit's attention. He was enormous – taller and broader even than Much. Slung across one shoulder he still carried the sledge-hammer he had intended to use against the Sheriff's men.

'That there is John Little,' the hetman said, following Kit's gaze and gesturing to the giant. 'And this is Conan,' he said, pointing to a stocky, heavily bearded man, who gripped a make-shift mace studded with nails. 'And next to him is—'

'I don't need to know your names,' Kit said. 'You have some-thing to say to me – what is it?'

'We want to join you,' said a fierce, gaunt-looking woman at the hetman's side. 'We want to fight.'

Midge scoffed. 'What good would you be to us? You and your hayfork.'

The woman faced him without visible fear. 'I've watched two sons die of lung-rot. I've dug in that soil, amid those stones, practically every day of my life. It might be I'm tougher than you think.'

'You're not coming with us,' Kit said. 'That's final. I won't lead lambs to the slaughter. Take my advice. Bury these soldiers deep. Pray the Sheriff never gets wind of what happened here. Go on with your lives.'

'What lives?' another woman called out. 'The Sheriff signed our death warrants when he destroyed the forest. Year by year the wastes creep further into our fields. His soldiers bleed us of anything we have left.'

'Then leave,' Kit said. 'Take what you can carry and go.'

'Where?' the hetman said. 'The land is dying. Or it's been fenced off by the barons, who hunt vagrants with dogs. Where is there left? The city? That's a true death sentence for the likes of us.'

'I'm sorry, we can't help you. No more than this.' Kit took from his backpack two purses full of gold pieces. He threw them at the hetman's feet. 'This will help you on your way, until you find somewhere better. Much, Midge, all of you, we're leaving.'

The wind had picked up once more and as he spoke it strengthened, tearing straw from the thatched roofs, slammed doors.

'Storm's brewing,' said Ira, looking back towards the wastes. 'We might be better sheltering in that barn till it passes.'

'We leave now,' Kit told her. 'There might be more soldiers crossing the wastes. We can't risk them finding Gaia'

'Little chance of that,' Midge said. 'Look what I found in the captain's backpack.'

He unrolled a scroll, laid it out on the ground. Sonskya knelt and helped hold it flat as the corners flapped in the wind. Kit studied the map. For there was no doubt that was what it was intended to be. There was a rough compass at the top. Around the outside were tiny symbols that looked like peasants' huts. These must denote villages on the edge of the wastes. Then there was a boundary line, within which a large, almost blank expanse represented the Lost Lands. This section was marked with a few wavy lines that probably indicated hills, and shaded areas that were perhaps old lakes or other depressions. But other than that it was featureless.

'See? Pathetic,' snarled Midge. 'All these years searching the wastes and they're as clueless as when they began.'

'They only need to get lucky once,' Kit told him. 'We've left Gaia unguarded long enough. We need to get moving.'

'Wait,' the hetman called after Kit and the others as they made their way out of the village. 'At least tell us it's true. Robin Hood. He's still out there, isn't he? He'll return.'

Kit had no answer to this. Lowering his head against the wind, his hood raised, he led the last of the forest fighters back into the wastes.

IV. Night Moves

Rex burned with night terrors. The whole world on fire, with nowhere to run. And beneath the roar of the flames, a voice whispers: *I see you. I know who you truly are.*

He woke with a gasp, breathing hard, to find a dark figure looming at his bedside. His mind raced and his heart thumped as he tried to make sense of this – was this still part of his nightmare?

But then the figure spoke, and the ruined side of his face glistened. 'Get dressed,' his father said in low tones. 'You are coming with me.'

What time was it? Where were they going? Through the high embrasure, the sky showed black and starless. Looking towards the doorway, Rex only now noted that two more figures lurked there. Rangers of the Guard, gripping spears.

'I told you to get dressed,' his father said. 'Do not make me repeat myself again. I shall await you in the Solar.'

Rex scrambled to pull on hose and tunic, with a dark cloak over the top, then hurried out of his chamber. His father turned and led the way down through the tower, with the guardsmen following behind.

As they went, Rex's father said: 'I know full well who released the creatures from my Menagerie. I am certain your mother goaded you into it. Even so, you have a will of your own, and you chose to play your part. I hoped you had grown out of it – these night-time escapades. But no. So – tonight it is our turn, you and I, to play a nocturnal game. I trust it will serve as a valuable corrective.'

Rex's heart clenched at these words, and tightened further when they reached the foot of the tower and stepped out to find another dozen rangers waiting, each of them armed with a spear and holding a flaming torch. And more ominous still – behind these men waited a dozen figures wearing red robes. Guy of Gisbourne's warrior monks.

At their centre stood the heretic hunter himself. As always, whenever he caught sight of Sir Guy, Rex stared at him with grim fascination. With a confusing mixture of repulsion and awe. This fearsome warrior went dressed, as ever, in the complete hide of a horse, the leather armour covering every inch of his colossal frame, even down to his boots, and including a cowl that masked most of his face. The hilt of a broadsword protruded from a baldrick at his back, while his hands, the size of shovels, clenched and unclenched at his sides, as though he could scarcely contain his own strength.

'This wind will mask the sound of our approach,' Rex's father told the guards. 'Even so, we go soft-footed. Woe betide any man who alerts our quarry. Sir Guy, lead on.'

Alerts our quarry? thought Rex as the party started towards the castle gates. *What is this? Why is the heretic hunter with us?*

What lesson was his father intending to teach him?

It was a ghostly night, the full moon scudded by quick cloud, its light a halo of yellow and silver and blue. In the distance, from the direction of the wastes, came the moaning of the wind – a low, breathy sound that could almost have been human.

On such a night, the upper city appeared deserted, the inns shuttered and dark, even the nightwatchmen nowhere to be seen. As they passed through the shadows of the big town-houses, here and there a bandog barked and rattled its chains, but otherwise the streets were as silent as they were still.

Ahead of Rex, the warrior monks were crimson shades, gliding across the ground without a movement out of place or sound to mark their progress. At their head went the hulking figure of the heretic hunter, monstrous in the moonlight, looking from behind like a stallion walking on hind legs.

All of this caused Rex's foreboding to grow and grow. As it did so, his arms began to itch, his vulcanism rising to the surface. He clasped his hands together, forced himself not to scratch, while the irritation burned beneath his skin.

At his side, his father looked wan and red-eyed. The effort of this brisk walking had left the Sheriff short of breath: Rex could hear him wheezing faintly with every inhale. Rex's own chest felt tight and he prayed and prayed that his cough would stay away as they crept on through the gloom.

The cobbled streets narrowed as the mercantile district led into the craftsmen's quarter, lined with its stalls and workshops. Here, was the occasional sign of life – candlelight at a window, low laughter from a tavern or dicing den.

The further they descended through the city, the narrower the streets became, until the party was forced to go single file through the lanes of the labourers' district. The cobbles beneath their feet had given way to packed earth, which now became mud scattered with straw as they entered the shambles, with its smoking sheds and slaughterhouses, the whole place stinking of fish guts and offal.

Still Sir Guy led them onwards, until they were in the shadow of the city walls. As they picked their way along rutted alleyways, Rex stared around him. He had roamed with his mother all through the city, and imagined he must have explored every nook and cranny. Yet here was a quarter that was entirely unfamiliar.

The houses here appeared to be hardly houses at all, patched together as they were with scavenged pieces of timber and cloth. The shacks were lashed together with rope, and leaned into one another for support, often sharing roofs and walls, so that it was hard to tell where one home ended and another began.

Here, Rex's father raised a fist and the party came to a halt. The guardsmen formed a circle around Rex and the Sheriff, spears ready.

'Scent them out, Sir Guy,' his father said. 'Be quick.'

While Sir Guy and his warrior monks fanned out, each moving down a different track, flitting away into the darkness, Rex's father turned to him.

'The people who inhabit this place,' he said softly, 'do you know where they come from?'

Rex looked at him. 'I . . . don't know what you mean. Aren't they citizens?'

'They come from the *land*,' his father said, spitting the last word. 'They are too weak and indolent to farm their fields, so they lay down their tools and flock here. They trick their way through the gates, claiming to have wares to sell. And then they stay, content to scavenge and to live on scraps.' He swept his gaze across the shacks with obvious disgust. 'They come here and live like rats. And like rats, they bring disease.'

Rex looked at him, startled. 'The plague?'

'Yes. But not of the body. It is a sickness of the spirit. A plague of the soul. That is what I brought you here to see.'

He turned to look at the heretic hunter, who was returning with his monks.

'Did you locate the source of the pestilence?'

Sir Guy nodded his massive head. 'It is as you suspected, sire. They are all gathered in one place.'

'A moon like this – they believe it gifts them some kind of power. Well – they shall see what it brings them. Lead the way, Sir Guy.'

The party set out once more, snaking its way between the low, tumbledown shacks. Ahead of them, Rex could now see a larger structure. It too appeared cobbled together from mismatched pieces of timber and fabric. From inside this makeshift hall, through thin cracks in the walls, showed the glimmer of firelight or the flicker of candles. As they drew close, Rex also heard sounds coming from within. It was a low hum, like conversation, only more rhythmic. It was singing – or chanting.

'So then,' his father said with quiet menace, again giving the signal to halt, before turning to Rex, 'now you will see what we are up against. While you run around with your mother, plotting childish pranks, our enemy gathers its strength. They are massing at our gates. No – closer still – they are here in our very midst.'

As he listened to this, Rex stared around him at the shacks, then at the meeting hall. The night suddenly took on a soft texture, unreal, as though he could no longer trust his own eyes. 'Enemy?' he said, swallowing against the fire that was building at the back of his throat. 'Who do you mean?'

Ignoring his question, Rex's father nodded to Guy of Gisbourne. Flanked by his warrior monks, their swords drawn, the heretic hunter strode forward with such shocking speed and power that Rex blinked and missed the instant that the door of the hall crashed inwards, splintering beneath the giant boot of Sir Guy. There were cries from within, and heavy thumping sounds, while rangers rushed in after the heretic hunter and his monks.

'Come with me,' Rex's father told him, 'and bear witness.'

With great trepidation, his breathing sharp and shallow, a crawling itch at the back of his throat, Rex had no choice but to follow.

Inside the hall, he saw people sprawled, many of them bleeding, some crying, holding one another. Rex's father

44

stepped between them, his hands clasped behind his back, while they cowered, and he swept his icy gaze.

'Be still, and quiet, all of you,' he said between wheezing breaths. 'The time for pleading is passed. You have made this cross for your own backs. Son, come here. See what these savages think of us and our laws.'

He had stopped at the far end of the hall, where dozens of candles burned. They were arranged on what appeared to be a makeshift altar. But set upon this altar, as Rex moved closer, there was no chalice or relics or holy offerings. Instead, it was laid with natural objects. A pair of crossed sticks; sprigs of holly; willow wands; blood-red berries.

'You,' his father said, pointing randomly at one of the shire-folk. 'Tell my son the purpose of this sacrilege. Of your so-called ritual.'

The woman he addressed shook with fear as she huddled on the ground, her arms wrapped around two weeping children. 'W-we were raised on the land – that's all it means,' she stammered. 'We gather here to r-remember our roots, nothing more.'

'Liar. You,' the Sheriff said, indicating another member of the congregation. 'The first person to speak the truth may yet receive clemency.'

'We mean no harm,' the second man mumbled, his face bloodied where a guardsman had struck him. 'We merely pay our respects to the Earth, and ask forgiveness.'

'Liars all.' The Sheriff spoke softly, but with enough venom to spread hush through the hall. 'You gather here to call on your savage gods. To summon your Earth magic.'

From the centre of the altar, he picked up the smallest object. A single nut, or seed. Rex's mother had shown him one of these once, and now his mind groped for what she had called it. An acorn. Yes. The seed of an oak tree.

'I am well aware of your ways,' his father went on, pacing once more through the hall, holding up the acorn, turning it between two fingers. 'After casting your hexes and speaking your incantations, you intended to take this out into the streets, where you would plant it in the mud. You mourn the loss of the forest. So much so that you would attempt to seed it anew, even here, in the heart of my city.'

One or two of the shire-folk tried to dispute this, or protest their innocence, but at a gesture from Rex's father the guardsmen silenced them with the butts of their spears.

'Even worse,' his father continued. 'You gather here also to invoke the name of Robin Hood. Even now, you grieve for the phantom outlaw. You dream he will one day rise again, together with his accursed forest. You bow down to him as if he were a god. *He is not your god!*' Rex's father suddenly raged, sending a shockwave of terror through the hall. '*I* am your god! Bow down to *me!*'

He stopped, short of breath, amid the huddled crying figures, sweeping his gaze from face to face. The fear now hung so thickly in the air that Rex could feel it as a palpable thing, like mist on his skin.

'But I am a just man,' Rex's father said, regaining his breath, 'and we find ourselves in dispute. You claim you gather here – against the laws of the land – merely as a mark of remembrance. Others would view this assembly as tantamount to treason. If you are found to be in the right, you will be granted quick executions. If you truly are conspirators, however, then your punishment must serve as a warning to others.'

This caused an outcry of terror and protest, which the soldiers again subdued.

'However, this is a straightforward ruling,' the Sheriff went on. 'Even a child could make it.' To Rex's horror, his father now turned to face him, before saying: 'My son shall pass judgement.'

All eyes now fixed on Rex. The black baleful glare of the heretic hunter, and the glassy sinister stares of his warrior monks, and, worst of all, the wide pleading eyes of the shire-folk.

'So then,' his father said, leaning close and dropping his voice so only Rex could hear. 'Pronounce their doom. Do it swiftly.'

Rex stared at him, then back at the shire-folk. 'But . . . how?' he mumbled. 'I . . . I don't know these people, or their ways. How do I know if they're telling the truth?'

'You would take their word over mine?'

'No – no. It's only . . .' He looked around him at these men, women and children, all of them stick-thin and dressed in rags. 'They're . . . starving. They . . . don't look like they could harm anybody.'

'You pity them.'

'Yes . . . No . . . I don't—'

'Let me assure you, these *creatures*, they are as wily as serpents. They feign weakness, while plotting our destruction. They would tear down everything I have built. Destroy your legacy. Make no mistake, they are the enemy. *Your* enemy.'

Rex tried to fix his father's words to the people he could see in front of him – these pitiful, wretched souls – but the effort only made his vision grow cloudy, as though he could no longer trust his own senses.

'Speak,' his father said in his ear. 'I have told you before, in those fated to lead, who walk the path of power, indecision can be fatal.'

But Rex doubted he could speak now even if he had known what to say. There was a hot pressure in his chest so intense it felt as if his ribs could cave in. The expectant hush in the hall seemed to suck in all the air, and he could barely breathe.

Finally, with a slight shake of his head and tightening of his jaw, his father turned away from him. He drew himself up to address the hall.

'My son has passed me his judgement. He upholds the laws of the city. At dawn, these rebels shall be hanged, drawn and quartered.'

'No, wait, I—'

'Silence,' Rex's father hissed at him, while the hall filled with wails of terror and cries for mercy. 'You had your moment to speak. Your chance to wield power. You surrendered it. Leave us now.'

In a daze, Rex did as he was bid, in truth fully desperate now to escape the hall, where in the shadows there were now scuffles and hard thumps as some of the shire-folk resisted their fate and were restrained by Sir Guy and his warrior monks.

Out in the night air, the world swam. His chest unlocked and his cough finally broke to the surface, leaving him doubled over as he rasped and rasped. By the time the fit subsided, his father was leaving the hall, flanked by his guards. Without glancing at him, the Sheriff swept back the way they had come.

With the world still unsteady at the edges, and the after-shock of the cough burning in his lungs, Rex hung his head and followed, watching his feet squelch in the mud.

As they retraced their steps up through the labourers' district and into the craftsmen's quarter, he kept expecting his father to call him forward, whisper to him some chastisement, promise him correction. But much worse – his father held his tongue, leaving Rex's imagination to devise its own punishment. Leaving him also to see, over and over again, those people in that hall, staring at him with vain hope in their eyes.

My son has passed me his judgement . . . At dawn, these rebels shall be hanged, drawn and quartered.

Finally, as they made their way up through the mercantile district, his father called his name. Rex hurried to his side.

'What do you imagine is my most powerful weapon?' the Sheriff said, between laboured breaths. 'Is it my troop of men, my arsenal, my war machines? It is none of these. My most potent weapon is my voice. These soldiers you see around you. Do you doubt, that should I order them to fall on their swords, any one of them would fail to obey?'

At this moment, utterly without warning, and to his dismay, Rex's cough resurfaced, and he fell behind as he hacked and hacked. Finally, he got the cough under control, held the last of it in his chest while he hurried to catch up with his father.

'By now you should be coming into your own power,' his father continued, staring dead ahead. 'But you squander it. You choose to hide. Even this cough of yours is a feigned weakness. You use it to mask inaction. As an excuse not to face your fears.'

At these words, Rex felt something stir inside him, dislodging his shame. He said through gritted teeth: 'I'm not afraid. I'll show you I'm not.'

'You misunderstand. I am not referring to physical courage. I watched you ride a charger when you were six years old. Even as a child you would stand against seasoned rangers in the combat yard. No, your fear is of a different breed. I see it when your opponent lies defenceless at your feet and you stay your sword. It is the reason you squeak when you should roar.' He looked at Rex, and his eyes glinted like ice. 'What you truly fear is your own power. Your own anger. You dread what might happen were you to set that anger free.'

Before his father could say more, his attention was drawn to a figure coming towards them, crossing the drawbridge of the castle. He was a thin, wiry man with a full moustache and a weaselly face. This was Gad Levins, the Chief Porter.

'Begging your forgiveness, sire,' Levins said, bowing low. 'Sentries were patrolling outside the city walls and they discovered a pair of vagrants. Scavengers from the wastes.'

'And this deserves my attention?' Rex's father said, striding onwards. 'String them up with the rest of the vermin.'

'That was our intention, sire,' said the porter, 'except . . . the girl . . . she keeps asking to speak with you. She claims to have made a discovery. The tale she has to tell – well, it is something you will wish to hear, sire.'

The Sheriff continued into the castle. 'Very well,' he said. 'But if they are wasting my time, they'll get worse than the gallows.'

All this came to Rex vaguely, the night around him suddenly unreal. What was he even doing out here beneath this phantom moon? Why had his father put him through that ordeal? What was it supposed to prove?

As the Sheriff headed towards the Throne Room, now intent on other matters, Rex slunk wordlessly away, allowing himself at last to rub his arms, the scratching only adding fuel to the flames, his skin burning as fierce and raw as his anger and his shame.

V. Buried Truths

Marian woke wine-sick, her skull throbbing and her throat on fire. She groped for a pitcher at her bedside but only succeeded in knocking it over, the last of the water dribbling into the rug. As she groaned and sat up, she became aware of two things simultaneously: it was still the middle of the night – and thumping crashing noises were arising from somewhere nearby.

Throwing off her coverlets, she stood unsteadily and stumbled from her chamber, all the while the thudding, cracking sounds becoming more distinct. When she entered the solar, she saw it was Rex. He was even now lifting a stool and hurling it against a wall, where it splintered. Elsewhere, flagons had been toppled, vessels smashed.

Marian smiled grimly. 'You are your mother's son. It doesn't help much, does it? And they always put it back exactly the way it was.'

When he set eyes on Marian, Rex stopped, breathing hard. He slumped down on a bench, his face in his hands. She crossed to him and sat at his side.

'What's he done now?'

'I don't want to talk about it.'

'You've left a trail of mud. Where have you been? Tell me . . . What happened?'

'I don't understand. What did they do to deserve that?'

His face was still buried in his hands but she realized now that he was crying, tears running between his fingers. It must have been years since she saw him cry, and seeing it now gripped her heart like an iron fist. She put an arm around him. At first he tried to pull away but she persisted, and finally he softened into her and sobbed openly against her chest.

'You need to tell me what he did.'

'Why? What does it matter? What can you do about it, or me? Nothing I ever do is enough. I . . . I don't even know what he wants from me.'

'He wants you to be afraid,' Marian said evenly. 'Whatever it is he puts you through, that's his ultimate aim. He wants you to live in fear, like he does.'

Through his tears, Rex scoffed, 'What's he afraid of?'

'Everything. The wilderness. His own weakness. You.'

Rex pulled away, blinking. 'What are you talking about? Why would he fear me?'

She laid a hand on his chest, over his heart. 'Because you carry in you something he'll never have – that he will never even understand. Because already you are stronger and braver and freer than he'll ever be.'

Rex shook his head, wiped away tears. 'I don't know what you mean. He's not afraid of anything. Everyone fears him!'

'Believe me,' Marian said quietly. 'I know him better than anyone else alive. Better than he knows himself. And I assure you of this – he's been frightened his entire life. That's where it all springs from. His rage. His hatred. His need to cage and control. It's all fed by fear.'

Rex glared at her with eyes that were red-rimmed and raw. 'How can you talk about him that way? Why did you marry him, then, if you despise him so much? Why am I here? I didn't ask to be born! I didn't ask to be the Sheriff's son!'

These words fell upon Marian with a crushing weight. Suddenly she understood, in that moment of silence between them, while the wind continued to howl outside, that everything had been leading to this moment – that it had all been building to a head, like a thunderstorm that must surely break.

And she knew, in that instant, that the time had come. She had long told herself that this was not something to be planned for – that she would know by instinct when the moment arrived. And now, here it was. Sitting here with her son, who only yesterday struck her as having become a man, seeing his face now crumpled and blotchy from sobbing like a child, his features etched with confusion and pain, she knew she could deceive him no longer. Tonight, here and now, she would tell him everything.

'Rex, listen to me, there's . . . something I need to tell you,' she said, hearing the words come out of her mouth, unreal, as if they were being spoken by somebody else. 'When you hear it, I want you to remember one thing: I hated lying to you. It's burned me all these years, keeping up this lie. I need you to know, it was only ever for your own good. To keep you safe. This truth . . . if I had told you when you were younger . . . you might not have understood. Or . . . or you might not have guarded it closely enough.'

Rex was now sitting very straight and still. 'What are you talking about? Why—'

'Please, don't speak, not until I'm finished,' Marian said. 'I've kept this to myself so long, buried it so deep, I'm not even sure I'll be able to say it. And for you, it won't be easy to hear. Not at first. This truth . . . it might seem to you like a burden. Like a weight to bear.' She wiped a tear from her cheek. 'But it isn't, you'll see. In fact, it's the greatest gift. Yes, think of it as a treasure.' She smiled and cried at the same time. 'Something infinitely precious to keep locked in your heart. The way I have, all these years.'

'Mother, I don't know what any of this means. Why are you crying? You look . . . different. You're not yourself.'

'I am,' she said, smiling through the tears. 'Right now, I am. This is the real me. And now I'm going to tell you about the real you. Gods alive, it's a relief. Already it's a relief. Now I just need to come out and say it. So then – here it is. Your . . . father. The man you—'

The blare of a clarion cut through her words, left her speechless. Rex scrabbled to his feet as the clarion sounded once more, from the foot of the tower.

'No – no,' Marian growled. 'Not now! Rex – wait – you can't leave! Please, I hadn't finished. This is something you need to hear.'

'I can't let him see me like this,' Rex spluttered, rubbing at his tearstained face. He flung his cloak around his shoulders, while doors slammed open below.

'Hide then, until he leaves,' Marian told him, as bootsteps echoed up the tower steps. 'We need to finish what we started.'

But Rex was already on the move, pulling up his hood as he darted across to the far wall. Quick as a squirrel, he scampered up to the high embrasure, shimmied through, took hold of the creeping ivy and clambered down out of sight.

Moments later, the sound of boots came marching outside the room and the Sheriff entered, accompanied by his bodyguards. The rangers positioned themselves around the chamber, while their master paced slowly towards Marian, his hands clasped behind his back.

'Prior warning of your visits would be appreciated,' Marian told him, 'especially at this hour.'

'My business cannot wait,' the Sheriff said. 'In any case, it was not you I came here to see. I am looking for our son.'

Marian shrugged. 'I haven't seen him.'

The Sheriff looked down at the floor, which was stained with mud. Then he turned to stare towards the oval embrasure. He coughed into a gloved fist. He coughed again, and kept coughing, his whole body wracking as the fit took hold of him.

His sickness was Marian's doing. Twenty years ago, when she had first been a prisoner of the Sheriff, she had tried to kill him with a poison known as dragon's tongue. She had sewn it into his clothing and it seeped into his flesh and blood. His apothecary discovered the plot and saved the Sheriff's life. But he had never recovered his full health. Looking at him now, shuddering like a man in his death throes, looking drawn and skeletal, she felt the stirring of an old hope that the aftereffects of the poison may yet still kill him. But no, it was a vain hope. He may look like a walking corpse, but he was animated by hatred. He would outlive them all.

Finally, his coughing fit passed and the Sheriff stood breathing heavily, his eyes glistening as he fixed his gaze on her. Unexpectedly, Marian found her limbs were trembling. A half-full flagon was sitting nearby; reflexively, she reached for it and took a slug of wine, expecting it to douse the fire in her flesh. But the trembling only grew worse. What was wrong with her? It had been a long time since the Sheriff's presence had evoked such a visceral reaction.

'As you see – Rex isn't here,' she said, her voice cracking. 'If that was all, I'd thank you to leave.'

As if she hadn't spoken, the Sheriff swept his gaze around the Solar, taking in the disarray. The smashed vessels and toppled furniture.

'These petty displays of pique,' he said slowly, turning back to her. 'Are you not ashamed? When I think what you once achieved. What you once were.'

'If you wanted to reminisce about the past, can't it wait until morning?'

'That day you came to my chambers, sixteen years ago,' the

Sheriff said, 'and you asked – no, begged – to be my bride, I took it as a sign that you had truly repented. That the savage spell of the forest was broken.'

He paced amid the splintered pieces of pottery and glass. 'Perhaps I was naive. Or blinded by dreams of grandeur. But who could blame me. The warrior queen of Sherwood. With you at my side, how might my power rise? Truly, we would be deities, you and I.' He paused, turned to look at her. 'After all, hadn't we already achieved God-like feats, when we destroyed the forest?'

Marian shook her head, gritted her teeth. 'How much longer will you cling to that lie? It was you who destroyed the forest, no one else.'

'I could not have done it without you. Any more than a fire can burn without fuel.'

'I've heard all this before,' she said, taking another swig of wine. 'Go away. Can't you see I'm busy.'

'Of course, now I understand the nature of my error,' the Sheriff went on, regardless. 'The warrior queen of Sherwood never did come to my castle. In body, perhaps. But not in spirit. The true Marian Delbosque remained in that godforsaken forest. Day after day, even here in the castle, I see you kneeling in your rose garden – do you imagine I don't know what you're doing?'

He spun and fixed her with a hateful glare. 'It is abominable enough that the little people should still worship the name of Robin Hood. But the Queen of Nottingham. My own wife. Even after all this time, even in death, he exerts a grip over you. It is a grip, I must finally admit, I will never succeed in breaking.'

He turned away. 'With you at my side – a faithless wife,' he spat the words, 'is it any surprise that final victory eludes me? That outlaws still roam the wastes? That a fragment of Sherwood still exists?'

'If I'm such a weight around your neck, why keep me here? Divorce me. I'll disappear. You'll never see me again.'

'No. That will never do. The people love you. The idea of you. They see in our union, I believe, the final triumph of order over chaos. Of the wilderness tamed.' Again, he fixed her with a cold glare. 'If only they knew.'

He paced away. 'In any case, you would never willingly leave without our son. And his place is here.' He paced once more, his hands behind his back. 'That is where you have disappointed me most deeply. In your corrupting influence on our son. You would have him masquerade as a thief and a blackguard, when he should be donning the robes of a prince.'

During this speech, Marian bit down hard on her tongue, and she kept biting, not trusting the words that might spill out should she start to speak.

'Well – no matter,' the Sheriff went on, as the wind howled against the tower and the candles spluttered. 'I have devised a physic for Rex. It will be bitter medicine, no doubt. As likely to kill as to cure. But you have left me little choice.'

'What are you talking about?' Marian said, rising to her feet, shaking.

'You know I don't believe in chance, Lady Marian, nor coincidence. No sooner had I understood, with certainty, what our son required, than the perfect opportunity presented itself.'

'What . . . opportunity?'

'Yes,' the Sheriff said, nodding to himself. 'Is it not fated? Our son must lead the expedition. He must go into the wastes and retrieve the bones in person.'

Marian gripped the back of a chair to steady herself. 'Wastes . . . bones?' she said, her voice faltering. 'What drivel is this? What do you mean?'

As if he hadn't heard her, the Sheriff strode towards the doorway, issuing orders to his bodyguards as he went. 'Search the grounds. Find my son. Be quick.'

'Wait! Tell me!' Marian stumbled after him. 'What are you planning? What's happened?'

The Sheriff paused, looked back at her. 'You mean you haven't heard? The news reached the castle an hour ago. It's been discovered, finally. The body.'

Marian groped once more for furniture to steady herself as the ground lurched. 'What . . . body?' she murmured. 'Whose?'

'The phantom outlaw, of course,' the Sheriff said offhandedly, as he turned to leave. 'The body of Robin Hood.'

VI. The Killing Wastes

'We daren't go much further in this,' Ira said at Kit's side, raising her voice against the wind. 'We're heading right into the teeth of it.'

'The cave isn't far from here,' called Sonskya, shielding her eyes from a fresh flurry of grit and sand. 'We could take shelter there.'

'He isn't going to turn, is he?' Kit heard Midge say at the rear of the group. 'Once and for all, our mighty leader proves he has a death wish.'

Kit didn't need telling they were taking an awful risk. He knew better than anyone that storms out here in the Lost Lands could prove deadly. With no trees or even shrubs to slow the wind, gales could build to phenomenal force. What was more, the heat of the Great Fire had baked the sandy soil into glass, which meant the ferocious storms could hurl dagger-sharp shards along with rocks and stones. But even knowing this, Kit couldn't bring himself to seek shelter, his every instinct insisting they return to Gaia as soon as possible.

He beckoned over his shoulder to the rangy figure of Eric O'Lincoln. The veteran tracker lowered his head into the wind and moved up the line.

'Those soldiers back in that village,' Kit said when he reached him. 'The Sheriff never sends just one scouting patrol, does he?'

'I've been thinking the same thing,' said Eric. 'But if there are more soldiers out here, we're a long way off their scent.'

'Why worry, with this storm rising,' said Jack, who was close enough to overhear. 'If there are more rangers out there, let the wastes take care of them.'

'They might get lucky and live through it,' said Kit. 'If they do, and they stumble upon Gaia—'

He was interrupted by a vicious gust of wind, powerful enough to send large rocks rolling and make the outlaws catch their balance.

'Nothing we can do for Gaia if we're dead,' Jack said simply.

'We don't all need to take the risk,' Eric said to Kit. 'I'd move quicker on my own in any case.'

Kit considered this, then nodded. 'Don't go far. Just see if you can pick up a trail before this wind wipes everything clean. Whatever happens, join us at the cave before nightfall.'

Stringing his bow, unsheathing an arrow, Eric loped away, while Kit led the others northwards towards the cave.

It was hard going, the wind now buffeting them from all sides, threatening to throw them off their feet. The rising dust was now masking the sun, and the day grew dimmer and dimmer until they were barely shuffling forwards, feeling with their toes for pitfalls and petrified roots and sinkholes.

Finally, though, the land rose ahead of them. And there it was: Robin Hood's Cave. Once the most secret and heavily guarded place in all of Sherwood. Now it stood gaping and exposed, a dark and jagged wound in the hillside.

Reaching the entrance, dropping to his knees, Kit led the way inside. It was a profound relief to be out of the wind, the relative quiet of the cave now ringing in his ears.

He groped around for the birch-bark torches that the outlaws stashed by the entrance – found one, lit it with his strike-a-light. Meanwhile, Sonskya and Jack had done the same, and by the flickering light the outlaws settled back against the flowstone walls.

A phenomenal gust of wind howled across the cave entrance, powerful enough to extinguish Jack's torch.

'It's building even quicker than we thought,' said Ira, while Jack rekindled the light.

'Eric shouldn't be out there on his own,' said Midge.

While the others stretched out to get some rest, their heads pillowed on their backpacks, Kit paced deeper into the cave, needing to be alone with his thoughts.

Midge was right, of course he was: Eric should be here, hunkered down with the rest of them. Why had Kit let him go off alone? Was his judgement slipping?

You've been away from Gaia too long, he told himself. It's always this way when you're out in the wastes. It leaves you drained.

So thinking, desperate to placate his stormy thoughts, he pushed further and further into the cave. It was always a strange sensation, coming back here. Like stepping into a different life-time. It was the smell, mostly – that dank aroma – it transported him back to those weeks and months following the Great Fire. Kit and the other survivors had taken refuge here, while outside the remains of Sherwood Forest still smouldered and ash clouds blanketed the sky.

It was a dreadful time of fear and darkness and frustrated fury. Several outlaws had taken their own lives. Many of the younger ones fell to blows over dice or some perceived slight, or simply from too long cooped up in the same space. Their duels often sparked feuds that led to yet more bloodshed. As time went on, one by one, others simply got up and went out into the wastes, never to be seen again.

By the time the blasted land outside stopped billowing smoke, and the survivors came blinking out into the sickly light,

Sherwood's once mighty outlaw army numbered fewer than two dozen souls.

And since then we've been dropping one by one, Kit told himself as his spirits sank ever lower. Lives lost to the Sheriff's men and to the elements. *And now look at us – down to the bare bones . . .*

He continued onwards through chambers that once housed dormitories of bats, but which now stood eerily empty. Only the sound of his own breathing and his scuffing footsteps. Even the rats seemed to have abandoned this once-hallowed place.

He came into a cavern so vast that the updraught sucked at his torch. He swept his gaze across glittering piles of gold and silver and gemstones: the fabled hoard of the outlaws. Following the Great Fire, when the outlaws had first taken refuge in the cave, many of the young bucks had come here and rooted through this treasure, thinking themselves richer than pharaohs.

Little good it did them, Kit thought grimly, kicking though a pile of gemstones which glimmered in the torchlight as they scattered. Here and there were gold coins splattered with blood, showing where outlaws had murdered one another over the choicest pickings.

Walking past caskets full of brilliants and emeralds, Kit crossed to the far side of the chamber where darker materials gleamed back at him. Here, scattered all around, heaped against the walls, were all the weapons the outlaws had claimed from slain enemies. Swords and maces and shields. Armour and battledress of every kind.

As he stood here, Kit again suffered a shift in time, as though years had suddenly slipped away. As a novice warrior, under the watchful eye of Eric O'Lincoln, Kit had come and trawled through this arsenal, equipping himself with the sword and leather armour he still wore to this day. The memory was so distinct that he turned, lifting his torch, expecting to find Eric standing behind him, nodding encouragement.

There was no one there, of course, but Eric was once again the prime thought in his mind, and it sent him hurrying back through the passageways. Certainly, his old mentor would have returned by now, and Kit would never be gladder to set eyes on him.

But when he reached the others his hope curdled in his stomach. They were all asleep except for Midge, who met Kit's gaze and curtly shook his head.

'He'll be back,' Kit told him, with as much confidence as he could muster, as he took up watch near the cave mouth. 'Eric knows the wilderness better than any of us.'

But another hour passed, and a third, and there was no sign of him. The wind continued to rise, until it was as fierce a gale as Kit could remember. It howled past the mouth of the cave, sending in flurries of dirt and dust. In the distance it moaned so low and hollow and demonic it truly might have been the Earth itself groaning in its death throes.

The other outlaws had all shuffled together for the body warmth, and even Midge was now sleeping. Kit sat alone, wrapped in his cloak. Despite the shelter of the cave, the temperature continued to plummet, until the cold was a livid thing gnawing at his bones.

But a far worse torture was in Kit's mind. Where was Eric? Had he found somewhere else to take shelter? Had he run into soldiers alone? What had possessed Kit to let him go off by himself in the first place?

Finally, just before dawn, the storm ceased. The wind dropped so suddenly that the silence roared. Forcing himself to move, his joints cracking with cold, Kit crawled out of the cave. He moved off into the badlands, while behind him the others started to emerge, dead-eyed, like reanimated corpses.

Kit had walked less than a hundred paces when he found Eric.

The veteran outlaw had floundered into a mud pit – one of the black and putrid pools that dotted this landscape. He had sunk up to his waist. There were signs of struggle where he had tried to thrash himself free. The sanctuary of the cave had lain so close. He could probably see it from where he died. He must have been calling and calling for help, but the others had been unable to hear him above the noise of the wind.

Kit's warriors gathered and stood around, staring at Eric in silence. Trapped there like that, he had been defenceless against the glass-storm. He had died from a thousand cuts, his clothes shredded, his skin perforated, the mud around him slick with his lifeblood.

Amid the howling silence of the plain, nobody uttered a word or wept. They had all seen too many scenes like this. Lost too many brothers and sisters in arms. Now, from most of his band, Kit sensed only a mute resignation. In Midge, though, a different energy was rising. He began pacing, like something caged – like a scared and angry beast.

'Eric was a warrior,' he said through gritted teeth. 'He should not have died like this.' He glared at Kit. 'He should not have died all alone.'

Kit drew himself up. 'Eric knew the risks. He volunteered to go.'

'Because you kept talking about more patrols. What patrols? You're seeing phantoms, and Eric died for it!'

'Watch your tongue, Midge.'

'What are you afraid of, mighty leader – that the soldiers will find Gaia?' Midge tore open his backpack, drew out the scroll they had retrieved the dead rangers. 'Well, look at this – look!' He waved the almost blank map in front of Kit's face. 'They barely know east from west. And for this –' he shoved the map closer to Kit's nose – 'for this, Eric is dead!'

'Step away from me, Midge,' Kit said in low tones. 'That's the last warning you'll get.'

Midge dropped the map but stood his ground, his fingers closing around the hilt of his sword. Kit stared into his misshapen face: the twisted lip, the cloven chin, the crushed cheek. His eyes burned red and murderous. Was he desperate enough to draw his blade?

And if he did, and Kit was forced to draw his own sword, what would happen then? Much would come to his son's aid, that was certain. Would other outlaws take Midge's side, or stand with Kit? How many of them might die here today? Was this how the rebellion would finally end, with the last of the forest fighters spilling each other's blood into this lifeless soil?

Thankfully, Midge's sword remained in its scabbard and finally his shoulders slumped. 'What does it matter?' he murmured, the fight suddenly going out of him. 'We're all as good as dead in any case. Maybe Eric was the lucky one.'

Spitting on the ground, he turned and trudged away.

Kit watched him go, then turned to the others, forcing himself to look each of them in the eye.

'Much, Jack, pull Eric out of there,' he said. 'The rest of you, find something to make a litter. We'll take him back to Gaia. I need to collect something from the cave. By the time I get back I want you all ready to leave.'

There was nothing he needed in the cave. Nothing but solitude. Once again, Midge had spoken the truth. Eric's death came down on Kit, of course it did. Now, as he sat here alone, he felt the full crushing weight of it. The loss of a brother-in-arms, and a mentor. But more, so much more. Another warrior of the Earth, gone. How much longer could they last? How long before the last flame guttered to nothing in the dark?

VII. The Unquiet Grave

Behind the White Tower, in a secluded corner of Nottingham Castle, stood Marian's walled garden. The Sheriff had gifted her this patch of land on the day of their betrothal. Over the years, she had made of it a small Eden of wildflowers and climbing plants. There was a shaded bower beloved of butterflies. There were aromatic walkways lined with narcissi and flowers of paradise. Elsewhere, Marian grew herbs and roots to make medicines for Rex's ailments.

But the centre of the garden – its original purpose and still its heart – was its bed of roses. Marian knelt there now, amid the petals and the thorns, the soil muddying her knees, while she sobbed into her hands. It had been a long time since she had cried, and now all those unspent tears were flooding out in a torrent, while her body shuddered, wracked with sorrow.

When she had come here and planted the first seedling, twelve years ago, she had done so in the spirit of hope. Back then, against all odds and reason, she still harboured the belief that Robin might still be alive. That by some miracle he had survived the inferno that incinerated Sherwood Forest. Even when she planted the second rose, and the third, and the fourth, she told herself she was only marking time before they would be together once more.

But on the seventh anniversary, as she knelt here digging yet another hole for another seedling, she finally admitted, with a sudden and terrible unearthing of grief, that she had been deluding herself. That Robin was gone and she would never see him again.

Since then, once a year, she had continued to plant these flowers as an act of remembrance, doing so with the greatest sadness but dry-eyed, telling herself that in a sense she had buried him at last. Except no. Because now this.

It's been discovered, finally . . . the body of Robin Hood.

Marian cried in great heaving sobs, tears running through her fingers and down her forearms. What was wrong with her? She had long ago accepted Robin was lost to her. Did this news make him any more dead, or less?

Whatever the reason, her grief had now burst to the surface, as fresh and raw as if she had lost him yesterday. She never got to say goodbye. He didn't even have a grave she could visit. All she could do, year after year, was kneel here in the home of his enemy, feeling as though half her heart had been torn from her chest.

In pain and rage, she lashed out at the roses, ripping at their petals and stems, trying to tear them from the soil. Their roots held, and all that tore were her hands, the thorns gashing her flesh.

Finally, she became still, staring down at her bloodied palms. Slowly, the physical pain became real. Her crying subsided, then stopped. As she wiped at her eyes with the back of her sleeve, her passion settled into calm sorrow.

Robin is dead. There is nothing you can do for him. The thought came to her with ice-cold clarity and was followed by another, equally sharp. *Rex still lives. He is your life now. He needs you.*

Yes. Because in the Solar the Sheriff had talked of Rex, too. He said he intended to send Rex into the wastes. Recalling this

– allowing herself, perhaps, to face the idea fully for the first time – sent icy fear crawling up Marian's spine.

No – he can't. I'd never see him again!

But for all her fear, and her fury, what could she do? This was the Sheriff's world, and his word was absolute. If he said Rex would journey into the Lost Lands, then nothing and no one could prevent it.

So thinking, shaking with her fear for him, she got slowly to her feet. Rex's path was set. So then – her own path was equally determined. No other course remained.

With a fresh stab of sorrow, sensing perhaps that she would never come to this garden again, she placed two fingers to her lips before placing the kiss on the petal of a rose. Telling Robin silently that she loved him, wiping away a final tear, she left the garden and went to prepare herself for the challenge ahead.

An hour later, when Marian descended from the White Tower, she was transformed. All outward signs of anguish were gone. Her skin was flushed and her eyes bright following an ice-cold bath. She wore her most regal attire, her brocade gown sparkling with brilliants, trimmed with sable. Her hair was brushed and oiled, and her eyelashes were darkened with kohl. Guards and stable hands and kitchen staff stopped to watch her pass as she made her way through the grounds.

She found the Sheriff in his Throne Room. Of all the gloomy, forbidding places in the castle, this one made her skin crawl worst of all. As sentries stood aside, and porters hauled open the iron-studded doors, and she passed inside, she felt the great weight of the black basalt walls looming over her. Outside, the day was bright and warm, but so chill in here she could see her breath.

As she made her way up the central aisle, her footsteps echoing to the rafters, she passed beneath the statues of past sheriffs, staring down from their plinths. Beneath her feet were the tombs of these dead tyrants, their names etched into the flagstone floor.

The flesh-and-blood Sheriff was sitting atop the dais on his black-iron throne. The seneschal was there with him, and several scribes, who hurried back and forth with scrolls for the Sheriff to sign and stamp with his seal.

He left Marian waiting at the foot of the dais while he went on signing these edicts and death warrants. Finally, the last of them was complete. With a wave of one hand, he dismissed his staff, who scurried away to the scriptorium at the rear of the hall, the door closing in their wake.

Only then did the Sheriff raise his head. His eyes lingered on Marian's hands, which she kept clasped in front of her. She had treated the lacerations, then covered the bandages with kidskin gloves. But now the Sheriff stared at those gloves as if he could see through them, and the secrets of her wounds laid bare.

'You are here to talk about our son,' the Sheriff said, before she could speak. 'You believe I am wrong in having him lead the expedition.'

'It's a fool's quest to begin with,' she heard herself say.

'On the contrary, it is vital. The little people must look upon the bones of their false god. Only then will they admit that he failed. That he is extinct.'

Marian bit her lip, already struggling to maintain her composure. 'But why send Rex? His whole life he's barely set foot outside the castle.'

'You make my argument for me. It is time for him to see how rotten the world is, outside these walls. It may serve as the spur he needs.'

'The wastes will eat him alive.'

'There will be peril in it, and hardship. But what doesn't kill us makes us stronger. You of all people appreciate that.

Besides, he will be well supported. A battalion of my finest soldiers will accompany him, alongside his own sword master, Alpha Johns.'

Marian scoffed at this. 'Your men were lost in the forest. From everything I hear, they understand the wastelands even less.'

Again she bit her lip, took a deep breath. She had not come here to draw battlelines; that would only make matters worse. She must be subtler than that.

'Well then . . . if I can't stop him going,' she said, almost shaking with the effort of keeping her voice even, 'at least give him a fighting chance. Let me go with him.'

The Sheriff pursed his lips, studied her. 'He has already been too much under your influence. Your presence would threaten to blunt his very purpose.'

Marian dropped her gaze, recalled her rehearsed words. 'It would serve a greater purpose. I . . . I've been thinking about what you said . . . about how part of me never did leave Sherwood. I see now . . . you were right. I've been living with ghosts. I never could truly accept that they're gone. Robin. The forest.'

She felt the Sheriff's hateful gaze burning into her as she forced more words across her tongue. 'I think . . . if I were to go there . . . where Sherwood once stood. Where Robin . . . where he died. It might become real. I'd be able to bury the past.' She dropped her head lower. 'Upon my return . . . I could be the warrior queen you need me to be.'

There was a long silence in that cold candlelit hall, after which the Sheriff said: 'There is some merit in your proposal. But tell me, if you were to join our son on his quest, what makes you believe you would be an asset? Even the sharpest of blades, when left idle, turns to rust.'

She brought her head up, and her eyes blazed. 'The wild is

in my blood. You know that. Besides, I'd die a thousand deaths before I'd let Rex come to harm.'

The Sheriff's lips twisted, perhaps in a faint smile. 'A mother's protective instinct. Is there any force on this Earth that burns fiercer? Very well, you have convinced me. Go. Slay your ghosts. Help our son through his ordeal. But understand this – it is *his* undertaking, not yours. Once you leave the castle you will be his humble servant, nothing more.'

Flooding with relief, and with a thousand warring thoughts, Marian could only nod. She turned and made her way back down the hall, the walk endless now with the Sheriff's gaze boring into her back.

When she stepped out of the Throne Room, she found that the sky was overcast and that a hot wind was once again blowing from the west, moaning mournfully atop the battlements. Feeling the first droplets of rain on her skin, she knew, by some long-buried instinct, that this wind was the harbinger of a powerful storm. It seemed prophetic, a heavy sense of doom settling upon her as she made her way back towards the tower. She had got her wish. She would accompany Rex on his quest. But only now did she truly accept what that meant.

After all these years . . . she would be going back to Sherwood.

VIII. Earth to Earth

Nobody could remember who had named it, or when, but the outlaws called this place Gaia. It was all that remained of the once titanic Sherwood Forest. Standing amid a sea of lifeless desert, it was a blessed island of green, consisting of perhaps five hundred trees.

The wildwood was encircled by a wide ditch – a moat Robin Hood had created with his forest powers, which had saved it from the Great Fire. Over the years, this ditch had grown thick with blackthorn and spear grass and lance thistle, which now guarded Gaia like the curtain walls of a castle.

After a long, woeful trek across the Lost Lands, Kit and his band finally closed the final furlong and approached the wildwood. Standing before the wall of greenery, Kit raised a weary hand and gestured with his fingers. In response, the blackthorn pulled in its thorns; the grass and thistle parted. With a wet rustling sound, a tunnel formed in the vegetation.

By now, a forbidding wind was once again rising in the wastelands, and with infinite relief Kit led the others into the opening. He gestured again and shoots and rootlets twined together to form a walkway, spanning the ditch like a drawbridge. The crossing creaked but held firm as Kit went over and the others followed.

Once the last of them were across, Kit opened his palms

and released his grip on the undergrowth. Again there was a wet, slithering, rustling noise, and the bridge fell apart and the tunnel closed. As it did so, Kit stumbled. Being out there in those wastelands had left him more drained than he realized, and now using his forest powers, even for those few moments, left him ready to drop.

But he fought for his footing and managed to stagger onwards through Gaia. The wildwood thrummed and hummed with insects, and warbled with birdsong. The air was humid and rich with fragrance, and the footpaths were striped with sunlight and shade. Out in the Lost Lands, there was little to mark the turning of the seasons; Kit had almost forgotten it was summertime. Now that fact came back to him with a sense that the world had regained its proper shape.

As he went onwards, life barking and scurrying and shrieking all around him, Kit felt steadier on his feet, this summertime energy seeping into him, his vitality already returning. At this moment he might almost be joyful – if it weren't for the task that faced him and his band this morning. Behind him, Much and Midge were carrying a stretcher. Laid upon it was the corpse of Eric O'Lincoln.

In silence, Kit led the funeral procession through cool misty hollows, along deer paths and badger runs, around moss-quilted boulders, over rotting tree trunks. Finally up a steep natural stairway, formed of rocks and roots that protruded through the soil.

At the top of the climb the group gathered, and Much and Midge laid down the stretcher. They were now standing at the foot of an emperor oak – the last of its kind. The outlaws called it the Mother Tree. It towered up from the centre of Gaia, its colossal limbs arching across the island like protective arms, its roots humping through the soil and running all the way to the boundary, as if binding the entire woodland together.

At the base of the great tree, its trunk was dotted with cavities, some as large as caves. Without a word, Much and Midge went to one of these openings and, ducking their heads, carried the stretcher inside. Shortly afterwards they came back empty-handed.

As they had when they found Eric's body, the outlaws simply stood there in silence, dry-eyed, with deadened expressions. Kit glanced around at them all; their hard, scarred faces. What could he say to these desperadoes that would make any difference?

In the end, he bowed his head and said simply: 'Eric was a warrior of the Earth. A guardian of the forest to the last. Now his flesh will feed this soil. May every one of us, when our time comes, have the chance to return to the forest.'

When he opened his eyes, he saw Midge was already storming away. Hanging his huge head, Much went after him, followed by Jack and Ira. Only Sonskya remained, standing silently alongside Kit, the pair of them facing the Mother Tree, staring into the ancient darkness of her hollow trunk.

Finally, Sonskya said: 'It wasn't your fault, what happened to Eric. No one blames you. Not even Midge. He's just scared. The same as the rest of us.'

Kit looked at her. 'Scared? You? I've seen you face death a dozen times. You're not afraid of anything.'

She shrugged. 'Not my own death, perhaps. But losing this,' she spread her arms to indicate the last forest, 'watching this die . . .?' She looked at him. 'What would we even be, Kit, once this is gone?'

Kit stared at the ground. 'That soldier back at the village – he said the Sheriff will never stop hunting Gaia, not until it's destroyed. And he's right, isn't he? It's only a matter of time. It's a miracle she's stayed hidden this long.'

'It's no miracle, Kit. It's you. It's us. We've driven off his soldiers, led them astray, killed any who've got too close. But we've paid the price in blood. Now there are only six of us left. We can't keep doing this all alone.'

'I know where this is leading. You're wasting your breath.'

'Those villagers out there – you saw them. They've got nothing left to lose.'

'It isn't their fight. *We* are the rebels of Sherwood. *We* are the guardians of the forest.'

'It's everyone's fight, Kit. With so much at stake, how could it not be?'

'Marian said the same thing when she recruited her peasant army. You were there, the same as I was. You remember how that went.'

'This would be different. Don't you see? Marian's refugees were living a soft life in the greenwood. And they thought they always would. I don't think any of them believed – none of us did – that the forest was truly under threat. Those villagers out there are different. They've *seen* what the Sheriff can do. What's more, they've lived through it. They've spent the past twelve years in the shadow of the wastes. They're the ultimate survivors.'

'They're not warriors.'

'You'd *make* them warriors. You'd forge them into an army.'

Kit heard himself laugh – a mean sound full of self-hatred. 'You overestimate me. I couldn't even lead the army I had. I couldn't stop it falling to pieces.'

'No one said—'

'You don't get it, do you,' Kit interrupted. 'I wasn't even supposed to be this.' He shrugged off his quiver, threw it to the ground, along with his bow. 'I never asked for any of it. One day I woke up and people were looking at me for leadership. I went along with it, telling myself I was just carrying the torch, biding time until our true leader returned.'

He laughed again, bitterly. 'That's my secret, Sonskya. All this time, deep down, I've been doing just what the peasants do – I've been hoping and praying for the return of Robin Hood. And where has it got me? Where has it got any of us?'

Sonskya started to speak again, but Kit turned his back on her. He stalked away from the Mother Tree, while the canopy of the forest churned in the wind.

Those villagers out there . . .

You'd forge them into an army.

How could she even suggest it? She was there that day, the same as he was. Behind his eyes now appeared a vision he had seen countless times, in sleep and waking. It was a memory from twelve years ago, before the Great Fire, when he returned to Sherwood Forest and stood at the foot of Major Oak. And there, hanging from the boughs, were dozens of bloody corpses. Every one of the peasants Marian had recruited to her outlaw army. Including all the young people from Kit's village. All of them murdered by Guy of Gisbourne, and strung up like so much slaughtered meat.

No – never – I won't let that happen again. I won't watch history repeat itself. There must be another way.

A crack of thunder made him look skywards. Above Gaia the sky was now very dark, boiling with purple-black cloud. It was hard to tell if this storm was also building out there in the Lost Lands, or if it was more localized. Gaia could conjure her own weather. Even whilst the wastelands baked beneath a heatwave, or withered through a drought, Gaia always managed to summon rain to water her soil and replenish her streams.

As thunder rumbled once more, and the wind roared in the treetops, Kit went on, following deer runs and badger paths through the dense undergrowth, until he climbed a steep slope and came finally to The Henge.

The Mother Tree might stand at the very centre of Gaia, but

The Henge was its dark and primal heart. It consisted of seven yew trees, each as old as the Earth, their trunks gnarled and twisted, their understorey shrouded in permanent mist.

Passing between the twin gateway trees, Kit entered the ancient circle. Its stillness and its gloom enveloped him. As always, it gave him the sense that the outside world had faded away to nothing, and all that now existed was this hallowed patch of earth.

Usually, the moment he stepped into this place, his passions began to cool, his doubts and fears dissolving into the timeless serenity of this refuge. But today he carried too much with him, felt it weighing on him heavier than ever as he paced from one side of The Henge to the other, while the primordial trees watched him and said nothing. Several of them were seeping red sap, making them look as if they were bleeding – or weeping blood from their ancient eye sockets.

Finally, Kit stopped and looked down at a patch of ground. Here was where Robin Hood had knelt when he fought his final battle – when he used the full might of his forest powers to wage war against the Sheriff's firestorm. Since that day, not a single blade of grass had grown where he had knelt – as if in reverence to his sacrifice.

On an impulse, having never done so before, Kit knelt on the same spot. Closing his eyes, he pressed his palms to the earth and he heard himself muttering a prayer.

'Please, if there's any hope . . . show me. Help me see the way. Show me what I need to do.'

In response came a thunderous boom and a cloudburst. The gathering storm broke with a furious passion, lashing the woodland with rain, thrashing it with wind. Even in the sanctuary of The Henge, Kit was buffeted by the winds, while the ancient yews found their voices at last, howling and moaning in their boughs.

Kit remained there on his knees, rainwater soaking his clothes, running down his cheeks, with the crushing sense that at the last even the forest had forsaken him.

IX. Warrior Within

All night Rex had lain awake, listening to the howling of the wind, his imaginings growing ever more tormented. That evening, his father had announced that tomorrow Rex would leave the castle and lead an expedition into the Lost Lands. Even as he was telling Rex this, another storm had arisen in the wastes and swept towards Nottingham. Since then, the storm had steadily built in power, until now it was a true monster. It roared through the city streets, tore at the castle with claws of grit and sand.

The fury of the storm was awesome. But it was not this that kept Rex lying here rigid, unable to even close his eyes. Instead, it was some separate noise . . . something below the wind, or within it. At first, Rex believed his sleepless mind was inventing it. But as the night drew on, it grew ever more real and distinct. Ever more *insistent*.

Yes, there it was again. Where the storm raged and howled, this other sound whispered. Yet it was clean and clear and unmistakable. It sounded like . . . a voice. A voice calling out to him . . . bidding him to take action, or to bear witness . . .

Finally, unable to resist this uncanny summons any longer, Rex rose, shrugged into a dark cloak and padded from his bedchamber. He climbed the spiral staircase, heaved open the trapdoor at the top and emerged onto the crown of the White Tower. Steadying himself against the onslaught of wind, shielding his eyes from a flurry of grit, he crossed to the edge of the parapet, where he braced himself against the low wall. There he stood and stared out towards the wastelands.

The world out there was turbulent and strange. There was a full wolf moon, but its light was refracted through clouds of dust and sand that had risen on the storm. From out of that maelstrom, with its eerie savage beauty, came the tormented howl of the wind, sounding now to Rex like something animal, and injured. And beneath that noise, or cradled within it, was that other sound, that *voice*, whispering its sweet dark secrets . . .

Lightning stabbed at the cursed earth, the flash so bright it pierced the dust clouds and illuminated the whole boundless plain. In that instant, near the horizon, Rex glimpsed something gigantic and black out there in the sand, crouched on its haunches. The light died and Rex stood there, petrified, with the afterimage burning behind his eyes.

There came a second lick of lightning, a forked tongue. The whole plain stretched ahead of him, clear as day. Rex's gaze was already fixed on the dark shape at the horizon. And this time it had time to form into a definite shape.

It no longer looked like a black beast. Instead . . . it was a patch of green wilderness.

An island of trees.

It must be leagues distant, yet in that moment he saw it with perfect clarity, its treetops churning, the full moon hanging directly above it, bathing it in moonbeams.

A gust of wind, carrying a handful of grit, hit him like a mailed fist. He cried out and recoiled, covering his face. Wrapping his cloak around him, raising his hood, he staggered back to the trapdoor, stumbled through, and heaved it closed against the gale.

He lay in the darkness of his bedchamber, his thoughts more turbulent than ever. He knew what he had seen out there was real, he was certain of it. He had seen Gaia. The fabled Last Forest. His father and his war-men had been searching in vain for it for years. Why had it revealed itself to him? Why now? What did that mean?

In fact, the expedition to the Lost Lands did not leave the following day. Nor did it set out the day after that, nor the next. The demon storm would not allow it. Night and day, winds raged out of the wastes. They brought with them blizzards of sand and grit, which battered the city and the castle like hailstones. Nottingham became a ghost city, the approach roads closed, market stalls shuttered and taverns bolted while citizens huddled in their homes.

Marian used the delay to prepare her body and mind. Each evening, she sent away rich platters of meat and cheese, demanding in their stead fresh fruit and fish. In the night, when she woke shaking and drenched in sweat, she bathed in icy water to defeat her cravings for wine.

During her years living in Sherwood Forest, she and her warrior girls had devised a strict system of training in order to stay agile and strong. Now, in her chambers at the top of the White Tower, Marian adopted a similar regime. It was clumsy work at first, but slowly she rediscovered all the old forms – wildcat, falcon, boar. She practised them over and over, hour upon hour, using the rafters of her chamber the way she used to swing from branches in the forest, and furniture to balance across in place of mossy logs, prowling and leaping circuit upon circuit until she was left panting and exhausted on her knees.

She was dismayed at how soft her body had become. Mere days of this training would not make her battle-ready. Even so, at least she was casting off her hateful sloth; hour by hour she sensed her old vitality returning.

In all this time, she had barely seen Rex. After that first night of storms, he hadn't even come back to the White Tower to sleep. She presumed the Sheriff must be keeping him close, putting him through preparations of his own. She loathed the Sheriff for keeping them apart, while also telling herself it was for the best. When she next saw Rex, she would be better armed to face the trials ahead.

The winds continued for a fourth day, and a fifth, bringing torrents of rain and gusts of ash that swirled like an eerie summer snowstorm. She went to the second floor of the White Tower, where there was an entire chamber stuffed with garments that earls and dukes had presented to her as gifts. Most of it was pretty and useless – ornate gowns and pointed shoes and jewelled surcoats – clothes difficult to even walk in, let alone to wear on horseback.

But now and again, over the years, perhaps in respect to her past reputation, some young baron or lordling had brought her an item befitting a warrior queen. After much searching, she recovered one garment that had caught her eye. It was a slim bodice, triple-layered and lacquered, strongly stitched with silk. The baron who brought it claimed it came from a tribe of warlike women in the Far East. And indeed, as Marian strapped herself into it, she found it was as tough and light as the leather armour she once wore in the forest.

She also donned a pair of wrist bracers, made of cordovan leather, and stiffened riding breeches, and goatskin boots. Over the top, to serve as a travelling cloak, but also intended to impress, she choose a hooded robe, which reputedly came from the palaces of Byzantium and which was thickly woven from cloth of gold.

As she clasped the robe at her throat and stood looking at

herself in the mirror, her hair tied back and her eyes bright and fierce, the wind suddenly dropped.

The abrupt silence stopped her breath. Slowly, she crossed to the oval window of the Solar. She peered westwards. Clouds of dust still hung over the Lost Lands, but they no longer swirled. Yes, the storm had abated.

Which meant there would be no more delay. And she found that she wanted none. She blinked and looked around the chamber as if seeing it for the first time. How had she wallowed in this padded misery for so long? How had she squandered so much time?

No – not squandered, she told herself. *You've been doing the most vital work of your life: raising your son, keeping him safe. All these years, you've played this hateful role for his sake.*

But now they were entering a new phase. So she must cast off this false skin. She must reveal the warrior she had buried deep within.

Because, in the days ahead, Rex would face a new breed of danger. But that wasn't all. Because this unlooked-for quest also contained opportunity. In these days of delay, Marian had come to see that with greater and greater certainty.

Yes . . .

Somehow, at some point, she would get her chance.

And when it came, she would be ready.

X. After the Storm

During those days and nights of savage storm, the outlaws lay low in Gaia. Its curtain wall of vine and thorn kept out the bombardment of grit and sand. Even so, Kit lay awake, spellbound by the power of the winds, which thrashed the forest canopy and bent trees almost flat to the ground, while the wood groaned fit to crack.

It seemed miraculous to Kit that any of these trees remained standing. But stand they did, shoulder to shoulder, leaning into one another and helping to thrust their brothers and sisters upright, and in this way weathering the onslaught.

Together with the wind came the rain, which lashed Gaia with such power that it made boiling cauldrons of the ponds and pools.

Finally, on the sixth day, the storm ceased. Kit's shelter was waterproofed with willow bark and holly leaves and birch resin, but even so he was soaked to the bone on the morning he crawled out and walked through the bright and steaming wood.

He climbed to a high plateau at the eastern edge of Gaia, which commanded a view across the wastes. Ira and Sonskya came up to join him, and they all three stood looking out in awed silence.

'It's a different world,' Ira said at last.

'No wonder,' said Sonskya. 'It hasn't rained out there for weeks.'

Kit swept his gaze once more, shielding his eyes against the dawn sun. Here in Gaia, the greenery had softened the power of the downpour, while the topsoil absorbed the deluge. The river and the streams, although gorged, were already settling back into their normal course.

Out there, in the badlands, the ferocious rain had fallen on bare, sun-baked ground. It had wreaked havoc. Great slews of mud were slouching down hillsides. There were landslides and rockfalls. Surface water gushed everywhere, gouging fresh gullies, pooling into dark sucking pits.

'Well, we won't be going out there anytime soon,' said Ira. 'I'm going back to sleep. Providing I can find anywhere dry to lie down.'

For two more days the outlaws were confined to their island of solid ground, encircled by a sea of shifting mud and sand. But on the third day it changed. Standing at his lookout post, Kit watched the mudflows begin to slow, and finally come to a stop. The ground steamed as the blazing sun evaporated the last of the surface water.

Kit walked down to the boundary, created a tunnel through the wall of vegetation and stepped out into the wastes. The ground crunched beneath his feet. It was once again baked solid, and was now covered in a whitish crust. In fact, it was harder and more forbidding out here than ever, the landscape gouged and gullied and saw-edged. Here and there were treacherous pools of sinking mud, which bubbled and popped, giving off a noxious stench.

The other outlaws emerged behind Kit, and for a while they all wandered aimless, circling Gaia, peering about themselves, getting their bearings.

Kit looked to the east. A rainbow was taking shape. It gradually became more distinct, until it was perfect; vibrant from end to end, dark cloud above it, bright blue sky beneath.

It had been a long time since Kit had seen a thing of real beauty out here in the wastes, and for a while he just stood and stared. But then something else caught his eye. Something on the cracked, grey ground ahead of him.

The tiny thing sparkled in the sunrays and gleamed, like an emerald.

He went forward and knelt and looked at it in wonder.

It was a green shoot.

A single stem, with two perfect miniature leaves.

Kit lifted his head – there was another one! He rose and went to it and knelt again, brushing the second shoot with his fingertips.

'I thought it was a mirage,' said Ira, as she and Sonskya came to stand over him. 'But you're touching it. It's solid.'

'Who would have known,' said Sonskya, 'after all this time, there's still life in this land after all.'

'Look,' said Ira. 'Is that another one – over there?'

The three of them went to look, and yes – here was another tiny plantlet, with three shining leaves, struggling up through the drying mud. The two warrior women skipped on, gasping with girlish delight, and found a fourth shoot and a fifth, and more.

Kit stood and watched them drawing ahead, following a trail from one plantlet to the next. They were moving away from Gaia in a straight line, travelling directly south east.

Could it really be . . . ?

Please, if there's any hope . . . show me. Help me see the way.

That was the prayer Kit had whispered to the forest, when he had knelt in The Henge, before the rains came. And now . . . here were these shoots.

This emerald trail.

'Where are they going?' Jack said, nodding towards Ira and Sonskya, as the others gathered.

Kit squared his shoulders, looked each of them in the eye. 'They're following a trail,' he said, with as much authority as he could muster. 'What's more – we're all going to do the same. These plantlets – see them?'

Midge sneered at him. 'Finally snapped, mighty leader? A trail of flowers? What exactly are we hoping to find at the end of it?'

'I don't need to explain myself to you,' Kit snarled in response. 'Gather your weapons, and pack provisions. Midge, if you don't stop looking at me like that there'll be hell to pay. Do what I say, and be quick.'

As the others trudged away, Kit asked himself why he had bared his teeth at Midge. Was it because he shared his doubts? Was it pure lunacy to follow this unknown path into nameless lands? Was it a path at all, or was Kit merely so desperate he was now seeing a way where there was none?

In the end, he dismissed these fears as he went to collect his bow and pack. Pure delusion or true hope, what difference did it make? It *was* a way forward. It was the only one they had. For better or worse, here was the path they would take.

XI. Relationship of Command

'Your force is assembled, sire,' Alpha Johns said. 'We are ready to depart.'

These words acted like a spell on Rex. Having barely slept for nights on end, the world this morning had appeared fuzzy and unreal. But now, in an instant, everything came into the sharpest relief. Rex looked at Alpha Johns, sitting tall in the saddle of his destrier, wearing the crested skull helm that marked him as Chief Rider.

He swept his gaze across the other twenty rangers gathered in the Great Ward, all of them armed and armoured and wearing the crimson cloaks of the Sheriff's Guard. And suddenly it seemed to him he could hear every breath of every horse, see every vein in every eye as the men looked back at him expectantly. As they waited for *him* to give the command.

Turning in his saddle, he looked towards the great gates of the castle, which stood open, the drawbridge lowered. Beyond the gates lay the sprawl of the city, the streets awash with grey sludge following the dust storm and the deluge, people emerging tentatively from their homes, the marketplaces and the taverns coming slowly back to life.

And beyond all this, just visible from this elevation, were the city's walls. And set into those walls was the gateway that would lead Rex and his war party out onto the road . . . which in turn would lead inexorably to the wastes . . .

Alpha Johns leaned close, dropped his voice low so only Rex could hear. 'I remember the first time I went into the Lost Lands,' he said. 'I won't pretend it was easy. But trust me, the waiting beforehand was worse. Nothing is ever as bad as the imagining.'

Rex looked at his mentor. His eyes were as grey as granite, but with none of the coldness. Although he could be a hard taskmaster, Alpha had always treated Rex with respect and fairness, even kindness. His presence on this expedition could not be more welcome.

'And I'll tell you something,' Alpha continued, 'you're better prepared, body and spirit, than I ever was. What's more, you're in the best possible company. I handpicked these troops myself. They are good men, and loyal. They will follow your every word without question.'

Rex looked again at the assembled rangers. To a man, they had polished their black half-armour until it gleamed with a dark lustre. The crest of the Sheriff – a wolf's head with its teeth bared – stood out stark and livid against their chests.

They are good men, and loyal. They will follow your every word without question.

Rex sat taller in his saddle. *Yes, and as well they might*, he told himself. *You are the Sheriff's heir. You were born to lead. It's in your blood. Now is your chance to prove it.*

All heads turned as a newcomer entered the Great Ward. She rode a beautiful silver sprinter, and her robe was woven from cloth of gold, so that she shimmered in the dawn light like something divine.

Rex stared, for a moment unsure whether this truly was his mother. She sat straight-backed and clear-eyed, her expression fierce and implacable. Rex was put in mind of a relief painted on the chapel ceiling which depicted warrior angels, their spears flaming as they swept into battle.

So impressive did she look, in fact, that as she approached he felt himself shrink a little in his saddle. He noticed the effect she had on the assembled troops, half of whom averted their eyes, as if they had glanced at the sun, the other half continuing to stare, but all of them seeming to grow smaller somehow as they shuffled aside to let her pass.

Rex shrank further as she drew near, and he saw the way she was scrutinizing him.

'Whose cloak is that?' she asked harshly, as she came to a halt.

Rex pushed back his shoulders. 'It's mine.'

'Where did you get it?'

'Father gave it to me. It's the one he wore when he first went into Sherwood.'

'I feared it might be. It doesn't suit you. Take it off.'

'What? No.'

'There's no shade in the wastes. And black absorbs the heat. You'll boil in your skin.'

Rex glared at her. When he was told his mother would be joining them on the expedition, he had never felt more conflicted about anything. On the one hand, even if he didn't want to admit it, having her at his side would be hugely reassuring. And yet, at the same time, he resented her interference. And now, here she was, before they'd even set off, undermining his command.

'Mother,' he said in a low voice, glancing towards the assembled war men, 'you need to remember this is my mission. Father entrusted it to me.' He narrowed his eyes. 'You don't think I can do it, do you? That's why you're here. You don't think I can lead these troops.'

She shook her head. 'I wish you didn't have to.'

'What's that supposed to mean?'

She looked about to respond but held her tongue, and finally let out a long breath. 'It doesn't matter. There's no stopping it now. '

She muttered something else to herself as she turned to inspect the war party. Her gaze lingered on a soldier named Sam Gorefield. Perched on the saddle behind him was the scavenger, a scrawny girl of perhaps eleven or twelve years old.

'Chief Rider,' Marian said to Alpha. 'I understood there were two scavengers – twins. Where is her brother?'

'I wasn't told,' Alpha said, 'and I didn't ask. The Sheriff said one guide would suffice.'

Marian creased her brow as she studied the scavenger. The girl was dressed in desert rags, with a pair of bone goggles perched atop her head. She wore a permanent grimace, as if in pain, even as she met Marian's gaze with a glare of defiance.

'Why wouldn't we take them both?' Marian tried again, addressing Alpha. 'What does he intend with the other?'

'What does it matter?' Rex snapped, hating the petulance in his own voice. 'Everything's prepared, Mother. There's nothing else to think about. We need to get underway.'

Forcing himself to sit tall, he faced his war-men. 'Bring the scavenger up front,' he called, flushing scarlet as he heard his voice break around the words. 'We've got a lot of ground to cover before nightfall, so we'll set a fast pace.'

With that, turning quickly away from them all, he dug his heels into his horse's flanks and led the way across the Great Ward.

Something made him look back towards the Keep. Standing there atop the parapet, watching him leave, was his father. He kept his gaze fixed on Rex, his expression as cold as iron.

You think I can't do it, Rex said silently, facing forwards. *You and Mother both. You think I'm afraid. You think I'll fail. But I won't. I'm not who you think I am. You'll see.*

As the party rode out through the gates, Marian too turned to look back. She also saw the Sheriff standing at the top of the Keep, watching them with that cold, dead stare. Seeing him there, Marian flooded with a rage that took her breath away.

How dare you put Rex though this ordeal. How dare you put him in harm's way!

Her fury grew fiercer still, until it clawed in her flesh. It was the wrath of a wildcat, standing over her cub, when mortal danger threatens.

For everything you've done, she promised the Sheriff noiselessly, *for everything you've cost me and Rex . . . I will destroy you.*

This idea materialized like a ghost from a different lifetime. Loathe the Sheriff as she might, it had been years since she had actively sworn vengeance upon him.

But her old self was rising. Her true self. If she had doubted that before, now she was sure of it. And she was glad. Because where they were going, she would need every ounce of her warrior spirit. She would need it to keep Rex safe. And she would need it too for her other objective. For her secret scheme.

That scheme now burned in her heart and mind, fierce and clear, as she followed her son and his war party out through the castle gates.

Unbeknownst to Marian and Rex, the Sheriff was not alone at the top of the Keep. As he watched the expedition start down through the city streets, he beckoned to a figure standing in the shadows. Guy of Gisbourne stepped heavily to his side.

'I trust your preparations are complete, Sir Guy. As soon as they are out of sight, I want you to follow.'

'You knew Lady Marian would insist on going,' the heretic hunter said from behind his mask. 'That was your intention.'

The Sheriff nodded. 'This expedition has assumed a triple purpose. It is vital that the little people should see the remains of Robin Hood. To understand that his power is extinct. At the same time, they must witness my son coming into his own power.'

After a moment, Sir Guy looked at him. 'And the third purpose?'

The Sheriff's eyes had taken on a watery sheen as he continued to stare westwards. 'I accused Lady Marian of living in the past,' he said at last. 'But I too have been guilty of that. For years I have lived with the idea of who she once was, rather than the reality of who she has become. What is worse . . . I have allowed her to corrupt my son. The damage can yet be undone, but we must act now.'

He turned his head suddenly, and his good eye was weeping. 'Do you see, Sir Guy, I am left no other choice. The people would never accept me breaking with my wife – not unless Death himself should rip us apart. Unless the cruel wilderness should tear her from my grasp.'

He stared once more after the dwindling party, which was now approaching the city gates. 'So go. Do what needs to be done. Ensure my son learns his lesson, and triumphs. And as for Lady Marian,' he added, in the barest of whispers, 'see to it she never returns from the wastes.'

Part Two
Unearthed

I. Return to Sherwood

Returning to Sherwood, when the moment arrived, was far worse than Marian could even have imagined. After leaving the castle, the party had ridden a full day across tattered farmland and scrub. It was a dismal, treeless landscape. A place of poisoned waterholes and razed copses and abandoned crofts. The fields were dry and the roadways were crumbling and the tracks overgrown with spear grass and saw thistle.

Back when she lived in the forest, Marian and the other outlaws had referred to this terrain, which lay close to the city and the toxic influence of the Sheriff, as the Shadowlands. Compared to their wildwood home, it appeared to them mortally wounded.

But it was nothing compared to what lay in front of Marian now. For the past hour, the soil had become increasingly sandy and cracked beneath the horses' hooves. What little life Marian could see or hear slowly ebbed away. The sky was now devoid of birds, empty even of insects. Even the spear grass and burn weed were thinning, only sparse clumps clinging here and there to the parched soil.

And finally even these remnants of vegetation gave way to nothing. As Marian stared and stared, horror-struck, she did not even realize that the war party had come to a halt, or that her own mount had stopped of its own accord.

They had come to the invisible boundary of the Lost Lands. Ahead of her, stretching away for ever, was nothing but bare, scorched earth. Here and there it was dotted with rocks, and with small heaps of animal bones, and it was scarred with crevices and gullies. As the sun lowered, it filled these fissures with shadow, making this hellscape appear all the more fractured and jagged.

Next to her, Marian was vaguely aware that Rex and Alpha Johns were talking between themselves. But for the moment her mind was unable to understand their words, or fully comprehend anything – least of all these terrible unreal deadlands that lay in front of her.

All these years she had lived with the awful knowledge that Sherwood Forest no longer existed. But perhaps it was true, what she had said to the Sheriff – that part of her had never truly accepted it. Only standing here now, staring into this barren desert – listening to this noiseless void where the great forest once scuttled and scurried and shrieked – did that knowledge finally and fully pierce her heart, stabbing at her with an intensity of grief that left her barely able to breathe.

A freak gust of wind swept across the plain with a heavy hollow howl. Such a sound, had it arisen in the old times, might even have gone unnoticed amid the cacophony of the forest. But now, moaning out of the void, this noise was terrible. It unsettled the horses, making them toss their heads, and the soldiers, many of whom muttered prayers. To Marian's horror-struck mind, it sounded like a mass howl of torment – as if all the lost creatures of Sherwood, countless legions of them, had risen from the dead to send up one last wail of anguish.

'We can't do it,' she heard herself murmur. 'We can't go in there.' She turned to address Alpha Johns. 'Chief Rider, leave us,' she said, her voice trembling. 'I need to speak with my son.'

Alpha looked at Rex, who nodded.

'Mother – what is it?' Rex asked as Alpha drew away, going to join the rest of the troops. 'You're shaking.'

'Listen to me,' she said, keeping her voice low. 'This is wrong. All of it. We can't go any further.'

'It's getting late, I know,' Rex said, 'but Alpha thinks we should push on while we can. He says it does the men no good to—'

'No – listen to what I'm saying! We can't go in there at all. Not now. Not ever. We shouldn't even be here.' She leaned towards him, shot a glance back at Alpha and the rest. 'You have to trust me. We need to leave. This wasn't the way I'd planned it. In my head, we would enter the wastes and bide our time. Go under the cover of darkness. But we can't wait. We have to go, now.'

'I don't know what you mean. Go where?'

'Anywhere! Anywhere but in there – or back to the city. We'll run, we'll hide, and we'll run again. We couldn't have done it before – not when you were a child. But now it's different. You're as good a rider as I am. You're quick and strong. They won't catch us, I know they won't. Together we can make it. We'll be free!'

'I don't understand.'

'Because I'm gabbling, and can barely think. But *please*, you need to see. This shouldn't be happening. None of it. You wearing the Sheriff's cloak, leading the Sheriff's men. It's all a mistake.'

Rex looked away. 'So that's it,' he said. 'This again. You think I can't do it. You think I'm scared.'

'No – yes – who cares! This is not your life. It's all a lie. It isn't you.'

'You're as bad as Father. He thinks I'm a frightened child.' He gave her a wounded glare. 'I'll show him. I'll show you both.'

As he spoke, another freak gust of wind arose, this one bringing with it a flurry of grit and sand, making Rex raise a hand to shield his eyes. With the wind came another demon howl – a sound straight out of hell, which set the horses stamping their feet and the rangers to muttering prayers.

Alpha Johns stepped over, struggling to control his agitated mount.

'Commander,' he said to Rex, 'if you mean to overnight here, give the word. If not, we should press on. This waiting favours no one, man or beast.'

'We continue,' Rex replied, his voice cracking. 'Onwards,' he called out to the troops. 'We can cover another league before nightfall. Gorefield – bring the scavenger to the front. Chief Rider, take the lead with me.'

And with that, he was kicking his mount into motion, and the war party was following in his wake. Marian was the last to move, her chest tight and her vision fuzzy with despair. Had that been their moment – their golden chance? Would they get another?

With such thoughts howling through her, and a deepening sense of doom, she had no choice but to spur her horse onwards and follow her son into the merciless wastes.

II. The Ghost Forest

Trailing the rest of the party, her heart so leaden it barely seemed to beat in her chest, Marian stared around her at the Lost Lands. Time and again, her memory flashed upon the old days – how entering Sherwood had always felt like a blessed homecoming, the greenwood greeting her with its panoply of rich scents and sights and smells, her senses dancing with the squirrel kits in the boughs.

This return, in stark contrast, was like drowning in mud – in nothingness. The single sound was the empty moan of the wind. The only aroma was of hot rock and baked earth. The stored heat in that leafless ground rose to meet her, harsh and unforgiving. Bridging a hand above her eyes, she swept her gaze once more across this vast trackless landscape, with a sorrow that left her hollow, and numb.

She knew she was not the only one. During the long ride across the scrublands, the soldiers had been loudmouthed, gregarious as crows. She had suspected their bluster was all show – a smokescreen to hide their nervousness. Now she knew it for certain. Because since entering the Lost Lands, the rangers had barely uttered a word between them. A full battalion, and it barely made a sound – only the clink of the horses' harnesses and the clomp of their hooves against the baked ground.

Even these sounds were unreal – too loud and staccato in this hollow landscape – each noise short and sharp and hard. Marian's own breathing and her heartbeat became the chief sounds to her own ears. These noises, in fact, were now so dominant that they gave her the eerie impression that she had grown to an enormous size – that she and Rex and the war-men were suddenly giants riding gargantuan steeds across this barren plain.

Yes – these deadlands distorted perception – already she could see that. When they had stood at the boundary, she thought she had spotted heaps of animal bones. But now, as they rode and rode across the plain, they did not reach the bones or pass them; they remained there in the near distance, barely growing any bigger. Now she understood: these were not the carcasses of animals, but the remains of fallen trees. Their trunks and boughs were strewn far and wide, the wood bleached bone-white by the relentless sun. In this blank landscape, with nothing to measure them against, their colossal size made them appear much closer than they were.

As they rode on, Marian's disorientation only grew worse. This sprawling empty landscape – it was hardly a place at all, but rather a non-place, a space where the usual rules of distance and direction did not apply. She thought she saw a line of hills rising at the horizon, but a moment later they were riding past this landmark and it was merely a low bank of sand.

She kicked her horse and rode to the head of the line, where Rex and Alpha Johns and the ranger Gorefield were riding in silence. Rex turned his eyes to her before once more staring intently into the distance.

Marian studied the scavenger, sitting in the saddle behind Gorefield. As she had for the entire journey, the girl looked deeply troubled, her face contracted as if in physical pain.

'I was told you have a twin,' Marian said to her. 'Where is he?'

'Don't start that again,' Rex said. 'I told you, it's not important.'

The scavenger herself said nothing, seemed only to grimace, looking more pained than ever.

'You've got no map,' Marian tried again. 'I've seen no landmarks. How do you know we're on track?'

Again, the girl gave no response, didn't even turn to face Marian, and in the end Alpha spoke for her.

'I keep asking her the same thing. All she'll say is, she knows. I guess we'll just have to trust in that. She grew up here, I suppose. It's her world.'

These words caused Marian to shiver. She stared again at the scavenger. How old was she? Certainly too young to have known the great forest. To her . . . this lifeless plain . . . it was normal. This idea struck Marian as truly dreadful. As they rode on in silence, the wastelands only seemed to her more abysmal and hostile. It appeared . . . unreal, and senseless – a landscape devoid of shape and meaning.

It grew more so as the sun lowered. The reddish light seeped into cracks and fissures, making the ground appear saw-edged and fractured. An evening mist was rising. It was a ghostly mist, with a greenish tinge, and stirred thickly around the horses' hooves.

Marian blinked into the mist, and into the dust-heavy distance, and her vision shifted . . . and to her profound disbelief she saw trees. Not deadwood, but upright, living trees! Beech and oak and elm and alder. Her heart lurched, lifted. The great forest wasn't extinct after all! Sherwood lived!

But then the mist swirled, and angled sunlight sliced through the phantom trees, cutting them to ribbons. Marian blinked once more and saw only bare, scorched earth swirling with dust. Again, her heart lurched and contracted, and she must have made some sound because Rex and Alpha were staring at her.

'Mother, what is it?'

Marian went on staring at the spot where the spectre of

Sherwood had arisen and dispersed. It had seemed so solid, so *real*, that she could weep from the fresh loss of it.

'What have you seen?' Rex tried again, narrowing his eyes, trying to follow her gaze.

She shook her head, looked at the ground. 'It's . . . nothing. I don't know what it was.'

For Rex's sake, she tried to keep her voice even. But in truth, that glimpse of the phantom forest had left her shaken. And as they went onwards, and the mist thickened, she suffered more visions.

Here – right in front of her now – so solid-seeming she might reach out and run her hands across their bark – were the mighty pillars of living trees. They were there, she could swear they were! But a moment later they were gone, taken apart as the dust swirled and the twilight pierced the mist.

Marian knew that many of the Sheriff's soldiers referred to the Lost Lands as the Ghost Forest. Now she fully understood why. Everywhere she looked she saw more glimmers of wildwood – stands of pine trees and sweeping reaches of beech and thickets of hawthorn. These mirages became ever more substantial, until she began to believe she could even *hear* the great forest – the whistling of birds, the yapping of fox cubs, the shushing of wind in the treetops.

My mind can't accept this landscape, she realized, suddenly knowing the truth of it, as a towering emperor oak rose then vanished. *This silence, this . . . nothingness. It doesn't think this place can be real. So it's filling it with sights and sounds.*

She knew she wasn't the only one beset by visions. All around her, the soldiers wore haunted expressions as they stared around them, some of them gripping lucky charms or crucifixes or muttering prayers beneath their breath. Only two people seemed immune to these phantoms: the scavenger and Rex.

'You don't see it, do you?' she asked her son.

'See what?'

'The forest. By the time you were born . . . it was gone. For you – it's like it never was.' Saying these words stirred in her a profound sorrow. 'Oh, Rex, I wish I could have brought you here. When the forest lived.' She paused, then said: 'There was a place in Sherwood called Elysium Glades. It had lakes and waterfalls and whistling frogs.' She rubbed at her eyes, smiling and wanting to cry at the same time. 'And there were halcyon birds – dozens of them. They drew rainbows with their wings.'

Rex looked at her quizzically. 'What's a halcyon bird?'

Marian sat back in her saddle. How could she even begin to answer such a question? She looked at Rex, and stared around her at the world he inhabited, that he had inherited, and her sorrow gave way to anger.

Her anger redoubled as Rex broke into one of his coughing fits. He coughed and coughed, doubled over on his saddle, the air rasping in his lungs. With Alpha and the other soldiers looking on, she resisted the urge to reach out and comfort him, but merely watched, her heart wrenching, until the fit subsided.

'The Sheriff,' she said through gritted teeth. 'He did this to you. He stole your birthright. The land you walk upon. The air you breathe.'

Rex turned his reddened eyes on her. 'You shouldn't talk about him that way.'

'It's the truth! He took everything from you, and you don't even know it!'

'Mother,' Rex snapped, glancing at Alpha, 'the men are listening.'

'I don't care – let them hear it! He stole it from them too. We've all inherited his world of ashes!'

'Stop it!' Rex said, shooting another glance at Alpha. 'Why are you even here, Mother? Are you supposed to be helping me? Is that it?'

'Listen to me. We need—'

'No, you listen!' he said, glaring at her, looking bewildered and scared and angry. 'Father set me a task. He sent me out here to retrieve something. I am not going back without it. I'd rather die out here. Do you understand?'

He straightened in his saddle, turned to address Alpha Johns. 'Chief Rider, order a halt. It's getting too dark to see. This terrain is treacherous. We daren't risk a horse breaking a leg. Have the men set up the shelters, then post sentries. We go on again at first light.'

All this came to Marian thickly, as if heard from a great distance. She watched her son barking orders with a drowning sense of disbelief. How did it come to this? Her own son leading the Sheriff's troops . . .

Her disbelief swelled into despair. She had joined this quest with a secret agenda – the idea that somehow she and Rex would find a way to escape the soldiers and make a break for freedom. In her mind, she had navigated the various challenges. They would steal away under the cover of darkness; they would race to the coast, before stowing away on a seagoing craft. They would take refuge in her ancestral lands of Castile.

Except she had neglected the first and most fundamental obstacle of all, which was Rex himself! To him, all that mattered was this farcical mission. How could she win him his freedom when he didn't even know he was caged?

She watched him moving now among the troops, he and Alpha deep in conversation, like old friends.

He is not your ally! she wanted to scream at him. *He is your enemy!*

Except how could he know this? She herself had kept him blinkered his entire life. Now what would it take to open his eyes to the truth?

III. Thicker than Water

After spending a dismal and sleepless night beneath cloth tents, the party rose at dawn and went on again. At first, having lain shivering on that iron-cold ground, Rex was glad to feel the warmth of the sun. But within an hour the heat was blazing off the leafless ground. By mid-morning every last trace of cloud had left the sky, and the day had become searingly hot. The sun quivered and appeared to drip, like molten steel.

'Conditions like these can kill a man,' Alpha Johns said at his side. 'And the horses won't fare much better. If it was me I'd call a halt, at least for the middle hours.'

Reluctantly, Rex agreed. The rangers once more unloaded the packhorses and erected the tents and the party took to the shade.

These shelters were open-sided, and there was a light breeze, but even so, sitting here, Rex had never been so discomfited or so miserable in his entire life. Needle flies stabbed at him, while mosquitoes buzzed and pinched.

Worse than any of this, though, was his vulcanism. Ever since they had entered the wastes it had grown steadily more intense, until now it crawled and burned across his skin and sank scalding into his flesh. His arms no longer felt like his own, but were some demon thing, detached from him, floating in a sea of pain. His hands refused to sit still, and against his will scratched and rubbed at his arms, sharpening his torment.

He stared across at his mother, who sat apart in a shelter of her own. No doubt she carried balms and curatives in her backpack. Yet even in the depths of his agony, something stopped him from going to her for aid. Was it simply that he didn't want to show weakness in front of his war-men? Or was it something else?

He went on watching his mother, who had her knees pulled up to her chest, her golden cloak draped around her. She was sitting very still, apparently unperturbed by the insects, and she was staring out across the wastes. What was on her mind?

I've hated lying to you, all these years.

This is not your life. It's all a lie.

Suddenly it was all coming back to him – all the things she had said to him in recent days. Some of it he had only half-heard at the time, or had immediately buried out of mind. Now it all came swimming to the surface, leaving him dizzy, his vision blurred, while ahead of him the plain quivered with heat haze.

Perhaps it was the effect of being out here in this twisted landscape, where distance and direction could not be trusted, where drifting sand made the ground itself shift beneath your feet, but suddenly he had the disturbing sensation that *nothing* was as it seemed. As if . . . as if all his life he had been viewing the world in a warped mirror.

He looked down at Alpha Johns, who was stretched out, his head pillowed on his backpack. 'Chief Rider. Alpha. Can I ask you something?'

Alpha sat up. 'Ask away,' he said, swatting at the side of his neck. 'I could use the distraction from these damned insects.'

Rex hesitated before saying: 'My mother. Before she came to the castle . . . and joined my father. Was she truly an outlaw?'

Alpha shifted uncomfortably. 'What does she say about that?'

'She never talks about any of it. I don't suppose I cared before. But now, somehow . . . it seems important.'

'Well,' Alpha said, carefully, 'if your mother chooses not to tell, perhaps it isn't my place either.'

'What if I ordered you to?'

Alpha laughed at that. 'Well then,' he looked over at Rex's mother. 'Yes, there's nothing truer. Lady Marian was an outlaw. The warrior queen of Sherwood, in fact.'

Rex gazed again at his mother, who still hadn't moved a muscle, as though she had sunk into one of her melancholies. 'What was she like? In those days, I mean. Did you ever fight against her?'

Alpha shook his head. 'I was a novice ranger back then. Same as the rest of these men. Mostly, our place was back at the castle. Cleaning out the barracks, guard duty.'

'You never went into Sherwood?'

Alpha slapped at the back of his neck, opened his palm to reveal the bloody remains of an insect. 'Never,' he said. 'I was stationed at a garrison for a while, on the edge of the forest. But that was as close as I got. We were desperate to go in, of course – or at least that's what we told ourselves.' He smiled grimly. 'Had we actually been ordered to go, it might have been a different story.' His tone darkened as he added: 'In the end . . . we thanked our stars we were left behind.'

'What do you mean?'

Alpha paused, then picked his words with care. 'The final attack on Sherwood. The methods your father used. Was forced to use. They hurt our side as much as they did theirs. We all watched friends ride out for the forest that day. Not one of them came back.'

Before either of them could speak again, a noise arose that made everyone raise their heads. It was the hollow groan of wind across the plain. It became louder, and deeper, until it sounded like a great exhalation – like the breath of some titanic creature waking out there in the wastes.

'This is what I feared most,' Alpha said, watching the eastern horizon, where dust had begun to billow. 'Out here the winds rise from nowhere, and can be vicious. These shelters won't be worth much in a glass storm.'

He stood and went to a neighbouring tent. With the toe of his boot, he poked the scavenger, who sat up and looked at him, hollow-eyed.

'You told me you and your brother passed gullies. Whereabouts?'

Mutely, Arora lifted one arm, pointed eastwards.

'How far?'

The scavenger shrugged. 'A league. Maybe. More or less.'

As the wind groaned once more, Alpha returned to Rex.

'Riding anywhere beneath this sun could be deadly,' the Chief Rider said. 'But I'd judge those winds pose the greater threat.'

Rex dragged his gaze away from his mother. 'Give the order,' he said. 'Make sure all the horses have been watered and fed. Then get us back underway.'

While rangers broke camp around her, and the wind continued to rise, Marian remained motionless, staring into the distance, weathering a storm of turbulent thoughts.

It's been discovered, finally.

The body of Robin Hood.

It seemed extraordinary, and struck her with shame and sorrow, that until they stopped here to shelter from the sun, Robin had not been on her mind. Since she left her rose garden, in fact, days ago, she had not thought of him once.

Had she intentionally put him out of mind, because the idea of him was too painful? Or had she simply been so focused on

Rex and the danger he was heading into that there was no room for anything or anyone else?

Either way, the thought of Robin had now returned with a vengeance. Her memories of him burned brighter than they had done in years. She recalled him as a boy, quick and brave and fierce, when they had lived together in their tower. She remembered his laughter, which came rarely, but was all the more wonderful for that. She relived the feel of his body against hers when they lay together on their lake isle.

These memories might almost make her smile. Except now that other fact hit her in full force – the reason they had come into these wastelands in the first place. They were here to retrieve Robin's corpse. At the end of this journey, should they survive it, Marian would be with him again. Only this time, and for ever, they would be separated by death.

To the east, the wind howled more ferociously than ever, shrieking through the fissures and furrows of the cracked earth.

'Work faster – all of you!' Alpha Johns was shouting, striding among the soldiers as they stowed the tents onto the pack-horses. 'This damned storm is rising faster than we thought. The scavenger knows a place we can take shelter. We must get there before it hits.'

In the distance, the wind howled once more, groaning long and low and heavy. To Marian, the noise sounded animal. Almost human. It was the voice of the land itself, moaning in its drawn-out death throes. This land that long ago had been struck a killer blow . . . which was mortally wounded . . . but which even now refused to breathe its last . . .

As such thoughts swirled through her, something gave way in Marian. Unbidden, the most fabulous idea arose. It was a tiny, fluttering hope, fragile as a newly formed butterfly. It was so precious, this notion, and delicate, that at first she dared not move unless it should break.

Finally, Marian blinked, and got slowly to her feet. Walking carefully, still with that idea of cradling something infinitely precious, she headed towards the scavenger. The girl was clambering into the saddle behind her escort.

'Scavenger – ride with me,' Marian said. 'I need to speak with you.'

'She can't do that,' said the ranger, Gorefield.

'She can, and she will.'

'I was given express orders.'

'And now you're being given new ones.' Marian locked eyes with him. 'I see your error. You've seen me around the castle, in my painted prison, and you've concluded that I've been defanged. Well, we're not in the castle now, and I assure you I can still bite. Stand up to me again and I swear by this cursed earth you will regret it.'

While she spoke, Gorefield tried to sit tall and hold her gaze. But Marian's old self was rising, the fire rekindled in her eyes, and she was not surprised when his defiance broke and he bowed his head.

'As for you,' she said to the scavenger, who sat slumped in the saddle, 'I can tell you don't like me very much. I could hazard a guess why, except I don't care. Get up on my horse, now, or you will shortly wish you had never been born.'

Arora climbed down and slouched after Marian. Soon the pair of them were mounted and underway, following at the rear of the procession as Rex and Alpha led them in a canter, and the wind howled.

'I'm going to ask you some questions,' Marian told the scavenger as they rode. 'A great deal rests on the accuracy of your answers, so I want you to think carefully before you speak. Do you understand me?'

Arora remained silent, only clinging to Marian as her horse stumbled across the rutted ground.

'Right now, you are not yourself, I understand that,' Marian told her. 'You are a scavenger of the wastes. To survive out here, you must be tough and quick and brave. Yet I've watched you since we set out, and I've barely seen a spark of life. You're a dead girl walking.'

'You don't know the first thing about me.'

'I know you're a twin. You've never been separated from your brother before, have you? And now it feels like half of you is missing. Like you've been hollowed out from the inside.'

The girl sat rigid, maintaining a stubborn silence. But finally she slumped. 'It's agony,' she murmured. 'I can't stand it. Please, tell me, why is he keeping us apart? What does he want with Lucas?'

'Your brother? I have my own theory about that,' Marian said. 'I'm keeping it to myself until you answer my questions.'

'Why should I trust you? We should never have trusted him.'

'I am not the Sheriff. If it was in my power, I'd see him writhing in hell. You can believe that or not, I don't care. Either way, you do not have a choice. You will tell me what I need to know. Firstly, you and your brother, what did you find out here?'

After a pause, the girl murmured: 'I already said what we found.'

'You didn't tell me. I've been told it was Robin Hood. How do you know it was him?'

Again, the scavenger hesitated. 'Our father used to tell us stories. About the outlaws of Sherwood Forest. He told us all about Robin Hood – what he could do and what he looked like. And when we crawled into that tree stump, there he was – we saw him with our own eyes.'

'Describe him.'

'Well – he was wearing the cloak. You know – the godskin. Beneath that . . . there isn't much to tell. He was just skin and bones.'

Marian swallowed. 'Bones? Is that what you found?'

'Well . . . in a manner of speaking. His corpse then. The flesh was still on him.'

Marian put her hand to her chest, cradling that fragile hope. 'And that flesh . . . was it rotting? Was it decomposed?'

'As a matter of fact . . . no,' said the scavenger. 'I did think about that. There weren't no smell, either. I suppose he must have died recent.'

Or he never died at all, Marian thought, the tiny fluttering hope fully fledging at last, opening its wings and flying free, leaving her dizzy and gripping the saddle for balance.

And why shouldn't she hope? Didn't it all suddenly make sense? If Robin had died in the Great Fire, he would have been reduced to ashes. If, on the other hand, he had somehow escaped the inferno and crawled away somewhere else to die, by now he would be nothing but a pile of bones. But that was not what the twins had found. The only other explanation was that he had survived the fire, and the intervening years, somehow wandering the wastes unseen, only to lie down and die in recent weeks. None of these scenarios seemed plausible.

So what did? She recalled Robin's deep connection with the Earth – his ability to send his essence into the green – to merge his mind and spirit with the greater being of the forest. She remembered watching him do this; he would become so still he was like something rooted. His pulse and heartbeat would slow to the point where they were barely perceptible, like a hibernating creature.

She had known him occupy such a state for hours, even days on end. But what if Robin's ability to exist like this had *no* limit?

What if . . . what if he could exist that way indefinitely . . . ?

As if in answer to this question, the wind rose to a new pitch, tearing across the plain with its deathless howl. Looking up at the sound, Marian's vision wavered with more images of the ghost forest: towering oak and beech trees conjured out of the swirling dust and mist.

This twisted, alien place – the gods only knew what was possible here. So why not? It was tearing her in two, this notion that was unthinkable yet credible, impossible yet true. Could Robin really have survived after all? Was this journey into the deadlands merely a quest to bring back his corpse . . . or was it a path of reunion? After all these years, might they truly be together once more?

As her mind swam with this glorious tormenting promise, and the wind howled, and dust eddied around her horse's feet, she suddenly became aware of something else. Some intuition crawled at the top of her spine, made her turn and look back the way they had come. And there, in the far distance, a plume of dust was rising. Could it be caused by the wind? No. This cloud of dust was too localized, and regular.

'What is it?' the scavenger said, craning her neck to see where Marian was looking.

'My theory about your brother,' Marian said. 'This is why the Sheriff kept you apart. He's sent a second party into the wastes.'

'We're being followed? Who is it? What do they want?'

'It's Guy of Gisbourne,' Marian replied darkly. 'Don't ask me how I know, I just do. I'd stake my life on it. As for why he's out here . . .'

Marian trailed off, her mind churning with dark possibilities. Had the Sheriff sent the heretic hunter purely as insurance – in case the first party failed to complete their quest? Or did he have another purpose?

About one thing she had no doubt: Sir Guy and his warrior monks were following in the footsteps of Rex and his men. Which must mean they were bound for the same destination.

Robin's resting place.

What would happen if Sir Guy should get there first? In

Marian's mind's eye, the impossible hope had become more and more real, until she had begun, tentatively, to picture the moment she reached Robin and discovered him alive. Now that image turned dark and bloody, blotted out by the shadow of Sir Guy.

'Mother – what are you doing? Wait – come back!'

Marian was barely even aware that she had kicked at the flanks of her horse and galloped up the line of soldiers. Even as she thundered past Rex, and he called after her to halt, she carried on riding hard, the world a blur.

The scavenger shrieked, held on fast. 'What are you doing? You're leaving the others behind!'

Marian kicked harder and they flew across the ground in a thunder of dust. The wind howled, pelting her with grit, while behind them Rex and Alpha shouted for her to stop.

I won't let it happen – I won't let them keep us apart again!

If some part of Marian knew this headlong rush was lunacy, the greater part of her didn't care. Two ideas burned through her with white-hot certainty: firstly, that Robin *was* alive. Secondly, she must reach him before Sir Guy. Nothing else mattered or even existed.

'Stop – please – you'll kill us,' the scavenger pleaded as Marian pulled back on the reins, making the horse jump a crevasse in the rutted earth. 'We'll fall!'

Other voices were hollering behind her, but she paid no heed. She only raced onwards, while the wind shrieked and pelted them with grit, and her eyes streamed.

'The dust storm,' the scavenger wailed. 'We're heading into the teeth of it!'

Yes – and Guy of Gisbourne would be insane to follow us!

And if Marian was insane herself – so be it. If this was madness – this unbridled dash towards Robin – then she welcomed it! After all these years of sitting numb with grief, of existing apart, of enduring this living death – at last, she was going to be with him again. Nothing and no one on this Earth could prevent it!

So thinking, while the world roared at her to halt, she flattened herself against her mount, kicked her heels, and plunged headlong into the storm.

IV. Flesh and Blood

Rex raced after his mother, yelling at her to halt. Alpha Johns galloped at his side, likewise bellowing into the wind, while the rest of the war-men thundered along behind.

'We're not gaining on her,' Alpha shouted to Rex. 'She's too good a rider – even with a passenger. We'll have to let her go.'

'What? No!'

'This storm will swallow us all. We passed those gullies a mile back. We need to turn and head there. It's our only chance.'

Rex raced on, regardless, while the wind tore at him, gouged his cheeks with claws of grit, and his eyes streamed. Ahead of him, his mother and the scavenger were little more than outlines amid the swirling sand. He tried to call out once more but dust lodged in his throat and made him cough and cough while he clung desperately to the saddle.

'Commander, my orders were clear,' Alpha tried again, as Rex fought to regain his breath. 'I am to protect you at all costs. She has our guide, but we must let them go. Nothing is worth more than your life.'

'Wait,' Rex shouted. 'I think . . . she's slowing. Yes – look – she's coming to a stop!'

They swept upon Marian. And now Rex understood it was not her choice to halt. Forced to gallop full tilt into this headwind, carrying two riders across this unforgiving terrain, her horse had simply come to a standstill, exhausted. Now it stood, dead on its feet, even while Marian kicked at its flanks and beat it with her fists.

'Move, damn you – he's coming! We can't let him get there first!'

'Who are you talking about?' Rex cried, while rangers fought to control their own terrified mounts. 'Why did you do this?'

'Commander,' Alpha broke in. 'We need to get you to safety, now.'

He took hold of Rex's reins, began to turn his horse. But Marian gripped the reins from the other side, pulled against him.

'No – we're not going back!' she spat. 'We can't!'

'Lady Marian – for the love of God. You'll condemn Rex along with the rest of us!'

'It's too late in any case,' Arora said, her voice trembling. 'We won't outrun the storm now. It's here.'

A ranger cried out as his horse bucked and threw him to the ground. Other soldiers were struggling to stay in the saddle as their horses whinnied and tossed their heads and started to panic.

'Dismount – all of you!' Alpha shouted. 'It'll be slow going afoot but we have no choice. I'm getting you all back to those gullies. Follow me.'

He tried to trudge away, leading his horse by the reins, but by now the wind was so powerful that he made no headway, could barely keep on his feet. Rex stared around him in horror as the dust whipped into whirlwinds.

Another soldier cried out and fell. A flying rock had caught him a blow to the head. From somewhere, another ranger was wailing that he couldn't see, blinded by the grit. Two horses won loose and bolted.

'What do we do?' Rex murmured, turning to his mother. 'Tell me. What now?'

His mother looked at him, blinking rapidly, as if waking from a dream. She stared around her, trembling.

'Rex – I shouldn't have – I didn't mean—'

A howling sheet of grit and sand came sweeping across them. Several rangers cried out in pain, holding their faces, while more horses bolted in panic.

Marian and Rex scrambled from their own frantic mounts. Rex took hold of his mother, shook her. 'Tell me! What do we do?'

'I don't know!' she wailed. 'I know the forest. I *knew* the forest. But this – I've never – I can't—'

Another wave of sand rolled over them, as sharp as pins. Rex found himself on the ground, covering his head with his arms, his horse fleeing.

His mother shrieked and threw herself across him as another wave of grit blasted them. Rex touched his cheek and his hand came away sticky. There was no pain yet, only a cold numbness in his face, and that alone was frightening.

On top of him, his mother was trembling, trying to shield him with her own body. Nearby, Alpha was staggering and stumbling, dragged this way and that like a ragdoll in the hands of a giant.

No – no! Rex screamed silently. *It can't end like this! There must be a way!*

With blurred eyes he peered through his fingers, desperately scanning his surroundings. There had to be somewhere they could hide – or something they could use to protect themselves. But where – or what? Through the swirling dust he could see only bare ground – a few rocks. And scattered upon this bare earth were the rangers, all of them curled up in a foetal position . . .

These are good men, and loyal. They will follow your every word without question.

A plan was in Rex's mind now. It was desperate, and repugnant. He tried to cast it aside. But he couldn't. It would not be unthought. He clutched at the idea like a drowning man clinging to a raft.

Struggling free of his mother's grasp, he stumbled to his feet, staggered among his war-men. Seeing them lying there, helpless and afraid, he again battled with himself, and at first he was unable to speak.

What is my most powerful weapon? It is my voice.

By now you should be coming into your own power. But you squander it.

His father's words stabbed at his heart, sent shame swirling through his veins, stoking his fear and his desperation. He stumbled on, and began hollering at his war-men.

'On your feet – all of you! Form ranks around me!'

His voice was all but lost amid the wind. No one paid it any heed, the soldiers cowering from a fresh onslaught of sand and stones.

You squeak when you should roar.

What you truly fear is your own power.

'I said form ranks! Do it! Now!'

Finally, a single soldier began to crawl and shuffle and stumble towards him. Once the first had moved, two more followed, then a fourth, and more.

'Mother – Alpha – scavenger – alongside me!' Rex yelled, kneeling next to his mother. 'The rest of you, form a circle around us, shields outwards. Two soldiers deep.'

Rangers stared at one another, shielding their eyes from the debris. Even Alpha looked uncertain, catching his balance as the storm roared.

'I gave an order!' Rex bawled, in a voice he didn't recognize, the words warped by fear. 'Kneel in a circle, facing away from us. Do it now!'

Finally, a soldier went to one knee in front of Rex, thrust the sharp butt of his shield into the ground. As before, it only took one man to act before the rest fell into line. Kneeling alongside each other, they planted their shields and interlocked their sword arms.

Soon, with Alpha and Rex and Arora and Marian in the centre, a double ring of men had taken shape, grit and sand and stones skidding off their shields and their skull-helms.

Rex's mother clasped him tight. She whispered something, but the words were lost beneath the howling of the wind and the clattering of detritus against steel. Now that it was done, the fury abruptly drained out of Rex. All that was left was the terror. And the remorse – yes, that too, as he listened to the rangers groan in pain, and he told himself over and over again that he had been left no other choice.

That most terrible of storms lasted all night. The wind brought with it freezing temperatures. Wrapped in her thick mantle, surrounded by the body warmth of the soldiers, Marian was still deathly cold. She held Rex as tightly as she was able, and she felt him shuddering.

Worse than the cold was the bombardment of detritus. Marian had lived through thunderstorms in Sherwood Forest, and they were always awesome, often frightening. But not like this. Back then, the trees and the undergrowth blunted the force of the winds. Out here, on this barren plain, nothing stood between these frail human bodies, huddled on the ground, and the full fury of the elements.

In all her years of living wild, and of warfare, Marian had never been more afraid. She could barely imagine Rex's terror. She gripped him and tried to tell him it would be all right, but she didn't believe it herself, and in any case, her loudest shout was swallowed utterly by the gale.

As the storm roared ever more monstrous, and Marian suffered stabs of pure panic, she imagined any moment that the circle would crack and the soldiers would scatter, leaving her and Rex defenceless.

And yet, almost against her own belief, as the nightmare hours crept on and on, each individual soldier held his position and the whole circle retained its shape, even as the wind slashed at them with sand sharp as glass and with stones like arrowheads. In spite of herself, Marian felt a creeping respect for the rangers' courage and forbearance.

Except it isn't courage, not really, she told herself, *nor forbearance. These men are slaves. They've spent their lives doing as they're bidden. Now it's so ingrained they have no will of their own.*

Even so, it was still a remarkable feat of endurance to weather this onslaught. Now and again she thought she heard one of the rangers cry out, or sensed one of them shudder, but mostly they remained as stiff as steel, and as muted.

Finally, blessedly, just as Marian was certain she would run mad huddled here, so cold and afraid and helpless, the weak sun struggled over the horizon, and as it did so the storm ceased. It died away even quicker than it had arisen, the last of the grit pitter-pattering against the soldiers shields – then silence. A silence so profound it seemed to roar even louder than the storm.

Slowly, Alpha and Arora stirred, uncoiling their huddled forms. Rex sat upright and lowered his hood and looked at Marian through eyes that were puffy and bloodshot.

'It's . . . over?' Marian thought he said, reading his lips.

'Yes, it's finished,' she said, unable to hear even her own voice through the ringing in her ears. 'You did it. We're alive. Come on, I'll help you stand.'

Standing, though, was not easy. Her limbs were stiff with cold and cramp, and she was wedged tight amid bodies. She shoved at Alpha and Arora and she wriggled amid the soldiers and finally she levered herself upright.

But still she was trapped, none of the soldiers shifting an inch to allow her out of the circle.

'Get out of my way – move!' she snapped, shoving at them, suddenly desperate to be free. 'What's wrong with you – can't you hear it's over?'

'They can't hear anything,' said Alpha, in a voice that was flat and chilling.

Marian looked at him, then stared around her at the soldiers, and finally she admitted the truth. These soldiers had not held their ground out of courage, nor sheer force of will, nor even blind obedience. It was simpler than that. Planted here on one knee, with their shields overlapping and their arms interlocked, no individual would have been able to move even if they had wanted to. No matter how terrified they might have been, or close to panic, it would have been impossible for any one man to shift even an inch. And so the whole structure had remained rigid, unbroken . . .

Even once the men started to die.

'All . . . all of them?' Rex murmured, gripping her arm. 'They're all . . . dead?'

Yes, they were, every one of them. The outer ring had likely perished first, Marian saw, as she fought her way over the corpses, hauling Rex with her out of the grim circle. Even huddled behind their shields, and wearing skull-helms, enough dagger-like stones and glass-like sand had got through to pierce eyes and slash throats. The second ring of men most likely died of cold, their bodies stiff with frost, the last of their body warmth having leached into the centre of the circle, where it helped keep Marian and the other three alive.

'I . . . I did this,' Rex murmured, stumbling. 'I killed them.'

'You saved our lives – that's what you did,' Marian said,

cupping his chin and making him look into her eyes. 'It was them or all of us.'

Marian looked over at Arora, who was standing with her arms at her side, staring into the distance.

'They're getting worse,' the girl mumbled, as though speaking to herself. 'Every storm is worse than the last. Soon there'll be no living on this land.' She turned to stare in the opposite direction. 'But Lucas survived it. I can feel he did.'

'All the more reason to get moving, if Guy of Gisbourne is still out there,' Marian said. 'How much further to go?'

The scavenger blinked at her. 'Well . . . now we're on foot,' she said quietly. 'A morning's walk. Maybe.'

'Right, so let's get started. Gather provisions. Rex, same for you. But no more than you can easily carry.'

'We . . . we need to bury them,' Alpha murmured.

'In this ground? You'd dig your own grave while you were at it.'

'But we can't just—'

'I said no! We don't have time. We're not the only ones looking for Robin. We need to get there before they do. Pack provisions, now. One light pack each. We're going to move fast.'

It took a lot more cajoling and persuading and threatening, but at last Marian got the meagre party underway.

As they moved clear, Marian spared one last glance back at the awful circle of dead men, kneeling there as if in prayer.

'You did what you had to do,' she told Rex. 'It was resourceful and brave and brilliant, you know that? If it wasn't for you, we'd all be dead.'

Rex only stared at the ground and trudged onwards. Marian sensed the anguish pouring off of him, and she cursed the Sheriff. Cursed him for making Rex come out here and endure all this. Cursed him for creating these killer wastes in the first place.

He won't get away with it. For everything he's done, for all he's taken from us, I will destroy him.

But first . . . Robin.

I'm coming for you.

Yes. That night of bitter survival – of living against all the odds – had washed away her final doubts. That flicker of hope now blazed. Yes – Robin was alive. Yes – they would be together again.

And then . . . for keeping them apart, for all his other crimes, for all he'd done to Rex, the Sheriff would pay in full.

V. Where Paths Converge

Time and again, as they slogged on beneath the molten sun, Marian turned to peer westwards. The horizon remained blank, the air shining hard and clear. No sign of dust rising. Could it be that Guy of Gisbourne perished in the storm, after all? No – that was a hope too far. Instinct told her, with absolute certainty, that the heretic hunter was still out there, dogging her steps.

'We're not going fast enough,' she told the others. 'Arora – move quicker. You too, Rex. We need to get there first.'

None of them gave any reaction. Rex in particular trudged along with his head lowered, lost in his own anguish, as he had done ever since they left the corpses of the soldiers out there on the plain.

'Come *on!*' Marian went back to him, dragged him by the sleeve. 'Alpha, if you're coming, move yourself. What's wrong with you all? We can't let him beat us!'

Finally, as she pulled him stumbling along, Rex blinked at her, his eyes heavy and red. 'Beat us? Who are you talking about?'

'Guy of Gisbourne.'

'The heretic hunter? Out here? He can't be.'

'Just hurry! Arora – how much further?'

Arora raised her bone goggles, pointed ahead. 'We're almost there. See where the land dips? It's just beyond that.'

'Come on then. Quicker. All of you.'

The scavenger led them onwards, Marian hauled at Rex, and Alpha trudged stupidly behind, and in this way they made faltering progress.

Eventually, the ground ahead of them dropped away. They stumbled down a shallow slope into a wide depression. Marian saw at once that this was an old dry lake. The ground was dotted with pebbles, polished smooth by water, and with the petrified imprints of fish and wildfowl.

Marian stopped yanking at Rex, and her own steps slowed. This place . . . it was more oppressive even than the rest of the wastes. It left her leaden-footed, as if it was bleeding her spirit.

She came to a standstill and swept her gaze. A few flies buzzed in the dust of the old lakebed, but otherwise it was as dead a landscape as she could imagine. Despite the sun, a greenish mist seeped out of its crevices and swirled like a sickly miasma. It carried a sharp, tangy aroma, almost metallic.

'Why did you bring us here?' she demanded of the scavenger. 'You said you'd take us to Robin. Well – where is he?'

'He's close,' Arora said. 'This is where we found it.'

'Found what?'

'The relic. See?' Arora opened a pouch at her waist and extracted an object. It was a piece of jade, shaped like an arrowhead.

Of its own accord, Marian's hand shot out and snatched the amulet.

'That's mine!' the scavenger yelled. 'Give it back!'

These words didn't reach Marian. She was staring in sweet sorrow at the long-lost treasure that lay in her palm. As her head swam, she fell back through the years. She recalled standing on the lake isle with Robin. She had taken his half-arrowhead amulet, tied it together with hers, before flinging them out into the water. Could it truly be . . . ? Yes – look at the fissure down the centre, where the amulet had once been divided in two. The heat of the firestorm must have fused the pieces back together.

All of which meant . . . as Marian stared around her once more, feeling unsteady on her feet . . . all of which must mean that this place, this dust-choked hollow, this hellscape of toxic mist and black ooze and dying flies . . . this must once have been Robin and Marian's paradise.

This is Elysium Glades.

For a brief moment, her horror-struck mind brought it all back to life. She could hear the waterfalls flowing once more, feel the fresh breeze off the ponds and the pools, hear the whistling frogs and the songbirds. She could see the halcyon birds trailing rainbows from their wings.

Then a gust of wind blew, stirring the dust and the dead insects, and the vision vanished, leaving only desolation and silence.

'Mother – what's wrong?' Rex was saying. 'Is it the sun?'

Marian realized she was sitting on the ground. Rex was kneeling beside her, looking at her with concern.

'Here, drink this,' he said, holding a flask, putting it to her lips.

She pushed it away, looked at him through tear-blurred eyes.

'Oh Rex, you've been here before.'

'What did you say?'

'There was an islet. It must be that hump of ground, over there. That's where . . . where your life began.' Tears streamed down her cheeks. 'For you, this should have been a . . . a homecoming.'

'Help me get her up,' Rex said over his shoulder to Alpha. 'We need to find shade.'

Marian shrugged them off as she got to her feet. She stared around her once more at this lost Eden, and she hissed between her teeth.

'He took everything from us,' she said to Rex. 'He stole your birthright before you were even born. I promise you this, he will suffer for it!' She spun to face the scavenger. 'Robin – where is he? Show me!'

'Once you give me back my charm.'

Marian thrust the amulet into her hands. 'I don't care – have it! Just take me to him, now!'

The scavenger hurried onwards and the others followed, Rex watching Marian with concern, Alpha trudging along behind without a word. As they went, Marian's eye fell upon something curious. It was a tiny green plantlet. The first green living thing she had seen since entering the wastes. Although minuscule, it blazed against the dead, grey land.

There was a second shoot – and a third. She could see now there was a line of these plantlets, running across the lakebed almost like miniature wayposts. As Marian and the others continued across the dust bowl, their own path merged with this emerald trail. Marian wondered at this briefly, but then pushed it aside, her full focus fixed once more on reaching Robin.

The land rose as they climbed out of the old lakebed. As it did so Marian recalled, with a fresh stab of sorrow, the beechwoods that once encircled Elysium Glades. Towering trees had reached up to the heavens, the light through their leaves bathing the world in a thousand shades of green. But no more. Because here were the remains of those majestic beings. Their trunks and limbs were burned and broken and scattered. Bleached by the sun, their skeletons were scattered far and wide.

As the scavenger led them into this boneyard, the air became still, and Marian detected a deep chill in spite of the sun. In the hush, she could suddenly hear every scuff of their feet, together with her own breathing and heartbeat.

Then came the soft sighing of steel across leather as Alpha drew his stabbing sword.

'Commander,' he said to Rex, uttering his first words since leaving his dead comrades. 'Something here is wrong.'

'What is it?' Rex said, drawing his own sword.

'I can't be sure,' he said softly, as they went onwards. 'But I think . . . people have been here before us.'

'Who? Have you seen tracks? Are they still here?'

The Chief Rider shook his head, stared around him. 'Call it instinct. Something here means us harm.'

'Look,' Marian said. 'What's that? See it?'

At first she had taken it for a mirage – one more phantom vision of Sherwood. But the breeze blew across it, shivering its leaves, and it remained solid. She moved towards it, unblinking. It was a green oasis: bushes and ferns and flowers of every type. At its heart, anchoring and sheltering the foliage, was an ancient tree stump. On the side facing them, a triangular fissure yawned, like the entrance to a cave.

Seeing this final detail, she stumbled to a halt. 'He . . . he's in there, isn't he?' she said to the scavenger, the words catching in her throat.

The girl merely nodded, and Marian went back to staring at the tree stump. Growing all around it and over it and out of it was verdant rustling life. On its leeward side, protected from the wind, it even cradled a nursery of saplings and two adolescent beech trees. This miniature patch of wildwood buzzed with bees and flashed with dragonflies.

Seeing all this, finally admitting without doubt that it was real, Marian felt giddy and had to catch her balance.

That seed of hope that had been growing inside her – the idea that Robin might truly have survived the Great Fire – now took root as immutable fact, as solid as ironwood. Seeing this blaze of green, this fountain of life, enduring out here amid the bones of a dead world, she knew for certain it was true.

Yes – Robin had survived too.

He's alive! He's here!

This certainty brought as much sorrow as joy.

Oh, Robin, I'm sorry. You've been here all alone, all these years. I never wanted to leave you – I had no choice.

'Mother – what is it? You're crying. You look . . . scared. I don't understand.'

Marian looked at him. 'You will. I'll explain everything. But right now there isn't time.' She pointed to the hollow stump and its cave-like entrance. 'I need to go in there. The rest of you stay here.'

'Wait,' Rex said. 'Father . . . He entrusted this to me. It's my responsibility.'

'No – it isn't,' Marian said softly. 'This is something only I can do. And I can't wait. Because Guy of Gisbourne is coming.'

'Why do you keep talking about him?' Rex said, taking hold of her arm, fear creeping into his voice. 'He's got nothing to do with this.'

'Commander.' Alpha spoke with quiet urgency. 'I think I heard something.' He was turning in place, his blade ready. 'We need to be on our guard.'

'Stay with Alpha,' Marian told Rex. 'You'll be all right until I come back. Please, Rex, let go of me. There isn't time.'

'Quiet, all of you!' Alpha snapped. 'There's someone here. We need—'

His next word broke into a wet strangled scream.

On pure instinct, before she even knew she was going to move, Marian broke free of Rex, dropped and rolled, coming up and taking hold of Alpha's sword, yanking it from his hand even before he hit the ground.

Shadowy figures were sweeping around them on all sides. One of them grabbed Rex from behind, pressed a dagger to his throat – and in the same instant Marian's own blade went to the neck of his assailant, hovering at his jugular.

The world froze in that shape. Rex's eyes wide with shock and fear. Marian holding the sword in a two-handed grip, locking eyes with Rex's captor, daring him to flinch.

Until finally, Kitwald Thorne spoke.

'Marian Delbosque, as the gods breathe, it truly is you.'

VI. Into the Dark

'Let go of him – now!' Marian growled, the tip of her blade pricking Kit's skin, so that a bead of blood rolled down the steel.

'Why . . . what is he to you?' Kit said, keeping his own dagger pressed to Rex's throat. 'And who's this?' He nodded towards the scavenger, who was simply standing there stunned. 'What were you doing with this red-cloak scum?'

Here, he looked down at Alpha Johns. The soldier was sprawled in a widening pool of blood, an arrow protruding from his throat, his legs kicking in their death-throes.

'I won't tell you again,' Marian snarled at Kit. 'Lower your blade. Or else I'll kill you where you stand. You will remember, I do not make idle threats.'

'Do what she says, Kit,' said a hushed voice behind her. 'Can't you see . . . ? It's Marian. She's come back to us.'

The voice echoed out of another lifetime. It was the voice of Ira Starr. But for the moment it meant little to Marian. She stared at the dagger pressed to Rex's throat, and she looked into her son's horrified eyes, and she felt a wrath so fierce that her entire body began to shake and more of Kit's blood trickled down her blade.

'This is your last warning,' she snarled. 'Release him, now!'

'Ira's right, Kit,' said another voice from the deep past, this one belonging to Sonskya Luz. 'It's Marian. What else matters?'

Kit turned his eyes to the warrior women, then back to Marian, before finally lowering his blade. Rex fell to his knees alongside the corpse of Alpha Johns.

Midge Millerson narrowed his eyes. 'Who *is* this . . . weeping over a dead ranger? That cloak he's wearing . . . I've seen one like it someplace before.'

Marian stared at Midge, then turned to face each of the other outlaws in turn, looking longest at Ira and Sonskya. How strange and disturbing it was to come face to face with these ghosts from her past. They had once been her sisters-in-arms. But now she barely recognized them. They were shaven-headed and battle-scarred and gnarled as old she-wolves.

'I knew you weren't dead,' Ira murmured. 'You couldn't be.'

'We heard you were the Sheriff's queen,' sneered Jack Champion. 'I could believe that even less.'

'Seems you owe us some answers,' said Midge. 'You're gone twelve years, then show up out of the blue, trailing a pet ranger.'

Ignoring him, Marian blinked again round the circle of outlaws.

'Is this . . . all?'

'What did you expect?' Jack leered, a scar splitting his face from chin to ear. 'It's not the greenwood out here, Marian.'

Rex rose slowly to his feet. He laid a hand on the hilt of his sword, and his eyes blazed.

'You didn't even dare face him,' he snarled at Kit. 'You killed him from the shadows. You're a coward.'

This ushered in absolute silence. Until finally, Kit said softly: 'I don't care who you are, or what you think you're doing here. Try calling me that again and the word will die on your lips.'

'Stop it!' Marian snapped. 'Rex, do not even think about drawing that blade. Do you hear me? Don't be a fool! This isn't the combat yard. These are not rangers. Do you know who these people are? They are the outlaws of Sherwood Forest.'

His eyes burning with rage, it took Rex a long time to release the grip on his sword. But when he finally did so, all the fight flooded out of him and his shoulders slumped.

'What do I care?' he spat, staring down at Alpha. 'I didn't ask for any of this!'

As he spoke, he tore the Sheriff's cloak from his shoulders and hurled it to the ground. Then he stormed away and disappeared behind a fallen tree trunk.

Watching him go, Kit said: 'Who is he, Marian?'

'You know who he is,' said Ira. 'Look at them both.' She gazed at Marian. 'He's . . . your son.'

Before anyone else could speak, Much Millerson gave a low whistle. He was standing lookout atop the remains of a beech tree.

'A dust cloud,' he called down. 'Horsemen. I'd say at least a dozen of them. Headed this way.'

Kit turned to Marian. 'You're being followed. Who by?'

'Guy of Gisbourne.'

Midge narrowed his eyes. 'How do you know? Why?'

Marian hesitated. 'I don't yet have all the answers. But I came here with a purpose. And I'm running out of time.' She looked towards the tree-cave, then turned to Kit. 'Did you go in there?'

Kit shook his head. 'We found this place just before you did. I was about to go in when you arrived.'

'It isn't your place,' Marian said. 'It's mine. And I need to do it before the heretic hunter gets here.'

Midge started to speak again, but she stopped him. 'Time has passed. We've all had to change.' She looked at Ira and Sonskya. 'But you know who I am, underneath. So, for now, I'm asking you to trust me.'

'Why should we?' said Midge.

'Because you're desperate,' Marian said. 'We all are. And there's hope buried here, I know there is. I think you can sense it too. You need me to unearth it.' Again, she locked eyes with Kit. 'Guy of Gisbourne. That's your part. I need you to hold him off, as long as you can.'

'Hold him off? Just like that?' said Midge. 'The six of us.'

'And for what?' said Jack. 'What are you meaning to do?'

Marian stared once more towards the stump and its cave-like opening. 'In all honesty . . . I wish I knew. This time, I'm acting on faith.' She looked at them all once more. 'What I do know is we're still on our feet – the seven of us. After all these years, in spite of everything, we're still fighting. And now something . . . or someone . . . has drawn us all here. Give me time and I'll find out why.' Again, she looked around the circle of outlaws. 'What other hope is there?'

As if to underscore these words, a powerful gust of wind rolled across the plains. It came with a long tormented howl, like a mother lamenting the loss of her cub, but deep and massive enough that it might be the Earth herself sending up her grief.

Finally, Kit stood tall and addressed his outlaws. 'Marian's right – we did not come here by chance. And we're not turning away now. All right, Marian . . . Do what you need to do. But whatever it is, be quick.'

Marian nodded, then turned and strode away. As she went, she kept one eye out for the scavenger, who had taken the chance to creep away while the outlaws faced off. By now, though, there was no sign of her, and Marian presumed she was in hiding.

She found Rex slumped against a fallen tree trunk, his arms wrapped around his knees, his head buried.

'Rex, listen to me, please,' she said, crouching before him. 'I can only imagine how confused you must be. You have a place in all this – a vital place. But you don't yet know what that place is. I'm going to help you find it, I promise.'

She reached out to touch his shoulder. 'But first I need to leave you, just for a little while. When the heretic hunter gets here, there will be fighting. It needn't concern you. Find somewhere to hide. Rex, are you listening to me?'

'Yes – I heard!' he blurted, lifting his head and glaring at her with reddened eyes. 'Do this, stand there – do exactly as I'm told! It's all laid out for me, every step! You and Father are just the same. Just go then. Leave me!'

Marian stood, her heart tearing in two, hating to leave him here like this yet knowing she must. 'I'm doing this for you, as much as anyone,' she told him. 'Afterwards . . . everything will be different.'

Turning away from him, she faced the ancient, living tree stump. Steeling herself, she walked towards it. She moved close enough to smell this oasis. Its dank, loamy aroma was a balm after the scorched dust and rock of the wastelands. Even so, as she approached, her footsteps slowed. The cave-like interior of the stump seemed to grow ever darker and more forbidding.

Something made her stop. She watched the darkness. Slowly, she moved to one side and took cover behind a fallen tree. Peering through a fissure in the wood, she went on staring towards the oasis.

She detected a stealthy presence moving to her side.

'You saw it too,' Kit said, softly. 'What do you think it is?'

Marian just went on watching the stump, and its opening. It was utterly black. And yet . . . she could just discern some shape, or movement . . .

There – yes, a shadowy shift – and a golden glint.

The glint became eyes. Golden eyes, slit down the middle, like the eyes of the fox. The face moved forward, took clearer shape.

Yes, it was her – the vixen-goddess. Only now did Marian allow herself to truly believe it. She always presumed the goddess must have perished in the Great Fire. But no. Because here she was, her head tipping back as her nostrils tasted the air, like an animal preparing to leave its den.

When she finally stepped out into the open and became fully visible, her appearance came as a supreme shock. Back in Sherwood, particularly in the late spring, her beauty was numinous. Marian remembered glimpses of her running barefoot through the bluebells, her fox-red hair blazing like flame-of-the-forest, the sight stirring in Marian complex waves of envy and lust and awe.

Now, though, the goddess was transformed. That once lustrous hair hung in ragged clumps. Her body was crooked and bone-thin, the ribs showing like veins in a leaf. She was covered in blisters and scabs, like burns that had refused to heal. All her old grace was gone; as she left the tree-cave she lurched and hobbled as if every movement caused her pain.

As Marian and Kit watched, holding their breath, the goddess moved around the tree stump. When she reached its far right-hand side, she came to a halt. After looking left and right, and sniffing the air, she went to one knee. She appeared to reach her arm into a hole . . . or a burrow, that opened between two of the roots. Yes – her arm went in as far as her shoulder – and when it came out again her hand drew out an object.

She stood, holding it. It looked like a vessel of some kind. A jug – or an amphora, like those used to store wine or elixirs. At the sight of this, Kit sucked in a breath, while Marian just went on staring, spellbound.

The goddess took the cork stopper from the neck of the amphora. Then she began circling the stump once more. Here and there she stopped, and she tipped the vessel, pouring liquid onto the roots and the soil, sprinkling it too on the leaves of the saplings and the ferns. The liquid appeared to be viscous, and dark in colour, glistening black or dark red.

The goddess went on in this way, like a gardener watering a herb garden, disappearing from view as she circled the stump, then reappearing as she completed the circuit. Finally, she appeared satisfied and replaced the stopper. She went back to the hidey-hole and secreted the amphora back beneath the earth. And then, still hobbling, but with surprising speed, she bolted back into the cave-tree and was gone.

Kit let out a long breath, then said in a bare whisper. 'It's true then, isn't it? If she's in there . . . he must be too. After all this time . . . we've found him.'

For Marian's part, she had no words. She simply stood and left Kit, moving once more towards the tree-cave. Her footsteps were leaden. After dashing headlong to get here, these final paces felt like leagues. What was it making her falter at the last? Was it seeing the goddess, and knowing she too was lurking in the dark?

No, it was thoughts of Robin. He was here, and he was alive, and those ideas were beyond glorious. But they were also daunting. Because they had been apart so long. Existing out here, all alone, in these twisted wastes . . . how would it have changed him? What might he have become? What would he think of her, after all she had been required to do?

She pushed aside such doubt. It was Robin. Her guiding star. They had nothing to fear from one another. Not now, not ever.

As she reached the cave-like stump, she took a storm lamp from her back pack, lit the wick. And then, allowing herself no more time for hesitation, she went to hands and knees and she crawled into the ancient deathless dark.

VII. The Physical Plain

After crawling into the tree-cave, Marian curled around her lantern, eclipsing the light, unable at the last to face whatever awaited her here in the dark. It took all her courage, but finally she forced herself to kneel, and to lift the lamp, and raise her eyes . . .

And to focus on the rear of the chamber.

As she did so, her breath stopped, and even her heartbeat seemed to cease in this moment outside of time.

Because he was here. It was truly him.

After all these years apart, of yearning and longing, or believing him dead and gone, here he was, in front of her . . .

Robin.

For the moment, where he knelt, on the edge of the lamp-light, he was little more than a shadowy shape. But she could see the outline of his wolfskin cloak, its fur glistening. And she could see too his wolf-head cowl, its eyes gleaming. And he was sitting perfectly still and upright and noble, just as always – and her imagination filled in the rest of the details, until he was exactly as she remembered him, in all his dark savage majesty.

'Robin, I'm here, it's me,' she managed to murmur, her throat tight with joy and anger and remorse. 'Oh, Robin, you . . . you've been out here waiting, all alone, all these years.' She shed tears, wanted to scream, as she lurched, crawled towards him. 'We . . . we've been living apart, and we should never have been. All this time, we could have—'

She came to a dead halt. The scream that had been building inside her now erupted, echoing within the cave-like space. It was no longer a scream of regret, or guilt – but one of pure grief. A tide of grief that engulfed her so abruptly and so utterly that she must surely drown in it, while a second scream burst from her lips.

Because now Marian had crawled closer to Robin, and the lamplight illuminated him. And she could see the reality. Yes, the wolfskin glistened, whole and hale . . .

But underneath the cloak . . . Oh, just look at him . . .

His face was ghastly, the skin as grey as old parchment, stretched tight across his bones. Veins bulged visibly in his neck and chest, and the blood in those veins was black and frozen. His limbs were skeletal and looked as brittle as kindling, while the hands that lay in his lap were withered claws.

Trembling, Marian raised her fingertips to touch his lips. There was no warmth. No hint of breath. She pressed one ear to his chest. No heartbeat. No pulse of lifeblood. Tears ran down her cheeks, and she was shaking, sobbing.

'Oh, Robin, I told myself . . . I told myself I'd find you living. I so wanted to believe it. I let the hope in – and now I can't stand it!' She wiped at her eyes. 'But listen to me – how dare I. What about you? How long have you been here like this? When . . . when did you die? You should not have died out here, all alone. Forgive me. That day . . . when the forest burned . . . I wanted to stay too. I tried to follow you. I was ready. But they stopped me. And now . . . now it's too late. Oh, Robin, I'm sorry.'

Putting her arms around his withered remains, here in the darkness of his tomb, she cradled him while she sobbed and sobbed, years of pain and yearning spilling out in a tormented torrent. Vaguely, at the very back of her awareness, she became conscious of another presence, here with them, but it was insignificant and tiny when measured against her grief.

Finally, a voice behind her rasped a single word: 'Pathetic.'

'Leave us be,' Marian said through her tears, squeezing her eyes shut. 'Even now you can't leave him in peace!'

'Correct – I haven't left him. I never did. Unlike you.'

'I had no choice! There was nothing I could do!'

The vixen-goddess laughed spitefully. 'The motto of your kind. Carve it into your gravestone. Burn it into the soil. *There was nothing I could do*. Bleating it like lost lambs while the world burns!'

'I did all I could!' Marian sobbed. 'Leave us alone! This is all the time we have left. Can't you at least grant us this?'

'Pathetic,' the goddess said again, her voice still disembodied, but closer. 'Even now you plead helplessness. How much easier to feign impotence than to embrace your power.'

'What are you talking about?' Marian whispered, opening her eyes, staring once more at Robin. 'I have no power over this. He's . . . dead.'

Again, the goddess laughed – a cackling, eerie sound. 'Dead? No, no – he isn't. Not exactly. But nor is he fully living. He exists somewhere in between.'

'Don't toy with me!' Marian hissed, turning, trying to lay eyes on the goddess. 'He's not breathing. There's no pulse. He's dead!'

'Flesh and bones. Blood and breath. Your kind – how narrow your view of existence.' Suddenly, the goddess appeared, so close that Marian gasped and recoiled. Her golden eyes sparkled in the darkness, but the rest of her was impossibly old and hideous. Her skin was as burned and ravaged as the soil out there in the wastes.

'See here,' she rasped through rotting gums, slouching close to Robin. 'See how he endures!'

The goddess lifted Robin's cloak where it pooled around him. Marian looked away, some part of her not wanting to see this, whatever it might be. But finally she forced herself to turn, and lift her lantern, and peer close.

She saw that this ancient stump not only nurtured life on its exterior, but also harboured life within. All around Robin grew lichen and moss and small plants. Robin was enmeshed in all this. Shoots and suckers had grown up over his feet and knees, and had twined up him like ivy climbing a tree . . .

Marian blinked heavily, her vision unsteady. She stared and stared and finally was unable to deny what she was seeing. Suckers and tendrils of vegetation were not only growing around Robin and over him . . . but also *into* him. Rootlets punctured his skin and wormed inside his flesh. She could see them bulging beneath the surface of his legs. With trembling fingertips, she traced their progress up into his midriff and his chest, where they stood out like engorged veins.

As she caressed these lifelines, not yet knowing whether to laugh or scream, she felt one of them throb. So . . . she had been wrong. Robin had a pulse after all . . . only it had been too slow to detect . . .

It was the heartbeat of the forest – sap pulsing in the trees.

'This tree,' she murmured. 'It's . . . feeding him. Breathing for him. '

'Yes, yes,' the goddess rasped. 'As I sustain the tree, the tree sustains him.'

Through eyes blurred with tears, Marian looked at the goddess, and she was suddenly sickened.

'Why? Why would you do this?'

The goddess put a hand to her heart, and smiled through blackened teeth. 'I thought you'd be pleased. Didn't you dream of finding him alive?'

'This isn't living – you said so yourself. You've . . . you've kept him here like this, all this time. Hasn't he suffered enough?' she sobbed, holding Robin. 'Why won't you let him die? He gave everything – he doesn't deserve this!'

'This is exactly what he deserves! Robin Hood holds a mirror to the world. Look what you did!' Her fire-ravaged face leered out of the darkness. 'Why should he rest in peace while I am denied mine?'

'You brought it on yourself!' Marian wailed. 'You welcomed the fire!'

The goddess retreated into the gloom, and slumped, suddenly looking so old she might be nothing but bones.

'Yes, I did,' she murmured. 'Because I thought that would put an end to it. I thought it would put us out of our misery. But there is no end, and no escape!' she blurted. 'My fate is tethered to the Earth – I wear its wounds upon my skin.' She pointed a claw at Robin. 'So does he. So do we all! We shall suffer with it for eternity!'

This last burst of passion exhausted the goddess; she shrank in on herself until she was a heap of skin and hair. She huddled there, unmoving, until Marian could believe she had expired at last.

With a heart full of sorrow and revulsion and pity, she turned back to Robin. Once again, she brushed her fingertips across the tendrils and rootlets that fed into him. She felt the slow, deep throb as they pumped him with sustenance.

The initial shock of seeing him like this was fading, and she began to think more clearly. Deep in her heart, that phantom hope rekindled and began to flame once more.

After all . . . it was undeniable that Robin was here in front of her – that he still existed. She could touch him. This place was not his tomb, but rather his hibernaculum.

And when a person slept . . . no matter how deeply . . . they could awaken . . .

'Oh, please let it be true,' she murmured, touching his face. 'Robin, I'm here. And I *do* believe it, I have to. I believe you can hear me. I'm here, and I can help you. Whatever you've suffered . . . you can heal. Robin, I *know* you're in there. Wake up. Please.'

'Silly girl, you won't reach him that way.' The goddess slouched closer, skin sloughing from her bones. 'You live and breathe on the surface of the world. You always did. He exists beneath. Within.'

Marian turned to her. 'But you're saying I *can* reach him . . . somehow?'

'Oh yes, yes indeed.' The goddess leered. 'As a matter of fact, I'm relying on it. I've tried bringing him back myself, but he denies my help.' She grinned horribly. 'He seems to believe I mean mischief.'

Marian narrowed her eyes. 'You wanted me to come here. You need him to wake. Why? What do you want from him?'

In response, the goddess only smiled, showing cracked teeth.

Marian turned away from her, studied Robin once more. A tiny voice somewhere inside whispered that she should kiss him on the cheek, say goodbye, and leave this place for ever. There were forces at work here that she could neither control nor comprehend.

But a far stronger part of her knew she could never turn her back on Robin, not even now. *Especially* not now. If there was even the smallest chance she might pull him out of this living death, then she knew she had to try.

She locked eyes with the goddess. 'Tell me. How do I reach him? What do I have to do?'

The goddess leaned close, and her ancient eyes gleamed. 'Sweet child, I told you, he has left the daylight world. He roams the realms between life and death. If you wish him to return . . . you must go there yourself.'

VIII. The Last Relic

'They're getting close,' said Jack, standing lookout atop the fallen oak. 'It's a big force. Two dozen at least.'

'What's this meant to achieve?' said Midge, standing with the others beneath the lookout post. 'It's nothing more than a death wish.'

'Marian needs us to stay,' said Ira. 'If it's our last stand, so be it.'

'I second that,' said Sonskya, a mad glint in her eye. 'What did you think, Midge, you were going to live for ever?'

'We don't even know what Marian's game is,' said Midge. 'She's been gone twelve years, and now we're throwing away our lives because she says so?'

'I don't know why you're all still talking,' said Kit. 'I told Marian we'd buy her time – that's what we're going to do. Jack, get down here. Take to your hides, all of you. On my signal, we unleash everything we've got. Take down the warrior monks first. Leave Guy of Gisbourne to me.'

Kit only wished he felt as confident as he was trying to sound. Surely Midge and Much were right. To stand against these odds was nothing short of suicidal.

As his outlaws loped away to their hiding places, he peered once more around the Giants' Graveyard. Certainly, the fallen trees would make excellent cover for an ambush and for the hit-and-run skirmishes that would follow. What other resources were there out here? Were there strategic advantages he might have missed?

'You're doing the right thing, Kit.'

Sonskya had not flitted away with the others, but remained standing behind him. Now she came to stand at his side. Together they peered out across the plain, watching the cloud of dust grow thicker, glints of dark steel showing here and there.

'This had to happen sometime. Somewhere,' she said. 'We couldn't go on like that for ever. Even Midge knows that.'

'You sound like you'd welcome it. The end.'

'Wouldn't you? Deep down. You've carried more than anyone.'

Kit said nothing, just stared at the enemy force sweeping towards them. He could feel the vibrations of the horses' hooves through the earth. He caught a glimpse of a warrior monk, and another, their scarlet robes like slashes of blood amid the dust.

Finally, Kit shook his head. 'I don't believe it ends today. Not this way.' He turned to stare at the ancient tree stump. 'Our path led us here for a reason. This is where our fate turns, I can feel it. All we need is—'

He broke off. He stared once more at the ancient tree stump. An astonishing idea had taken root, leaving him speechless.

What other resources are there out here?

'Kit? Where are you going?' Sonskya called. 'They're almost on top of us!'

'Go – take cover!' he called back, as he ran. 'Wait for my signal.'

Kit sprinted to the oasis, with an out-of-body feeling that his actions were not his own. After circling the stump clockwise, he stopped in the same spot where he had seen the goddess kneel.

Scanning the ground, he could see that in fact multiple

holes opened up amid the roots of the old tree. Picking one at random, he dropped to one knee and thrust his hand into the dark space beneath the earth. With his arm buried to the elbow, he groped around inside. His fingers found only damp soil and something brittle like ancient bones.

While his heart thundered, merging with the thunder of hooves as enemy horsemen came sweeping across the plain, he yanked his arm back out and plunged it in again, groping around in a second subterranean chamber. This time his hand brushed against something scaled and coiled, which hissed at him.

With rising fear, the enemy thundering down upon him, he thrust his arm into a third burrow, and a fourth, finding in one a huddle of furred creatures, and in another a scattering of broken fragments, like beetle casings or eggshells.

In the fifth hole he tried, Kit's hand touched something solid. His fingers closed around the object and he drew it into the open.

Yes, here it was. This was the vessel he had seen the goddess use.

Still barely daring to hope, he shook it and heard thick liquid gloop inside. He took the cork out of the neck and sniffed the contents. The aroma – a sharp, coppery tang – was enough to dispel his last doubts.

He held the vessel aloft – cupped in both palms like an offering – and for long moments all he could do was gaze at it in awe.

Many years ago, so legend told, when Robin Loxley had first entered the wildwood, he fought a deranged old wolf god. In victory, Robin claimed the god's shadow, and its skin, using them to battle the enemies of the forest. Later, Robin also took possession of the god's teeth. They helped him combat the Great Fire. It was because of Robin, and the potency of the god-teeth, that Gaia had survived the inferno. That any hope remained to the world at all.

But the legends said that the teeth were not the last of these powerful relics. One piece of the wolf-god remained. All these years it had lain buried, unclaimed.

Until now . . .

Because here Kit was, holding the last of Sherwood's great relics.

The blood of a forest god.

He fixed his gaze on the ancient tree stump, with its coating of moss and rustling undergrowth. This fountain of life that existed here in the wastelands. The goddess had created this oasis, sustained it – and Kit had seen her use a mere sprinkling of the blood.

Yes – it will work, he told himself. *It has to work. It is our only hope.*

Staggering to his feet, with the hooves of the enemy quaking the ground beneath him, Kit took the amphora and sprinted towards the edge of the Giants' Graveyard, praying beneath his breath that it wasn't already too late.

IX. The Underearth

'You say he's left this world, but how can that be?' Marian asked the goddess. She cupped Robin's stone-cold chin in her hands. 'He's . . . here. I'm touching him.'

The goddess smiled through rotting teeth. 'This is his outer form, merely. An empty skin. Like I said, his essence roams other realms.'

Marian clasped her hands together to stop them from shaking. 'And you think I can journey there too. How?'

'There are many doorways – many paths,' the goddess rasped. 'See here – this is the quickest. Although it is also the most perilous.'

The goddess reached out, and with blackened fingers parted the night-flowers that grew around Robin's feet. Marian looked closer. Nestled amid the flowers were tiny clusters of mushrooms. Their caps were luminous hues of red and green and blue.

Marian examined them, perturbed. Among the outlaws of Sherwood, her herblore had once been legend. There was not a plant or flower or fungus she did not know how to brew into a curative or a palliative or a poison. Yet now, as she examined these mushrooms in detail, she failed to identify their name or their nature. In all her years living in the forest, she had never encountered these particular types growing anywhere.

'You want me to eat these? I won't do it. They could be deadly.'

'Could be?' The goddess smiled. 'No doubt. In one way or another – a certainty.'

'I didn't come here to die.'

'But I told you,' the goddess said, gazing at Robin, 'your love walks a path between life and death. How can you even dream to lure him back –' she narrowed her eyes at Marian – 'if you won't taste death yourself?'

Marian stared at the mushrooms. The longer she stared, the larger they seemed to grow, glowing here in the gloom. Green and blue and red.

'Which one?' she murmured.

'Ah, well now, that depends,' the goddess said, her golden eyes sparkling in their ancient sockets. 'One will stop your heart in an instant – and there our game ends. Another will kill you just as surely, but will drive you to madness first. The third will take you where you wish to go. That is your portal to the Underearth.' The goddess grinned. 'I would help you choose . . . except, in truth, I can no longer remember which is which!'

The mushrooms now loomed so brilliantly in Marian's awareness that nothing else existed in this tree-cavern. They were adamants sparkling against black velvet. They were stars flaming against the infinite blackness of the heavens.

Could one of these truly take her to Robin? And if so, what then? Even if she managed to find his spirit, could anything or anyone truly bring him back to the world of the living? Was it lunacy to even try? Was it worth risking her own life?

She had seen people die from deathcap and belladonna and other plant poisons – it was hard to imagine a death more agonizing. She envisaged herself choking and thrashing here in her death-throes, all alone but for the hateful presence of the goddess.

Most of all, she thought of Rex. He was out there in that desolate bone yard, awaiting her return. He had already lived without a father – his real father. Could she really risk leaving him an orphan?

You'd be doing this for Rex as much as anyone, she told herself. *He can't go on the way he was – living a lie, inhabiting the Sheriff's world . . .*

So thinking, she brushed her fingertips across the mushrooms. The green. The red. The blue. As if of their own volition, her fingers tightened around the stem of the green. And already the decision had been made – she was plucking the mushroom from its bed of mulch – and she was watching in dread fascination as her hand brought it towards her mouth.

Then the tangy musty taste on her tongue . . . and she was swallowing it into her throat . . . and it was done.

For a moment, nothing. The goddess tipping her head, watching her with a slight frown.

Then a tingling in Marian's hands –

A coldness in her skull –

And a tightness in her chest that gripped so suddenly and viciously that breath and pulse went out of her in an instant as she slumped to the ground and was swallowed into boundless black.

Beneath the relentless sun, with the relentless noise of armed horsemen bearing down upon him, Kit stuck to his task. He circled the Giants' Graveyard, stopping every few paces to tip the amphora. Its viscous contents splattered onto the scorched ground.

He glanced back at the slick slug's trail he had left behind him. The god's blood glistened atop the baked topsoil. It stirred thickly amid the dust. It did nothing more than that.

But it will do something – soon, he insisted to himself. *It will work – it has to.*

153

Out there, across the plain, Guy of Gisbourne and his war party galloped ever closer, warrior monks and rangers now clearly visible even amid the thunderhead of dust.

Kit focused once more on his task, dribbling his black-red trail upon the ground. He shook the amphora. There wasn't much left – but enough. Only this last stretch to go. He hurried onwards, casting the droplets of blood, like a farmer sowing seeds.

Finally, he completed his circuit. There was now a dark band of god's blood marking a boundary around the entire Giants' Graveyard.

He dropped the amphora and headed back towards his outlaws. As he passed between the skeletons of the trees, a face peered out at him. It was Marian's guide, the scavenger.

'Whatever your part in this, it's finished,' he called out to her. 'You've still got time to run. Get as far from here as you can.'

The girl shook her head, went on staring towards the advancing horde. 'I'm waiting for my brother,' she said blankly. 'He needs me.'

Kit shrugged, went on his way. He had bigger things to worry about than a couple of wastrels of the wastes.

A little further on, he spotted Much, only the whites of his eyes visible amid the remains of a shattered trunk. He carried on past Jack, then did a tour of the other outlaw positions, nodding to each in turn.

'I don't know what you were planning, mighty leader, but it hasn't worked,' said Midge, raising his head as Kit passed. 'Now it's too late. We're trapped like rats in a barrel.'

Ignoring him, Kit strung his bow, then went to take his place behind a barricade of sun-bleached timber. Peering over it, he watched the perimeter. There was the ring of blood, glistening. Still nothing stirred within it.

The enemy bore down, closer and closer . . . and *still* nothing . . .

Had he made a terrible mistake? Had he been fooling himself, all along – dreaming up hope where there was none? If so, then Midge was right, and he had doomed them all.

X. The Unknown Path

The supreme moment – the instant of death – was more frightening than anything Marian could have imagined. It was a falling, but not through empty space, but rather *through the Earth*. Through soil and rock and root, the pressure in her chest and skull intensifying with every heartbeat, the crushing weight above her growing ever more terrifying as she plummeted down and down and down . . .

She tried to scream, but her mouth was full of earth and her lungs were squeezed breathless and her heart hammered so hard it would surely burst.

Her heart. It was still beating.

She could hear it thundering like galloping hooves. She could feel the pulse of blood pounding in her ears.

So, then – this wasn't death.

But what was it?

The downward rushing of darkness began to slow. The worst of the panic eased. She was no longer in freefall, but rather . . . she was floating.

Floating underground.

She had the impression of opening her eyes.

The blackness remained. She turned her head. Blackness in every direction. Blackness and weight. Buried alive.

The panic surged, re-energized, more potent than ever. She thrashed her phantom limbs, trying to wrestle free – to swim for the surface – but the darkness only seized her tighter, until once again she was unable to breathe, until the pressure squeezed so heavily upon her skull that surely it would collapse in on itself.

She had never known such fear. Such desperate helplessness.

The fear itself would stop her heart – that was certain. She would die down here in the darkness, separated for ever from Robin and Rex.

No – you can't allow that, came a tiny voice, perhaps her own. *You can't let the darkness have you – not yet. They need you – Rex and Robin both.*

A memory drops into her like a gift – like a lifeline. A recollection so vivid she might be living it at this moment. She has stepped into The Henge, a dark circle of yew trees at the heart of Sherwood Forest. And lying there on the ground in front of her is Robin. The god-shadow has turned against him, snaking up from his arm and wrapping itself around his throat. It is choking him to death.

Screaming in fear and fury, Marian tries to fight the shadow, but it is like wrestling with mist – it wisps between her fingers even as it constricts, stopping Robin's breath. Finally, when all else fails, Robin insists they stop fighting. He forces himself to lie still, and simply waits. Faced with no resistance, the shadow finally falls apart and lets him breathe . . .

Yes – you remember – that really happened. Surrender saved Robin. You must do the same now. Stop struggling. Stop feeding your fear. It's like a nightmare – it has no substance. It can't hurt you unless you allow it to. Let it pass. It's your only chance.

Talking to herself this way, with the sensation she had closed her eyes, she gave herself over to her fear and her panic, admitting she was powerless against it, inviting it to do its worst.

Taunted, her fear redoubled, the blackness and the weight

pushing in heavier than ever. Resisting the urge to fight back, summoning the greatest strength of will she had ever known, she merely floated, just breathing, and finally managed to relinquish all will entirely.

She could *see* her fear now. It was a red and ravenous thing. It wrapped itself around her, squeezing. But now it found no purchase. It thrashed and flailed, impotently. It was shrinking, burning itself out, like a wildfire deprived of fuel. Finally it dwindled to nothing and was extinguished.

The peace that followed was so profound that Marian might willingly have suffered the panic in order to experience this state of bliss. She floated free and disembodied, opening her eyes and watching the blackness turn and shine as deep and wondrous as the heavens.

Perhaps this was death after all. If so, she might almost be glad. It was glorious!

It was as though her spirit had fallen clean through the Earth and now floated far out amid the stars. Yes – look there – those twinkling spots in the darkness. More and more of them blinking into view. Whole constellations. A whole firmament. The stars shining white and yellow, or softly pulsing red and blue and green.

She had never known anything so beautiful, or so serene. There was a silence here so deep it was musical. As she floated, gazing in rapture, the starscape appeared to change – or she began to make more sense of her perceptions. She could see now that none of these points of light were separate. Instead, they were joined, each one to the next, by glistening threads.

Marian blinked. The filaments were as thin and insubstantial as gossamer; she only caught sight of them when they glimmered. But they were there – countless multitudes of them, joining every star to every other, forming a never-ending web, surrounding her on all sides, above and below, rippling away into eternity.

The scale of it might have been terrifying, if it weren't so sublimely beautiful. No – there was nothing here to fear. She looked down at her body, floating in space, and was not surprised to find it was made of the same radiance that surrounded her. These shimmering strands rippled through her too, threading her into the infinite, numinous web.

'Robin – are you here?' she whispered. 'I . . . I think you must be. I don't know where this is, but at the same time . . . I . . . I *recognize* it. Like I belong here. Or . . . I've always been here, in a way. I think you must be here too. I . . . I don't think this could exist without you.'

As she spoke, the nodes of light within her and all around her glowed brighter, and the threads connecting them glimmered along their lengths, glistening blue and green and red. The effect was so spellbinding that Marian laughed in delight. Her laughter rippled outwards through the web, making her laugh again, sparking yet more cascades of brilliant light.

What is this? she thought, dumbstruck. *Where am I?*

With deepening awe, she saw it wasn't only her voice that sent colour rippling through the starweb. Her very thoughts shimmered outwards, zipping from one node to the next, painting the firmament with her thought patterns.

'Is this . . . am I inside my own mind . . . is that it?' she murmured to herself. 'Or . . . or is this Robin's mind? Or the mind of the world?'

'All three are true – they are all the same,' came a voice from everywhere and nowhere. 'There is no division here.'

It was the voice of the vixen-goddess. Although it had changed. It was no longer cracked and rotten as it had sounded in the ancient tree stump. Here, in these everlands, her voice was a symphony of coloured notes, the sounds playing upon the strands of the cosmos like strings upon a harp.

And when the goddess appeared, she was not the deathly

husk she had been above. In fact, here she had no form at all – at least none that was solid. Instead, she was light, pure and protean. She swirled around Marian, and into her, their bodies merging.

'You and I . . . We're the same,' Marian said in amazement, suddenly knowing it to be true. 'We're . . . the same thing.'

The goddess just laughed at this, but there was no malice or derision in the laughter. There was no rancour between them here. How could there be?

'This place,' Marian whispered, watching her words paint the firmament. 'If Robin found his way here . . . he would want to stay. He *deserves* to stay.' A single tear rolled down her cheek, fell away as a perfect gleaming brilliant. 'I shouldn't have come. How could I take him away from this? I want him back so much. But I can't ask him to leave this place. I won't. Not for anything.'

'Ah, yes . . . that would have been a dilemma,' the goddess said, her voice shimmering away to eternity. 'A dilemma many others have had to face. But not you. Your beloved is no longer here.'

'What do you mean? Where else could he be?'

'He acted too much at the surface,' the goddess said, her light-body swirling around Marian now, like heavenly fireflies. 'At the same time, he left too much unfinished. Words unsaid, deeds undone. He came here weighted with regrets, and remorse. To find him, we must tread deeper depths. Come, I shall show you the way.'

The light of the goddess unwound from Marian and drifted off through the blackness. Marian remained in place.

To find him we must tread deeper depths.

Marian couldn't imagine – or didn't want to imagine – what this might mean. It was too taxing to even try. She only knew one thing with certainty: she had found the place where *she* belonged. A place she never wanted to leave.

All of a sudden, she could barely even recall how she had ended up here, or why. It couldn't be important. What was there to do, other than drift amid the ageless stars, watching them turn, listening to the music of the spheres?

'You cannot dwell here – not yet,' the goddess said, reading her thoughts. 'You too leave acts unfinished. Come. We must proceed.'

This command was irresistible. Of its own accord, Marian's spirit-self drifted after the goddess. As it did so, Marian's mind began to clear, and with a stab of something like guilt she remembered her purpose.

Robin. And Rex.

Yes. She had come here for them.

For their sakes, she must go on, and she dare not fail.

XI. Defenders of the Earth

The war party was almost upon them. At the head of the charge came Guy of Gisbourne. He was dressed head to foot in his horse-hide armour, and he was riding his giant destrier. To Kit, through the dust, man and horse appeared to be one, the heretic hunter galloping across the plain like a mighty centaur.

Seeing this, as Kit gripped his bow, a wave of despair washed over him. He stared at the boundary of the Giants' Graveyard. The trail of god's blood glistened there, but still nothing stirred in that barren soil.

It hadn't worked. Kit would die here today. And so would his band of outlaws – the last of the forest fighters. After today, the Sheriff's iron rule would be absolute, with no one to stop him destroying the last pockets of true wilderness.

No. I won't allow it. This cannot be the end. Not like this.

So thinking, without yet knowing what he was intending, Kit moved out from behind his barricade. With his bow at his side, he walked steadily towards the advancing war party.

'Kit! What are you doing?' Sonskya called out as he passed her hide. 'They'll cut you down where you stand!'

Kit kept going, regardless, keeping his head held high, his stride as even as he was able, as he moved through the Giants' Graveyard.

As he approached the boundary, Guy of Gisbourne fixed his black gaze upon him. He slowed his horse, raising a hand for his followers to do the same. The war party came forward at a walk.

Kit halted at the boundary, and looked down at the glistening trail of god's blood. He knelt and pressed his palms to the Earth.

'Please,' he heard himself whisper, 'you led us this far. You're with us, I know you are. Please, give us the strength we need.'

He stood, and fixed his gaze once more on Guy of Gisbourne. The giant warrior was now no more than three bowshots from the boundary. He watched Kit intently, hatefully, as he led his war party onwards.

Kit became aware of a presence at his side. It was Sonskya. Ira was here too, on his opposite flank. And then the entire band had gathered, standing shoulder to shoulder, their weapons lowered.

'I always said he had a death wish,' Midge muttered. 'Now he's done for the lot of us.'

They were the words Kit might have expected, but they lacked their usual spiked edge. Instead, his tone was one of resignation, perhaps even relief.

'We won't die in vain,' Much said, a flash of fire in his eyes, glancing at his son. 'If we can take the heretic hunter with us, our lives will be well spent.'

Two bowshots short of the boundary, Guy of Gisbourne raised a fist and his force ground to a halt. Beneath his horse-hide cowl, his eyes blazed black with hatred, while his bull-like shoulders flexed and his massive hands twitched.

'So then – what do we find here?' he growled, the words thick and guttural, carrying clearly across the dead plain. 'The famed outlaws of Sherwood. I have hunted you from bolthole to burrow. And now you come to me willingly?'

'This place is under our protection,' Kit called, keeping his voice as steady as he was able. 'None may enter.'

'Six of you?' the heretic hunter scoffed. 'You cannot protect even yourselves. All that remains is the manner of your destruction. Lay down your arms and I will grant you the swift blade. Resist us and you will suffer.'

'You have been warned,' Kit said. 'Come no further.'

The heretic hunter considered. 'These are stalling tactics. They can serve no other purpose. Where is Lady Marian? Where is the boy prince? We found the force they travelled with, and we know they came this far. Tell me where they are, before I grow angry.'

He studied Kit with eyes like a pair of black stars, infinite in their malice. 'You keep looking at the ground. What is it you have drawn there – a spirit fence? Do you imagine I will be defeated by superstition?'

Kit cursed himself. He had been trying not to look at the trail of god's blood. But his eyes kept dropping to it. Because something was changing there, he was almost sure of it . . . some stirring in the blood-darkened soil . . .

Yes – there – look! And there – tiny heads of green were popping up, glistening. There was another one – and another! More and more of them, sprouting out of the earth, growing as he watched . . .

'Kit, what's happening?' Sonskya breathed. 'Is this . . . is this your doing?'

Kit stood tall. 'Be ready,' he told his outlaws. 'It will happen fast now. I can feel it rising.'

'Look!' gasped Ira. 'And another there, see? It's—'

She broke off with another gasp as greenery burst up through the cracked earth – suckers and saplings shooting upwards all along the boundary line. Shield ferns and lance thistle and spear grass grew up and out, bushing thickly with dry, slithering, rustling sounds.

'Demon tricks! Earth magic!' Guy of Gisbourne hollered, kicking his destrier into motion. 'Flay their godless hides!'

His host of rangers were slower to react; for long moments even his warrior monks remained mesmerized, staring at the upwelling of wilderness. Briar bushes sprouted and branched and intertwined. Python vines snaked through gaps and twisted into cables. A curtain wall of vegetation was growing before their eyes.

'With me!' Guy of Gisbourne bellowed, thundering towards the perimeter. 'Destroy them all!'

Kit locked eyes with the heretic hunter. Forced himself to stand there rooted even as the colossal warrior on his giant steed came thundering directly towards him.

Between them, the green curtain wall grew thicker, higher. Already it reached the height of a man, and it was still rushing skywards. Saplings interlocked their branches. Blackthorn bushes bared their spikes.

Kit closed his eyes, bowed his head. Breathing deeply, he focused his attention inwards, allowing the outside world to drift to silence, even as the enemy drew near.

He sent his awareness into the green, his mind tunnelling through tendril and stem and rootlet, his being merging with the wall of thorns . . .

Guy of Gisbourne reached the boundary, shouted, swung his broadsword, crashed in among the greenery—

And in the same moment Kit raised his head, opened his fists, punched both his palms outwards. The green wall surged, took hold of Guy of Gisbourne, tore him from his saddle and flung him back out of the Giants' Graveyard.

The heretic hunter landed hard, his blade flung to one side. Without missing a breath he was back on his feet, had retrieved the sword and was thundering into the attack once more, hacking and slashing at the living barricade, while warrior monks and soldiers joined the attack.

Kit bunched his fists over his chest, then punched them outwards. Suckers seized the invaders and thrust them back out onto the plain.

'Take them down!' he shouted to his band. 'I'll keep them out as long as I can.'

The outlaws didn't need this command. Having shaken off their own shock, they had drawn their weapons and were already prowling the boundary, looking for shots between the greenery. There was a death-wail where Ira's arrow found a soldier in the throat. A warrior monk died, Midge cracking his skull with a rock from his slingshot.

But the onslaught had only just begun. The enemy were now trying to break through on all sides. Closing his eyes, Kit struck back with his forest powers, causing vines to whiplash and briars to thrash. He ensnared two soldiers in a net of thorns, while branches beat down a third. And all the while he battled Guy of Gisbourne, who came on like a battering ram, crashing time and again against the green wall.

How long can we hold them off? Kit asked himself, already feeling the drain of tapping his forest powers.

He turned his eyes towards the tree-cavern. *Whatever you're doing in there, Marian, it had better work. And soon. Otherwise, this place will be a graveyard for us all . . .*

XII. Deepening Realms

At first, as Marian's spirit-self drifted after the goddess, this otherworld remained unchanged. It was a beautiful infinity of blackness, populated by a starscape of glittering light and the gossamer threads that glistened between them. She herself was formless and perfect, indivisible from this perfect formless world.

But gradually, as they went onwards, Marian detected a shift. The sensation of weight settled upon her. Solid ground beneath her feet. With a sense of profound loss, she realized she was once more tethered to a tangible form. She was walking forwards. And downwards. Because this path they were following was sloping, steeper and steeper.

At the same time, her perception of the world around her changed. Above and all around, she could still see those strands of light glistening like a vast web. But now they were more substantial. They put her in mind of rootlets – and the tiny hair-like filaments that interconnect the rootlets. As she went on they became thicker still; here and there they were as chunky as taproots, and sometimes as tangled as root balls. Suddenly it seemed to her she was somehow walking *within* the earth, beneath a great forest, weaving through the vast network of its root clusters.

Beneath a forest, or through it? Dizzy now, and disorientated, her perception shifted again, and the shapes around her seemed more like the branches of trees. Yes, here were all the tangled forms of the wildwood – except ghostly, as if viewed through mist. She had the sensation she was scrambling over something slimy – a mossy boulder. She gasped as a thorn snagged her skin.

'What is this . . . ? Where am I?' she murmured aloud. The deep serenity she had experienced before had vanished now, to be replaced by a creeping fear. 'How did I get here? I feel like I'm in my own body, but . . . but I can't be. I left my body above.'

'It is all the same,' the goddess called back. 'Light and shade. Blood and dust.'

'What did you say? Wait! I can't keep up!'

Marian was running now, pushing through undergrowth, battling thickets of thorns. Ahead of her, the goddess too had taken on a solid form. She was a young woman, pale-skinned and graceful, with flowing fox-red hair.

'Wait!' Marian shouted again. 'You're moving too fast. I'll get lost down here!'

The goddess flitted on, regardless, Marian scrambling in her wake. Meanwhile, her surroundings grew ever more substantial, until she was ducking under low boughs and hurdling rotting logs and scrambling down rocky paths and sweeping through woodland clearings. The darkness lifted, to be replaced by soft sunlight, which bathed the trees in an autumnal glow.

As she ran, she stared at all this in wonder, with the feeling she had slipped back in time, and was now running through the greenwood. Yes – where could this be except Sherwood Forest? Here it was, the great forest – in fact it had never gone – nothing had ever been lost!

A laugh made her stumble to a halt, and turn. That was not the laughter of the goddess. It had come from a human throat. Listen – more laughter, and voices. Voices she recognized!

Before she even realized what she was doing, or could stop herself, she was running in the direction of these blessed sounds. It was true – nothing was lost – it was all still here! *They* were still here – she could *hear* them!

She reached a wide river and came stumbling to a halt, her arms cartwheeling to prevent herself plunging into the water. She caught her balance and stared. They were there, playing on the opposite bank, their hair sparkling in the sun. Eight . . . nine . . . ten of them – everyone!

'I'm here!' Marian called across, lost in the wonder of this, everything else forgotten. 'Aimee, Minnie, Lyssa! It's me!'

The young women gave no indication they had heard. They went on with their games, teasing one another, wringing water from their hair, while Marian stood and stared. Eventually, Elfen and Petronilla turned to leave, and others stood to follow.

'Wait – don't go!' Marian called. 'I'm coming across!'

'I wouldn't do that if I were you,' said a voice behind her.

But Marian was already scrambling down the bank and wading into the fast-flowing river. The cold was shocking and the power of the current almost knocked her off her feet. But she kept going, fighting for firm footing on the polished rocks of the riverbed.

Halfway across she slipped and went under. Gasping for breath, thrashing her arms, she came back to the surface. But the current seized her, and again she floundered, while on the far bank she saw the last of her sisters stand and move away.

'Wait!' she tried to shout, choking. 'Come back! I'm here!'

The last of these words were gargled underwater. The world rushed over her, turned her upside down. She flailed and thrashed, sucked desperate breaths as she resurfaced – then down once again, her lungs tightening in her chest.

Her flailing hand came up against something solid. She pulled against it and found herself back at the bank where she had begun. She was gripping the exposed roots of a willow tree. She coughed up water and sucked air into her lungs.

'That wasn't very wise,' the goddess said, looking down at her from the bank. 'Be warned – if you die here, you will wish you had taken the poison that stops your heart.'

Marian dragged herself up onto the grass, where she coughed on hands and knees. Only . . . why was she coughing? She was no longer short of breath. Already the cold of the river had left her, and when she sat upright her hair was dry.

'Why am I here?' she snapped at the goddess. 'What good will it do? None of this is real. It's just illusion.'

'Oh?' The goddess smiled. 'And you would know the difference?'

Marian stared around her. It all *seemed* so lifelike. The trees glowing in their autumn coats of red and russet and gold. The woodnotes of songbirds and the humming of bees and the croaking of toads. The aroma of damp moss and dank loam.

She bowed her head. 'What difference does it make? Even if Robin is here . . . how can I help him? This isn't my world. Minnie and the others . . . they couldn't even hear me.'

'Very well,' the goddess said, kneeling. 'Yes, I understand. It's best you go no further. You don't really want to see what lies down here.' She opened her fingers to reveal a mushroom, luminous blue, resting in her palm. 'Take it,' she said. 'Go back to the world you know. Leave the rest buried.'

With trembling fingers, Marian reached out and took the mushroom. She thought about her body – her real body – up there, slumped and defenceless. She thought of Rex, awaiting her return.

'You were right,' the goddess said. 'You should never have come here. You'd better return now – while you still can. Go any further . . . and you will no longer have the choice.'

While Marian turned the mushroom in her fingers, a tremor

rippled through the world around her, quaking the ground and shaking the trees. Birds took off from their roosts in alarm.

Marian looked up. Something told her that the disturbance originated at the surface – in the world of the living. What was happening up there? Had Guy of Gisbourne arrived at the Giants' Graveyard? Were the outlaws standing against him?

These questions, together with another quake from the surface, steeled Marian's resolve. She glared at the goddess.

'We're wasting time,' she snapped. 'You said you'd lead me to Robin. So where is he?'

The goddess showed her canine teeth. 'I told you – your beloved carried a great weight. He sank through these realms long ago.'

'So . . . we need to go deeper?'

'Oh, yes – and deeper still. Come,' she said, turning. 'I cannot take you there, exactly. But I shall point the way.'

Marian stood on the riverbank, the water glistening in the twilight, otters diving after fish. For a moment, all was peace and harmony.

Then another violent tremor rumbled down from the world above, shaking leaves from the trees and panicking the birds.

Marian pictured Guy of Gisbourne fighting his way to the ancient tree stump, crawling inside and finding Robin's body, wasted and helpless.

So thinking, with the under-forest quaking once more, she tossed the blue mushroom into the river, where it was borne away by the current. Then she hurried after the goddess, resolved to follow this darkening path no matter how deep it might run.

XIII. Last Stand

While violence raged all around him, Rex remained motion-less, locked in shock and disbelief. Hugging his knees, he stared unblinking at the wall of thorns. He had watched these green battlements rise up before his eyes, yet still his shocked mind refused to accept that it was real.

This shouldn't be happening. None of it . . . It's all a mistake.

This is not your life. It's all a lie.

Crossing the wastes, he had suffered the awful, bewildering idea that *nothing* in his life made sense. Now that idea resurfaced and redoubled, until he was drowning in it. The very ground beneath him felt soft, his own body unreal.

This is wrong. All of it.

I've hated lying to you all these years.

His mother's words floated back to him, as insubstantial as everything else. As untrustworthy as these sounds ringing in the air: the grunt of warrior monks and soldiers trying to cut through the wall of thorns; the hollering rage of the heretic hunter; the *thwip thwip* of arrows where the outlaws stood their ground.

I need to leave you, just for a little while.

Afterwards . . . everything will be different.

Blinking, he finally managed to turn his head. He stared

at the ancient tree stump. What was she doing in there? Why had she insisted on going inside in the first place? What did any of this matter? What was so important about Robin Hood's remains that they should draw all these warriors here, and provoke such violence? How had Rex become ensnared in it all?

These questions, and countless others like them, plunged Rex deeper and deeper into doubt and confusion. Until finally, truly drowning, he flooded with fear. His fear, in turn, morphed into rage. Grinding his teeth, he staggered to his feet.

At first, his fury was aimless – it thrashed around, looking for a target, lashing out at his father for sending him into these wastelands, and at his mother for leaving him out here all alone, and even at Alpha Johns for abandoning him.

But finally his rage found its mark. He became deathly still once more, staring at one warrior in particular. He was standing out by the green barricade. He was locked in some kind of battle with Guy of Gisbourne.

It was the one they called Kit. Leader of the outlaws.

Alpha's murderer.

Hissing between his teeth, Rex stalked towards the outlaw chief.

As he went, he almost stumbled over a corpse. It was a ranger. He had evidently broken through the wall of thorns, before falling prey to the outlaws. They had clubbed him to death, his head staved in and his brains spilling out.

Rex took in this grisly scene without fear or revulsion – his fury was now a white heat, burning through all other emotion. Without hesitation, he snatched up the dead ranger's crossbow. It was already fully wound, and fitted with a quarrel.

He took the weapon and continued to prowl towards the leader of the outlaws.

You have a place in all this – a vital place. But you don't yet know what that place is.

His mother had said that too. But it wasn't true. For a while, trapped in his own misery and confusion, Rex had forgotten his place.

But now he remembered.

He had come here as commander of the Sheriff's troops. He had come to retrieve the bones of Robin Hood. Perhaps that prize was denied him. Well – here was one far greater. He would return to his father in triumph, bearing the head of the outlaw chief.

He would personally bring the rebellion to an end.

XIV. Phantom Fears

As the goddess went onwards, and Marian followed, the ground beneath them sloped downwards ever more steeply. Their path twisted sharply left and right, and doubled back on itself, winding into a shadowy labyrinth.

With every footstep, so it seemed, the world around Marian had been changing, the other-forest becoming darker and quieter. She could no longer hear birdsong, or woodnotes of any kind. This place now put her in mind of the wildwood in the grip of midwinter, the trees she glimpsed through the mist standing like skeletons, white and spindly. Or here and there, their limbs were pink, like bones freshly skinned. The gloom thickened further, until Marian was groping her way forward with arms outstretched. Unseen branches tugged at her hair, while thorns clawed at her flesh.

As they descended, the goddess was changing too. Her fox-red hair no longer gleamed but grew dull. She was shedding her hair, clumps of it hanging from briar bushes in her wake. Her posture was slumping, her graceful movements giving way to a shuffling gait. She glanced back over her shoulder and Marian sucked a breath to see her decaying face. The skin was flaking from her cheeks, like the bark sloughing from a birch tree, revealing pink bone and sinew beneath.

Noises behind Marian made her spin in place. The snapping of twigs. The cracking of branches. Something was crunching through the undergrowth.

Holding her breath, narrowing her eyes, Marian tried to see what it might be. But the shape was barely discernible amid the shadows. And now it was drawing further off and its noises were fading and it was gone.

'There was nothing there in any case,' Marian murmured to herself. 'There can't be. This place isn't real.'

'No?' said the goddess, stepping back to her, smiling through wasted gums. 'Then you won't mind if I do this.' Her hand flashed out and she scoured claw-like fingernails down Marian's forearm, making her cry out and recoil. 'Don't worry, it's just imaginary,' the goddess said, grinning madly, before turning and going on.

Marian cradled her arm, blood beading through the claw marks. She stared around her at the twisting forms of the nether-forest, thorns glinting amid the mist like teeth, fireflies drifting in pairs like eyes.

She ran to catch up with the goddess. 'This is all in my mind,' she said defiantly. 'I know it is because this is exactly how I used to see Sherwood Forest. I jumped at every shadow, until I came to know what it was I was looking at. I *made* the fear. And that's all I'm doing here.'

The goddess smiled back at her toothlessly. 'I'm glad to hear you so certain, and brave. Because we have reached our parting of ways.'

'What? No! You promised to take me to Robin!'

'I promised to point you in his direction. I can do no more.' The goddess limped onwards, more decrepit with each passing moment. 'I'm a trespasser here – even more than you are.' She flashed Marian another gruesome smile, a final tooth falling from her gums. 'From here on . . . you're on your own.'

'Wait . . . No!'

But the goddess was already collapsing, falling to the earth as strands of hair and sloughs of skin and heaped bones. Marian recoiled, horrified, as the steaming remains began to decompose, melting into the mulch of the forest floor even as she watched. Within moments there was no trace of the goddess, or any sign that she had ever existed.

Marian hugged her arms, peered around her. The mist was dense now, and icy cold. It was no longer merely quiet, but entirely silent.

'Robin?' she called, her voice a choked whisper. 'Robin – are you here? I . . . I've come to find you.'

What was there to do but go onwards? The only light came from a pale glimmer in the distance – the meekest midwinter sun. With no other point of reference, feeling desperately afraid and alone, she began groping her way in that direction.

As she went, the nether-forest became ever more sinister. Its trees were now standing deadwood, their branches breaking wherever she brushed against them. Beneath her feet brittle detritus snapped and crunched. She dared not look down, the idea growing in her that these were not sticks cracking underfoot but instead a litter of bones.

'Robin . . . I'm here,' she murmured. 'I've come to find you.' She wiped a tear from her cheek. 'I'm so scared, Robin . . . and I don't even know why. I've faced death a thousand times, but this is . . . this is different. I feel so alone. So . . . far away. From everything. From myself. Robin, this place, I don't know what it is, but I need to get you out of here.' She wiped again at her cheek, and her words were so choked she could barely hear them with her own ears. 'I'm so sorry, Robin. I'm sorry I left you here . . . all by yourself . . . for so long.'

As she continued towards the glimmer of light, it grew more distinct. Finally, she saw that it was not the glow of daylight.

Instead, it was the flickering of tiny fires. Here the nether-forest was bleaker than ever. The ground was a burned and blackened crust. The standing remains of trees thrust up through the blasted soil like the grasping fingers of the dead. The bones of other trees lay scattered about, and it was these that flickered with flame. In the mist, these flames hissed and spluttered, like sickly candles.

Marian spun around. She had heard – or sensed – something move. It was swift and stealthy – gone almost before she knew it was there, leaving her with nothing but a dark afterimage.

'Robin?' she called. 'If that was you – please, show yourself. She said you were down here.'

She edged towards a copse of standing deadwood. The movement she had glimpsed had disappeared near there, she was almost certain.

She stared at the deadwood as she approached, then faltered when she thought she saw something shift in its shadows. She forced herself to keep moving forwards, imagining now she could see a faint redness glimmering beneath the trees. Yes, there was something there. It was crouched low, like a predator preparing to pounce.

'Robin . . .' she croaked. 'I don't know if it's you in there, but if it is I want you to come out. You don't need to hide from me. Whatever this place is, whatever you've been through, we can face it together.'

She watched the shadowy shape amid the trees. As she approached, she saw it draw back, deeper into the darkness of the copse. It appeared to watch her with reddish eyes.

She forced herself to keep walking, with dread wonder growing inside her . . . with the swelling certainty that this somehow *was* him . . . that she had found Robin.

'I . . . I'm coming in there,' she murmured. 'Whatever this place has done to you . . . no matter what you've become, it makes no difference. I've lived too long without you, and you without me. We can't do it any more. I won't leave you down here. Understand? I'm coming in, and I'm not afraid.'

'You should be,' a voice growled out of the darkness. 'You do not belong here. You should not have come.'

Death was coming for Kit. He understood that with a sudden cold clarity. So far, he and his outlaws had held their ground valiantly – with a desperate ferocity. But there were so many invaders, and they were relentless. It was only a matter of time . . .

In front of Kit, Guy of Gisbourne continued to hack and slash at the green barricade. He tore through tendrils and sliced through vines, his nostrils flared, like an enraged bull.

Kit closed his fingers, seized the heretic hunter with ropes of ivy. With a colossal effort, straining every sinew, Kit raised his arms and lifted the giant warrior off the ground – before flinging out his hands and slinging him back out into the wastelands.

The heretic hunter rolled over in the dust, then lay still. His great body heaved with every breath, and Kit dared to hope that this time he might be badly injured, or unconscious. But then he rose implacably from the ground and moved steadily to pick up his sword.

Then he came thundering into the attack once again, swinging his giant blade, hacking and hacking at the living barricade. Kit struck back with pollards of ash, stiff as spears, and shards of daggerwood, dagger-sharp.

Meanwhile, the rest of Kit's band were roaming the boundary, targeting the enemy wherever they threatened to break through. Half a dozen rangers were dead, hanging amid the thorns like grisly puppets. But the rest of the soldiers and the warrior monks kept coming, wave upon wave.

'Over there – quick!' Kit heard Ira holler behind him. 'They're coming through!'

Glancing back, Kit saw two rangers had cut a hole in the wall of vegetation and were dragging themselves into the Giants' Graveyard. They barely had time to steady themselves before Midge and Jack were upon them, clubbing and stabbing them to the ground.

Warrior monks were rushing around the perimeter, heading for the breach. Interlocking his fingers, Kit caused branches to meet like crossed swords. Closing his fists, he made vines intertwine and creepers knot. The opening was sealed.

The effort was exhausting. Kit sagged, but kept his feet. He turned his full attention back to Guy of Gisbourne. Taking advantage of the distraction, the heretic hunter had made deep inroads.

Kit wrestled against him with every scrap of strength he had left. But by now his forest powers had begun to wane. Tapping his Earth strength sucked the life out of him.

He suddenly felt so drained he could hardly lift his arms from his sides.

He turned his eyes to the tree-cave. Since Marian had gone in, Kit had heard not a sound from that black interior, nor glimpsed any sign of movement. Nobody had come back out. Nothing had happened.

What exactly had he been expecting? What miracle had he been awaiting?

From behind him, more shouting, and the *zip-thwack* of arrows finding their mark, and death-wails. The outlaws were fighting their last fight with ultimate ferocity, to the last drop of blood. But it would not be enough.

On all sides, rangers and warrior monks cut and slashed their way through the barricade. Ahead of Kit, the heretic hunter came on with the force of a thunderstorm, wielding his mighty blade as though it were weightless.

Movement to Kit's right made him swivel his eyes. At first

glance he thought a ranger must have broken though undetected. But no.

It was the boy, Rex. Marian's son.

He stepped around Kit, until he was in clear view.

He was holding a crossbow, and it was aimed at Kit's chest.

'I should shoot you in the back. Murder you in cold blood,' Rex spat. 'But I'm not like you.' He dropped the crossbow, drew his sword. 'You think I'm afraid of you, but I'm not.'

'Get away from me, child,' Kit growled. 'This isn't your fight. Do you even know what any of this means?'

'I know enough. I know Alpha Johns was a good man.'

'He was a ranger of the Sheriff's Guard. A defiler of the Earth.'

'You killed him.'

'And a hundred others just the same.'

Rex snarled, advancing. 'If you don't face me, I'll cut you down where you stand.'

Perhaps I should let him, Kit thought vaguely, as another wave of exhaustion washed over him. He stared once more at the relentless heretic hunter, and the depthless hatred in his eyes. *If the boy's strike is true, at least it will be a swift end.*

But even as these thoughts passed through him, and Rex stalked forward, hefting his blade, a surge of passion rose up in Kit. He knew this feeling well. Over the years, time and again, when Kit had found himself on his knees, ready to accept death, this instinct had arisen to save him – this fierce, desperate will to live.

Even now, as depleted and soul-weary as he was, that savage survival instinct showed its teeth, and from somewhere unimagined Kit drew yet more power up through the Earth. With a deathly groan, bunching his fists, he made suckers snake out from the wall of thorns.

The suckers seized hold of Rex. The boy cried out and

dropped his sword as his arms were pinioned at his side. He gasped and struggled as tendrils wrapped tighter, and tautened, dragging him backwards towards the boundary. More suckers reached out for him, hauled him into the green wall. The vegetation closed over him, like a colossal carnivorous plant devouring its prey.

Kit felt no great animosity towards the boy, but nor did he feel any particular pity. He was too exhausted for either. And so as Rex disappeared, choking, into the wall of thorns, Kit simply turned away from him and once more faced Guy of Gisbourne.

Kit's surge of survival fear had rippled all through the green barricade, and had thrust the heretic hunter back several yards. But already he was making up the lost ground, hacking and slashing tirelessly, driving onwards. And now Kit's last reserves of energy were truly depleted. Exhaustion and a sense of futility almost dropped him to his knees.

No doubt the heretic hunter scented his weakness. Because now he thrashed and roared more violently than ever. The green wall split asunder as the giant warrior made inroads, his eyes blazing with black hatred.

Yes – death was coming for Kit. It had dragged its feet, drawing out his suffering. But very soon it would be here.

XV. Dark Twin

You do not belong here. You should not have come.

The meaning of the words meant nothing to Marian. It was the sound of them. The sound was everything.

That voice . . .

Unheard all these years . . .

It belonged to Robin.

'Y-you're here,' she murmured. 'I've . . . found you.'

'You should not have come. Go. While you still can.'

Again, the sense of the words meant little. It was only the sound – that glorious sound. His voice was rough and guttural, like metal left to rust. All the same, it was *his* voice. In all the realms of heaven and Earth, it could belong to nobody else.

'You're truly here,' she murmured again, stupidly. 'It's really you.'

'This is not your place,' the voice said, low and heavy. 'You must leave.'

Marian stumbled forward, staggered into the copse of deadwood, groping onwards in the gloom.

'Robin – I know it's you – I know you're here. It's me. Show yourself, please!' She wiped a tear from her cheek. 'Oh, Robin, I'm sorry. I should never have left you like this, all alone.' She stumbled through the darkness. 'Where are you? Why won't you come to me?'

She fixed her gaze on a dark creature-shape. As she stumbled towards it, the shape drew deeper into the shadows.

'What are you doing? It's me – don't move away!'

'You should not be here,' the voice growled. 'Don't come any closer. I'm warning you. I . . . I am not what I was.'

'Warning me? What do you mean? I'm here. Let me see you, please!'

She struggled through the snaggled undergrowth, stumbling in the gloom.

'You should not have come,' the voice said, as the creature-shape retreated into darkness. 'You do not belong.'

'I do! If you're here, I do! I should never have left you in the first place. We should never have been apart.' She stumbled forward, while the black shape receded, slouching heavily through the copse, branches cracking in its wake.

'Robin – where are you going? What is this? Why would you hide from me? Let me touch you – let me hold you!'

'Get away from me!' the voice spoke, so deep and menacing that Marian faltered and almost fell. The creature-shape shifted, turned its head. As it did so, she saw twin orbs of red, like demonic eyes.

She hesitated, just for a moment doubting whether she was following Robin after all. Could this truly be him, wrapped in these blackest shadows, wearing that dread skin?

But that voice. *His* voice.

The sound of it echoed in her mind and drew her onwards through the copse. She approached that dark huddled shape, wanting – yearning – to touch him, to hold him. She stepped closer, reached out—

'I said leave me!'

As the guttural voice roared, shaking the trees, the redness of the eyes shifted, together with a mass of black. With the

184

cracking of branches, a sinuous form powered up and out of the copse and was gone.

Shrieking at him to stop, shaking with desperation, Marian dashed after the creature-shape. She burst from the trees and sped across the hellish plain.

Trying to focus through tear-blurred eyes, she sighted something massive surge ahead of her. Again and again she caught a glimpse. But it was always so quick – the shadow of a ghost – leaving only a fleeting afterimage.

Crying, stumbling, Marian ran in pursuit, staggering and scrambling over the scorched ground between flickering beds of flame.

'Robin – come back,' she called out. 'You don't want to run from me! You've been here too long. See what it's done to you! Oh, Robin, you shouldn't be here at all.'

'This is where I belong,' his voice rumbled back to her. 'This is what I deserve.'

'No – you're wrong!'

'Witness what I did to the world.'

'That was the Sheriff,' she shouted, running, stumbling. 'It was his doing, not yours!'

'I fought him. And the forest burned.'

'You tried to save the forest! You stood against the flames. You are the Earth's protector. That's who you truly are.'

As the black form loped ahead of her, she got clearer glimpses. She knew now it was a colossal wolf, blacker than a nightmare, with gleaming red eyes.

'This skin you're wearing – it isn't you,' she called after him. 'Down here . . . it's like . . . a dark reflection. Everything is twisted. Your true self is golden. I've seen that, over and over. All this is a trick. A mirage. You don't need to believe it – not any more.'

He paid no heed. The monster-wolf loped on through the

nether-land, and Marian's spirit-self raced after it, the hellish air burning in her lungs, the soles of her feet scorched and blistered.

'Wait for me, Robin, please. Come back with me to the surface. Together we can do anything. We can make you whole again. We . . . we can live.'

At some point, as this agonizing chase continued, Marian realized that the monster-wolf had slowed. Even though her own running was laboured, she was gaining on it.

As she drew closer, she noted that it ran unevenly, as though injured. Glancing down, blinking in the gloom, she saw its paw prints stamped into a track of soft ground. The prints were filled with blood. Yes – it was leaving a thick trail of blood in its wake, along with clumps of bloody fur where it brushed against boulders or the trunks of trees.

'You're hurt,' she murmured, scrambling after him, shedding more tears. 'It must have been agony, all this time. It's too much suffering – it has to end! Lie down, please. Rest. I'm here now. You don't have to go on all alone.'

Finally, the Robin-wolf slowed to a near standstill – then slumped to the ground, exhausted.

Stumbling, almost ready to collapse herself, Marian slowed. She approached cautiously. At close quarters, in the open, the demon-wolf looked colossal, and so black it was like a hole in the world. She watched its massive back rise and fall with laboured breathing. She stared at its ragged fur, matted with blood. She listened to the low, rumbling sound of breath, rasping between teeth and jaws.

'You fear me,' the Robin-wolf said, without lifting its head, its top lip curling back as it spoke. 'Even you fear me now.'

'No – never,' Marian said, approaching him as steadily as she was able. 'I could never fear you.'

'You should!' the beast snarled, suddenly swinging its

huge head around, showing teeth stained crimson. 'You think you know me – but I am not what I was! I don't even know myself!'

Marian stood her ground, forced herself not to recoil. 'I know who you are,' she insisted. 'You are me, just the same as I'm you. We always used to say that, even when we were children. And it's still true.'

The great wolf growled. 'Neither of us are what we were. We have both done too much.'

Marian hugged herself, took another step forward. 'We did what we had to do. But we are still us. We have nothing to be ashamed of.'

'Liar!' The colossal head came forward, until it was almost touching her, and its nostrils flared. 'You wear the stench of the Sheriff.'

She put her head in her hands and sobbed. 'Oh, Robin, he had nothing of me. My flesh! All that matters is yours and always will be!'

'You are as tainted as I am,' said the nightmare-wolf. 'We have despoiled ourselves, just as we despoiled the Earth.' The head swung away, slumped down onto front paws. 'I should devour you now. Put an end to it all.'

Marian stood there with her head in her hands, weathering a storm of shock and shame and remorse. Finally, it passed, and when she raised her head she found herself strangely calm and defiant.

She walked around Robin's wolf-form and knelt at his head. She reached out and placed one hand on the creature's muzzle. This caused it to growl, its upper lip curling back and quivering against its teeth. Undaunted, she kept her hand there while she spoke gently.

'You're frightened,' she said, suddenly realizing it was true. 'You couldn't say those things to me unless you were scared.

187

You've taken this form not because you're angry, or feel betrayed, but because you're afraid.'

The Robin-wolf made a sound that was a cross between a howl and laughter, while the hell-plains moaned with a scorching wind. 'Look around you. Do you imagine there's anything left for me to fear?'

'Not down here, no,' Marian said evenly. 'But it's not staying here that frightens you. That's easy. That's nothing but hiding. Up there – living – *that's* frightening. I know, because I've been hiding too. In a different kind of hell. I told myself I needed to hide. That there was no other way. Maybe some of it was true. But I know one thing for certain – we've been hiding too long. We need to go back. To face the world we've made. All of it. The good and the bad. Because we're not finished. We need to fight.'

The great wolf closed its eyes. 'We fought before. We lost everything.'

'Except that isn't true. I've been telling myself the same thing, all these years – that there's nothing left to fight for. But I see now, that was just an excuse. What we mean is, we don't *want* to fight, because we've been fighting for so long, and it's hard.'

She lay one cheek on the muzzle of the monster-wolf, a tear dripping from her eye to mingle with the fur.

'The world up there is dying. I won't deny it. But it can heal. We can help it heal. There's *always* a reason to go on fighting. There's always new life.'

She paused, before saying in a softer voice: 'You have a son, Robin. Oh – you don't even know. *We* have a son.'

She paused once more, sobbing into his fur, and for long moments neither of them moved or spoke. Finally, she felt the Robin-wolf shift beneath her and words rumble in its throat.

'A . . . son? A child? How *dare* we?'

'What? No! Wait until you meet him! He's everything!'

'We brought a child into *this* world?'

'No – no. It's not like that. We didn't choose him. He chose us. He wanted to live!'

'How can he? What hope have we left for him?'

'He *is* the hope!' She sat up straight, blinked away tears. 'Maybe . . . maybe it took coming down here for me to see it, but that's exactly what Rex is. He is hope. He is life. And they're the same thing. Do you understand? Life can't just stop. Even up there in those deadlands, life is poking through. It hasn't given up, and it never will.'

She pushed herself against the Robin-wolf, crying. Once more the beast became still, only the movement of its breathing and the sound of its giant heart pounding slowly in its chest. That heartbeat . . . it was slowing, softening.

Finally, Robin murmured: 'A son.'

'Oh, Robin, I've dreamed of you meeting him. He's beautiful, and strong, just like you. He has your wild spirit, and your courage. Only it's been so hard for him. He's grown up in barren soil. He's never known the forest, or the wild places.'

'And he never will. The forest is gone.'

'No – it isn't. Don't you remember? Sherwood didn't die. You guarded the heart of it, saved it from the fire. The forest still exists.'

She fell silent, her eyes closed, and for long moments there was nothing. Not a word from Robin. Not even the sound now of breathing. Finally, though, she detected a shift. The texture of him beneath her palms and her cheek – it had changed.

She opened her eyes, sat upright. The monster-wolf was gone. In its place was Robin. He was naked and pale and bleeding, swaddled in his wolfskin cloak. Marian spread her arms and lay across him, sobbing.

'Being down here,' he murmured, curling into a foetal position beneath her, 'there's so much I've forgotten. Is it real? Sherwood lives?'

'Yes,' she sobbed, 'yes it is. I've never seen it for myself, but I've heard the stories, and I know they're true. There's an island of wildwood, out there in the wastes. They call it Gaia. It holds everything. All that we are, that we remember.'

Something gleamed in the corner of her eye, and she turned her head to look. Squinting in the fire-spotted gloom, her gaze came to rest on a single moonflower, its petals shining white and blue.

'Oh, Robin, I see it now, even down here there's hope.' Her hands went to his skinny chest. Beneath his ribs his heartbeat was strong, and matched the rhythm of her own. 'You feel it too, I know you do. After all the time that's passed, and everything that's stood in our way, even now we've been drawn back together. The love between us, it burns as fierce as ever. Fiercer. Despite the darkness. *Because* of the darkness.'

These words poured out of her heart without touching her mind; the first she knew of them was when she heard them with her own ears. Even so, she knew them for absolute truth. In spite of everything, she could feel the love between her and Robin rising like wildfire.

All the yearning and grieving she had done for him over the years now only fanned the flames, until it seemed to her there was a physical light and heat blazing off both of them, illuminating the gloom.

It burned brighter still, spreading outwards – a golden, purifying fire, transforming this underworld into a sunlit paradise. The cracked and barren ground turned to fertile soil. Grasses and wildflowers sprang up, rustling. Bees and dragonflies shone in the golden light.

'What is this?' Robin murmured. 'What's happening?'

'I don't know,' Marian told him, looking around her, suddenly feeling quite calm. 'But everything is going to be all right. Just keep hold of me.'

Green life continued to sprout out of the ground. Saplings took root, grew upwards, becoming mature trees in a matter of moments.

Marian gasped as the ground bulged beneath her and the soil ruptured, and an oak thrust upwards. It lifted her and Robin, cradling them in its boughs.

As it did so, Robin shifted, sprouted fur. 'No – leave me!' he growled. 'This is where I belong!'

'You don't – you never did. You belong with me. And with Rex. We need you. The world needs you.'

As the great oak continued to bear them up, he twisted and snarled. But she gripped him and soon his strength was exhausted and he slumped in her arms, fully human once more.

'Even if we make it back, what then?' he murmured weakly. 'What more can I give?'

But he no longer tried to wrestle free. They merely clung to one another, and clung to the branches, as the great tree creaked and groaned and grew wider and taller.

Even if we make it back, what then?

Marian had no answer to this. Every step of this journey had been a leap of faith. All she could do was continue to trust in fate as the great tree thrust its way through the darkness, carrying them up and up and up.

XVI. Blood Sacrifice

As he poured out the last of his life-force in defence of the perimeter, Kit spared a glance for Marian's son. He was surprised to see the boy was not already dead. But it would not be long. Rex was fully enmeshed in the wall of thorns, struggling in vain, like a fly in a spider's web. A python vine was wrapped around his throat, and his face was turning blue.

Why should Kit care? When so many had died, what was one more death? What could he possibly do for the boy in any case? He was using every last ounce of his forest powers to hold Guy of Gisbourne at bay.

He turned his eyes back to the heretic hunter. The giant warrior was severing shoots and vines with focused ferocity. Kit felt each hack and slash in his own skin and bones, as though his nemesis was already here in front of him, hewing him down.

Elsewhere, soldiers and warrior monks were likewise puncturing the green barricade. Soon they would break through en masse and overrun the Giants' Graveyard.

No – there was nothing more Kit could do to save even himself or his fellow outlaws, let alone Marian's son. It would end here, today, for every one of them.

A figure appeared behind him. It must be a soldier, or a

warrior monk. Several had now broken through the outlaws' defences and were roaming the graveyard.

So then, is this how it would end – not hewn down by his nemesis, but struck down from behind, by an unknown assassin . . .

Kit was far beyond caring.

He shut his eyes and waited for the blow to fall.

But then the figure behind him spoke.

'They're breaking through on all sides,' Sonskya said in a flat tone. 'We held out as long as we could.'

Kit hung his head. 'It's over.'

'Not for all of us,' she said, quietly, stepping to his side. 'Not for you. I'm sorry. Ira has found a safe path out of here. You need to go with the others.'

Kit shook his head. 'This was our final hope. You know who's here, don't you? Robin Hood. I thought . . . I thought Marian could bring him back to us.'

'Then you've been fooling yourself,' Sonskya said. 'Even if Robin did return . . . he wouldn't be what he was. How could he be?' She glanced towards the ancient tree stump. 'No. Whatever Marian is doing in there – that's her business, not ours.'

'How can you say that? We need him more than she does.'

'No, we don't. This isn't about one man. It can't be.'

'One man? Robin was the guardian of the forest. The mightiest warrior who ever walked the Earth.'

'And he failed,' Sonskya said, her voice hardening. 'Have you forgotten that part? Don't you see – even he couldn't stand against the firestorm – not on his own.' She touched his arm, and her voice softened. 'Robin's greatness went far beyond his strength of arms. It went beyond anything he might have done, or said. It will outlast his death. Robin Hood is a symbol, don't you see that – for every one of us who would stand up and fight. That's the true source of his power. Nothing and no one can ever destroy that.'

'But . . . who will even remember,' Kit murmured, 'if we die out here in the dust?'

'That's why you can't die. Not yet,' Sonskya said. 'You still have a part to play. That greatness of Robin's – to inspire strength in others – it lives in you too, Kit.'

'Me? I failed you all. I'm nothing.'

She put a hand to his face then, ran her fingertips across his cheek and chin. 'You still don't see it, do you? Or you don't want to. Who you truly are.' She smiled ruefully. 'Maybe it doesn't matter. All I know is, you've brought us this far. Others will rise to light the way – we have to believe that. But for now, it's you. You've got to keep carrying the torch.' She craned her neck and kissed his cheek. 'That's why you must live. No matter the cost.'

With these words, with no more warning than that, she drew her twin stiletto daggers, and before Kit could lift a hand to stop her she had dashed away towards the green barricade. With a banshee wail, she threw herself amid the vines and thorns, and she flew at Guy of Gisbourne, attacking him with such shrieking wild ferocity that the heretic hunter was put on the back foot, raising a bloodied hand to defend himself while Sonskya jabbed and stabbed at his face and neck. The pair of them stumbled backwards in a macabre dance, the net of thorns constricting their limbs and making their movements jerky as puppets as she drove her adversary back and back.

'No – Sonskya!' Kit hollered, staggering towards her. 'You can't!'

'Too late – it's done,' Ira cried, appearing at his side. 'Come on, Kit. We've got an escape route. We have to go!'

'I can still save her. I—'

He tried to send out his forest powers, but they were spent. He only succeeded in stumbling to his knees. Ira hauled at him, trying to drag him to his feet.

'There's nothing you can do. Come *on*! If you let her die for nothing, I'll kill you!'

She was dragging Kit, and now Jack appeared and started hauling him too, and as exhausted as he was he could no longer resist their will. He stumbled to his feet and together the three of them staggered through the Giants' Graveyard.

At least a dozen soldiers had now broken through the wall of thorns and were stalking forward, their weapons bared. With the other two supporting his weight, Kit staggered away from them, losing them in a maze of fallen timber. A crossbow bolt whined overhead, while another struck a trunk to their left, but they kept going into the deepest shadows, while soldiers called out and gave chase.

Finally, the three of them reached a secluded corner of the graveyard, screened behind a heap of fallen branches. Here, the other outlaws stood waiting, breathing hard, blood splattered on their clothes and faces.

Without a word, Much nodded to a hole that had been cut in the green barricade. Around this breach, two rangers and three warrior monks lay dead. Stepping over the corpses, Midge darted into the opening and fled out into the wastelands. Much followed, then Jack. Ira shoved Kit after them but he resisted.

'Marian – and Robin.'

'There's nothing more we can do. Come on, Kit – go!'

'Sonskya, she's—'

'She's dead, Kit! She did it for you – for us! Don't let it be for nothing!'

She shoved and thrust at him, until finally he submitted, turning and groping his way through the green barricade. Then he was staggering out into the open wastelands and running with the others, their heads down.

As depleted as Kit was, all this was happening in a blur.

The world around him was a smear of shadowy forms, a dirge of sounds.

The world of his imagination, in contrast, was razor-sharp. It showed him three faces. Sonskya. Marian. Robin Hood.

All of them lost. And with them the final flicker of hope.

XVII. The Return

As the great oak continued to grow and grow, bearing Robin and Marian up and up, Marian found herself passing back through the realms she had experienced on her descent. Here was the tangled, gloomy wereforest, which twisted with ghostly shadows and echoed with the voices of lost souls.

As they swept through this realm, wintry branches reached out for them like skeletal fingers. Marian gasped as blackthorn clawed at her, snagged her clothing, almost tore her out of the oak. But she clung to its branches, and to Robin, and the thorns gave way and they continued upwards, while the ghostly trees moaned and howled in their wake.

Finally, they were through this shadowy realm, and abruptly the mist dissipated and the trees budded and burst into leaf. There came the sound of birdsong, and the aroma of blossom, and the warmth of sunshine on Marian's skin. Here was the idyllic greenwood, where she had watched her lost friends play at the water's edge.

'What is this?' Robin murmured. 'These smells . . . and sounds. I . . . I remember them. But it's been so long. Where are we?'

'We're slowing down,' Marian said. 'I think we're stopping.'

Yes – their upward momentum now ceased. With a tremendous

rattling of boughs and creaking of wood, the great oak rustled to rest.

Easing her grip on its trunk, Marian peered around her at the tree. It was now a fully mature emperor oak. Its countless leaves basked in the sun's rays, while its branches scurried with life and warbled with woodnotes.

'I don't think it's going to carry us any further,' Marian said. 'If we mean to go on . . . we'll have to climb.'

She looked upwards – and up and up – the great oak appearing to pierce the heavens.

'Such a long way to go,' the vixen-goddess taunted. She was sitting cross-legged on a branch, in the form of a beautiful young woman, her fox-red hair falling around her. 'In any case, you've done enough. You've rescued your beloved from his awful plight. Why go any further?'

'Ignore her,' Marian told Robin. 'I don't know what her game is. She wanted me to find you. Now I don't know what she's up to, and I don't care.'

Robin merely sat there slumped, his head bowed. She could hear his breathing, which was short and ragged. Peering once more skywards, she suddenly knew it was futile. Think of all Robin had endured down in that Hades. He was a shell. There was no way he had the strength to climb to the surface.

Shouldn't this idea fill her with sadness, and fear? Somehow . . . it was almost the opposite. She inhaled deeply. The scents of lavender and narcissi and flowers of paradise. From far off, reverberating off water, came human voices – people laughing.

She stood and walked along the branch. All around her and below her were more mighty boughs, so substantial that they were carpeted not just in moss but with grasses and wildflowers. They were just like the sky gardens she and Robin used to explore back at Major Oak. She walked on through clouds of butterflies, her bare feet cooled by the spongy moss.

'This place could be yours for ever,' said the goddess, her claws skittering along a branch above. 'Far better than that nasty world above.'

As she said this, the branch trembled. The whole tree quaked, making Marian gasp and catch her balance.

'Don't worry yourself about that,' the goddess said, sitting down to lick herself clean. 'Just ignore it.'

A second tremor hit the tree, shuddering down its length from its crown to its roots, shaking loose a shower of leaves.

'Robin – are you all right?' she called back to him. 'Up at the surface – they're fighting.'

The tree shook a third time, its canopy churning as if beset by a mighty wind. The sky above was now swirling with black and purple clouds. They flashed with something like lightning – except silver, like blades clashing. And the sounds rumbling out of these clouds were more like cries of pain than thunder.

Marian clamped her hands to her ears, not wanting to hear. She closed her eyes and buried her head. And by the time she stood straight once more, and cautiously lowered her arms, the battle-storm had abated. The sylvan paradise was restored. Squirrel kits played in the boughs, and birds sang their spring-time joy.

Blinking, Marian peered across the sky garden. Her eyes came to rest on a cluster of bushes. Their branches bristled with cloudberries.

'Look – Robin!' she said, grinning, heading towards them. 'Just like the ones we used to harvest back in Sherwood. But these are the ripest ones I've ever seen!'

With juice still dripping down her chin, she took handfuls back to Robin.

'Here. You've got to try these! It's been years. I'd forgotten how good they taste. And there are more here than we could eat in a lifetime.'

'They're not real.'

He mumbled these words, and she brushed them aside like an irritating fly as she went to gather more fruit. Let him sit there grumbling. Why should it bother her? What could trouble her in this blissful place?

A young man's face tried to materialize in her mind's eye, but the image was vague. What was the young man's name? Ralph? Reg? She found she couldn't remember. What did it matter in any case? She listened to the leaves shushing in the breeze, and the aimless forgetful burbling of the stream, and she found there was no need to remember anything, not any more.

'All you need do is step off this branch, fall to the forest floor,' the goddess breathed in her ear. 'You won't be hurt. Nothing will be able to hurt you ever again.'

Marian walked to the edge of the branch. She looked down. Wasn't this all that she ever wanted? To live here in the First Forest, together with the dryads and the nymphs and the fauns? She closed her eyes, stepped out—

But a hand held her back. It was Robin. He was standing at her side, gripping her arm.

'Robin – what's the matter? Don't you want to stay here with me?'

'This is wrong.'

'No, it's not. It's as real as anything else. We'll be happy.'

'It's no different to where I was before. In a way, it's worse. You can hear what's happening above.'

An aftershock shook their branch and Robin braced his weight to stop Marian falling. She closed her eyes, refusing to look up, knowing that monstrous storm of hatred was once again swirling above the tree.

'It's all right,' she said. 'Nothing can touch us here.'

His grip tightened, urged her away from the edge. 'You were right before,' he said, his voice slow but steady. 'I was a coward. I didn't want to face the world we made. But now you're here . . . and I'm brave enough. Marian, can you hear me? I need you. I won't make it on my own.'

Finally, his words reached her. She opened her eyes and blinked at him, seeing him clearly for the first time since they entered this false paradise. And yes – it was false, wasn't it. How had she not seen that before? As another rumble rolled out of the heavens, the trees all around her quivered, like heat haze. Some disappeared entirely, or swapped places, or looked hollow, like mist in sunlight. That laughter she could hear echoing through the trees – it was the same sound over and over, an endless loop. There was no joy in that sound. It was mere imitation – like a caged bird trained to mimic its master.

She stepped away from the edge of the branch, and Robin slumped. Only now did she realize what effort it had cost him to hold her back.

'That wasn't me,' she told him. 'It was the goddess. That's what she does, isn't it – worms into your mind.' She scanned the boughs. 'I think she's gone.'

Robin shook his head. 'I gave up trying to understand her games long ago. But . . . I'm grateful to her for one thing. She led you back to me.'

For the first time since she had found him, he sounded like his true self, and it brought tears to her eyes. They held each other close. Clung to one another as the tree shook, showering them with leaves and twigs. Marian looked up at the swirling storm of violence.

'If we do this, if we go back to the surface, things will be worse,' she said. 'Worse than they've ever been.'

'All I know is, you were right, we can't just go on hiding.'

'Do you think you can make it?'

'I must.'

So saying, Robin found a toehold in the trunk of the great oak, and he grasped the branch above, and with great difficulty he hauled himself up.

Marian followed, and slowly, agonizingly, they clambered skywards, heading for the surface, and all that awaited them in the real world above.

Guy of Gisbourne hacked through the last strands of hex-grass and demon-weed, and finally he was free of the wall of thorns. He burst into the Giants' Graveyard, dragging with him the corpse of the female outlaw.

He knew they were possessed, these rebels, driven mad by their worship of the wilderness – but even so, the savage ferocity of this one had taken him off guard. A dozen times she had opened his flesh with her dirks, before he finally managed to disarm her, take hold of her neck and snap it. Now he felt the urge to tear her body limb from limb. Her attack had stalled him, kept him entangled in that godforsaken barricade.

He looked back at it. In all his years battling these savages, he imagined he had grown accustomed to their Earth magic. But even now, to have witnessed this wall of thorns growing up before his eyes . . . it stirred in him such revulsion, such fury, that his grip tightened upon the dead outlaw and he had to fight the urge to defile her corpse. No – he must not lower himself to the level of the savages. He must focus his fury to best use. There was still much work to do.

He scanned the battleground. While he had been locked in combat with this she-witch, the outlaw chief had fled. Where was he now?

A ranger came hurrying towards him. It was Garp Speer, captain of this battalion. As he approached, Guy of Gisbourne flung the corpse of the outlaw, which landed wetly at the captain's feet, making him jump back.

'Where are her fellows?' the heretic hunter growled. 'I see dead soldiers. Why don't I see dead outlaws?'

Captain Speer dropped his head. 'Sire, we've just found a tunnel through the barricade. We think they went out that way.'

The heretic hunter surged forward, and quick as a snake he closed one giant hand around the captain's throat. He lifted him off the ground while the man struggled and choked.

'You had them surrounded, and you let them get away?'

The captain tried to speak, clawed at Sir Guy's fingers, kicked. But his sounds and his movements became increasingly feeble, and finally they ceased.

Guy of Gisbourne flung the corpse on top of the dead outlaw. The killing rage was upon him now and he scanned the battle-field, looking for other means to vent his fury. His eyes came to rest on a pair of rangers. They were guarding the boy scavenger who had guided them across the wastes.

The heretic hunter strode over to this trio, who shrank away from him.

'You! Tell me,' he said to the boy. 'Where are the remains?'

The boy was terrified, yet somehow managed to look him in the eye. 'F-first, I want to see my sister. You said she'd be here.'

At the heretic hunter's feet lay a crossbow, wound and loaded. He picked it up and aimed it at the scavenger's chest.

'Take me to Robin Hood. Do it now. I will not tell you again.'

Before the trembling boy could respond, two more rangers came hurrying across.

'S-sire,' one of them stammered. 'We think we've found the place. Robin Hood must be inside.'

'Is that so?' Sir Guy growled. 'In that case, we have no further use for a guide.'

So saying, without turning back to face the scavenger, he discharged the crossbow. The boy made no more sound than a sharp intake of breath – but from elsewhere arose a tortured scream. A girl broke cover and came rushing, stumbling towards them. It was the scavenger's sister. She fell upon the stricken boy, weeping and wailing.

But by now the heretic hunter had lost interest in the twins. He was staring into the near distance, where a knot of rangers had gathered around an island of greenery.

'So then – is that the place?' he asked the ranger, who nodded. 'Very well. We've wasted enough time. Let us do what we came here to do.'

XVIII. Love and Death

The final part of the climb was torturous. Each branch was harder to reach than the last, each toehold more difficult to find. There were many times when Marian knew, with cold hard certainty, that it was impossible – that she could not go on. But each time, Robin paused and reached down an arm and helped haul her upwards.

At other times it was Robin who appeared defeated. The life would go out of him and he would slump against the great oak, barely able to lift his head, let alone continue the ascent. These were the times, strangely, when Marian felt her strongest. With a surge of vitality, she took hold of Robin and heaved him physically towards the next handhold, the next sure footing, all the while whispering words of encouragement. In this way, they took turns to lift one another's spirits, and to coax one another up the sweeping reach of the tree.

Above them, the thunderhead swirled red–black, like spilled life-blood. Silver lightning flashed within the storm, like the clashing of steel. The clouds churned and a rumble of thunder came rolling downwards, making the oak shake and sway. Robin groaned and almost fell, but Marian held his weight.

'I . . . I can't,' he murmured. 'I thought I could, but I can't.'

'You can. You have to.'

She held him and felt afresh the shock of his wasted form. If anything, as they climbed closer to the physical realm, he had only grown more frail. Now he was a gutskin filled with chicken bones. Shaking off her shock, she cupped his chin in her palm.

'You listen to me, Robin. All this,' she poked at his spindly arms and legs, 'all this is just flesh.' She laid a palm upon his chest. 'In here – that's where your strength lives. You are a lionheart. You've never given up once in your life. And you're not going to start now.'

'If you hadn't caught me I would have fallen.'

'I could say the same about you. And not just today. Back in Sherwood – back when we were children, even. That's what we've always done, isn't it? Helped each other keep going.'

'But what's it all worth?' he said, as far above the thunderhead swirled colours of fire and flesh. 'Even if we do make it back – what then? More violence? More bloodshed? The whole cycle begins again.'

'Maybe it does,' she said, her grip tightening upon him. 'Maybe that's all we'll ever have. But we know one thing for certain. Rex is up there. Our son, Robin. For his sake, we can't give up. He needs us. He needs the forest.'

At these words, Robin straightened his back, lifted his head. 'The forest . . . it truly still exists? Down there . . . it was so hard to tell what was real and what imagined. But it's true . . . Sherwood lives?'

'Yes – yes, it's true, as I live and breathe. The Sheriff has been hunting for it – wants wipe it off the map. But we can stop that happening, Robin. You and me. I can't imagine how, not yet, but together we can do anything. We can rid the land of the Sheriff's poison. We can start to grow a new world. A world for Rex to live in. Where he can breathe, and trust the ground beneath his feet.'

Slowly, she watched these words take root in Robin. He rose, and without another word he resumed his climb, now with renewed vigour. Marian went after him, finding her next toehold in the trunk, grasping the next branch, and hauling herself up.

Robin was moving faster now, and for a horrible moment she thought he might leave her behind. She willed her depleted spirit to keep pace, and somehow she managed to stay on his heels as they heaved and struggled their way upwards.

Just this bough, then the next. Marian's world shrinking now to the sensation of climbing. One handhold, one footing, then again. And again. Over and over. For ever and ever. Until she achieved a sort of oblivion in the effort. Everything else fading to the background. There was no worry, or pain. She was simply climbing, that was all.

'We're doing it,' she laughed through tears. 'We're going to make it! Oh, Robin, it wasn't only you I found down there – I see that now! All these years, I've been soul-sick. I've been hollow. And now . . . I've never felt more whole! More alive!'

The struggle had become strangely easeful, as if it were being enacted by somebody else. In fact, as absorbed as she was, she didn't at first register that the sensations had changed. There was no longer a feeling of rising through space. Her body was still moving through the motions of climbing, but there was something solid pressed against her back.

It had become much darker. She stopped moving and turned her head, blinking. With a flash of panic, disorientated, she realized she could no longer see Robin.

'Where are you?' she gabbled, her voice muffled and echoing. 'Robin! Are you here?'

Her eyes focused on a cluster of tiny stars. For a moment she imagined she was once more free-floating in that space-like otherworld. But no. Because these stars had tiny caps, which glowed red and green and blue. They were mushrooms.

'Robin – we made it!' she gasped, scrambling to sit upright. 'We're back!'

Beside her, she heard a sound like a groan. It had come from Robin! Not the spirit-Robin of some underworld, but the real flesh-and-blood Robin kneeling beside her, right here and now! Throwing herself upon him, she pressed her head to his chest.

'Your heartbeat!' she gasped, tears spilling down her cheeks. 'I can hear your heartbeat. And you're breathing! Robin, you're waking!'

She scrabbled for her storm lantern. With shaking fingers she managed to find her strike-a-light and to reignite the wick. She studied him in the flickering light, and was shocked anew at his physical frailty – he was a desiccated husk. But nonetheless he was real and really here and waking up!

'That's it – you're doing it,' she breathed, as he twitched and groaned once more. 'You're coming back to me.' She wiped away tears, then put a hand to his face. There was warmth there – and breath at his lips!

While he groaned, and tossed his head, like a child stirring from the deepest of dreams, her fingertips explored his face and neck, revelling in the rising warmth and the pulse trembling beneath his skin. At first the pulse was weak and uneven. She rested her palms atop his heart, as if nursing a fragile flame, and already she could feel it strengthen.

'Just breathe,' she whispered. 'You're coming back to me. Oh, Robin, you're going to live!'

For the moment, nothing existed beyond this charmed circle of light and Robin's breathing. If there were other noises nearby, she refused to acknowledge them.

But finally, little by little, the outside world began to seep into her awareness. The heavy tread of boots, and the clinking of armour. Armed men circling the ancient stump.

With one hand still resting on Robin's chest, Marian closed her eyes and bowed her head.

'No – not yet,' she murmured. 'We need more time. Please.'

More movement outside the tree-cave. And voices.

She opened her eyes, gritted her teeth. 'Robin, can you hear me? Can you move? Our enemies . . . They're here. We need to do something. We need to hurry!'

Beneath her hands, Robin spasmed and groaned. But he made no attempt even to lift his head, let alone stand. How could he, as weakened as he was? Marian's eyes darted around the chamber.

'Robin – if you can hear me – I've got an idea. Our only chance. We need—'

She broke off as movement and light and malice burst into the tree-cave. A hulking figure was here on his knees, a lantern swinging in his giant fist.

'No, no, no,' Marian whispered. 'Please. Not now. Not when he's coming back to me.'

The shadow-man shifted his bulk, came nearer.

'No – no! Get away from him!'

Screaming these last words, Marian launched herself across the chamber, swinging her lantern like a club.

Guy of Gisbourne blocked the attack with the back of his hand, and in the same motion swatted Marian aside. The blow sent her sprawling. She cracked her head against the far wall of the chamber.

She lay, dazed, unable to untangle her limbs. Through blurred eyes, she watched the heretic hunter draw close to Robin. He knelt and lifted his light and studied him, his black eyes glistening above his mask. Robin moaned as the heretic hunter prodded at his arms and chest with obvious disgust.

'Please,' Marian murmured, crawling closer. 'He's waking, but he's weak. He mustn't be moved. He'll die.'

'In order to die, he must first be alive,' the heretic hunter growled. 'What we see here is not life. It is a travesty.'

He closed his giant fingers around Robin's neck.

'No – don't!'

The heretic hunter rose to his feet, taking Robin with him, wrenching him from his resting place, rootlets snapping and popping as they were torn from the earth.

'No!' Marian screamed, throwing herself forwards, claws bared.

Without turning his head, Guy of Gisbourne swatted her aside once more. This time the ironclad back of his hand connected fully and with ferocity, and Marian was catapulted backwards with such force that there was a moment of blackness.

Once it passed, she found herself on her back, her eyes swivelling, struggling to focus on a double image of the heretic hunter. Hanging from his fist, Robin was a broken puppet, severed roots dangling from him and raining soil.

'No – you can't!' Marian tried to scream again, but the words were mangled noise. She tried to attack the heretic hunter once more, but her limbs refused to even carry her across the chamber.

'Listen to me, listen,' she pleaded, her mind racing desperately. 'Do you want him to die? Does the Sheriff? Isn't he worth more to you alive?' She struggled to her knees, tried to steady her voice. 'I'm *ordering* you! I . . . I'm the Sheriff's queen. Put him down, now!'

All the while, Guy of Gisbourne went on holding Robin high in one fist. He shook him, side to side, like a cat toying with a mouse. Robin groaned but did not lift an arm or even raise his head. Finally, he laid Robin upon the ground.

'You needn't concern yourself,' he growled. 'The phantom outlaw has endured this long. He will endure a while longer. At least long enough to fulfil his purpose. As for you.' He came towards her. 'You outlived your usefulness long ago.'

'What do you think you're doing?' she murmured. 'Y-you wouldn't harm me. The Sheriff will have your hide.'

'On the contrary. These are his express wishes.'

From his belt, he drew a mace. It had a short handle and a studded iron head.

Staring at this vicious weapon in the heretic hunter's fist, Marian's vision narrowed, became dark. A blackness yawned open ahead of her and she was terrified of going into it without Robin and Rex.

'No – wait – please,' she heard herself beg. 'I'm not ready. Not yet.'

The words didn't touch Guy of Gisbourne. He took another heavy step towards her, his hulking muscles braced to swing the weapon.

In desperation, looking at the last for divine salvation, Marian's gaze darted around the chamber and came to rest on a pair of golden eyes, watching her from the darkness.

'Please,' Marian mouthed to the goddess. 'You can stop this, I know you can. It shouldn't be happening.'

The goddess only tipped her head, her features masked in shadow, impossible to read.

If the heretic hunter was aware of the goddess's presence, he gave no sign of it, nor was moved by Marian's pleas.

He merely closed the remaining gap between them. And without blinking, with no more hesitation than if he were crushing a fly, he swung the mace in a short powerful arc, the weapon connecting perfectly with the side of Marian's skull, killing her instantly.

XIX. Life for a Life

It's stopped – it's truly stopped. I'm going to live!

With a surge of relief bordering on lunacy, Rex finally admitted the truth of this. He could not have said how long he had hung here, terrified, teetering on the thin line between life and death. At least three times, as a noose of vines tightened around his throat, the world had begun to blacken and he had felt his life-force ebbing away. Each time, somehow, he had kept on sucking the thinnest of breaths, and his eyes had blinked back open – only for the desperate struggle to begin again.

But now it was finished. Because the wall of thorns had stopped writhing and constricting. The vines and suckers had come to rest.

It's over. I'm alive!

Wriggling one arm free, he finally managed to reach his boot knife. He used the blade to saw through vines and tendrils.

Hacking and slashing, he finally cut his way out. He half-stepped, half-fell into the Giants' Graveyard.

As he stumbled away from the wall of thorns, he saw, as he suspected, that the battle was over. He stared at dead rangers lying in pools of blood. He staggered past one dead outlaw, a she-warrior, her head bent at an unnatural angle.

Ensnared as he had been, fighting for his own survival, he had not witnessed the battle play itself out. Where were the rest of the rebels? Were they dead, or had they fled back into the wastes? Where had his mother been during all this?

He staggered towards the heart of the Giants' Graveyard. As he approached the tree stump, with its crown of greenery, he saw it was surrounded by rangers and warrior monks.

He limped closer. There was movement now amid the Sheriff's men. Rangers were stepping back, making way for someone. And there – crawling out of the ancient stump – a hulking figure. It was Guy of Gisbourne.

The heretic hunter stood to his full height, and Rex stumbled to a halt at the sight of what he carried with him. As warriors backed off, or stood and stared, Guy of Gisbourne held it up for them to see.

This thing – this creature – was bloodless and limp. It might almost be an empty skin, or a slain fox. But Rex knew it wasn't. He knew who this was.

It could only be him. The blind bowman.

Here was Robin Hood.

Rex's mind spun. Wasn't the forest king long dead? Hadn't they come into the wastelands to recover his bones? Yet here he was, limp as a ragdoll but whole. Was he still alive? If so, then barely. Beneath that wolf-skin cloak, Rex glimpsed limbs as thin as sticks; skin as pale as ice. If he wasn't already dead, then he certainly soon would be.

Despite the import of all this, Rex's shock was short-lived; already his mind had returned to his mother.

'Lady Marian; where is she?' he demanded of the nearest soldiers. 'Tell me where she is.'

As the men looked back at him blankly, and a creeping dread worked its way up from his stomach, he charged towards Guy of Gisbourne.

'What's happening?' he demanded. 'Where's my mother? She went in there. Why hasn't she come out?'

The heretic hunter lowered his mask and fixed his black gaze on Rex.

'She has not come out,' he said evenly, 'because it is her tomb. Your mother was a fool. She should not have gone in there alone.' He flapped Robin Hood like an empty skin. 'A dying beast is the most dangerous of all.'

Because it is her tomb.

The ground dropped away from Rex, and he was falling. When the darkness stopped spinning, he found he was on his knees, clutching at his chest.

'Y-you don't know what you're talking about,' he spat, as he fought for breath. 'You're wrong!'

Guy of Gisbourne shrugged. 'Go and see for yourself. Your mother is dead. Robin Hood killed her.'

'It's not true! Why would he?'

'Why does the fox kill the chicken? This . . . abomination,' again he shook Robin, who groaned, 'its nature is murder and mayhem. Your mother should never have trusted such a creature. Now she has paid for it with her life. Go. See with your own eyes. But be quick. We have our quarry. We must hasten back to the city.'

These words were mere noise now as Rex crawled towards the ancient stump. His vision was fuzzy, and the dark entranceway was unreal. It opened wider to swallow him, and suddenly he was inside the tree-cave.

The heretic hunter had left his storm lantern, and in its pool of light Rex could see a human figure lying on the ground. Shaking, he crawled towards it.

'Mother?' he whispered, the sound rasping from his throat. 'Mother . . . what is it? W-we need to get underway. The heretic hunter made a mistake. He thought that you . . . He said . . .'

214

Rex trailed off as he reached the body. He forced himself to look at his mother's face. The skin was white. Apart from at her right temple, where a vicious blue-green bruise splintered outwards like cracks in ice. Her varicoloured eyes of grey and green stared away into nothingness.

Rex sat back on his knees, just watching her, for the moment experiencing no grief or fear. No anger or shock. All of it was washed away by confusion and disbelief. That sensation of unreality, which had come upon him when they first entered the wastes – it had grown stronger and stronger, and was now complete. The last fragments of certainty had splintered away, until nothing around him held any meaning, nor ever would again.

Where was she? Where was his mother? This wasn't her. This inanimate thing lying here, as still and cold as rock. His mother was the most vital person he had ever known; she overflowed with lifeforce. She was fire and fury; even her melancholies were deeper and more potent than anybody else's. No way could this mere shell ever have contained all that she was. So where had she gone?

'It's time to go, my prince,' the heretic hunter called through the entranceway. 'Your father expects you back at the city.'

The voice broke Rex out of his stupor. He collapsed upon his mother's body, the touch of her making everything real and solid once again, as he wept and wailed and wished for death himself, cursing the very lifeblood running in his veins.

Part Three

The Returned

You draw breath into your chest – a breath that burns. On your tongue is the stench of the world – stale and scorched and barren. Your innards twist with a gnawing famine you share with the Earth . . .

These sensations, so long forgotten, so hateful. To inhabit this body is torture.

To inhabit this mind is worse.

Because you are back in the world of the living – and she has left it.

No – no! Can it be true? After all that time alone . . . she came for you. And now . . . can you truly be separated once more? The world of flesh and blood is wretched enough. If you must dwell here without her . . . then you will truly be damned.

Yes – and let the world be damned with you! You will tear it apart with your bare hands!

Your wrath rises, flicks its tail, flexes its claws. Your physical form rattles its chains.

But the movement is weak and leaves you exhausted. What use your rage? Your body is as wasted as your spirit.

Even if you could break your bonds and wreak havoc, what purpose would it serve? She is gone, and nothing on this Earth can bring her back.

Retribution, revenge – what are these but petty distractions?

No – for you now, there is nothing left. No hope. No future.

Only the waiting. And the suffering. And the yearning for death.

I. Triumph

'**R**ide forward, my prince,' Guy of Gisbourne called over his shoulder as the party neared the city gates. 'This is your triumph. Claim it.'

As numb as he was, these words failed to register in Rex's mind. He sat slumped in his saddle, staring blankly at his hands.

The heretic hunter slowed his horse and dropped back down the line. 'Come, take the lead, my prince. Your people must witness your moment of glory.'

If there was a sneering tone to Sir Guy's voice, Rex barely noticed it. Ever since leaving the Giants' Graveyard, the world had been a blur. During the entire arduous trip out of the Lost Lands, the only thing that had truly existed was an absence. An empty space where his mother should be. Was this real? Could he truly be returning without her?

When Rex again failed to respond, the heretic hunter pushed back his shoulders, and his voice hardened. 'Excessive grief shows weakness in a man,' he growled. 'It will reflect badly on the rest of us. I sent word ahead. The citizens know we are coming. Ride forward. Now.'

Numbly, lacking the will to resist, Rex found himself obeying. As the war party snaked along the western approach road, he worked his way up the line. Soldiers turned their eyes to watch him pass, while warrior monks sat as deathly still and expressionless as ever.

On the way, Rex would pass the cage. As he approached, he blinked at it, and it slowly came into focus. It was one more unreal thing – this cage, and that shadowy form within. As he drew closer, he gripped the reins of his horse as his hands began to shake.

The cage was sitting on the back of a long cart, which was pulled by a pair of packhorses. Inside the cage, suspended upright by chains, was Robin Hood.

Rex forced himself to look at the outlaw king. Strung up there like that, his head hanging to his chest, he looked more decrepit than ever. He looked like a depiction of Famine, his skin stretched so tight across his chest it seemed impossible that his ribs had not burst through it. The rootlets that had grown into him – that kept him alive while he was rooted into that ancient tree stump – had now withered and died. Where they had dropped out of his arms and legs they had left red welts, like stigmata.

Could it actually be true – had this pathetic specimen truly murdered his mother? Would he even have possessed the strength? Think of all his mother had been – fire and guile and passion. Could this wasted scrap of a creature truly have overpowered her?

What other explanation was there? His mother had gone into that tree-cave. And when Rex finally crawled in after her . . .

Grief washed over him with renewed power – with such vigour that he became dizzy, almost fell from his horse. He steadied himself, angrily wiped at his eyes. Grinding his teeth, he turned away from the cage, spurred his horse and continued to the head of the line.

He got there just as the procession reached the hulking West Gate. Rex passed through the towering stone entranceway, and he entered the city . . . and was met by a thousand staring faces.

This sight was so unexpected that he again had to grip the saddle to hold his balance. For the first time since leaving the Giants' Graveyard, the world came into sharp focus as this great sea of people looked back at him.

He swept his gaze across the citizens. They lined the roadside, three people deep. Here and there, dotted among them, were soldiers of the Sheriff's Guard, their blood-red cloaks stark amid the colourless crowds.

Eerily, these people barely made a sound. As Rex led the procession between them, he heard not even a cough or a shuffle of feet. The people stood there expressionless, motionless, more like statues than flesh and blood.

And then, as one, all heads turned. Without looking back, Rex knew why. The cart with the cage had just rattled through West Gate.

Robin Hood, the blind bowman, the phantom outlaw of Sherwood, had entered Nottingham. Chained and cowed, he was slowly borne up through the streets.

As he passed, the crowd remained silent. These were the outer reaches of the city – the slum districts. The lowborn citizens who lived here stood outside their shacks and hovels, and they barely seemed to breathe. From somewhere, a lone baby was crying, and further off a dog barked, but otherwise there was not a sound.

If Guy of Gisbourne had expected this return to be a triumph, or a celebration, he had been much mistaken. The people here were far from jubilant. As they stared at the phantom outlaw, they looked downcast, even sorrowful. They met Rex's gaze with something like defiance. Yes, there was hostility here, Rex could feel it in the air. Yet it was not directed at Robin Hood, but rather at his captors.

What had his father said to the lowborn folk, that night he took Rex into the slums?

You gather here to invoke the name of Robin Hood. Even now, you grieve for the phantom outlaw. You dream he will one day rise again, together with his accursed forest.

Yes, if Rex had doubted that before, he could see it now . . . These people venerated Robin Hood. With the Sheriff's Guard scattered among them, gripping their bludgeons, they dared not show it, but Rex could feel the despair and anger washing from them as they stared at the wasted figure in that cage.

The atmosphere was so intense that Rex was desperately relieved when the procession finally left the slum districts. The horses' hooves began to clop across cobbles as they worked their way up through the craftsmen's quarter.

They had crossed an invisible line, and the world around Rex now began to change. There were few soldiers here. The citizens were gathered freely, dressed in their finest clothes. Children ran around, excitable, while a murmur of voices arose.

As the procession continued up through the city, townhouses towered over them, and the streets widened into the mercantile district. Again, the world around Rex seemed to shift. The murmur of voices hardened, and was interspersed with angry shouts.

A clanging noise came from the cart. Looking back, Rex saw that a rock had rebounded off the bars. A second rock struck a cartwheel, while more people shouted curses. Someone threw a lump of dung, which splattered across Robin Hood's arm. People jeered and hurled more missiles, while the packhorses whinnied and the cart lurched.

A boy with a catapult shot a stone that gashed Robin Hood's cheek. The wildwood king hung there as passive as ever, while people pelted him with rotten fruit and pots of night-water and lumps of offal, and they jeered and mocked and hollered, the crowd now rising as one in a furious uproar.

Rex stared around him at the citizens, their faces twisted

with animal hatred. He looked again at their defenceless victim, his bare skin gashed and bleeding, his wolf pelt splattered with mud and dung.

'Stop it!' Rex heard himself shout. 'Leave him!'

His voice was swallowed by the baying of the crowd, while more missiles rained.

'I said leave him! I'm ordering you to stop!'

Again his words were lost, drowned by a fresh upswell of hatred, while another rock struck Robin Hood and drew blood.

'Stop!'

'You would defend the savage?'

Guy of Gisbourne had ridden up the line and was now walking his horse at his side.

'He . . . is our prisoner,' Rex mumbled. 'He can't fight back.'

'You think he deserves a fighting chance, after all he has done? He murdered your mother. The people's queen.'

Rex had no more words, was unable even to compose his thoughts. It was settling upon him once more – the same idea he had suffered in the wastes – that all this was somehow a dreadful mistake. That *nothing* here made sense. As though . . . as though he was trapped in a dark mirror that reflected his life backwards.

This idea intensified, made everything blurred, as a new noise arose from the crowds. The people were chanting a single word, over and over. Finally, he realized it was his own name.

'Rex!'

'Rex!'

'Rex!'

The ovation fed on itself, people cheering and applauding and calling his name, the noise reverberating off buildings and echoing through the streets.

What are you doing? Stop it! Rex wanted to scream. *Don't you see – my mother is dead! She's still out there in the wastes! Stop!*

223

The world swimming around him, he lifted his head and looked towards the castle. And he saw his father. Standing at the top of the barbican tower. He was staring down at Robin Hood, and at Rex, his expression impossible to read.

Rex hung his head, closed his eyes, while his horse carried him up through the streets, and the city echoed with his name.

'Rex!'

'Rex!'

'Rex!'

II. The Legend of Robin Hood

K it knelt at the centre of The Henge, utterly still, his head bowed. He had remained this way for hours, unable to stand or even move a limb beneath the crushing misery of defeat.

Outside The Henge, aspen leaves rustled in the breeze. But within this sacred circle not so much as a mote of dust stirred. Encircling Kit, the ancient yew trees sat huddled in their shadows. They loomed over him. Seven black-robed judges pronouncing their doom.

You failed us, their silence spoke.

We showed you the way.

You were weak.

Kit squeezed his eyes tight. But it was no good. Behind the lids, as vividly as though it were happening at this moment, he saw Sonskya charge into the wall of thorns, raising her blades against Guy of Gisbourne. Giving her life so that Kit and the others might escape . . .

And what had her sacrifice been worth . . . ?

Robin Hood was gone.

After all these years of hope – of praying that Robin might one day return – Kit had discovered his refuge. But then he had failed to protect him. He had allowed his enemies to seize the wildwood king. And now what hope remained to the world?

This isn't about one man. It can't be . . .

Kit jerked upright, opened his eyes. Sonskya's words had come back to him so distinctly he could almost believe she was here with him, whispering in his ear.

Robin Hood is a symbol, don't you see that – for every one of us who would stand up and fight . . .

It was all flooding back to him now – every word Sonskya spoke in the moments before her sacrifice. And one thing she said echoed over and above everything else, so clear and powerful it was irresistible.

You still don't see it, do you? Or you don't want to. Who you truly are . . .

Kit put one hand to his chest, over his heart, and in that moment all the pieces of his life slotted into place, and finally he understood.

His wildwood powers. The vixen-goddess. Marian's jealousy. They all added up to one thing . . .

I am Robin Hood's son.

The idea arose from nowhere and everywhere. The instant it did so, Kit understood that this knowledge had always been there, buried deep inside him, like a seed waiting to germinate. Now, in an instant, it sprouted and grew and bloomed into absolute truth.

Yes – I am Robin's son.

Why had he not unearthed this truth before? Why had he kept it hidden, even from himself?

Because you fear your own power, the answer came out of the deep silence of the yews. *Because you saw all that Robin Hood was fated to carry. You are scared to bear that same weight. Afraid of all you might have to do . . .*

'No – you're wrong,' he heard himself call out into the trees, rising to his feet. 'I'm not afraid! I'll do whatever it takes. I'll never stop fighting!'

In a daze, he found himself stripping off his wrist bracers

and his padded jacket and the rest of his leather armour, letting it all fall to the forest floor. He removed his tunic and breeches, then strode out of The Henge and through Gaia entirely naked. The other outlaws were sprawled in the shade by the stream, nursing their wounds and their grief. Kit felt their eyes on him as he passed, but they held their silence.

As he reached the boundary of Gaia, he paused at a boulder to peel off a length of silver fork moss. Carrying this with him and nothing else he used his forest powers to open a tunnel through the curtain wall of vegetation. Then he passed out into the Lost Lands.

The cracked soil was hot underfoot, and within half a mile the soles of his feet were beginning to blister. The late-morning sun beat down on his bare back. But he kept going, across old dry riverbeds and dust-filled gullies. Over shingle that sliced at his skin, and baking rockflows that scorched him, and through beds of lance thistle and burn weed. Mile upon mile through this shimmering hellscape, only pausing now and again to suck moisture from the strip of moss he carried.

Until finally, in the late evening, he came once again to Robin Hood's Cave. Gratefully he crawled into the chilly gloom, his sunburned skin sighing as he rested his back against a damp flowstone wall.

He located his stashed strike-a-light, together with a seed-head torch, and soon he had a light to guide his way deeper into the cave.

He made his way along passageways and through caverns, until finally he entered the vast central chamber that once served as the outlaws' arsenal and war chest. His torchlight glinted across the great hoard of scattered gold and gemstones, then shimmered back at him more darkly as he passed the great stacks of swords and maces and battleaxes.

Kit ignored all this and headed into a corner of the cavern, packed with barrels and baskets and chests. These were full of plunder of a different kind. Kit's light fell upon heaps of lambswool, and piles of kidskin boots, and stacks of beeswax candles.

There were goods here from all around the world: rugs from Arabia; wine from Champagne; cloth from Sicily. All of it had been twice stolen, the Sheriff's taxmen and bailiffs confiscating it from merchants; the outlaws, in turn, ambushing the Sheriff's caravans and taking it from his soldiers. Given time, Marian would have sold all this plunder, using the funds to swell her war chest. Except she never had the chance. And so all these lavish wares and fine materials had been left here to rot.

Kit searched through it all, turning over baskets, shoving aside arks and reliquaries, until finally he found what he had come here for. It was a large cedar chest, which contained dozens of furs. They had come from Bavaria, and were mostly the skins of bears. But Kit had been on the raid when the outlaws captured this shipment, and he remembered, very distinctly, seeing something more interesting.

Something that had made him think, even back then, what if . . . ?

He hauled out the last of the bearskins – and yes, at the bottom of the chest, there it was. It stared up at him with its dead eyes, its mouth snarling.

The pelt of a wolf.

Kit laid it upon the cave floor. Then he searched some more until he found thick thread, and needles made from slivers of bone, and a clothier's knife and a tanner's shears. Propping up his torch, he immediately set to work, shivering now in the cold of the cave, as he began to cut and sew and stitch . . .

It was just after dawn the following day when he returned to Gaia. The other forest fighters were eating their breakfast in silence, gathered around their home fire.

As Kit stepped into the clearing, they were instantly on their feet. Midge's slingshot was whirring. But then he let the rock drop. Ira released the tension from her bowstring, and for long moments that followed there was only the sound of birdsong.

Finally, Kit moved closer. He kept the wolfskin cloak wrapped close around him, his head lowered, the snarling cowl masking his face. Behind him, the sun glimmered huge and pale through the mist. He stopped and let them stare before raising his head.

'Sonskya helped me see,' he said. 'Her final gift to me. They may have taken Robin Hood's body. They might take his life. But he is more than either of those things. The people out there never stopped believing in him. Neither should we.'

Midge stepped around the fire, came closer. Kit was waiting for him to sneer, or challenge him. But instead, he said simply: 'What are we going to do?'

'We are going to bring the rebellion back to life,' Kit said. 'We will make it blaze fiercer than ever. Here's how we'll begin . . .'

III. The Terrible Dawn

Standing on the parapet of the White Tower, Rex watched the first flare of sunrise, and he groaned from the pit of his stomach. He had stood up here all night, unwilling to take to his bed and face his nightmares. It had been the blackest of nights, thick cloud smothering any glimmer of moonlight, and at some point in the hour before dawn, delirious through lack of sleep, Rex had entered a trance-like state in which the whole world had disappeared. He heard not a hint of sound from the castle or the city; he felt no weight or sensations of any kind from his own body. Time might have ended, or he might be dead himself. It was not a frightening sensation; quite the reverse: it was the first inkling of peace he had known since he had left his mother behind in the Lost Lands.

But now the sun was rising, spreading its fire across the horizon, piercing the blackness of his mind. Time juddered back into motion.

Again, Rex groaned, grief welling up so powerfully that he felt dizzy, catching his balance against the low wall that encircled the parapet. He toppled forward against the wall . . . then tipped further . . . feeling the fall tugging at him . . .

What if he were to simply let go?

Would it even be his doing?

He opened his eyes and peered at the cobbled courtyard forty feet below. What would it be like – the fear as he fell? Would his heart fail before he reached the ground, or would he experience every terrifying moment? Would the pain of the impact pass in an instant, or would it last and last?

He drew back, shaking, disgusted with himself. Was that the only reason he didn't do it – the fear? Surely that made him the ultimate coward: unwilling to face life, but too frightened to bring it to an end . . .

Behind him, he heard the clack of the trapdoor and the creak of the ladder. Without turning, he sensed his father climb up into the parapet.

The Sheriff came to stand at Rex's side. He was breathless from the climb, wheezing audibly. For long moments that was the only sound, the pair of them watching the fiery cloudscape.

Finally, Rex turned his head. To his surprise, he saw that his father's eyes were puffy and bloodshot.

'You've . . . been crying.'

The Sheriff looked at him. The corner of his mouth twitched. 'Did you imagine me immune to grief?'

Rex turned away. 'I only ever heard you two fight. But you loved her, didn't you?'

'More than you could ever imagine,' his father said quietly. 'I have just come from the chapel. I lit a candle for her. It was the hardest thing I have ever done.'

There was another moment of silence between them, before the Sheriff said: 'When she first came to the castle, your mother would stand up here every day. I would see her as I was leaving morning prayer. She appeared to be at peace, just standing here, watching the sunrise. Or perhaps that was just what I wanted to believe. Looking back, as much as I hate to admit it, I know there were times she when she was tempted to jump.'

Rex turned and stared at him, horror-struck.

'You must understand, the forest had cast a strong spell upon her,' his father went on. 'Living here, in spite of every comfort I could provide, she felt . . . confined.'

Rex stared at his hands, clasped them together as they started to shake. 'So why didn't she do it? Why did she go on living?'

'Because of you, of course.' He looked squarely at Rex, and now there was cold fire in his eyes. 'After you were born, she suffered whole seasons of melancholy. Yet still she endured. For your sake. And now, this morning, I see you standing up here, just as she used to do, ready to throw your life away. Is that how you would repay her? Is that how you would honour her life, and her sacrifice?'

Listening to this, Rex's own anger rose. 'What else am I supposed to do?' He pointed a shaking finger towards the Lost Lands. 'I went out there, like you wanted, and what did it prove?'

'It proved that you are a born survivor,' the Sheriff said, evenly. 'It showed the world that you possess fortitude and courage.'

It was a mark of Rex's delirium that he openly laughed at these words. 'Courage? How little you know me, Father. I'm more afraid than I've ever been. I daren't close my eyes lest I see their faces.'

'And you believe your fear makes you weak?' his father said. 'Look at me. Do you suppose I live without fear?' He pointed towards the wastes. 'See? There is my fear made manifest. I lie awake at night listening to the howling of the wilderness, just as I once listened to the shrieking of the forest.'

Rex heard this with a strange sense of release. It was as if . . . as if for the first time he could remember, a piece of his world slotted into its proper place.

'Mother . . . She told me this. She said you lived your life in fear. I didn't believe her.'

The Sheriff looked at him, the ruined side of his face livid in the dawn light. 'I would admit as much to no other living soul. Your mother likely understood it before I did. But yes, in this life, fear has been my constant companion. You might even say it is my true essence. But has that fear made me feeble? On the contrary. Fear has been my greatest ally – the wellspring of my strength. Without the fuel of fear running in my veins, I could not have built all this . . .' he swept an arm to indicate the castle and the city beyond. 'Without it, I could never have driven back the forest.'

He turned back to Rex, and his blue eyes burned coldly and the air rasped in his chest. 'You have inherited that fear. It is your birthright. Do not deny it. Embrace it. Wield it as your trusted blade. Use it to slay your enemies.' He stared once more towards the Lost Lands. 'Because now you have seen your enemies, have you not? The outlaws – are they not as godless and savage as their wilderness?'

Rex followed his father's gaze out to the wastes, which were black beneath low banks of cloud, and his brief sense of certainty, of having solid ground beneath his feet, now slipped away. Everything that had happened out in the Lost Lands . . . he still hadn't even begun to understand it all. The only part that seemed real was when he crawled into that ancient tree stump . . . and found his mother lying there . . . her eyes like painted marble . . .

'Robin Hood,' he murmured. 'Where is he?'

'Imprisoned in the dungeons,' the Sheriff replied. 'But he must not remain there. False gods grow stronger in the dark.'

'Will you kill him?'

'Certainly. But it cannot be done furtively. The little people still idolize Robin Hood. With their own eyes, they must see their false god turn to ashes. See there – we have begun to construct his pyre.'

Looking where his father had pointed, Rex peered out over the city and the curtain walls. In the dim morning light, he could see movement out on Gallows Field, a wide stretch of land that lay between West Gate and the river. Carters were arriving there with loads of timber, and packhorses were pulling winches into place, and labourers were arriving by the dozen.

'It must be a blaze worthy of the occasion,' his father said. 'The greatest fire since the forest burned. The flames must be seen across the Sheriffdom. The last of the outlaws – I wish them to see it – wherever they may be hiding.'

The last of the outlaws.

Wherever they may be hiding.

Once more, Rex turned his gaze towards the Lost Lands. It was so gloomy and full of cloud-shadow he could barely make out any detail – it was a vast, dead desert. Except Rex knew that was not entirely true. His memory took him back to that night of storms, when he had stood up here and stared across the wastes, and in a flash of lightning he had glimpsed an island of trees . . .

'I must go and oversee preparations,' the Sheriff said, turning away, as the shriek of saws and knock of hammers began echoing up from Gallows Field. 'Make yourself look more presentable, then join me. From now on, the people must see us side by side.'

'Father – wait,' Rex said, making him pause near the trapdoor. 'There's . . . something I need to tell you.' Rex stared out towards the Lost Lands, and after one last moment of hesitation, he heard himself say: 'I know where they are. The outlaws. I've seen their refuge.'

Slowly, Rex's father returned to his side. 'You've *seen* it? The Last Forest?' He studied Rex sceptically. 'My rangers have scoured the wastes for years without success.'

Rex went on staring into the dust-billowing wastes. 'Perhaps they didn't know how to look.'

Following another pause, his father said: 'And you believe you could locate it again?'

Rex nodded. 'Mother . . . She taught me things. How to read the stars. Navigate by the moon. The night I saw the wildwood, the moon was directly above it. On a clear night, I could find my way there.'

The Sheriff appeared to be holding his breath, before finally saying: 'You suffered much in the wastes. Yet you would be willing to return, and so soon?'

Again, Rex nodded. 'I would,' he said, his voice quiet but even. 'I will. I think . . . I need to.'

His father closed his eyes. 'Then the stars have truly aligned. At the next full moon, we will once again bring cleansing fire to the world. Not one blaze, but two. One here to obliterate Robin Hood. Another in the wastes to wipe out the last of his acolytes. We shall remove every trace of them, past, present and future, together with their accursed forest.'

He looked at Rex. 'As I foretold, your trip into the wastes has left you transformed. Already the people view you with fresh eyes. Succeed in this undertaking, strike the killer blow, and you will prove once and for all that you are worthy to be my heir.'

With that, he left the parapet, while Rex remained standing there, his mind churning. Had he done the right thing, telling his father about Gaia? What bloody deeds might follow? Could he really summon the courage to return to the wilderness?

Yes, he could. He had to. If he was going to live, he must act.

He must walk the only path that remained open.

IV. Lifeblood

'Admit defeat, sis. You know as well as I do, I'm already dead.'

'Don't say that! And don't be such a weakling. It's just a scratch.'

In spite of the pain, Lucas smiled grimly. He was lying flat on his back at the foot of the ancient tree stump, in the shade cast by the ferns and the saplings. His face was now so pale it was almost grey. His every breath was slow and laboured.

The crossbow quarrel had struck him in the midriff, missing the vital organs. But the bolt was barbed, designed to hook into flesh. It had taken Arora an hour to cut it out, while Lucas's agony echoed through the Giants' Graveyard. Arora had wadded and wrapped the wound as best she could, but it would not stop bleeding.

'Hold still,' she told him. 'I'm going to clean it again.'

Arora lifted a drinking bladder, preparing to pour water on the wound. But as she peeled away the bandages she froze, holding her breath. The ragged hole in Lucas's middle had begun to look sickly, greenish at the edges.

'So – you've finally got it through your thick skull,' he mumbled, trying to smile. 'I can see from the look on your face. I'm done. So will you please . . . just sit with me.'

'Stop saying that!' Arora hastily rebandaged his wounds, then leaped to her feet. 'You are not going to die – I won't allow it! I'm going to find curatives and I'm going to make you better, do you hear me?'

'You've looked everywhere. There's nothing.'

But Arora had already turned away and was storming through the Giants' Graveyard. As she had done twice before, she went one by one to each of the rangers who died fighting the outlaws. Their corpses were stiff now and withering beneath the blazing sun.

Ignoring the putrid stench, and the clouds of flies, she rifled once more through their backpacks and their clothing. There had to be something she had missed – there *had* to be! But with each body she searched, her fingers trembling with desperation, the more she became certain she was fooling herself. These soldiers carried only killing things, nothing healing.

'Please,' she wept, falling to her knees. 'There has to be something I can do. There must be a way . . . *Please!*'

Abruptly she fell quiet and sat upright. She stared at the wall of vegetation that still encircled the Giants' Graveyard. That towering, rustling wall of life . . .

Where until this morning no life had existed . . .

Before the battle began, from her hiding place, Arora had seen the chief of the outlaws extract an object from beneath the earth. With growing awe, she had watched him patrol the bounds, sprinkling a dark-red liquid upon the ground. She knew full well what this liquid must be. It could be none other than the fabled blood of the wolf-god. And soon it was proved beyond doubt. For where the blood fell, bush and briars and saplings sprang up.

The god's blood had poured life back into this lifeless ground.

And if it possessed the power to do that . . .

Holding her breath, barely daring to hope, Arora was back on her feet, and she was stumbling, charging, running towards the wall of greenery. This was the spot – this was where the outlaw chief had completed his circuit, she remembered distinctly. Once he had finished with the vessel, he had simply dropped it. The wall of vegetation must have grown over it, but she was certain it must be—

Yes! There! An object half visible within the mass of undergrowth. Dropping to her knees, she tunnelled her way in, heedless of the thorns and the thistles and the burn-weed. She scrabbled and fought and reached – until finally her groping fingers closed around something smooth. Yes – here it was – the amphora!

She wriggled and crawled her way back out of the wall of thorns. She sat up straight, holding the vessel, barely daring to move, praying beneath her breath.

Finally, bracing herself, she shook the container.

And she heard nothing.

No – no – no!

She pulled out the stopper and tipped the vessel upside down, shaking it over her cupped palm, praying for even a single droplet. But no. The outlaw chief had drained it entirely.

'No!' she hollered at the sky, flinging the useless vessel back into the undergrowth, before falling once more to her knees. Burying her face in her hands, she swore and cursed, wishing death to the Sheriff and his rangers and the heretic hunter, and even to the outlaw chief for using every last drop of the—

She sat up straight, became still.

Had he, though, used every last drop of the blood?

How did she know that to be true?

Scrambling to her feet, she sprinted back to the ancient tree stump. Ignoring Lucas, who called out to her weakly, she circled the oasis of greenery. She stopped when she came to a hole in the ground that opened between the tree's roots. Falling to her stomach, she mimicked the outlaw chief by thrusting her hand into the hole and groping around in the space beneath.

She found only mulch and damp soil. Springing back to her feet, she dashed further around the stump, until she spotted another opening. She thrust her arm in once more, burying it to the elbow. Furry creatures lived inside this burrow – she brushed against one and heard the rest scatter.

Jumping to her feet once more, she went to a third earth and a fourth, growing increasingly desperate. She wasn't as tall as the outlaw – what if another vessel lay underground but her arm wasn't long enough to reach? Should she try digging with her knife? Even if there was more blood buried here, would Lucas be dead before she could find it?

Even as she was thinking this, her fingers brushed against something hard and smooth, and once again her breath stopped. Groping carefully for the object, she finally got a proper grip on it and drew it carefully up into the light.

She stood, cradling the prize. It was an amphora, made of fired clay, simple and unadorned – identical to the one the outlaw chief had used. Except for one crucial difference. This one was heavier. She was sure it was. Closing her eyes, she forced herself to shake the vessel and . . . Yes! Liquid sloshed inside!

Clasping it to her chest, she hurried back to her brother. He opened his eyes as she knelt next to him.

'What have you got there? Something else to torment me with?'

'Don't speak. Close your eyes.'

'Why? What are you—'

'Shush. Just do it. Trust me.'

Arora removed the cork stopper from the neck of the amphora. With trembling hands, she peeled away Lucas's bandages, then raised the vessel above his wound. Slowly, she tipped it, and the blood trickled out. Where it landed on his wound, it hissed, and Lucas opened his eyes and gasped.

'Please, sis, no more, I—'

'Quiet!' Arora snapped, her whole body shaking. 'Hold still. I think . . . Yes – it is – it's working!'

The blood took effect with wondrous speed. Where it dribbled onto Lucas's injury, his flesh began to warp and convulse, to bubble and writhe. The wound started to shrink, to knit itself closed, to fold in on itself like a night-flower closing at sunrise.

Within moments, while Arora stared awestruck, the process was complete. Lucas's midriff was now whole and unblemished, his skin shining like a newborn infant's.

'W-what did you do?' he murmured. 'Th-the pain – it's gone. Is this – am I . . .'

'Shh, it's all right,' she spluttered, fighting back tears, laughing at the same time. 'Everything's all right. Take a look – you need to see.'

Still lying on his back, he stared up at her. The agony had unstitched itself from his features, and colour was returning to his cheeks. Slowly, he sat up, and with eyes that were wide and glistening he stared down at his midriff. He raised a shaking hand and laid it on the spot where the wound used to be.

'Where . . . what?' he mumbled stupidly. 'How did you . . . ?'

Snapping out of her own astonishment, Arora flung her arms around him, and for the first time since their father died she cried and cried. She kept crying while Lucas closed his arms around her and murmured his wonder into her hair.

'How, sis, how?'

'What does it matter,' she sobbed. 'It's a gift. That's all. I thought you were going to leave me, and I couldn't stand it. But it worked. You're healed. You're going to live!'

V. Fresh Blood

The villagers had pulled down the statue of the Sheriff. It lay shattered on the common green, its head hacked from its shoulders. When Kit and his band arrived, just after nightfall, the villagers were all gathered on the green, sitting around a communal cooking fire, roasting meat.

Leaving the other outlaws at the boundary stone, Kit approached them alone. For now he remained in the shadows, outside the ring of firelight, while they went on with their feast. He sensed that a great change had come across this place. Every single peasant, even the smallest children, had lying next to them a makeshift weapon: a reaping scythe; a fencing maul; a catapult. But it was more than that. As he moved closer, and their heads turned, he detected in their eyes a haunted hollow look that went beyond despair, into something deranged and deadly.

'You're too late,' spat a gaunt-faced figure whom Kit recognized as the hetman. 'My son went back to the burrows. The soldiers left a mantrap. He bled to death out there all alone. There's nothing for you here. You'd better leave.'

Kit stood and watched the hetman, meat fat shining in his beard. He and the rest of the villagers went on tearing at their chunks of flesh, the twisting firelight making their features look demonic.

These people were starving. Where did they get so much meat?

Even as Kit was asking himself this, he knew the answer. He remembered the outlaws' ambush, which left twelve soldiers lying dead. He looked towards the slaughter shed; through the slats he glimpsed hanging, bloody slabs.

No wonder these people looked changed. They have crossed a line. Perhaps I should turn and leave after all.

But no. He had chosen a path. To turn back now would mark the death of all hope. In any case, did he expect to recruit angels? Weren't these desperadoes exactly what the uprising required?

'I was wrong to deny you before,' he said, moving closer but stopping short of the firelight. 'This is your fight, as much as it is ours.'

'Don't concern yourself. We intend to fight,' spoke up a fierce-looking woman at the hetman's side. 'When his soldiers next come here, we'll fight to our last drop of blood.'

'There's a better way,' Kit said. 'Follow me, and others will join us. Together we can do more than give up our lives. We can make them count for something.'

As he spoke, he finally stepped into the ring of firelight. He kept his head lowered, the wolf-head cowl draped across his face, the pelt of the beast wrapped close. The silence was broken only by the crackling of the flames, and a lone owl hooting in the distance.

Eventually, the hetman said: 'You're not Robin Hood.'

'I'm his heir,' Kit said, gripping his bow across his chest. 'I've taken up his burden. I carry his strength.'

'Yeah?' the hetman snarled, his eyes bloodshot and crazed. 'Then prove it. John Little. On your feet. Give this imposter a thrashing.'

On the far side of the fire, a man lumbered upright. Kit remembered this colossal figure, built like an oak, with hands like mauls. He was holding a quarterstaff as thick as Kit's arm.

Kit shook his head. 'I don't fight with staff.'

'You do today,' the hetman snarled. 'Our village, our rules.'

Another villager stood with a second quarterstaff, tossed it to Kit.

'Fine,' Kit growled, catching the weapon and sweeping his gaze across the villagers. 'I'll fight your giant. And when I beat him, you will all swear an oath to me. Never again, on pain of death, will any of you question me ever again.'

An hour later, by the light of the rising moon, Kit and his band trudged back out of the village, with fifteen new recruits in tow. Kit was bruised and aching, and trying not to limp. John Little had proved a formidable opponent, his blows shaking Kit to his bones and twice leaving him sprawled and breathless. But Kit was quicker, and more cunning, and driven by a wild will not to be beaten here in front of his followers, old and new, and eventually he managed to fell the giant and disarm him and stand victorious.

Once he had done so, an abrupt change came over the hetman and the other villagers. They had packed their scant possessions without a word and were now following Kit as meek as lambs.

Lambs to the slaughter, Kit couldn't help thinking as he glanced back at them. *They may be desperate, and willing, but they are untrained and unskilled. How many of them will live to see another spring?*

Well, it was too late to think that way. There was no turning back. Kit had embarked on the only path left open to him. Come what may, he must follow that path to its bloody end.

VI. Dead Unburied

'All right, sis, we're ready. So what are we waiting for?'
Arora remained sitting with her back to a fallen oak, staring across the Giants' Graveyard.

Lucas put down his pack and knelt at her side. 'What is it? What are you thinking?'

Slowly, she turned her eyes to meet his. 'I've got this feeling. Like we're being watched.'

Lucas hugged his arms. 'I felt that the moment we stepped into this place. I wish we'd never found it.' He stood. 'Let's leave, right now, and never think of it again.'

Arora remained sitting. 'But we did find it, didn't we? Why?'

'Dumb luck.'

She shook her head. 'Father didn't believe in luck, and neither do I.'

'Sis . . . where are you going? We said we'd head east. That's the wrong way.'

Her brother's words barely registered. Arora found herself walking towards the centre of the Giants' Graveyard as if compelled – as though invisible threads were drawing her towards the ancient tree stump.

'Wait,' Lucas said, taking hold of her shoulder. 'What are you doing?'

'I need to go in there,' she said, staring at the cave-like entrance. 'I need to see.'

'What? Why? It's none of our business.'

'It is,' Arora said, shrugging off his hand. 'We're tied up in it, as much as anyone. After all that's happened, we can't just walk away.'

'We can! We have to!' He winced and held his side where he was injured. 'Haven't we suffered enough?'

Regardless, Arora was moving forward once more. And now she was reaching the ancient stump, and going to hands and knees, and crawling inside.

Kneeling in the gloom, she reached into her backpack and drew out her strike-a-light, together with a tallow candle. She lit the wick, then held up the flame and blinked around the cave-like space. Her eyes came to rest on a human shape. A female figure, lying flat on her back. She was as motionless as stone, and her skin was white, and her hair was fanned out like a dark halo.

Lucas came scrabbling into the tree trunk, his movement making the candle splutter and the light waver, the figure on the ground seeming to shift as it did so. Lucas became very still, holding his breath.

Finally, he murmured: 'Is that . . . ?'

'Lady Marian. Yes.'

'She's . . . dead. How? Who?'

'When she saw Guy of Gisbourne was following us, she was afraid. He killed her. I know he did,' she hissed between her teeth. 'Just like he would have killed you.'

'But he didn't,' Lucas whispered. 'So rejoice. The rest has nothing to do with us.'

'It does,' Arora said. 'That's what I've been trying to tell you. Think about it. Why you and me? Of all the people in the world, why did *we* find Robin Hood? Why did *I* find the blood of the gods? We didn't choose any of this. It chose us.'

'Even if that's true, we played our part. Now it's finished.'

'No – it can't end here. Not for us. Not for her.' She crawled closer to Marian, knelt over the corpse. 'If you'd heard what she said to me, out there in the wastes. I see it now. The Sheriff is poison. Marian – and Robin – they're the cure.'

'Robin is gone. And Marian – she isn't anything any more. Sis . . . what are you doing? Why are you holding that?'

Arora had reached into her backpack and taken out the amphora containing the blood of the gods.

'Oh no,' Lucas whispered, as she removed the cork stopper. 'No, no, no.'

'It worked on you.'

'I was *hurt*. This is a different thing! You can't even be thinking it. Sis, please!'

'I have to. I don't know how I know, but I do. This is . . . putting things straight. Restoring what's out of place.'

'No, sis, please. I'm begging you!'

But Arora could not have held back now even if she had wanted to. All this time, it had been growing stronger – that sense that she was no longer master of her own actions, but was merely enacting a long-determined fate.

In this serene state, she watched her own hands lift the amphora above the prone figure of Lady Marian. And then she was watching, fascinated, as the amphora tipped . . .

And the crimson liquid dribbled . . .

Dripped onto those cold, blue lips.

In that moment, time ceased, and the world blazed brighter and more real than Arora had ever known. She stared at droplets of blood, glistening stark and terrible and beautiful against Marian's snow-white teeth.

Then the timeless moment was shattered – Lucas gasped, screamed, as Marian's tongue darted out to lick the teeth clean.

In the same instant, Marian's chest heaved. She sat bolt upright, seized Arora by the throat, and her eyes blazed like wildfire.

'Where are they?' she snarled. 'Robin – and Rex. What has he done with them?'

VII. Baptism in Blood

Looking across to the next hilltop, Kit saw sunlight flare off bare steel. There was a pause, then two more flashes of white light, and finally a fourth. Using the flat of her blade, Ira had sent the signal.

Kit got to his feet. 'It won't be long now,' he said to the others. 'Much, go and man the log-fall. Stay alert. Timing will be crucial. You other two, come with me.'

Trailed by Jack and Midge, Kit made his way along the wooded ridge. Every ten paces, they passed a pair of new recruits. They were dug into the undergrowth, each of them gripping a makeshift club or spear, their faces darkened with mud and charcoal. A few of them turned their heads as Kit passed, but the majority remained admirably still, and not one of them made a sound.

Since going to that first village, where Kit had fought John Little, the outlaws had trekked miles through the scrublands, picking up new recruits as they went. Never again had Kit faced any challenge or resistance; on the contrary, he found the shire-folk only too ready to leave their homes and join the rebellion. With Kit at the head of the procession, wearing his wolf-skin cloak and cowl, the outlaw band had steadily grown and grown, each hamlet and village offering up another five or six or a dozen fighters. It had all happened so quickly. And now, blinking along the ridge almost in disbelief, Kit saw an entire rebel army.

An army or a rabble? he corrected himself, running his eyes once more across the mob, seeing youths barely out of childhood, and grey-haired men, and mothers alongside their sons. *Wolves of war or lambs to the slaughter? Well – now we find out.*

Positioning scouts on high ground, the outlaws had tracked a battalion of soldiers for the past ten miles. The road they were following would lead them directly below this wooded ridge. Out in these scrublands, this spot provided rare tree-cover. It was the perfect place for an ambush – and the perfect way to blood new troops.

'These rangers are either stupid or in one hell of a hurry,' said Midge. 'Probably both. Either way, they're playing right into our hands.'

'They don't expect us to be out here,' said Jack. He grinned as he ran his gaze back along the ridge. 'And they don't know there are so many of us. Aren't they in for a pretty surprise.'

'You're right, though, Midge,' said Kit. 'It looks like they're heading for the castle, and in a rush to get there. That usually means the Sheriff has fresh plans. See if you can bring me a live one to question.

'All right, there's the final signal,' he said, looking across to Ira's lookout post. 'Get to your positions. These recruits are an unknown quantity, so be ready for anything.'

While Jack and Midge flitted away, Kit went to take his place at the head of the line. It was essential, as ever, that he lead by example and be the first into the fight. But today of all days it would leave him vulnerable. He looked along the ranks once more. He had seen some of the green recruits passing drinking horns between them, bolstering their courage with strong grog.

But what if it wasn't enough? It was one thing to vow vengeance; the reality of charging armed and armoured troops was another thing entirely. What if their blood was to run cold and they sat frozen in the undergrowth, leaving Kit's meagre band to confront a battalion all alone?

Well – it was too late to think that way. Here they were, and this was happening. Any doubt or hesitation on Kit's part now would certainly spell disaster.

And now there was no more time for thinking of any kind. Kit's mind went blank as his battle instincts took command. Because there on the road below, now passing into the shadows of the ridge, was the battalion of soldiers. They were riding hard, their cloaks flying, their horses grimy with dust.

The moment they appeared, Kit raised a hunting horn to his lips. He gave two short blasts. An instant later, from the other end of the ridge, came a rumbling splintering crash where Much let loose the log-fall. At the sound and the sight of tumbling timber, the lead soldier hauled on his reins, his mount rearing and the horses behind him sliding to a halt and thrown into panic.

But to Kit, all this was mere surface noise. He had sunk fully into his battle-self, his every nerve focused on his first target, his bowstring drawn as he slipped down the slope quick and silent as a shadow.

As he let loose, and the first soldier fell screaming from his horse, he was aware of a hollering roaring cry filling the air as the new recruits, led by Jack and Midge, came thundering off the ridge, and the shocked and bewildered soldiers were swamped by the new outlaw army.

And an army they proved themselves to be. In the aftermath of the ambush, as Kit stepped through the battlefield, looking down at slain soldiers, he saw he had been utterly wrong to doubt the new recruits. Sonskya had been right – what she had said to Kit all that time ago – these peasant warriors were nothing like Marian's greenwood troops. Living a life of relative ease and safety in Sherwood, Marian's conscripts had been soft, even slothful.

Kit's makeshift warriors were of a different breed. For the past twelve years, ever since the Sheriff destroyed the forest, they had lived on the edge of the wastes, hewing a meagre existence from dying soil. They had endured drought and famine and sandstorms; they had lost elders to pestilence and children to lung-rot. Those who survived, season after season, had become as tough and unforgiving as the ground upon which they walked. They might be untrained, but pure desperation made them formidable.

And here was the proof. The new recruits had set upon the soldiers with raw fury, hauling them from their horses and hacking and bludgeoning them to death. One peasant warrior had been killed by a crossbow bolt; another trampled beneath the hooves of a horse; but those were the rebels' only losses, while a full score of soldiers lay slaughtered.

'So much for a live one to question,' said Jack, nudging a mangled corpse with his toe. 'These men are all very much dead.'

Yes, that was Kit's one regret: the rebel peasants had paid no regard whatsoever to taking prisoners. Indeed, many of them were so possessed with berserker fury that they went on hacking at soldiers long after they had taken their last breath.

This put him in mind of that first village they had visited – where they had found the peasants at their grisly feast, blood on their teeth and a wild madness in their eyes.

What have we started here today, he asked himself, as he continued through the killing field. *What have I unleashed?*

Earlier he had worried that the new recruits would lack the

stomach to fight – now he was questioning whether they were too bloodthirsty!

Well, it was pointless musing in either direction. What was done was done. Kit had chosen the bloody path. And now they were truly underway.

VIII. Deeds Undone

Standing at the edge of the Giants' Graveyard, Marian hugged her arms. She looked out across the unreal landscape, feeling unreal. Through the wall of vegetation, she watched the plain shift and warp with heat haze. Her vision shifted with it and she felt dizzy, the ground uncertain beneath her feet.

Perhaps there had been a mistake. Maybe . . . when the heretic hunter struck her, she had merely been knocked unconscious. The twins had done nothing more than help her wake.

But no, she could not fool herself that easily. Reaching back into her memory, searching for those lost hours, she found no trace of dreams, nor even the foggy emptiness of deep sleep. Instead, she found . . . *nothing*. A nothingness so profound it could mean only one thing.

She hugged herself tighter. She breathed the scorched-rock smell wafting off the plains, and felt the hot breeze on her skin. All of it so distinct, so tangible. There was no denying it. Here she was, back in the world.

Unbidden, she remembered what the goddess said about Robin. *He left too much unfinished. Words unsaid, deeds undone.*

And what did she say of Marian? *You too leave acts unfinished.*

Was that it then? Was that why they had both been allowed

to return? Or should she say *forced*? Was this second chance a blessing or a curse?

She shook her head at this useless rumination. Putting her hand to her chest, over her heart, she felt the pulse of her lifeblood. She existed. So did Robin and Rex. So did the world around her. She knew these things. They were the only true facts she had. They were all she needed. Now all that remained was to act.

So thinking, she turned and went back through the Giants' Graveyard. On the far side of the ancient tree stump, the twins were arguing.

'See sense, sis. It's pure lunacy.'

'She won't find her way across the wastes, not without us.'

'That's not our problem. We've done enough. Too much.'

'We're not finished. It's like I told you, we're tangled up in this for a reason. We couldn't turn our backs on it now even if we wanted to.'

'You should listen to her,' Marian said.

At she stepped into view, Lucas recoiled, and as she approached he backed away.

'You're scared of me,' she said to him, stopping with open palms. 'Perhaps you regret what you did. Maybe . . . I'll come to regret it too. But what's done is done. Here we are. And now . . . I need your help.'

Lucas shook his head. 'What can we do? This is your fight, not ours. We're just scavengers. We're nobody.'

Marian paused, then said: 'Before the Great Fire, Robin tried to tell me something I didn't want to hear. I wanted to believe the world revolved around me and him. He tried to tell me our struggle was far bigger than that. Now, at last, I can see it's true. Your sister senses it too. There are forces working upon us we can't even begin to comprehend, let alone control.'

'What's that got to do with going to the city?' Lucas said. 'Even if we get there, what then?'

'We're going to stop the cycle,' Marian said simply. 'All this,' she raised her arms to indicate the Giants' Graveyard and the wastes beyond, 'the Sheriff brought this upon the world. He cursed the Earth. That curse won't be lifted until he's destroyed.'

At this, Lucas squeaked a fearful laugh. 'And who's going to destroy him? You?'

'Yes,' Marian said. 'Me and Robin and Rex.'

'Robin Hood? You don't even know he's still alive.'

'He is. I can sense it. Once we're back together, we can do anything. Trust me,' she said, holding Lucas's gaze. 'That is our part to play. His and mine. We are going to bring the Sheriff's reign to an end. I think . . . that's why I was spared. The world needs us to finish this. And there is nothing that can stop us. Not the Sheriff's army. Not his castle walls. Not death.'

These words left Marian's mouth without passing through her thoughts, but the moment she heard them she knew them for truth. Perhaps Lucas heard the truth in them too, because he offered no further objections, but merely bowed his head.

Arora grinned. 'Besides, little brother, we've got nothing to worry about. Death can't touch us either. Not when we've got this.'

She held up the amphora containing the blood of the wolf-god.

'I'll take that,' Marian said, reaching for it.

'Oh no,' Arora said, clasping the vessel to her chest. 'That's my one condition. This is mine.'

'Once we reach Robin, it's the only thing that will heal him.'

'*If* we reach him,' said Arora. 'Until then, it stays with me.'

Marian locked eyes with the scavenger. 'You know I could take that from you, as easy as taking a breath.'

'You wouldn't be breathing if it wasn't for me!' Arora snapped, glaring back at her. 'Take a step closer and you can find your own way across the wastes.'

Finally, Marian showed her palms. 'Fine. But just remember, we all walk the same ground. Robin is the cure, for all of us. All right then, let's get underway. Before it gets too hot.'

As the morning had drawn on, the temperature had risen steadily, the heat haze now making the plain swim like liquid. Looking out at it, considering the journey ahead, Marian's sense of destiny wavered, and she suffered a stab of doubt. Just the three of them. On foot. What if they got caught in another glass storm? What else might lay in wait between here and Nottingham? Would she ever see Rex and Robin again?

Yes – you will, she told herself. *What you told Arora is true – nothing can resist you or keep you apart from the ones you love.*

As the three of them picked up their packs and headed west, towards the boundary of the Giants' Graveyard, a noise made Marian pause. It was coming from behind that fallen tree trunk. At first, it sounded like the scrabbling of claws. But now it was a soft mewing. Like an animal in distress. Or . . . a child in tears.

Telling the others to wait, Marian walked around the trunk. And there, sitting with her knees pulled up to her chest, her face buried in her hands, was the goddess of the forest. She was in human form, and small – girl-shaped. With her fox-red hair spilling around her like a cloak, leaving only glimpses of her pale skin exposed, she might have been an ordinary orphan, abandoned to the wastes.

'You're leaving, aren't you?' she sobbed, as Marian stood over her. 'Go on then – see if I care! Leave me. Everyone else always has!'

Marian looked back at the ancient tree stump, then swept her gaze around the Giants' Graveyard, looking at the corpses scattered about.

'You shouldn't stay here,' she said, 'not all alone.'

'He'll come back – you'll see!' the goddess sobbed. 'He needs me. I look after him.'

'Robin?' Marian shook her head. 'He's not coming back.'

'How do you know? Where's he going to go?'

'I don't know. But whatever happens . . . he won't be coming back here.'

At this, the goddess buried herself deeper in her hair, wailed into her hands. Marian watched her shudder and shake like a lost child. Like a child woken by nightmares.

'You can't stay here,' she heard herself say. 'You . . . should come with us.'

Abruptly, the goddess stopped crying. As she raised her head, her hair fell away from her face and her burn-scars glistened. She blinked, her eyes slow and puffy.

'You mean it?' she murmured. 'You'd take me with you? Wouldn't I be a burden?' She smiled weakly. 'Wouldn't I cause mischief?'

Seeing her canine teeth – that fox-like smile – Marian shivered. Part of her knew it was insane, inviting the goddess to join them. But another part of her looked down at this scared, scarred little being, all alone in this bone-white graveyard, and she knew she could not leave her here.

And now this part of Marian was reaching down . . . feeling the warm trembling touch of the goddess as their hands met . . . and she was helping her to her feet. Then she walked back towards the others, and the goddess came with her, sniffling, rubbing at her eyes.

Both Arora and Lucas stared at the goddess as the group came together. Lucas looked so startled that Marian feared he was going to turn and flee, and his sister would follow.

'This is new territory for us all,' she told the twins. 'But it's like I told you, this is bigger than us. We don't need to understand. We just need to play our part. The rest will take care of itself. Arora, do you hear me? We need to get underway.'

Finally, Arora snapped out of her wide-eyed stupor and

she headed across the Giants' Graveyard, dragging her brother with her. Marian went next, with the sniffling goddess trailing along behind.

They reached the wall of vegetation and in single file crawled through one of the breaches cut by the Sheriff's men. Then they moved out onto the dazzling plain, the twins wrapped in their sand-coloured robes, Marian keeping her head low and her hood raised.

As they went onwards, she glanced back at the goddess. Already she had made a full recovery from her distress, stopping here and there to pick up stones, gasping and gazing around her in delight, as if all this was some wonderful game.

You couldn't just abandon her, Marian reassured herself. *Besides, she still has a part to play too, she must do.*

A series of sounds arose from behind them. They all stopped to look back, staring at the wall of vegetation.

It was collapsing in on itself. Wilting and withering before their eyes. With slithering, sucking sounds, the briars and the ferns and the vines mulched down into the ground, turning brown as they decomposed. Within moments there was almost nothing left, just a few rotting remnants and some leaflitter scattering in the breeze.

Marian could now see the ancient tree stump at the heart of the graveyard. Its greenery had likewise collapsed into mulch, leaving behind nothing but bare deadwood.

'This phase is finished,' she said, while the twins gawped and the goddess giggled unnervingly. 'This place has served its purpose. Now we need to look forwards.'

So saying, beckoning for Arora to scout their trail, she led her strange fellowship deeper into the wastes, and whatever her fate held in store.

IX. The Coming Storm

Using the flat of his sword, Kit slapped the rump of the messenger's horse. With a snort, the beast ran away into the scrublands, disappearing into the long grass and the gorse. Gathering his wolf-skin cloak around him, he went back to the others. There was scant cover here – a mere ribbon of trees bordering an old holloway. The rebel peasants were staying out of sight as best they could, their eyes following Kit as he passed.

'Organize a watch,' he said to Midge. 'Send scouts out to those hills. I can't say how long we're going to be here, and I don't want rangers catching us unawares.'

As Midge moved away to carry out his orders, Kit went down into the holloway. Ira was already here, in the gloom beneath the elm trees, kneeling on the soft ground.

'Well?' Kit asked.

'Don't rush me,' Ira said, her forehead creased in concentration. 'Elfen lost a finger once, trying to open one of these.'

In front of her was a strongbox, banded with iron. It was studded with locks, but these would be dummies, booby-trapped, and Ira ignored them. Instead, she had both hands under the box and was gently tipping it side to side, front to back. From inside, Kit heard the faint sound of an iron ball rolling against wood. While Kit began to pace, Ira went on patiently tipping the box, lowering one ear, listening, guiding the ball through its invisible maze. Finally there was a click, a clunk, and the clasps sprang open.

'There – got it!' Ira said, grinning, sitting back. 'Told you I could do it.'

While Kit knelt at her side, she lifted the lid of the strongbox. Inside were a dozen or more scrolls, each sealed with the Sheriff's emblem of a wolf's head. Ira broke one seal, Kit another, and they unrolled both scrolls on the ground. Squinting in the gloom of the holloway, Kit saw that they were both covered in dense, arcane symbols.

'What do you think?' Kit said.

'I can try.' Ira rubbed at her eyes. 'I wish Sonskya was here. She was better at these than I'll ever be. But these crossed swords, we've seen those before, and this skull. So there's something to work with.'

'Do what you can. I'll go and see what our friend has to say.'

Kit stood and went to the Sheriff's messenger. Bound hand and foot, he was hanging upside down, the vine-rope slung over the branch of a tree, the free end pegged into the ground. Flanking him were two enormous figures. One was Much Millerson; the other was the greenhorn that the other outlaws had taken to calling Little John.

With his wolf-head cowl raised and his head lowered, Kit approached with measured steps, allowing the messenger to stare and stare, his fear swelling until he was physically writhing, like a worm on a hook. Coming to a stop, Kit raised his head and let the man look into his eyes.

'Wh-who are you?' the man gabbled. 'Y-you're not the blind bowman.'

'You're right, I'm not,' Kit growled. 'I'm something much worse. The first Robin Hood was shaped by the forest. He contained light, as well as shadow. I was forged in the wastes. I am the wrath of the Earth. Tell me what I need to know or you will experience the full truth of this.'

'I-I told you – I told these men,' the messenger shuddered, 'I don't know what's in the box! Messages! I don't know what they say!'

'Where were you told to deliver them? How many other riders did he send?'

'P-please – if you even knew what he'd do to me!'

'You have nothing more to fear from the Sheriff,' Kit said evenly. 'You've lived your life in his shadow. Now you pass beyond his reach. There is no way on this Earth you are leaving this place alive. So you may speak freely,' he said, as the man shook all over. 'Depending on what you tell me, your suffering need not be prolonged.' He nodded towards Little John. 'In his past life, this man was a butcher. He can snap your neck so you'll barely know it. Or . . . he can remove your skin, strip by strip, while you are yet still living. So, which is it to be . . . ?'

Sobbing, hopeless, the man's resistance broke then and he began to gabble, listing the garrison commanders to whom he was ordered to deliver his missives. He told Kit that a score of other riders had been dispatched, sufficient to visit every garrison, fortress and outpost in the Sheriffdom. The man had begun to repeat himself, and talk drivel, when Ira called out behind him.

Nodding to Little John, Kit turned and went back to her. As he knelt at her side, she met his eyes. Her face was pale.

'They've found it, Kit,' she said quietly. 'They know where it is.'

After his interrogation of the messenger, Kit already dreaded what was coming, but even so, a tightness rose up in his throat so he could barely speak the word.

'Gaia.'

Ira nodded shakily, the scroll taut in her rigid fingers as she stared down at it. 'The gods only know how – but it says so right here. He's calling in the troops, from all across the shires. He intends to send an army into the wastes.' She looked up and her eyes met his. 'This is it, Kit. They're coming.'

Leaving Ira, Kit strode out of the holloway.

'On your feet, all of you,' he called to his outlaw army. 'Jack, Midge, fetch in the sentries, and be quick.'

'So then, it begins,' he announced, once all the recruits were assembled. 'The Sheriff has located our refuge. The Last Forest. The only place left where any of us can truly be free. Where we can breathe as the Earth breathes. The Sheriff intends to raze the forest to the ground. In order to stop him, we will pay a high price. Many of us – perhaps all – will lose our lives. Those of you who would turn back should do so now.'

His makeshift warriors gripped their homemade weapons and barely blinked, not one of them uttering a word of dissent. He knew then, truly, that these people inhabited a world beyond doubt – beyond courage and fear – in which there was only one thing left to lose.

'It was my intention to take you to Robin Hood's Cave, to equip you with proper blades and train you in their use,' he went on. 'But there is no time. You must stand or fall by your fury alone. I trust it will be enough. So then, steel yourselves, we march fast. We must reach Gaia before the enemy, or all will be lost.'

X. Cheating Death

'We need shade,' Arora said. 'That gulley we passed – we should head back.'

'We're not stopping,' Marian said. 'We've barely made any progress.'

'We've come two leagues, at least. Too far in this heat.'

'What's wrong with you?' Marian said. 'You've spent your whole life scouring the wastes.'

'And I didn't survive this long by staying out in the midday sun. It'll bake us in our skins.'

Marian kept going, regardless. For the past hour she had put up with this – Arora bleating about rest and refuge. It wasn't that hot, was it? She held out her bare hands and saw they were reddening with sunburn. Strange, she didn't yet feel any pain.

Well, what of it? she thought, quickly pushing the idea aside. *You're toughening up against the elements, that's all.*

Keeping her cloak wrapped close, her hood raised, she trudged onwards. Had they really covered two leagues? With each step, her body insisted she was in motion. Yet just look at that dazzling plain, unchanging and never-ending; every time she lifted her head her eyes vowed she was going nowhere. That she was marching in place. Or might even be moving backwards. What might the Sheriff be doing to Robin while she was locked in this endless hell? Was Rex safe?

'This is ludicrous,' Arora grumbled behind her. 'We'll all get sun-fever.'

'I think you're right, sis,' Lucas mumbled. 'I . . . don't feel well.'

'Right, that's it,' Arora snapped, spinning in place, taking hold of her brother. 'Come on, Lucas, we're heading back to that gulley.'

'Back?' Marian said. 'You can't!'

'Just watch us,' Arora called over her shoulder. 'You do what you like.'

Marian stood and watched the twins draw away. What now? Should she continue alone? They were heading due east. It was easy enough to navigate whilst the sun blazed. But what if the sky should cloud over? She might wander this wilderness for days and get nowhere.

Scanning the ground ahead, her eyes came to rest on the vixen-goddess. In her guise as a young girl, she was kneeling upon the bare earth, poking at something with a stick. In contrast to the twins, the goddess had bounded along with enthusiasm. Sometimes she had skipped so far ahead that Marian had begun to suspect she had left them for good. But always she came running back to show them some sparkling shard of glass she had found, or a serpent's skin, or a sand lizard.

As Marian approached, she saw the goddess was now kneeling next to an overturned rock.

'Fire ants,' she grinned. 'My favourite. Watch how they pop!'

The goddess lifted a piece of sand-glass, which she used to focus the sun's rays upon the frantic insects. They began to explode in tiny flares, while the goddess laughed.

'Strange to think I used to be afraid of you,' Marian said. 'You were only ever playing. It's just what you do.'

'It's all a game,' the goddess giggled, as more insects burst into flame. 'Why do so few of you figure that out?'

'Do you know your way across the wastes?' Marian said, kneeling. 'Could you show me the way to the city?'

The goddess looked at her quizzically, her golden eyes sparkling. 'City?' she said slowly, as if tasting the word on her tongue.

Marian shook her head. 'Never mind.' She stood and turned away, while the goddess went back to her game. 'The others are sheltering. I suppose I'll join them.'

By the time Marian reached the gulley, Lucas was asleep. Arora put one finger to her lips as Marian entered the shade beneath the rock overhang.

'He's burning up. And it's your fault,' Arora hissed, glaring. 'We stayed out in the sun too long. Well, now he'll rest as long as he needs.'

She wetted her scarf from her waterskin before pressing it to her brother's forehead. Marian saw now that Lucas's face was pale, and his breathing was shallow and uneven. Was his sister right: was he simply in the grip of sun-fever?

Arora had told her what had happened: how she used the blood of the wolf god to heal a wound that otherwise would have killed her brother. Marian thought about that now as she watched Lucas struggle for breath, beads of sweat standing out on his cheeks and neck. An unwelcome idea tried to swim to the surface, but she held it under.

You've been doing that a lot today, she told herself as she found a place to settle back in the shade, her back against the shingle. *Sooner or later you'll have to face facts.*

But not yet. For now she would rest. Perhaps Arora was right after all: they had trekked too far beneath that blazing sun. Because suddenly she could barely keep her eyes open. Well then, why was she even trying? What a relief, while the outside world quivered with heat, and these deep shadows sat cool and still, to pillow her head on her backpack and drift into a dreamless sleep . . .

When she awoke, with a start, the world outside was dark – and someone was screaming—

Reflexively, as she scrabbled upright, she drew her boot knife. Then she froze, blinking into the gloom.

It was Arora who was screaming.

She was crouching over her brother. His eyes were still closed and his breathing came in rapid spasms, as if he were trapped in a vicious nightmare. He groaned and shuddered in pain. As Marian's eyes adjusted further, she saw his clothing was stained black-red. They were soaked in blood.

Arora was now tearing at his clothing. As she peeled the rags away from his sticky flesh, she screamed once more, then moaned in anguish. Because Lucas's midriff was split open, his innards glistening.

'No – no – how?' Arora groaned. 'He was healed – he was whole!'

She scrabbled for her backpack, tore it open.

'He needs more – that's it – that's all it is. I didn't give him enough.' She was now holding the amphora containing the blood of the wolf-god. 'Hold still, hush,' she murmured to her brother. 'You're going to be all right. I've got more of the stuff here. This is what you need.'

Having removed the stopper, she carefully dribbled the blood onto his wound. It hissed and bubbled where it fell upon the torn flesh. And while Lucas groaned, the flesh began to writhe and spasm. The wound folded closed. Within moments it was done, Lucas's midriff once again whole and hale. He blinked up at his sister with watery eyes. She lay across him and hugged him and cried.

'Why?' she murmured, when she eventually sat upright. 'He

266

was fine, he was healed. Why did it happen again? He'll be all right now, though, won't he?'

She was staring at Marian now, with a pleading look in her eyes. But Marian had no answers to give. Her mind was once again filling with questions of her own – questions too vast and frightening to face.

Before anyone else could speak, the goddess of the forest suddenly appeared. She was dangling from the rock overhang, her head upside down, her fox-red hair spilling to the ground. Instantly, Marian saw that she had changed. Her girlish features had matured; if she were truly human she might now be eleven or twelve years old. And when she fixed her gaze on Marian, her golden eyes were knowing and mischievous.

'Sleepyheads,' she said with a laugh. 'Awake at last. Come – quick. The moon is rising. It's a new world! Who knows what we'll find?'

With that, as graceful as a snake, she slipped back the way she came.

The goddess is changing – as she always does, Marian said to herself, while the twins stared at one other in silence. *By the time we reach the city, what might she have become?*

But that was merely one more thing not to think about. One more question to bury. In any case, no amount of thinking would change the future, one way or the other. Answers would come, or they wouldn't. What mattered now was to act.

She rose to her feet, shouldered her backpack. 'Lucas is healed. The sun is gone. So then, we go on.'

Her tone left absolutely no scope for doubt or dissent. As disturbed as they might be, the twins stood as one and followed her out onto the moonlit plain, and in troubled silence they continued their torturous trek towards Nottingham.

XI. Idiot God

The wilderness was unnervingly still. Marian had become accustomed to the wastes as a place of turbulence – of sudden gales and dust gyres and sandstorms. Tonight, though, as far as she could see across the plains, not a mote of dust stirred. Bathed in bluish moonlight, it lay frozen, its surface cracked and glistening, like a lake locked in ice.

Something this way comes.

Marian's own thoughts were shockingly loud amid the hush.

The forest was always like this, before the Sheriff's men invaded. As if it was holding its breath. It could sense the coming violence, even before we did.

The wastes are the same, she realized now, as she trekked onwards. *They know we're nearing the end. The final storm approaches.*

'We need to go quicker,' she called over her shoulder. 'Who knows what's happening in the city while we're out here dragging our feet.'

It was futile. Arora and Lucas were lost in their own private nightmare. Ever since leaving that gulley, the twins had barely uttered a word, had hardly lifted their eyes from the ground as they shuffled onwards.

They're holding their breath too, Marian thought, looking back at them. *They know it will come again, and the waiting is torture.*

Marian looked beyond the twins to the vixen-goddess, who was moving even slower. Her girlhood was long past now and her mood had turned sour. She dragged her feet through the dust, kicking at stones, looking mean and sullen.

'If we don't hurry, all this will be in vain,' she called out to them all. 'Can't you feel it? We're running out of time!'

Getting no response, she shook her head in exasperation and trudged onwards. The night drew on, and the others lagged ever further behind. She cursed them beneath her breath, and repeatedly turned to berate them.

But at some point, as the moon rose higher and brightened, she found her own steps slowing. She gazed ahead, and stood in wonder, seduced by the eerie beauty of the plains. It was happening again – she could *see* Sherwood, just as it used to be. All around her were emperor oaks, hulking and majestic; queen beech, towering towards the heavens; groves and glades, glimmering bright and perfect.

She stopped and stared, moonstruck, at one particular sight. It was a lake, ringed by trees tall as temples. She felt she knew this place. Did it remind her of Elysium Glades, where she and Robin would go to be alone when they lived in Sherwood Forest? Perhaps. But even more so it made her think of Titan's Lake, one of the secret places from their childhood. It gleamed blue and frozen, just like in winter when they used to come here to skate upon the ice.

Marian was drawn towards the mirage. She knew it was a mirage, of course, yet some part of her did not know, or did not care. She was grinning, heading towards this place that came before everything else – before the cruelty and the separation and the loss. This place of first freedom. Of unadulterated joy.

As she hurried closer, she slipped back in time. She could *hear* their voices now – she and Robin as children – their laughter reverberating off the icebound lake. The vision had become so vivid that the doubting part of her admitted defeat. This *was* Titan's Lake – and *there* was Robin – look, kneeling at the water's edge! For the moment he was indistinct, half hidden by reeds, but it *was* him, it had to be!

'Robin – I'm here!'

Her own voice gave her a stab of fear. The fleeting suspicion that she was running mad. She had followed Robin into the Underearth, found his spirit there, but this was a different thing entirely – a net woven from yearning and desperation – a snare for mind and spirit, from which she might never escape.

But this shadow of fear could not live long against the blaze of her delight. She saw now that Robin was working at something in his lap – probably whittling fiddlesticks ready for a game! She laughed and called out to him.

But he didn't run to meet her, or even look up. And now she saw that something was wrong. He was wearing his wolf-pelt. He shouldn't be wearing that. Not yet. All that waited far in the future – after the blinding and the bloodletting and the rest of the horror.

In fact . . . as she ran closer, staring at him . . . was it even a wolf-skin he was wearing? It looked too bulky at the head. Those branches above him . . . they weren't branches at all . . . but antlers.

Marian's steps faltered. The moonlight shifted, and with a slumping in her heart as heavy as grief, she saw this was not Robin. It was an old man. Except, no – he was only part man. He was also part king stag, part forest. He was wearing a cloak woven from grass and vines, and on his antlered head sat a crown of thorns.

A short distance from him, Marian slumped to her knees. She had never met this being in person, but she knew well enough who he was. Robin had talked of him often. He was an ancient god of the forest. He was called Cernunnos.

'I presumed you perished in the flames,' she heard herself say, her voice ghostly in this ghostly place, the shades of the lake and the trees fading in and out of existence. 'I thought you'd have no more part to play.'

Cernunnos didn't even appear to detect her presence; he just went on working at the object he held in his lap.

Now she had a clearer view of the old god, she saw he was truly decrepit. His cloak of green was rotting and shot with holes, while his antlers were missing several tines. His skin was pale and drawn, and his busy fingers were thin as sticks.

'Perhaps you did die in the fire,' Marian murmured. 'Maybe you're just another figment.' She peered around her. 'I'm finding it hard to tell what's real and what's not. I'm no longer . . . what I was.'

Suddenly the old god laughed, startling her.

'Did I say something funny?'

Cernunnos laughed once more – a long, croaking cackle. Then he raised his head at last. He looked through her with eyes that were whitish and clouded, like sour milk.

'I don't even know what I'm doing here,' Marian said, getting to her feet. 'How did I let you distract me?'

'A distraction, am I?' the vagrant god croaked. 'I've been called worse. Yet here you are.'

'It was an accident – a misstep.'

The old god cackled.

'You're not what I'm looking for,' she said.

This made Cernunnos laugh louder than ever – a mad bellowing roar.

'Worry not – I know your heart, better than you know it yourself. I know what you truly seek. And I can help you find it! Yes, yes indeed – I can guide your path.'

'You? Guide me? How? In any case . . . why would you even want to help me? After . . . after everything we did.'

'That's the dance!' the old god cackled. 'I cannot help myself, and neither can you. It is in my nature to give, and it is in yours to take – and take and take and take! Here, look, take *this*!'

He held out his hand. Resting in his palm was the object he had been shaping. It was a ring, fashioned from antler bone.

'Pieces of old gods hold great power, even now.' Cernunnos grinned, showing rotten gums and cracked teeth. 'I gave one of these to a young man, once, and it helped him – it did, it did!'

Marian stared at the ring, stepped forward to study it more closely.

'I wouldn't touch that if I were you,' said a voice behind her.

The vixen-goddess was standing with her arms crossed, looking mean.

Cernunnos chuckled. 'My sister never did think much of my gifts. Hers were always more . . . grandiose. But trust me, this is just what you need. It will take you where you yearn to go. It will speed your course, swift as an arrow!'

'He lost his mind when they took his forest,' the goddess said, tossing her hair. 'I wouldn't accept anything from him.'

Marian turned on the goddess. 'What's it to you? You can't show me the way.' She stared back the way they had come, picked out the tiny stumbling figures of the twins. 'Those two get slower by the hour. If he's willing to help me, why shouldn't he?'

The goddess shrugged, turned her back. 'Do what you like. As you say, why should I care.'

As she was saying this, a shrill noise cut across the plain. It was the twins. Lucas was wailing in agony, while Arora shrieked with anguish.

'It's happening again,' Marian murmured to herself. 'They'll never make it to the city. Even if they could, they'd be too slow.'

So saying, she turned back to Cernunnos and she snatched the antler ring, while he grinned at her madly.

'I don't expect a thank you,' he called after her as she stormed back towards the twins, stashing the ring in her pack as she went. 'All I ask is that you come back soon. It's the dance, don't forget! Take, take, take, give, give, give!'

By the time she reached Lucas, his screaming had ceased and his wound was healed. But the terror of it still showed in his eyes. His sister was kneeling at his side, her hands shaking where they gripped the vessel containing the god's blood.

As Marian joined them, Arora glared at her resentfully. 'Why doesn't it happen to you? You took the blood too. Why don't you need more?'

Marian shook her head. 'The goddess talked about deeds undone. Maybe . . . this world isn't finished with me yet.'

'What's that supposed to mean?'

'You know what it means, sis,' said Lucas, sitting up. 'You were the one talking about destiny. Well – it's obvious, isn't it? The blood wasn't meant for me.'

'No – don't get up! You need to rest.'

'I'll rest soon enough,' he said grimly, steadying himself on his feet. 'In the meantime, you wanted to reach the city. So let's get on with it.'

He staggered away. After shooting another accusing glare at Marian, Arora went after him, looking frantic.

As Marian followed, she heard in the distance a screeching, bellowing yowl. It sounded like a fox fighting, together with a grunting that might have been a stag or might have been the laughter of a mad old man.

Already, her encounter with Cernunnos had taken on the texture of dream. But when she opened her pack, reached inside, there was the ring the old god had given her, solid and real. She took it out. It weighed heavy in her hand, as if it was

273

made of lodestone, not antler bone. Would it really show her the way to go?

She pictured the ancient god. His rheumy eyes, his idiot grin. She drew back her arm, preparing to throw the ring into the sand. But then she watched the twins, Lucas dragging his footsteps like the walking dead. She could not rely on them much longer.

What other choice did she have?

Pieces of old gods hold great power, even now.

She thrust the ring back into her pack as she hurried after the twins.

XII. Angel of Mercy

'I can't keep going through that, sis, I can't!'
   'I know it hurts. We'll learn to live with it.'
'It isn't the pain. That's not what I'm talking about. It's the waiting. Mortal fear, sis. Watching the sun set and *knowing* I'm going to die.'
'But you don't die!'
'The fear is the same! A person should only suffer that once. Not night after night. I can't keep going through it, I can't!'

A short distance away, Marian stood listening to the twins. As dusk had fallen across the plain, it had happened once again. Lucas had dropped to the ground and his wound had burst open, as raw and ghastly as a freshly dug grave.

Arora had been ready – immediately she doused him with god's blood, and his flesh was healed. There was no remedy, though, for his deeper wounds, Marian was now certain of that. He remained stricken on the ground, inconsolable, while his sister's own anguish rose to a fever pitch.

'You think it's fun for me, seeing you like that?' Arora was saying now. She put a hand to her own midriff. 'You think I don't feel it?'

'I know you do, sis,' Lucas said more quietly, 'and that's another thing I can't stand. I can't keep putting you through it.'

'Don't you dare put it on me! I'm not the one talking about giving up.'

While they went on pleading and cajoling, Marian hesitated. Finally, she went and knelt at their side.

'I can ease the pain,' she told them. 'I can take away your fear.'

Arora glared at her. 'How?'

Marian reached inside her backpack, took out a mushroom, its cap a vivid red.

'Oh, you'd love that, wouldn't you,' Arora said through gritted teeth. 'He's slowing you down – so just get rid of him!'

'It would be quick, and painless.'

'For you!'

'Sis, listen—'

'No – I'm not listening – not to you or to her!' Arora hissed at Marian. 'Get away from us! I see what you are!'

'She's trying to help us,' Lucas said, sitting upright. 'We need this.'

'You'd do anything to get your own way!' she snarled at Marian. 'Now here's your chance!'

'You're wrong,' Marian said evenly. 'Maybe that was true once. But I'm not what I was. This is for him. And for you. If you should choose.'

So saying, she laid the mushroom on the ground, then moved a short distance away. She heard Arora cajoling, begging, and Lucas pleading.

'Please, sis, you're making this harder for me. You think I want to do it? You think I'm not afraid? I . . . I can't do it without you. I've never done anything without you . . .'

Marian stared into the distance, trying to think about nothing, but visited by memories of Robin and Rex. She hugged her arms, suddenly feeling very lonely and afraid out here on this deathly plain.

At some point, she realized Lucas was calling to her. She went back and knelt alongside the twins. Arora looked away, wiped at her face. Lucas blinked at her slowly, his eyes slow and puffy.

'What's it like,' he said quietly, 'the other side?'

Marian closed her eyes, tried once more to summon anything from those lost hours after the heretic hunter struck her – and once again she found only blankness. But that wasn't the only time she had crossed over, was it? She had eaten the goddess's mushroom, and sunk into the Underearth.

She cast her memory back to those spirit realms. She recalled the frightening wereforest, with its icy shadows. The Elysian greenwood, bathed in eternal springtime. She remembered a star-field, and the musical silence that connected everything. Except . . . was she recalling that correctly? They weren't stars exactly, were they? And the word *music* didn't fit, any more than the word *silence*.

Finally, she shook her head. 'I can't even begin to describe it. Besides, I think . . . it will be different for everyone. But I can tell you one thing. I found Robin there, waiting. In the end . . . that was all that mattered.'

Arora turned to look at her then, her eyes red and intent. Eventually, she said quietly: 'Leave us. We want to be alone.'

This time Marian moved further off. She could still hear the twins' voices, but not their words. Once or twice Arora raised her voice, but increasingly she spoke in quieter tones. She heard both of them crying, and the occasional incongruous laugh.

Staring out across the plain, Marian caught the edge of movement – a reddish streak – the vixen-goddess flitting away? Marian had seen no clear sign of her, nor heard a word, since her encounter with Cernunnos. Had she forsaken Marian because she had accepted a gift from her brother?

She opened her pack and took out the god-ring. Without daring to hesitate, desperate to distract herself if nothing else, she slipped it onto her finger. Instantly, the night shifted, appeared to spin in place, Marian catching her balance. Once the giddiness passed it was as though everything had settled into a clearer shape. Marian looked due east. Yes, that was the way she needed to go. She felt that in her bones, as if an invisible thread were tugging her in that direction.

She turned back to the twins. They were whispering now, barely audible. Then the voices stopped altogether and there was only the crying. Then that stopped too. Marian stood with the silence, and her own heartbeat. Finally, she returned to their side.

Lucas's head was resting in his sister's lap, his eyes closed. Arora stared out across the plain, her face grey and drawn.

'You know, you're fortunate, in a way,' Marian said gently. 'The day of the Great Fire, Robin was ripped away from me. We couldn't say goodbye. For years, I didn't even know if he was alive or dead. The not knowing was agony.'

She trailed off, meaning to say more, but not finding the words.

After a while, Arora said in a dead tone: 'I'm not going any further with you.'

'I know,' Marian said. She touched the ring on her finger. 'I can find my own way.'

'You want to take the blood.'

Marian nodded.

Arora looked at her. 'I'll make a trade. One of those mushrooms.'

Marian shook her head. 'Your brother wouldn't want that.'

'Don't you talk about Lucas,' Arora said, without passion. 'You didn't know him.' She picked up a nearby rock, held it over the amphora. 'Will you give me what I want, or not?'

Sighing, Marian took another red mushroom from her pack. She tossed it to the scavenger. Arora put down the rock and handed Marian the blood of the wolf-god.

Marian stood to move away, then paused.

'Your brother feels a long way away right now. But it won't stay that way, trust me. He is you, just the same as you're him. That's real. That's the most real thing there is.'

These words may not even have reached Arora. The scavenger went on staring across the plain, one hand resting on her brother's head, the other gripping the deadly fungus.

There was nothing more Marian could do for her. It was Arora's path to tread. Marian must look once more to her own fate.

The fate of Robin, and of Rex.

With the ring of the gods upon her finger, her rightful way stretching ahead as clear as a summer's road, she set out on the last leg of her journey alone.

XIII. Devastators

The waiting had been torture. But now, at long last, they were underway. Following days of delay, while they waited for garrison troops to come in from the outposts, Rex's war party was finally assembled and provisioned and on the move. Tinkers and tradesmen and carters hurried to clear the roadway as the cavalcade came clattering and rumbling out through the city gates.

Rex turned in his saddle to look back at the column of soldiers, all of them riding the finest, fittest horses to be found anywhere in the Sheriffdom. The rangers' half-armour gleamed blackly in the dawn light, the wolf-head insignia polished to a fine sheen upon their chests. Guy of Gisbourne and his warrior monks rode in the vanguard, tall and implacable as Fate itself.

Most impressive of all, to Rex's eyes, were the war machines. Six of them. Catapults and trebuchets. Huge engines exuding power, even at rest. Yoked to huge draught horses, the vehicles crunched along the cracked Roman roads. Behind them came six long carts, all loaded with incendiaries.

Once again we will bring cleansing fire to the world.

As he remembered his father's words, Rex had a sudden vision of the near future: he pictured the war machines hurling flaming missiles into Gaia, the Last Forest erupting in fire. And he envisaged too the aftermath: the land wiped clean, only ash eddying in the breeze.

How had this fateful act fallen to him? What was it even meant to achieve?

He turned his head and looked towards Gallows Field. Labourers had been working day and night to construct Robin Hood's pyre. By now, the construction was so massive that they were using cranes to winch timbers and stacks of firewood into place.

The greatest fire since the forest burned. The flames must be seen across the Sheriffdom.

Why? To what purpose? Justice? Vengeance? Would it bring back his mother?

It was happening again. This was what Rex had endured, over and over, ever since telling his father he would lead an army to Gaia. He had lain awake in his bed, or paced the White Tower, asking himself such questions, tormented by the idea that there had been some terrible error – a mistake he could not name or even begin to rectify.

And now, as the war force surged away from the city, rumbling like thunder, this doubt and confusion spiked, until he was almost dizzy with it. His mind took him back to the start of all this – that dreadful night when he followed his father into the slums, and they caught those shire-folk at their wildwood ritual.

They are the enemy. Your enemy.

He pictured those pitiful peasants gathered in their make-shift hall. He saw, too, Robin Hood hanging in his cage, and his mother's face, and Alpha Johns lying in a pool of lifeblood, all of it swirling together, making him grind his teeth and grip the saddle to hold his balance.

In that moment, Rex was horribly afraid. But what was the true source of his fear, and his fury? Who was he supposed to hate?

He looked to his right-hand side. Guy of Gisbourne was staring at him, his eyes black behind his mask. Rex faced forwards, flicked the reins of his horse. He kept his gaze set dead ahead, but he felt the heretic hunter studying him still. Sir Guy could sense weakness, Rex had always thought, the way animals can sense fear.

Well then, Rex would show him no weakness. He vowed, from this moment onwards, to cast off all hesitation and doubt. It was all futile in any case. If ever there was a chance to turn back, or choose a different path, that time was long past.

With the war force behind him, feeling now its great weight pushing him forwards, he knew truly that his fate was sealed.

XIV. Shades of Sherwood

This blasted plain must truly stretch on for ever. As she stared into the empty distance, Marian caressed the ring Cernunnos had given her, turning it on her finger. The god-gift was even more potent than she had first imagined. Not only did it show her the way to go, lighting her path as unfailingly as a lodestar, it also sped her progress, energizing her and quickening her steps, allowing her to cover league after league swiftly and tirelessly.

Yet still, the same vast emptiness stretched out ahead of her. Surely by now, having trekked night and day, she must be nearing the edge of the wastes. But narrowing her eyes, staring into the distance, she saw no hint of a roadway, or habitation, or any other sign that she might be approaching the boundary.

Another day was coming to a close, the sunset painting the plain in shades of orange and red. An almost-full moon was rising, adding its mysterious shimmer to the deepening dusk. In this strange half-light, the plain appeared to ripple and morph, revealing its subtler layers. Once more Marian gazed upon the Spirit of Sherwood, trees appearing to stretch away as far as the eye could see.

This phantom forest was more vivid than ever – so real it seemed to twist perspective. Suddenly it seemed to Marian she was walking high above the ground – looking across the treetops, just as she had once done standing atop her Sky Palace in the boughs of Major Oak.

The sensation was vertiginous; she stopped to catch her balance and her normal viewpoint was restored. But as twilight deepened into night, and moonbeams cast their purple shadows, she suffered more distortions. One moment it was as though she were moving backwards, ghostly pine trees marching past her on both sides. Then she was walking forwards once more, but time sped up, the moon sweeping upwards on its arc, the ground rushing beneath her feet so swiftly she might be a hawk on the wing.

Once more she stopped, gathering her breath and her wits. She held up her left hand, peered at the antler-bone ring. Was the god-gift causing these warps in perception? She wriggled it off her finger – and instantly regretted it. The wastelands spun around her, the night reconfigured, and by the time it came to rest she was more bewildered than she had ever felt in her life. Truly, in that moment, standing all alone on that empty plain, she could not have identified east from west, left from right, barely knew up from down.

She had experienced being lost in the great forest, and it was always horrendous. That sickliness that crept from groin to belly to chest. This was the same, only a hundred times more intense. Out on this endless, featureless plain, with no real point of reference, nothing solid to anchor her, she was *truly* lost, and it was terrifying.

She was so frantic to put the ring back on that she dropped it, her panic spiking as it rolled away into the dust. Gasping, she scrabbled after it, and with blessed relief saw it gleam in the moonlight. Snatching it up, she thrust it back onto her finger.

Again the night lurched, spun, and once it settled, it was as though invisible pieces had slotted back into place. She once again sensed her correct path unwinding across the wastes. She hurried on her way.

But as the night drew on, she once more began to suffer doubts. This trek would never end. She would be doing this, taking one step after the next, for eternity. Even though she felt no fatigue, her feet and legs and then every inch of her became numb, until she might be floating bodiless.

She must be dead. Where else could this be but Purgatory? Look at this place. This limitless, lifeless plain. Here and there she glimpsed the Spirit of Sherwood. But the ghost-trees were no longer shimmering with autumn finery; rather they were bare skeletons: the wildwood in the grip of midwinter.

And now there was something else . . . something she didn't want to look directly towards. It was a phantom glade, filled with shadowy figures. The figures were people. The shades of people. There was a ring of them, kneeling, their hands pressed to the Earth. At their centre was a woman as gaunt as the wilderness.

As Marian walked past, watching from the corner of her eye, she had the chilling impression she recognized this woman. Her mind groped for a name, dredging it up from a different lifetime . . .

Blodwyn Kage.

Surrounding her were her wildwood warriors: the outlaw band once known as Hydra's League. Marian shuddered, hurried onwards. These people perished twelve years ago in the Great Fire. They could not truly be there.

Yet they appeared so real.

She could even *hear* them, she suddenly realized. Yes, they were chanting something, in unison, their voices rising ever louder on the dead air.

'The wolf did not fail.'

'The wolf did not fail.'

That was all they kept saying – this one mantra, over and over.

'The wolf did not fail.'

What does it mean?

'It doesn't mean anything,' Marian answered herself, aloud. 'It doesn't even exist. Your mind is playing tricks.'

'So you're still clinging to that,' a voice said at her shoulder.

Despite her sneering tone, Marian was almost glad to have the vixen-goddess sneak up on her. Anything was better than wandering out here all alone, with only ghosts for company.

'They don't exist,' Marian insisted, as she hurried away from the shades of Hydra's League, their haunting mantra drifting after her. 'It's just another form of doubt. Another test.'

'You're quite certain of that?' the goddess said, slouching after her.

'Yes. My mind hates this place. This emptiness. So it's filling it with things I once knew – or half remember. Or it's trying to distract itself, or – I don't know, and I don't care! All I know is, I need to get off this plain or I'll go mad.'

At this, the goddess laughed. 'So then – madness it shall be.'

'Is that why you're back, to taunt me?'

'What else is there to do out here? I thought I'd play with my brother for a bit.' She yawned. 'He used to be fun to tease. Now he hardly seems to notice. And you're no better.'

'Should I have left you behind in the Giants' Graveyard?'

'It's all the same. I thought you were going to speed the arrow. Raise hell, like before. But now you're just going in circles.'

At this, Marian suffered a stab of fear. That lost-child feeling creeping up from her groin into her midriff.

'I am not going in circles,' she growled, marching away from the goddess. 'I'm going to the city. I'm going to Robin and Rex.'

'Whatever you say.' The goddess yawned once more as she walked at Marian's side.

'You don't know what you're talking about.' Marian touched the ring from Cernunnos. 'Your brother gave me this. It's showing me the way.'

'Oh yes – it certainly is,' the goddess said with a smirk. 'The only question is . . . the way to where?'

The sickly lost-fear intensified, her mind frantic.

I know your heart, better than you know it yourself.

I know what you truly seek.

As far as she could recall, she now realized with a jolt, neither she nor Cernunnos had specifically mentioned the city, nor Robin, nor Rex. Had Marian been so desperate to find the way that she had ignored the old god's actual words, in favour of what she wanted to hear? Did Cernunnos – dispossessed decrepit old god that he was – even know his own meaning?

'I told you not to accept gifts from him.' The goddess smiled, licking her lips, tasting Marian's mounting panic. 'But would you listen? Oh no. And now look . . . You're no further on than when you started.'

As she said this, Marian stumbled, almost fell to her knees. Because there ahead of her, taking shape amidst the moonbeams, was a startling mirage.

And it *was* a mirage – nothing more and nothing less – it *had* to be. Marian would prove it was! She would tear it to pieces with her bare hands – rip it to shreds like the moonlight and shadow she knew it to be!

She was running now towards the vision. It took the form of an island of trees. An emperor oak stood at its centre, looming ever higher as she stumbled and staggered closer. Surrounding the island, she now saw, was a wide ditch, growing out of which was a wall of briar and blackthorn.

'No – no – no! It isn't here!'

As she closed the final distance, she scooped up a rock. With a wail, she flung it at the illusion.

The rock did not pass through it, like sunlight through shadow. Instead, the woodland swallowed the rock with solid sounds of rustling greenery.

'No . . .' Marian whispered, the fight sucked out of her.

She fell to her knees at the edge of the ditch. She could no longer deny it. She was really here.

In front of her was Gaia. The Last Forest.

Gaia . . . which lay at the very centre of the wastes . . .

As distant from the city as the Giants' Graveyard.

'I can't do it,' Marian murmured to herself. 'I can't begin again from here. Even if I could, I'd be too late. I've failed them both.'

She had no idea how long she remained there like that, shrouded in black despair, her eyes closed and her forehead pressed to the unforgiving Earth.

But at some point something changed. Noises began to pierce her awareness, like stars pricking the firmament. They were noises that, like so many things since she'd entered the wastes, drifted to her like dreams from another lifetime. It started with a lone chirp, followed by a flurry of tweets, and then a surging wave of warbles and flutes and whistles.

She opened her eyes and sat up. Night had passed. The rising sun was glowing at the horizon. And Gaia had come alive with its dawn chorus – such an orchestra of wild noise as Marian had almost forgotten existed. A thousand times a thousand voices washed out of Gaia to roll across the wastes and rise up towards the heavens.

After spending so long in the soundless wastes, this was as shocking as it was glorious. Marian was spellbound – as though she was here witnessing the very first noise – the world building itself in sound even as she listened. And with all this, arising as unbidden as the sunrise, came strange and powerful thoughts.

Nothing's gone wrong. There's been no mistake. At this moment, you are exactly where you are supposed to be.

At her side, movement startled her. It was the vixen-goddess. She had come to kneel beside Marian. She had both hands pressed to her chest, above her heart. Her nostrils flared as she sniffed at the air, and she gasped.

'Oh yes, it's true – they come!'

'What?' Marian said.

'The wheel will turn after all.' The goddess grinned. 'Soon it will begin!'

'What are you talking about? Who's coming here? The outlaws?'

'Oh yes – and the other ones,' the goddess said, turning to look Marian in the eye. 'The clashing of worlds! And we are here to bear witness!'

With that, as quick as a vixen, with a flash of red hair, the goddess darted to the wall of thorns and, with a rustle, disappeared.

So Marian was left all alone, more bewildered than ever, feeling a thousand leagues from Robin and Rex, yet also harbouring that strange feeling that somehow, in some indescribable way, this was exactly where she was meant to be.

What could possibly have given her that idea? Why had blind fate led her back to the forest? Who did the goddess sense approaching? Where did her destiny lead from here?

XV. The Promised Land

'I see it! There it is!'

'Just a mirage, must be.'

'No – it's real!'

'Yes, it's there. Look! See?'

Shimmering with heat haze, as if viewed through the depths of time, Gaia had materialized on the distant plain. As it did so, Kit's peasant warriors, who until now had endured the long trek across the wastelands in near silence, began one by one to gasp their amazement and delight.

'It's all true. It exists!'

'Never thought I'd see it with my own eyes!'

'The forest lives!'

For Kit's part, the sight of Gaia brought with it the most profound relief of his life. He had forced the march as fast as he dared, not even pausing to cover their tracks, some of the younger recruits looking dead on their feet as they trekked league after league. Even at this pace, the journey back seemed to take an age, while the fear grew and grew inside Kit that they would be too late – that the Sheriff's troops would get there first – that they would arrive to find the last wildwood going up in flames.

But now this fear-fantasy dissolved like morning mist as he listened to the wonder of the peasants setting eyes on Gaia for the first time, and he led them all towards it with the familiar blessed sense of coming home.

As the last miles dropped away, and the wildwood loomed ever larger and more solid, the peasants' babble became hushed murmurs before lapsing into silent awe. They could hear the wildwood now – a yapping, yowling cacophony of life washing across the lifeless plain. They were close enough to see the leaves on the trees, glistening with rain after a recent cloudburst.

Kit continued to the wall of thorns, stood before it. Opening his palms, he spread his arms wide. Behind him, peasant warriors gasped as the vegetation parted, an archway forming with a soft wet slither.

Kit led the way into the opening, through the tunnel of undergrowth, across a vine-bridge that sprang up at his feet. A few of these grizzled desperadoes were weeping now as they followed him into the wildwood. They gazed around them at this moss-quilted paradise, alive with clouds of butterflies and warbling birdlife. Kit watched them closing their eyes, inhaling this lush green aroma that they remembered, perhaps, from their childhoods.

Kit knew then, listening to their sobs of joy, mixed with murmurs of loss and sadness, that thus far he had seen nothing of his peasant army. If he had thought them formidable before, they were now on home soil. Already he could feel them drawing fresh energy from it, and a renewed will to fight.

He led them all to a coppice of ash and daggerwood. This was where the outlaws came to craft quarterstaffs and fresh arrows.

'You all need rest,' he told them as they gathered, facing him. 'But that must wait. The Sheriff will bring war machines, as he did before when he besieged the forest. It is vital that we halt their progress. First we need to cut stakes. Much, Midge, show them what to do.'

Soon the rebel peasants had set to work, the knocking of axes and rasping of bowsaws reverberating through the wood. Meanwhile, Kit took himself off alone.

Twice since entering Gaia, tell-tale signs had caught his eye. They weren't much: a bent twig; a scuffed patch of moss. Anyone else might have dismissed them as the passage of a badger, or a fox. But Kit's forest-lore was acute; he knew every track and scat of every creature of the wild. And something here was out of place and significant.

Going to one knee, he ran his palm across a rock, detecting a faint crushing of the lichen on its surface. Yes, pressure had come down here, no doubt. The step had passed quickly, and lightly: his quarry was something swift-footed, at home in the woods . . .

A little further on, at the edge of a mire, he found a distinct footprint. This led him to a cracked stick, and a crushed fern, and more scuff marks on the bole of a tree. By now, he was certain: these signs had not been left by accident. They were a lure, drawing him onwards.

Entering a small glade, pine trees shadowy at its edge, he came to a standstill. A stream sparkled before disappearing into the gloom beneath the trees. A magpie cackled.

'So – I'm here,' he called out. 'Why don't you show yourself? What are you afraid of?'

'You know, I could kill you for wearing that skin,' a voice replied from the shadows. 'When I first saw you, I thought it was him.'

'Why the game of cat and mouse?'

'I wanted to talk to you alone.'

Finally, Marian appeared. Her grey-green eyes materialized first, before the rest of her stepped out into the light.

She looked very different from the last time Kit saw her. She still wore her cloak of silver and gold, but now it was so tattered and grimy it looked like the rags of a vagabond. A vicious bruise covered her left temple and cheek, rippling outwards like a blue and purple spiderweb. Where her skin was exposed it was sunburned and blistered.

'I thought the heretic hunter was after your blood. How did you escape? How did you find this place?'

'It wasn't my intention,' Marian said, coming to stand on the bank of the stream. 'I . . . got waylaid.' She stared into the trees, looking pensive and conflicted. 'Honestly . . . I don't know what to make of it. But I know one thing,' she said, meeting Kit's eyes once more. 'Robin is alive. I need to go to him. I want . . . I want you and the others to come with me.'

Kit shook his head. 'We're needed here. The Sheriff is sending an army.'

'You won't stand against it. Robin is our only hope.'

Again, Kit shook his head. 'For too long I thought like that. I was waiting and waiting for Robin to return. But this isn't about him. It can't be about one man.'

'You'd leave him to his fate?' Marian locked eyes with Kit. 'You know who he is. Who you are.'

Kit looked away. 'It makes no difference. It doesn't matter about me, or you. It's bigger than any of us. Robin understood that, didn't he?' He peered around him at the wildwood. 'You talk about saving Robin. But what would he even be without this? Would he even exist? Don't you see? Fighting for Robin and fighting for the forest are the same thing.'

All the while, Marian said nothing. She was no longer even looking at Kit. She had never expected him to leave with her, had she? Did she even truly want him to? Her request had been half-hearted, as if she no longer knew her own mind. Kit could almost believe this was not Marian at all, but some imposter wearing her skin.

'Wait here,' he said. 'I've got something that might help.'

When he returned, Marian had lowered herself to her knees, and had become very still. She was apparently watching her own reflection in the stream, the light playing across her expressionless face. Stepping across the water, Kit knelt with the objects he was carrying.

'The day of the Great Fire,' he said, laying them down, 'you dropped these. Ira and the others collected them. They kept them, all these years.'

Marian didn't even turn her eyes to look at the bow or the leather armour.

'I don't need them.'

'I've built an army,' Kit said. 'They're raw, but they've got a chance. If they were to see the wildwood queen in their ranks . . . it might tip the balance.'

Marian didn't stir, gave no indication she had even heard these last words. Kit stood, looked down at her. He had no idea what she must have endured all these years, or even since they last met. Perhaps the warrior queen of Sherwood truly was dead. In any case, she was only one person; he had far bigger concerns.

He went back across the stream and headed out of the glade, going to oversee the preparations for war, leaving Marian there on her knees, the shimmering of the stream reflected in her faraway eyes.

XVI. Warring Spirit

For the rest of the evening, and all through the night, while the moon shone its blessed chill on their labours, the rebels continued to construct their defences.

They carried armfuls of ironwood stakes out onto the plain. Each one was sharpened like a spear. They drove the butts of these stakes into cracks in the ground, slanting them outwards, creating barricades. Meanwhile, inside this outer ring, they began to dig trenches, using farm tools and swords to widen natural gullies.

In the upper reaches of a beech tree, Marian sat still as a hawk and watched all this. Even as the night drew long, and crept towards dawn, she didn't stir, feeling no fatigue or hunger. Perhaps she no longer needed to eat, or sleep. She wondered briefly about this, then put it aside. She had more important matters on her mind.

She fondled her old bow, turned it in her hands. She could see it had been oiled and polished, over and over, so that it looked as strong and trustworthy as the day it was crafted. Her armour too had been lovingly cared for, the deep red leather as supple and strong as it had ever been.

Fighting for Robin and fighting for the forest are the same thing.
It's bigger than any of us. Robin understood that, didn't he?
Kit's words echoed once more, and this time she admitted

they were nothing less than the truth. She had been there that day when Robin stood, to the last, against the Sheriff's firestorm. To him, there was no life without the forest. What would he want from Marian at this moment? Would he want her to set out into the wastes, in the vain hope of reaching the city? Or would he wish her to stay, and help defend this last true patch of wilderness?

'How delicious,' a voice whispered. 'You're going to do it, aren't you?'

The goddess of the forest had come to perch on the branch above. Her features were briefly feathered, before settling into the face of a young woman.

'You're going to take sides,' she said with a hawkish smile. 'But which side will you choose?' She licked her lips. 'Delicious,' she said once more. 'My cub versus yours! And the prize? No less than possession of the Earth!'

My cub versus yours.

This was something Marian had been trying very hard not to think about.

'We don't know he'll be with them.'

'Oh, but he will – he must! How else will the wheel turn?'

Marian looked up, glared. 'And I suppose you'll be watching it all. The bloodshed. The fire. And you won't lift a finger.'

The goddess laughed. 'You complain when I show my hand and you complain when I don't. It's all the same. One day you'll learn – but not until the whole world burns.'

With that, following a strange shift that made Marian blink, and a quick flurry of wings, a merlin dropped from its perch and the goddess was gone.

My cub versus yours.

Marian groaned as her heart wrenched, feeling as though she were being torn in two.

You're going to take sides.
But which side will you choose?

Part Four

Blood and Soil

I. First Blood

Gaia materialized with the dawn. As Rex and his troops continued towards it in silence, the island of wildwood appeared to rise, shimmering, out of the ground, like some mythical lost city emerging from the depths of the sea.

For Rex, it was a disorientating experience. Ever since he had caught his first glimpse of Gaia from the top of the White Tower, on that storm-wracked night, it had taken root in his imagination as a grim and menacing place – a monstrosity lurking out here on the these godless plains. Indeed, he had been told all his life – his father had whispered it at his bedside – that Sherwood was a hexed and blighted wilderness, infested by demons and shades.

But now here he was, looking upon Gaia with his own eyes, and what he saw was so opposite to his imaginings that it made perspective look twisted. The forest, he had always been told, was a place of danger and darkness. But look at it – and listen! It glistened with fresh leaves in every shade of green, from the brilliant sheen of emeralds to the dark lustre of jade. Here and there it flared opal orange and ruby red.

But it was the noise that poured out of the wildwood – a riotous flood of yammering, bellowing shrieks – that made Rex hold his breath. It was so alive, this wilderness, that it suddenly seemed to him that until this moment his entire world had been dead. That only with this dawn had he himself awoken to a world newly born.

What madness was this he felt seizing him? It tugged at him bodily, gave him the strange sudden urge to kick his horse into a gallop and go racing devil-may-care towards the wildwood.

Fighting this impulse, he pulled up on his reins, raised a fist, brought the war party rumbling and grinding to a halt. He stood there, staring at the forest, flocks of birds flapping and cawing above the treetops.

Guy of Gisbourne stepped alongside him. The hulking muscles of his shoulders twitched. His fingers flexed, balled into fists.

'Our quarry is in sight,' he growled behind his mask. 'And now . . . you hesitate.' He turned his black glare on Rex. 'A warning, my prince. I have waited twelve long years for this. I will allow nothing and no one to stand in my way.'

This was enough to break Rex out of his daze. He locked eyes with Sir Guy, his habitual fear of this man battling his loathing, and mixing with something new: something like repugnance or disdain.

'Watch your tongue, heretic hunter,' he heard himself say. 'You admit to twelve years of failure. Now I will finish what you couldn't. I will destroy the wildwood.'

So saying, he gestured to his troops, and his war party clanked and clattered back into motion, Rex leading them forward at a walk.

I will finish what you couldn't. I will destroy the wildwood.

Whose words were these? From what source had they arisen?

As Rex continued towards Gaia, which was shrieking and warbling and whistling ever louder, and he listened to the clanking rumble of his war machines, those imaginings returned to his mind's eye: he heard himself give the word to let loose;

he saw the flaming missiles arcing into the wildwood; the trees bursting into flame. And he saw the aftermath, so vividly it layered itself upon the real world, wiping away the trees in front of him, leaving only ash billowing across the plain . . .

And with the imaginings returned all his doubt and confusion, deeper than ever. Was this really his destiny, to carry out this irreversible act? Why him? Why now? How had he been fated to wield this flaming sword? To visit such destruction upon the world?

Ahead of him, his eye fell upon something that shook him out of his thoughts. Once more, he raised his fist, bringing his legion grinding to a halt.

He stared at the mystery shapes lying there upon the ground. At a greater distance they had looked randomly scattered; he had taken them for fallen branches or other detritus, perhaps shaken out of Gaia by the wind. But now they began to look more uniform in size and structure.

'Barricades,' Guy of Gisbourne growled, coming to his side. 'Evidently, the outlaws have prepared for our arrival. It will not help them. They are foxes gone to earth. They will burn with their accursed forest.'

Rex stared towards Gaia, then back at his massed ranks. 'They must know they can't stand against us,' he murmured. 'Sticks and stones, against fire and steel.' He straightened in the saddle. 'They must be given a chance to surrender. You,' he called, pointing to a tough-looking old ranger. 'Run a message to their leader. Tell him to lay down arms and come before me. If he does it quickly, I may show clemency.'

'A futile gesture,' Guy of Gisbourne said as the messenger rode uncertainly towards the barricades. 'The outlaws expect no quarter, just as they would give none. You have just proven, my prince, once and for all, that you do not understand the nature of our conflict.'

These words came down on Rex like hammer blows. The undeniable truth of them. What did Rex know of this war? It had been raging since before he was even born. With a sudden start, he realized he didn't even know how it began, let alone how it had come to consume half the world. And yet, somehow, here he was, at the centre of it, preparing to strike this final earth-quaking blow.

Such thoughts froze Rex's blood, made his vision blurred. Time must have jumped, because already the messenger was returning in a cloud of dust. Rex blinked, trying to focus on the rider more clearly. In his numb state, he could not at first say what was wrong with this ranger. But there was something about the way he sat in the saddle, or the way his arms hung stiffly at his sides . . .

The dust swirled and Rex's vision cleared, and he saw that the messenger was headless. Blood fountained from the stump of his neck. As his maddened mount galloped closer, Rex saw why the corpse had not fallen. Arrows speared his legs, at the unprotected spots near his knees, pinning him to the saddle.

'So then, you have the outlaws' answer,' Guy of Gisbourne growled at his side. 'Already you have cost us a soldier.'

Rex barely heard these words, lost as he was in disbelief and doubt. All his life, this idea had lain dormant – that somewhere in his past there had been a profound mistake, a wrong turning in the road – almost that he should never have been born at all. But ever since he first entered the wastes, on the hunt for Robin Hood's bones, this germinal idea had grown and grown. Until now, as he watched the headless horseman gallop away across the plain, and he stared at the shimmering forest he had come to destroy, the idea bloomed in its full and terrible glory. *None* of this was supposed to happen – he should not even be here – *nothing* in his life or his existence was what it appeared to be.

'They say, my prince,' Guy of Gisbourne said menacingly, leaning in, as Rex remained mute and rigid, 'that a man's true nature is revealed only in extremis. So then, here you are, for all the world to see.'

The heretic hunter straightened, turned in his saddle. 'You five,' he said, gesturing to a pack of young, nervous-looking rangers. 'Stay here to coddle the prince. His blood runs cold. Even so, our master will be displeased if he fails to return to the castle. You two,' he pointed to another pair of soldiers. 'Run a message to the city. Tell the Sheriff we have located the wildwood. Soon it shall burn.'

He drew his broadsword, raised it to the heavens. 'The rest of you – with me to glory! The deeds we do here today will echo through eternity!'

The rangers brandished their weapons and sent up a gargled war cry, while Sir Guy's warrior monks simply drew their slender blades and looked back at him, dispassionate.

All this, Rex heard and saw. Yet something lay between him and it all, like a pane of glass, keeping him separate. No – not glass – he was trapped under ice. These events were happening far away on the surface, while he sank deeper and deeper, drowning.

With a final bellow of hatred, Sir Guy led the cavalcade forward. And still Rex floundered. All he could do was watch as this great killing force gathered momentum. As it clanked and rumbled towards the wild's last true fastness, intending to erase it for ever.

All this was his doing. It had been fated to him, after all. Whether he lifted another finger or not, it was him who led this army here.

He was the one who brought this devastation upon the world.

II. The Besieged Wild

'Perhaps we should have received their envoy after all,' Jack said grimly, as the outlaws crouched on the edge of Gaia, watching the enemy force grow and grow beneath its dust cloud. 'Suddenly I feel the burning desire to talk terms.'

'He's sent his whole damn army,' Midge muttered. 'They'll smash straight through that barricade.'

'They won't,' Kit said, with as much assurance as he was able. 'The war machines won't get past those ditches.'

'They're not even going to try,' Ira said. 'Look – they're stopping short.'

It was true. The Sheriff's host was now crunching to a halt. Peering through the undergrowth, Kit watched this with puzzlement, together with a creeping dread. He'd expected nothing less than a direct assault, the Sheriff's troops trying to batter their way through to Gaia through sheer weight of arms. So what was this?

Scrutinizing the enemy, he could just make out tiny specks dressed all in red – warrior monks. And there was the hateful figure of the heretic hunter himself. He appeared to be riding along the line of troops, pausing now in front of one of the siege engines, then riding on to the next. Why the delay? Why wasn't his nemesis coming on full force?

'You've made a mistake,' said a voice behind him.

All heads turned. Everyone stared. Marian was dressed in her dark-red leather armour. She was gripping her shortbow, a quiver of arrows at her back. Seeing her standing there like that, her eyes banded with warpaint, giving her the sharp-featured look of a bird of prey, was like greeting someone back from the grave.

Finally, Kit broke the silence. 'How do you mean . . . a mistake?'

Coming to his side, Marian dropped to one knee. 'I should have realized it sooner. The barricades – they're too close.'

'How so? It's five hundred paces. What can they do at that range?'

'We faced the Sheriff's catapults before,' Marian said. 'But that was twelve years ago. His armourers never cease.'

'Meaning . . .' Midge murmured, 'these are not the same machines.'

'It's true,' Ira whispered, as the dust settled around the siege engines. 'Now they're closer you can see. They're . . . huge.'

'They don't have to cross the barricade,' Jack breathed, as a shocked silence spread through the rest of the outlaws. 'They can rain fire on us from where they are.'

A dreaded clanking clunking noise began echoing across the plain. It was the sound of war machines being wound, their great arms sinking beneath the skyline as they arced back and down.

Much was the first to speak. 'So that's it,' he said, lumbering to his feet, gripping his giant quarterstaff in both hands. 'We need to take the fight to them.'

'On the open plains?' said Jack. 'It's a death wish.'

'Better than staying here to burn,' said Midge, dropping a rock into his slingshot, standing with his father. 'At least we'll take some of them with us.'

'They're right,' said Ira, on her feet with daggers drawn. 'It's the only way. Marian, if you're with us, we need to move. Kit? We need to attack while we still can!'

Her voice came to Kit as muffled sounds, as though heard underwater. He was drowning in hopelessness.

We made a mistake.

They can rain fire on us from where they are.

'Kit, come *on*,' Ira urged, tugging at his wolfskin. 'We need to get moving!'

Kit tried to stand, failed. He was unable to even open his eyes, or raise his head. What was wrong with him? Ira was right. They had to act, and act now. But another part of him knew it was already too late.

Already the creaking clanking noise of the siege engines had ceased. The hurling arms were in position. Soon the bombardment would begin, and the flames would rise. Nothing the outlaws might do could prevent that now.

Knowing this, Kit's canker of helplessness swelled and swelled, until finally it burst into hatred and rage. A rage more potent than anything he had ever experienced. A rage that could not be contained, but surged outwards, quaking the trees in their roots, sending birds bursting from their roosts.

'Kit – what is this?' Ira shouted, as ground creatures wailed and shrieked and leaves rained from the trees. 'What good will this do?'

The tempest intensified, raging like hot wind through the wildwood, hurling detritus and panicking birds and beasts, while new recruits shielded their eyes and cried out in shock and fear.

'Go,' Kit said evenly, without looking up. 'Leave me.'

'What? No!' said Ira.

'Burning with your forest?' said Jack. 'Noble gestures get us nowhere.'

'The greenhorns need to see you in the fight,' said Midge.

'They will,' Kit said darkly, in a voice he didn't recognize. 'We all have our part to play in this. Ira, I want you to lead the attack.'

'You lead it,' Ira snapped back. 'What do you think you can—'

'I said, leave me. We're running out of time. Go!'

Although Kit kept his voice low, it sent a heavy quake through the wildwood, cracking boughs and sending crows cawing into the air.

It was enough to startle the outlaws into action.

'Ready the new recruits,' Ira told Midge and the others. 'Split them into five groups. Marian, if you're with us, you'll lead a band too. Kit, we'll need a route out.'

With a tiny part of his forest-mind, and a twitch of one finger, Kit opened tunnels through the curtain wall. At the same time, vine-bridges sprung up to span the ditch.

Once this was done he strode off alone through Gaia. Through the blessed dells and glades, beneath the sparkling beech trees. His actions composed at the surface, while deep within him that phenomenal rage lay coiled, awaiting release.

He reached The Henge. Passing between the twin gateway trees, he entered the deep, dark stillness within. He went to the hallowed patch of ground where twelve years ago Robin Hood had knelt to battle the firestorm.

Kit went to his knees on the same patch of ground. As he did so, he felt a rush of cold clear certainty. All this was fated. Every moment of his life had been leading him here. This calm conviction deepened, until he was enveloped in pure silence.

And within that silence – the very wellspring from which it arose – he detected an awesome presence; a vast, dark power. For years he had tapped the strength of the earth. But never had he reached a seam this deep. Already he understood that. He sensed it in every last leaf of every tree that surrounded him, in every watercourse and tendril, every fibre of his own being. This power had been here for ever, waiting to be unleashed.

This was the same power Robin Hood had summoned on the day of the Great Fire. It helped him safeguard the heart of the forest.

But that was a long time ago. Robin was gone.

Which meant this final desperate defence fell to Kit.

Kneeling here, waiting for the assault to begin, he could only pray he was equal to the test.

III. Skyfire

'There are five war machines, five of us,' Ira called to Marian and Midge and the rest as they left Gaia behind at a run, each outlaw leading a band of peasant warriors. 'Target one each. Take them apart any way you can. Leave the rest of the new recruits in their foxholes. We'll need—'

She broke off and Marian stumbled at a dread sound. A whooshing whip-crack. It echoed across the plain and down the years. It was the sound of war machines letting loose. The last time Marian had heard that noise, all the fires of hell were soon to follow. And now, once again, the Sheriff was bombarding the forest.

Except this time, he had brought even deadlier weaponry to bear. Those siege engines of twelve years ago hurled payloads of gunpowder, which lay inert until it could be ignited with a flame. As these new machines hurled their projectiles, Marian saw that each one trailed a fiery tail, like a comet. They were fuses, which fizzed and flared along their length as the missiles flew. These new machines threw flying bombs.

Seeing this, the forest fighters and the rebel peasants stumbled to a halt, all of them staring upwards in horror, while Marian stood there rooted and hopeless.

I'm sorry, Robin. We failed you. We failed the forest.

The battle was lost before it had even begun. Any one of these incendiaries, dropped into Gaia, might be enough to spark an inferno. And already five of them were whistling overhead.

All Marian could do was watch in mute shock as the first of them reached the apex of its arc, then dropped towards the treetops . . .

It was making a yawning, yowling sound now as it hurtled towards Gaia . . .

As it thundered lower and lower—

Until, abruptly, it veered away, like a bat changing direction mid-flight.

It crashed down upon the dead plain, where it exploded harmlessly in a shower of dust and flame.

It happened so quickly, and so unexpectedly, that it looked like a trick of perspective. One moment the flying bomb was hurtling directly for Gaia – the next it was falling in the desert. How had it missed?

The next two incendiaries were now screaming towards the wildwood, dropping in tandem. The first exploded in mid-air, its fuse too short. But the next screamed onwards. Marian stared, not shifting her gaze even a fraction. And this time she saw it happen . . .

Just as the bomb dropped to the treeline, a python vine snaked up out of Gaia. It rose out of the curtain wall of vegetation, its head swaying, like a serpent guarding its nest. With a whiplash, the vine swept the flying bomb from the sky, deflecting it out onto the plain, where it erupted with a *whump* and a spray of sand and dust.

It's Kit! Marian realized, her head spinning, as more vines swatted away the fourth bomb, and the fifth. *He's doing what Robin once did. He's channelling the might of the forest. He's standing against the firestorm.*

'The Earth Mage summons his dark magic!' Guy of

Gisbourne's voice rasped across the plain, cracking the stunned silence. 'Acolytes – with me. Dig him out of his bolthole. Why have the machines stopped? Reload, damn you! Burn the cursed wood to the ground!'

'Let him through!' Ira hollered, running once more towards the barricade, Marian and the others stumbling in her wake. 'Don't try to stop him – it's futile!'

The heretic hunter and his whole pack of warrior monks were now charging towards the barricades and the peasant troops in their foxholes. Ira was right. These defences might be enough to halt regular rangers, but the heretic hunter in full flight, in full fury – never.

'Let him pass,' Ira shouted. 'Leave the heretic hunter to us.'

But it was no use. The peasant warriors were doing as they had been told: lying in wait until the enemy was practically on top of them. From within their foxholes, Marian could see the tips of their spears, and the glint of their axes.

Guy of Gisbourne and his monks hurdled the deathpits, crashed through the outer barricade as if it were so much kindling. The peasant warriors burst from the trenches, weapons poised. Only those weapons were like children's toys against the sweeping broadsword of Guy of Gisbourne – against the quicksilver blades of his acolytes.

In one sickening rush of blood it was done, a dozen green-horns shorn of heads and limbs, left spewing guts in the dust, while Guy of Gisbourne and his warrior monks galloped on towards Gaia, their swords already back in their scabbards.

'So much for our first line of defence,' Midge spat. 'Now?'

'We continue as we were,' Ira said. 'They're reloading the siege engines. We have to stop them.'

'What about the heretic hunter?' said Much.

'We'll just have to hope Kit can hold him off. Once we take down those machines, we'll double back to help. All right?' she said, as they slipped through the barricade and headed towards the siege engines, 'Marian, take the one of the far left. Midge, that's yours in the centre. Much, Jack, head east. Marian, did you hear me? There's your target, get going!'

For the moment, Ira's voice was vague. Marian was here but not here, her limbs acting of their own accord. As they neared the enemy line, she scanned the ranks of soldiers.

Your cub versus mine.

Could Rex really be among them? No – she refused to believe it. No matter how strange her destiny might be, no twist of fate could be so cruel, so perverted, as to bring them both here to this battlefield, to pit them against one another as enemies.

A cracking whiplash of sound yanked her from her reverie. The war machines had let loose once more. Looking skywards as she ran, Marian tracked the flight of the bombs as they arced up and out before dropping towards Gaia.

At this distance, across the shimmering plain, the island of wildwood suddenly looked to her like a tentacled creature. Multiple vines snaked up above the treetops, swatting at the incendiaries as if defending itself from venomous insects.

The first two bombs were batted harmlessly aside, to erupt in the dust. The third exhausted its fuse just as it reached the treeline. It exploded in mid-air, incinerating the vine that had whipped out to meet it. This caused panic in the treetops, birds bursting from their roosts as thick as flies, cawing and shrieking and beating their wings. From deeper in the wildwood erupted howls and bellows and wails.

Waving the stump of its amputated tentacle, screeching in a thousand voices merged into one, the wildwood seemed more than ever like a single giant creature, wounded and enraged. The final two projectiles it batted away with renewed vigour, slapping one with such force that it ricocheted back almost as far as the invading host.

'The forest is defended,' she called to her rebel band as they ran on once more. 'But Kit can't hold out for ever. We need to dismantle that machine.'

Standing guard in front of the trebuchet were ranks of soldiers. They had formed a shield wall, their spears lowered, while war horns blared.

'They have the numbers, but their will is weak,' she told her followers as they readied their makeshift blades and bludgeons. 'They have no cause but destruction. You fight for the very world you inhabit.'

She meant this as a rousing call to arms, but her voice fell flat. She felt strangely dispassionate as they ran onwards. Where was the fear and fury of battle? She tried to summon hatred for these invaders, but found something closer to sorrow. From her sunburned skin to her hollow heart, she felt . . . nothing.

This is not you, not any more, the thought stabbed at her. *This is what you were, not what you've become. This is not your part to play . . .*

She shook her head. It was too late for thoughts like that. Ahead of her, with a great fiery roar, the war machines let loose a third volley, while rangers braced themselves for battle. Behind her, desperadoes readied their weapons, their faces etched with dread rage.

Whatever forces had brought her to this point, she was here and this was happening. With her bow at half-draw, she met the eyes of her enemy, as after all these years she prepared to wage war once more.

IV. Enter the Web

'Earth Mage – show yourself! You cannot escape your doom. Your gods have deserted you. Face me, coward!'

As Guy of Gisbourne and his acolytes hacked and slashed at the wall of thorns that surrounded Gaia, the heretic hunter hollered a tirade of curses and taunts.

In spite of these provocations, Kit remained perfectly still, kneeling at the centre of The Henge, the yew trees dark and silent around him. He could not allow his concentration to waver, even for an instant. Even now, a fresh volley of flying bombs was screaming its way towards the wildwood. Five seeds of fire that must never be allowed to germinate.

Raising his palms, Kit coaxed tendrils from the forest floor. He caused them to snake up above Gaia. With a flick of his wrists, he made the tendrils whiplash, right and left, slapping at the flying bombs, swatting two from the sky, then a third, causing them to spin out over the plains and erupt in harmless flame.

The last two projectiles fell in tandem. Closing his hands together, interlocking his fingers, Kit caused two python vines to intertwine, and bunch, forming a ball at their tip. Sweeping his own balled fists, Kit swung the vines and batted the bombs from the sky, catching them with such force that they exploded in mid-air, the fiery fragments raining into the wildwood, hissing as they were extinguished in streams and ponds.

He turned his attention back to Guy of Gisbourne. While his energies were directed toward the bombs, he and his warrior monks had made inroads, hacking deep into the wall of thorns.

Interlocking his fingers once more, Kit thrust his palms outwards. In response, the undergrowth rose up, surged like a tidal wave, tumbled the heretic hunter and his acolytes back out onto the plain.

No sooner had Kit regained his wits, recovered his strength from this skirmish, than another whip-crack echoed across the plain. The war machines had let loose once more, another fiery hailstorm screaming towards the wildwood.

Kit steadied himself, took two long breaths, then raised his arms and flicked the tip of a tendril like a whip at the foremost projectile. He whipped the vine again, and again, sending four flying bombs spinning out across the wastes, where they exploded in flight or erupted with a muffled *whump* in the dust.

Rather than bat the fifth bomb aside, he caught it, wrapping tendrils around it as it dropped. Using the momentum, he swung the vines outward, hurling the bomb like a rock from a slingshot. He intended the missile to return to the Sheriff's men, but it fell short, dropping on the outlaws' own barricade.

Kit shook his head, silently chiding himself. *Careful. These powers are heady. Don't forget who you are. Remember your task.*

He shifted his attention back to Guy of Gisbourne. He and his acolytes had once again burrowed deep into the defensive ditch. Summoning suckers and tendrils, Kit plucked them out one by one, before flinging them out onto the plain.

They had penetrated deeper than he had realized, dug in tighter than ticks, and the effort of expelling them left Kit breathing hard, his arms hanging heavy at his sides. He recovered his wits just in time to meet another volley of projectiles, raising vines to swat them aside.

'Poor child – his labours take their toll,' said a voice behind him. 'How much longer can he carry the world on his shoulders?'

'I don't have time for your games,' Kit snarled, without turning. 'I've got work to do.'

'At this rate, that work will be the end of you.'

'So be it.

'But don't you see,' the goddess whispered, kneeling at his side, 'there's a better way. Why be a breeze, fanning the flames – when you could be a gale, feeding the inferno!'

'What are you talking about? Leave me be.'

'Fine,' she said sulkily, standing and drawing away. 'If you don't want my help, you can do it all by yourself.'

'Wait,' Kit said, despite himself. 'What . . . help are you offering?'

She laughed, bounding back to him. 'Nothing more than this. The wisdom of the wild. The old rules of predator and prey. Those men out there – don't you see – you shouldn't be shutting them out. You should be inviting them in.'

'You're talking madness.'

'No – no! Think!' she said, the burned side of her face livid in the gloom of the yews. 'This is your place of power, not theirs. You forget yourself. You were born to play the hunter, not the hunted.'

Kit bowed his head, closed his eyes. Bitter experience told him to block his ears against the goddess's words. But it was too late. Some part of what she said had already pierced his heart and buried itself deep.

This is your place of power, not theirs.

Yes. Kit is a child of the forest, with wildness in his blood. *These interlopers know nothing of the grace or the power of the Earth – that is why they fear and loathe it.*

You were born to play the hunter, not the hunted.

Yes, yes. Compared to him, these invaders were insects. Feel them, pricking his skin. Burrowing into his flesh.

From the shadows, the goddess laughed in delight. 'You know I'm right, sweet child. What would you do without me?'

But by now, Kit was paying her no heed. With all the anger of the wounded Earth surging through him, his decision had already been made. So much so that he had to restrain himself from flinging wide the gates and inviting all his enemies in at once. No – that would not do. He must not startle his prey. He must lie still at the centre of his web, as patient as a spider, laying his trap thread by thread.

He focused on a pair of warrior monks. They had hacked open the beginnings of a tunnel, and their efforts had separated them from their companions. Yes, these two would be perfect.

Spreading his fingers, Kit widened the tunnel. Drawing in thorns, like a wildcat sheathing its claws, he made the tunnel longer, and straighter. Leaving just enough vegetation for them to battle to allow them to think they were making this progress themselves, he led the monks along this passageway . . . up and out of the ditch . . . and into Gaia.

Emerging from the undergrowth, stepping into the criss-cross of light and shadow, the warrior monks stood to their full height, squinting.

'We made it – we're through,' one of them murmured, his voice unevenly pitched and cracking from disuse.

His companion turned back the way they had come, shouted for others to follow. Kit masked the noise with a bellow of his own, borrowing the growls of ground creatures and the shrieks of birds.

'We should go back,' the first monk said, 'show them the way.'

'Go back how?' the second man replied. 'I don't see where we came in.'

317

Both men searched, thrashing their swords, but found no trace of the tunnel that led them here.

'Let's just find him,' one of them muttered, his voice breaking. 'Get this over with.'

So saying, their bared blades flashing in and out of the dappled sunrays, they made their way deeper into the wild-wood.

Both men glanced up as a projectile screamed towards the treetops – then veered out and away from the forest as Kit batted it clear with his green fists.

'This damned dendromancer. Where are you, Earth Wizard?' The first monk raised his voice. 'You failed. You couldn't keep us out. Now show yourself.'

'I'm here,' Kit said softly, allowing his voice to carry through the whispering aspen leaves, the murmuring of a stream. 'I'm all around you. Open your eyes.'

The two warrior monks spun in place, swords raised.

'That voice – you heard it?'

'It came from over there.'

'No. It was behind us.'

'I'm everywhere,' Kit said. 'You've spent your lives hunting me – and now you don't recognize my face.'

The warrior monks turned about, slashing at saplings and ferns and the trunks of oaks.

'Where are you? What are you?'

Kit laughed, setting magpies cackling in the boughs, a stag grunting in the distance. 'I am the wild,' he howled, 'and now you shall know my wrath!'

In one swift motion, Kit reached down with sucker-limbs and tendril-paws, thorns his claws, and he swept both men off the ground, whipping them high into the boughs.

They were trying to scream, but already their mouths were gagged, Kit wrapping them round and round with python vines, like a spider encasing flies. Dangling upside down, they rocked gently as the boughs settled and the wind died.

This is your place of power, not theirs.

Yes. And today Kit would prove it. He would do more than defend himself from his enemies. He would feed on them. Use their blood to bathe his wounds.

Delirious perhaps from killing rage, from the fatigue of using his forest powers to take life, these thoughts swirled through Kit as though they were not his own. As if something greater and more terrible than himself was speaking through his mind.

But in any case, thoughts mattered little, nor words – their time was past. Now, with all that stood at stake, only actions held any significance.

And already Kit was committing his next act, raising more tendrils above the treetops and swatting more incendiaries away from Gaia. At the same time, he was drawing a mark on the other warrior monks, and on Guy of Gisbourne most of all.

Your time is short, he whispered to his nemesis, the words rippling through the undergrowth as the hissing of snakes and the buzzing of wasps. *Soon you too shall be invited in. And the forest shall feast.*

V. Demon Queen

The fury and ferocity of the rebel peasants – Marian had known nothing to match it in all her experience. Neither had the Sheriff's men. Time and again, levelling their spears, the soldiers tried to advance and drive the rebels away from the war machine. But each time they were overrun by the howling mob, peasants hacking and slashing with their make-shift weapons, beating rangers to the ground, forcing the rest to regroup and retreat.

It didn't come without cost. Marian stepped over the corpse of a rebel who lay in a tangle of his own innards, looking like some surprised sea creature. Further up the line, another peasant lay leaking brains.

But the rebel host absorbed its wounds like a mythical multi-limbed beast: with each blow struck against them, they merely hollered their pain while seeming to grow stronger and fiercer yet, throwing themselves at the wall of soldiers as though possessed – as though their bodies were not their own but merely puppets acting out the rage of the Earth.

'Nothing can stand against you,' Marian called, urging them on. 'The Sheriff would leave you with nothing but ashes. Destroy his infernal machine.'

Not for the first time, as she shouted, soldiers shot glances in her direction. She was certain she detected a widening of fear, even horror in their eyes.

What had they been told back at the castle? What did they think had befallen Marian Delbosque? What did they think to see her now on the battlefield? Was her very presence helping to unman these soldiers, and keep them on the back foot?

If so, she was happy to feed their fear. She paused alongside a slain soldier. After dipping two fingers in his blood, she drew battle-streaks on her cheeks and her forehead. With her bow at half draw, she let any soldier who dared meet her glare as she stalked forwards, a blood-smeared demon queen.

She realized something then: since the fighting began, she had not let loose a single arrow. It was enough to prowl the battlefield, helping to break the rangers' nerve, while stoking the peasants' fury.

Not that they needed much encouragement. These rebels were rudely equipped, vastly outmatched in skill and experience, yet for all that they were driving the rangers back and back. They were a seething mass, like human fire, sucking in the oxygen of battle, blazing fiercer with every death-wail.

As she advanced with them, something made her glance eastwards. Her eye fell upon mounted figures. Maybe half a dozen. They were just sitting there, perhaps three bowshots beyond the battleground.

At this distance it was hard to make out details, but amid the crimson cloaks of the Sheriff's Guard, it appeared one of the figures was dressed all in black. Her heart lurched. Could the Sheriff have come in person? No, it had been years since he had even set foot outside the city. There was no way on this Earth he would brave a journey into the wastes. So then, in that case, could it be—

No – no, no. She refused to admit that idea into her reality. She yanked it out at the root. Turning away from the mystery figures, she forced herself to focus on the battle ahead. It had reached a pivotal stage. The defending soldiers were now backed up against their war machine. They had locked shields and were somehow holding formation as the rebels threw themselves into the attack again and again, snarling like wild beasts.

Then all of a sudden it happened. A giant rebel swung his quarterstaff, batted a ranger to the ground, and the shield wall cracked. Marian herself leaped into the breach, her bowstring at full draw, hollering for others to follow.

All was chaos then. The enemies' discipline fell apart, leaving knots of soldiers isolated and panicking as the rebels swarmed on all sides, hacking with their mattocks and swinging their scythes.

The engineers were the last to lie down. Standing atop their machine, one of them loosed a crossbow bolt that lodged in a peasant's throat. But that was to be their last act. The peasants were upon them now, snarling wilder than ever, hacking and beating and stabbing the enemy into a grisly pulp, with a blood-thirsty ferocity that made even Marian catch her breath.

What have I helped to unleash? some part of her whispered then. *I thought we could bring the cycle to a close. But we're opening up something new.*

In the grip of their battle lust, the rebel peasants made no distinction between man and machine – once the engineers were dead they merely went on hacking and hammering at the trebuchet, sawing at its ropes with their blades and smashing its wheels with their mauls.

'Shake yourselves – collect your wits,' she called out to them. 'Other machines are yet operational. So catch your breath. We fight again.'

So saying, gathering her rebel band around her, she set off across the battleground, leading them towards the next siege engine.

As she drew nearer, she locked eyes on Midge. He was urging his troops on, flinging rock after rock from his slingshot, the missiles careering off shields and skull helms as the rangers shuffled forward behind their wall of steel.

'They're a stubborn bunch.' He leered at her, his hair matted with blood. 'Every time we crack their line they pull themselves back together.'

'Keep them occupied,' Marian told him. 'We'll loop behind and try to get at the machine.'

'It's good to have you back, Marian,' he said, loosing another rock, which struck a ranger between the eyes, while his band roared their battle frenzy.

Gesturing to her troops, calling out commands, Marian led her band in a wide arc, intending to outflank the soldiers' defences.

As she went, she couldn't help peering once more towards that group of mystery soldiers. Were they senior officers? Why were they just sitting there, rather than directing their forces? Did they have some secret strategy they would yet bring to bear?

And what about the Guy of Gisbourne? She spared a glance towards Gaia. Sir Guy was there, with his warrior monks, dwarfed at the treeline. So far, thank the gods, they had played no real part in the battle, obsessed as they were with cutting their way into the wildwood. But what if that should change? How long would these rebel peasants stand against Sir Guy and his acolytes should they go on the rampage?

Forget all that, she told herself, leading her band now in a direct charge for the siege engine. *Focus on your task. We're going to do it, Robin. We're going to beat them. We'll protect the forest. Then I'm coming for you, I promise . . .*

VI. Blood Brothers

While violence raged across the plain and rangers died, Rex remained trapped in his own body, hating himself for his inaction. He felt incapable of lifting a finger, or uttering a word.

In those fated to lead, who walk the path of power, indecision can be fatal.

The outlaws were winning. Even in Rex's numb, hazy state, he understood that well enough. The siege engines were being overrun. Rebel peasants swarmed like frenzied insects, while soldiers scattered in disarray.

They needed leadership. They needed Rex to ride among them, redeploying troops and issuing new commands. All this lay within his power. Since he was six years old, he had been taught the art of warcraft; he had studied plans of battlefields and learned endless stratagems. But now, instead of calling on that knowledge, using it to rally his forces, he remained immobile and silent, leaving his men to be slaughtered.

You had your moment to speak, his father's words came back to him. *Your chance to wield power. You surrendered it.*

Was it fear that kept him paralyzed? Perhaps. But not fear of death. Rather, it was the sense of teetering at the brink. Sitting here, he remained on the edge of this war – of this timeless struggle he barely understood. The moment he raised his sword and used it to battle outlaws, he would be sucked into that struggle once and for all. He would embark fully, and irreversibly, upon the dark path his father had laid out for him.

He broke into a coughing fit. He coughed and coughed, while the six rangers of his bodyguard sat watching him, uncertain. Rex scratched at his arms, his skin flaking and agonized. All his old afflictions were crowding back in, tightening the cage around him, his chest so tight he could barely breathe.

Through blurred eyes, he stared towards Gaia. It glistened black-green, like deep water. While these wastelands burned beneath the sun, and rang with murderous violence, everything as red and raw as his skin, the Last Forest was a soothing balm merely to look upon . . .

'Sire – where are you going?' a ranger of his bodyguard shouted. 'Your orders, sire!'

Rex barely heard this voice. He was barely even aware he had snapped out of his reverie at last, and spurred his horse forward into a gallop. Suddenly, all that existed was the forest. He kept his gaze fixed on it, mesmerized. All around him, as he entered the battleground, were the wails of killing and dying men. But to his ears there was only the noise of the wildwood – its cacophony of howls and bellows and shrieks – drawing him on like a siren call.

He galloped through a breach in the outlaws' defences, where the barricade had been smashed. As he did so, carrion crows scattered from his path. Pieces of dead men lay scattered about, as if they had been torn limb from limb by wild beasts. Their lifeblood soaked the cracked earth, running into every fissure and rivulet.

But Rex barely noted any of this. Every fibre of his being was focused on the swaying sprawl of wildwood. As he drew near, its flood of sound became a palpable thing, hitting him like a hot wind, making him slow his mount. He stared into the deep darkness between the trees, the shadows seeming to shift with unknown movement, and glint with quick eyes. Suddenly, for the first time, the aliveness and wildness of this place was daunting, making him slow further as he approached the ditch with its wall of thorns.

'Sire – what are your orders?' the chief of his bodyguard said, breathless, as he and the other rangers caught up. 'Did you come for Sir Guy? I saw him further up that way.'

Yes, Rex had spotted the heretic hunter. But for the time being he meant as little to Rex as anything else. Anything other than this – the hulking mysterious body of the forest, with its haunting wild calls and its shimmering shadowy depths.

'Sire,' the chief of his bodyguard tried once more. 'We're in a vulnerable position. We should return to—'

'Guard my horse,' Rex said, dismounting, handing him the reins. 'Stay here and wait for my signal. Not another word.'

Dumbfounded, the ranger did as he was bid, the bodyguard standing their horses a safe distance from the wall of thorns, men and beasts equally unnerved.

Rex continued around Gaia on foot, staring through the curtain wall and between the trees. Its gloom glinted with thorns the size of meat hooks, and shone with berries the colour of blood. But ideas were in him now, merging: this place was alien and daunting. Yet at the same time it was enticing, and strangely intensely familiar, as if he had been here many, many times in the past. Almost as if, in fact, he had been here always . . .

With such phantom thoughts playing through his mind, Rex at first thought his eyes were deceiving him. The wall of thorns appeared to be twisting, shifting. Hanging vines drew aside, like curtains parting. With one last slithering suck it was complete: to Rex's profound disbelief, a passageway had opened amid the greenery.

As Rex drew his sword, stood with it braced in both hands before him, a noise drifted out of the tunnel. At first, it came to him as snarls and chirps and the rustling of leaves. But then, contained within these sounds – or somehow composed of them – came human words.

'Lay down your blade. You may enter.'

'Who is that?' Rex demanded, the tip of his sword wavering. 'Who's there?'

'You know who I am, brother.'

I know that voice. It's him. Kit. Chief of the outlaws.

'Come, brother. Welcome.'

Rex ground his teeth. 'Don't call me that. I'm no brother of yours.'

'Oh, but you are. I failed to recognize it the first time we met. But from here I see clearly. The blood of the forest runs in your veins, just as it flows in mine.'

'I don't know what you're talking about. I'm the Sheriff's son. I'm his heir.'

'You are a child of the forest,' the voice insisted. 'That truth has been hidden from you. Enter – and learn your true nature.'

Rex's world shrank, until nothing else existed – nothing except this shadowy gateway into the wildwood.

Enter – and learn your true nature.

The words held him spellbound. All his life there had been something missing – an absence he could not begin to clarify. As if he had been born lacking a vital piece of himself. Or rather, as if the very ground of his life was not to be trusted – all the sights and sounds of his existence mere surface appearance, while the fundamental truth of the world remained buried, forever out of reach.

And now here was this invitation. This promise.

Enter – and learn your true nature.

Was he sun-crazed to even consider it? How could he ever

hope to find answers to questions he couldn't even articulate?

And yet . . . where had his life been leading, except here? What did he have left to lose? What might he stand to gain?

He dropped to his knees, crawled through the archway. He heard shouting behind him as the chief of the bodyguard came running, trying to stop him. But already the tunnel was swallowing the ranger's words – was shutting out all murmur of the outside world. Rex was alone, with only the sound of his own breathing and the thumping of his heartbeat. The passageway rustled with the unknown and sparked here and there with fireflies as it led him deeper and deeper into the gloom.

It became so dark he was as good as blind. As he groped his way onwards, finger-like twigs clawed at him on either side. The scurrying sounds in the undergrowth and the shrieking from the trees twisted in his mind, becoming ominous as the crawlspace stretched on and on, curving first downwards then seeming to bear him up and up.

The peace that had initially enveloped him dropped away, turned to creeping unease, and finally to fear. He thought about trying to go back. But he had come too far. The wildwood had swallowed him – he had fallen for its enticements and now he would crawl down here until he ran mad . . .

With fear pumping through his veins like venom, his movements became frantic – he was scrabbling forwards, panting like an animal – until suddenly he burst out of the tunnel into clear green air. He lay blinking and breathing hard on a bed of moss, bathed in rays of sunshine that filtered between the trees.

Shaking himself, Rex got to his feet and stared. The wildwood. From a distance it had appeared mystical. From closer range it had looked daunting, even if strangely enticing. But now a new face revealed itself. Because here . . . within the forest . . . it was *glorious*.

Trees stretched above him the height of cathedrals, their leaves gleaming and turning the sunrays numinous – like the divine light that streams through stained-glass windows. Everywhere everything chirped and chattered and chirruped.

He never dreamed the world contained so much sound. He never imagined it held such a suffusion of smells. Rain-kissed soil and sodden moss and animal scents of countless kinds, along with aromas he could not even begin to identify. He could only stand here, awestruck, his senses overwhelmed.

'Welcome home, brother.'

The voice came from everywhere and nowhere, whispering out of the boles of the trees, out of the birds' nests and the burrows. In any case, for the time being Rex didn't care where the Earth mage might be. It didn't even rankle to be addressed once more as 'brother'. What could any of it matter?

He wandered forward aimlessly, his whole body soothing, the misted air extinguishing the fire in his skin, relieving his raw lungs. He pulled off his skull-helm and felt the soft warmth of sunshine and shade.

Peace. Yes, that was it. Until this moment peace had been merely a word, never a lived part of his experience. But yes – for the first time in his life, he knew what peace truly meant as he trod the mossy path across a bee-loud meadow.

A sharper noise stabbed at his serenity, made him look up. A blunt shape was dropping out of the sun. It was a flying bomb. It screamed earthwards, trailing its comet's tail – until the forest rose up to defend itself, towering tendrils reaching into the sky and slapping the projectile away. In the distance came a muffled *whump* where the bomb erupted in the desert.

'You see what the Sheriff would do to our home, brother?' the outlaw chief spoke through the forest. 'Is that truly the path you wish to follow?'

'You don't know anything about my path,' Rex said, sweeping

his gaze through the treetops. 'You call me brother, so why won't you show yourself?'

'I must keep my place. Join me here. The forest will show you the way.'

Rex walked on, across a rustling glade, a chill breeze shivering his skin. 'Join you?' he said. 'Why? So you can kill me, the way you killed Alpha Johns?'

'I mean you no harm. You carry the forest in your heart. How could it be otherwise? We can be allies, you and I. We can sow peace in this land.'

'You don't want peace,' Rex said, continuing through the wildwood, his steps guiding themselves. 'You want victory. You'll do anything to get it.'

'You're wrong,' the phantom voice said. 'I do what is necessary.'

'My father says the same thing.'

'Your father,' the voice echoed, with a mocking edge. 'And you – what do you say?'

Rex had no answer to this. He came to a standstill as he entered another small glade. This one held a different atmosphere from the others he had passed through. It was encircled by dense pine trees which shut out most of the light, and even the sound.

Rex saw a lone serpent slither into the undergrowth. Crows sat watching him in silence. He tried to re-conjure those blessed feelings from before. Where had it gone, that deep peace? What was this sense of menace he now felt creeping at the back of his neck?

'You needn't be alarmed,' the Earth Mage whispered, as Rex hurried onwards, out of the gloomy glade. 'Sometimes the forest must be cruel to be kind. Death feeds life. This is the way of the world.'

'I don't know what you're talking about,' Rex said, his voice cracking. 'I don't even know what I'm doing here. My father warned me about your kind – you talk with a forked tongue. Every word is a lie.'

'The Sheriff is the one who has deceived you. Your mother too.'

'Don't you dare talk about my mother!'

'She did it to protect you. But you don't need that armour any more. Join me here. The heart of the forest. Learn who you truly are.'

'I know who I am,' Rex murmured, hugging his arms, suddenly cold and afraid. 'I am the Sheriff's son. I am his heir. I don't know what I'm doing here. I shouldn't have come.'

He spun about and began to retrace his steps.

'What is this? Turning back? But you've barely begun.'

'Why did you bring me here? If you mean to kill me, just do it! Or leave me be!'

'I don't desire your death. You are not like these others. They have long since made their choices. You can still change your path.'

You are not like these others.

Rex came to a standstill. He had entered once more the shadowy glade, encircled by pine trees. He could hear now the cawing of the crows and the shushing of the wind, every sound very clear and distinct.

But there was something else here – it was pushing at the edge of his perception. He realized now that some part of him had known it was here all along.

Finally, unable to stand the tension in his bones, he slowly raised his head and looked up into the boughs. And there, suspended in the trees, were four dangling objects.

They were uncanny, his mind unable to fit them into any pattern of his experience. They were like fruit, only swollen and monstrous. They were like the cocoons of insects, only far too massive. Their cases were green and thorny, like vampire vines.

From inside one of these objects, Rex heard a muffled noise – a moan. He glimpsed a mouth, an eye. Human faces.

And finally his mind admitted the truth. These were funeral shrouds. And the men encased inside were still alive – like flies awaiting the return of the spider.

Rex was running then – he was scrabbling, staggering, blundering back through the wildwood, blind now to his surroundings, instinct alone guiding him back the way he had come.

'There's no need to run,' the phantom voice said, keeping pace, as though scampering through the boughs above. 'The forest must cleanse itself. But their fate need not be yours. Join me. We can put an end to all this.'

Rex fled back through the sunlit glade, along pathways, bolted for the tunnel where he had come in.

'Stop – I insist,' the voice said, hardening. 'I offered you refuge. Now you must stay, and learn the truth.'

As Rex dived for the tunnel, its mouth was already beginning to close. Rex scrambled through, his clothing snagging on thorns, and he kept scrabbling, racing onwards, while the tunnel crunched closed in his wake, snapping at his heels like monstrous jaws.

'So be it. Go then,' the phantom voice snarled in the dark. 'I granted you safe passage and I keep my promise. Go – and never return!'

With a slithering, crunching rumble, the tunnel finally collapsed along its length, sending a convulsion that swept Rex up and spat him out into the wastelands, where he landed breathless and senseless.

At some point he became aware of movement above him, and voices. The rangers of his bodyguard.

'Sire – are you injured?'

'It's a trap,' Rex mumbled, staggering to his feet. 'They're dead.'

Dazed, he stared out across the plains and listened. The sights and sounds of warfare hit him with such piercing clarity it was as though he had just surfaced from underwater. Soldiers were dying. The outlaws would kill them all.

'It's a trap!' he hollered, stumbling around the edge of the wildwood. 'Cease this. Come out!' he shouted to the warrior monks. 'Free yourselves! Now!'

Rex's shouts were matched by the voice of the wildwood – a furious shrieking howl that rose into the uppermost boughs.

'You betray me, brother,' the riot seemed to roar. 'I offered you truth, and fellowship, and this is how I am repaid!'

'It's a trap!' Rex hollered, regardless. 'He's luring you in one by one. Sir Guy – cease this, now! All of you – come out!'

The warrior monks, trained their entire lives to obedience, did as they were bid. They struggled and slashed their way free of the ditch and came to stand out in the open.

The heretic hunter himself, however, seemed oblivious. He remained locked in his private war with the wall of thorns. And now, with the warrior monks free, the vegetation was tightening around him, tendrils squeezing like pythons embracing their prey.

'Your master. Help him!' Rex hollered to the warrior monks. 'The rest of you,' he shouted to his bodyguard, 'with me. Set him free!'

They rushed in to attack the undergrowth, trying to reach Sir Guy. Rex feared the wildwood would swallow them all, so fierce was this struggle. Every time he swung his blade, loped off a vine, he was faced by two more. Each severed limb sprayed sap like green blood, while the forest sent up shrieks of pain and rage.

'Sir Guy – halt! I'm ordering you to follow me!'

333

'I told you before, my prince,' the heretic hunter growled. 'I've waited a long time for this. I shall destroy the savage sorcerer and his accursed forest.'

'You're a fool! He's toying with you. Four of your monks are dead.'

'They are ready to give up their lives, as am I.'

'Then he'll win! Don't you see? He's trapped in there. We don't have to dig him out. We can wait.'

Whether his words finally cut through Sir Guy's fury, or whether the wildwood itself could endure this torturous struggle no longer, Rex would never know. With a roaring bellow that came from the heretic hunter's throat, or from the forest, or both, the undergrowth surged and swords slashed and the world spun, and Rex found himself back out in the wastelands, sprawled on his back, warrior monks and soldiers groaning around him.

As Rex staggered upright, he saw Sir Guy was already back on his feet, brandishing his giant blade.

'If you go back in there you're a bigger fool than I took you for,' Rex spat at him. 'You'll throw away your life and victory with it.'

Slowly, while the wildwood shrieked, Sir Guy turned to face him. 'Twice you have called me fool,' he said darkly from behind his mask. 'No matter who you are, when the time comes, you shall reckon for it.'

'We don't have time for your threats, or your idiocy,' Rex said, shaking, forcing himself to hold the heretic hunter's black glare. 'Look at it out there. See for yourself. We will lose here today, unless we act now.'

The sounds of warfare rang across the plain. Finally, Sir Guy looked one last time at the wildwood. And then, without another word, he went to his horse, leaped into the saddle, and charged towards the battlefield, his warrior monks in his wake.

Ordering his bodyguard to follow, Rex took to his own mount. And then he was galloping after the heretic hunter, drawing his sword, preparing to do battle with the outlaws.

And so the choice had been made. He had stepped over the brink. Ahead of him his bloody fate yawned open like an abyss.

VII. God of War

Marian had seen this before. When the tide of war turns, it does so with startling speed and brutality. One moment she and her rebel horde were closing in on the third war machine, the last of its defenders practically on their knees – and she was glancing across at the other remaining siege engines, seeing that they were similarly besieged and would soon surely fall – and in the next instant all was turned on its head, and the enemy was surging back to life with the savagery of a wounded beast.

First, in the near distance, came the thundering of hooves. Turning, she saw a cloud of dust sweeping across the plain, heading towards the furthest trebuchet. From within the dust came the flash of red robes. And at the head of this charge was a giant mounted warrior garbed head to toe in the hide of a horse.

Holding her breath, Marian watched the heretic hunter come sweeping into battle, cloaked in his cloud of dust, like some god of war descending upon mortals, swinging his broadsword, lopping off heads.

Behind him, the blades of his warrior monks flashed in the sun. In their wake came a smaller band of soldiers, who loosed crossbows from horseback. But Marian barely glanced at them. Her full focus was locked on the heretic hunter and his acolytes. Already, they were cutting a swathe through the rebel ranks.

'Midge – do you see?' Marian called. 'This is what we feared. It'll take all of us to stop him. We need to get over there.'

'What about here?' Midge yelled back, hurling a rock from his slingshot. 'We can't leave this machine operational.'

It was true. Their own target was vital. She looked once more across the plain. Jack and Ira had now joined forces, she knew, marshalling all their peasant troops into the push for the fourth siege engine. Would their combined forces be enough to resist Guy of Gisbourne?

She watched the giant warrior turn his destrier and thunder once more into battle, swinging his sword in one hand, then the other, cutting left and right, scything down rebels like so many sheaths of wheat. Following his lead, his warrior monks cut down survivors with efficient zeal.

No – these peasant warriors had come this far on pure fury and thirst for vengeance – but that would no longer be enough. The heretic hunter matched their rage, ounce for ounce, and added to it a lifetime's experience of bloodshed.

'They can't stand against him,' Marian insisted to Midge. 'They need us.'

'We've got our hands full here,' Midge shouted, letting fly once more with his slingshot. 'These dogs were about to lie down. Now look.'

This was true, too. Sir Guy's reappearance on the battlefield had sent fresh fire coursing through all the Sheriff's troops, restoring their morale and whetting their courage. The soldiers they were facing had closed ranks, locking shields and beginning a slow march forward, spears lowered.

We were so close! If only we could reach that machine, destroy it. We'd break their will and win free at the same stroke.

And that was when she saw it. Scanning the defensive line, she spotted her chance – and already she was up and running.

'Hold them off,' she shouted back to Midge. 'And be ready!'

'Ready for what? Marian!'

She dashed with her head down, directly for the shield wall. Soldiers readied their spears to meet her charge. At the last moment she veered away and skirted their lines. A crossbow bolt skimmed her arm but she kept running, past outlaws and soldiers who were locked in skirmishes, hurdling injured men and dying men and corpses.

'Marian – what is this?' Midge's voice reached her faintly. 'You'll never reach the engine on your own!'

But she wasn't targeting the engine. So far, this entire skirmish had been focused around it. Meanwhile, close behind it was a long cart, loaded with projectiles. In the heat of battle it had been overlooked, and stood relatively unguarded.

Re-sheathing her arrow and strapping her bow across her back, she darted between rangers, dodging one blade, ducking the next, weaving and sprinting for the cart, throwing herself beneath it as crossbow bolts hummed and thudded into the wood of its wheels.

The ranger's commander understood what Marian was planning now and was shouting orders, sending men to stop her. Beneath the cart, Marian tore upon her backpack, pulled out her strike-a-light. She groped around inside the pack once more and – yes, thank the gods, here was a tinder pouch, unused and dry.

Gripping the strike-a-light, she clashed the flint against the firesteel, but failed to get a spark. She tried again, and again, in vain.

'Come on,' she whispered to herself as more crossbow bolts ricocheted off the cart and soldiers came running.

She clashed steel and stone, over and over, and finally – yes, a spark landed on the little pile of tinder, set it aflame. Breathing on the precious fire, forcing herself not to hurry even as nailed boots thundered close, she scooped up the burning tinder, heedless to the burning of her palms.

She wriggled out on her stomach and stood at the rear of the cart. She swept the flame across the projectiles – two, three, four of them – their fuses fizzing into life. She lit a fifth, a sixth, before the soldiers were upon her.

She drew her dagger and her boot knife, slashed wildly left and right, snarling at her attackers, keeping them at bay, a wildcat with claws of steel.

The outlaws came rushing to her aid – Midge and a dozen others, setting about the soldiers with their own blades – and everything descended into a melee of fury and blood and screams and thrashing limbs.

'Get clear of the cart!' Marian shouted to Midge and the others. 'Run!'

Lunging at a soldier, spinning past another, she opened space for herself and leaped into it. Hurdling a fallen ranger, ducking a flailing blade, she lowered her head and ran, hollering for the others to do the same.

Then the world turned over, cracked apart into shards of black and yellow and red, and the Earth was roaring at the sky, and Marian found herself on her back, staring at the blackened sun, while fiery fragments of wood fell down upon her like hot rain.

Her vision was blurred and the ground was soft and there was an angry buzzing in her ears. Sucking lungfuls of burning air, rolling over, she found herself staring into the face of a soldier. His eyes were wide and still, his head cleaved by a shard of flying timber, which lay lodged in his skull, and still flickered with flame.

Other victims lay scattered about, or stood around stupidly, clutching at lost limbs. Or they rolled over in the dust, their cloths aflame, trying to tear off their cloaks and their armour, their mouths open in muted screams.

Somebody stumbled to stand over her. It was Midge. He was blood-spattered and burned, one ear charred and twisted. As he reached down to her he said something, but his words were swallowed by that buzzing that filled the world.

Marian took his hand and staggered upright. Other rebels were here, looking stunned but on their feet, some still gripping their weapons, others searching around for fallen blades or for missing parts of themselves.

Marian nodded to Midge. She tried to speak, then gave up and merely pointed towards the second battlefront. Those who were able took her lead and together they staggered and limped away from the scene of devastation, lone soldiers watching them in a daze.

Marian blinked, almost fell. Ahead of her the world was an unstable mix of colour and shape. It drifted into two halves, came back together, slipped apart once again. It was the best she could do to keep her feet as they stumbled onwards. She was aware Midge was saying something at her side but his voice was a distant murmur, as if heard underwater.

She tried to focus on the battle ahead. Events swam together, resolved, revealed pieces of themselves. There was Guy of Gisbourne, riding his giant destrier. To Marian's stunned mind, man and mount were one – a monstrous centaur galloping across the plain, trampling rebels underfoot, splitting others open with great swings of its sword. Riding in his wake, his warrior monks were demons, wearing robes of flame, wielding shards of lightning, slaughtering mortals at will.

We won't survive this, her shocked mind murmured. *Not with untrained troops – not caught in the open . . .*

Even as she was thinking this, figures came towards her and

Midge. It was Jack and Ira, trailed by a scattering of peasant fighters. Jack's mouth was moving – shouting – and Marian knew he was calling a retreat. Fall back to the wildwood, regroup. Midge resisted, but Jack took hold of him and kept yelling, and finally they were all fleeing towards Gaia.

As they ran, Marian looked back towards Guy of Gisbourne. He had dismounted his horse and was battling somebody, one-on-one.

It was Much Millerson. He had stayed behind, with a handful of peasant warriors, to keep the enemy occupied while the other outlaws withdrew.

Now this truly was a massacre. While she ran, and the world spun, Marian glanced back once more, saw two more rebels fall, ridden down by red-cloaked rangers.

Much was still on his feet, swinging his massive quarterstaff, he and the heretic hunter battling there on the plain like a pair of giants.

But then, as she looked back again, she saw a warrior monk charge Much from behind. He was forced to turn and parry, and in that instant the heretic hunter struck, taking Much's head from his shoulders.

Midge glanced back too. He reeled and fell to his knees, sending up a wail of pain and fury loud enough to whet Marian's blunted senses, the sound sharp and real and terrible to her ears.

Jack took hold of Midge, dragged him upright, forced him to keep stumbling onwards. The remnants of the peasant army followed, while Marian staggered along at the rear.

Looking back once more, she saw Guy of Gisbourne re-sheath his sword, remount his horse. He turned his masked face towards the retreating outlaws, while his warrior monks finished their efficient slaughter.

Surely now the heretic hunter would come thundering after

them, try to stop them reaching the wildwood. Why was he just sitting there?

She noted now that a figure had come to his side. A young man riding a destrier, wearing a black cloak. This young warrior looked in her direction – stared straight at her.

From this distance he might have been anyone – and to her shocked and ringing mind he might not have been there at all, but merely one more mirage of the wastes – yet at the same time he was real and really here and could be nobody else.

And so she could no longer fool herself. Here he was. The commander of the Sheriff's forces. The face of her enemy.

Rex.

VIII. War Child

'My prince, your orders,' the heretic hunter snarled. 'If we pursue them now we may yet have their hides before they reach their bolthole.'

When Rex sat mute and immobile, staring across the wasteland at the retreating figures, the heretic hunter straightened in his saddle, growled behind his mask.

'You called me a fool, but now see how you are deceived. You believe that was her. I assure you, it was not. The outlaws are as sly as snakes. They dress their chief in a wolfskin and parade him as Robin Hood, reborn. Now they do the same with their fabled warrior queen. That was not your mother, my prince. Your mother is dead. That was merely one of her warhawks, wearing her old skin. A mummer's trick to rally the troops. Or to deceive you.' He lowered his mask to spit in the dirt. 'And it worked. Now they have escaped us.'

These words were distant and unreal. Out there, across the battlefield, Rex had seen his mother. He had met her eyes. Nothing could be more certain than that. And yet, at the same time, it was not true. It could not be. These two certainties warred within him, tearing apart his reality, making everything false – even the ground beneath him and the sky above – mere figments, simply shadows of a dream.

Your mother is dead.

That was merely one of her warhawks, dressed up in her old skin.

Was that it then? Was that what he had seen? The outlaws were masters of deception, he had witnessed that for himself. Hadn't their chief tried to beguile Rex with false promises in order to lure him into a death trap? So, yes, they were capable of this too, of course they were. This depravity – this sacrilege – using the image of his dead mother against him. How dare they! His heart burned and tears of rage stabbed behind his eyes, while above him a lone buzzard circled, its piercing call merging with the cries of the dying scattered across the battlefield.

The chief engineer stepped forward to address him. 'Sire, two of the war machines have been destroyed. Another has suffered damage but can be salvaged. Shall I recommence the bombardment?'

Rex was grinding his teeth so hard that at first he could not speak. Eventually, he shook his head and said: 'We regroup, rearm, then hit them in full force.' He pointed to a senior ranger. 'You – pick three men. Take spare horses and ride hard. Report back to the city. Tell my father we have broken the outlaws' resistance. But it may take time to burn them out. Tell him we need reinforcements. Replacement siege engines, more ordnance, and provisions for a siege. If we must remain out here for a year, so be it. We shall annihilate the outlaws, raze their forest to the ground, no matter how long it may take.'

IX. The Power of Hatred

Robin existed inside a well of nothingness. His body still hung here, chained deep beneath the ground, but his spirit had long since left him. Rats gnawed at his wasted flesh without him feeling their teeth. Cockroaches crawled across his open wounds, looking for warm places to lay their eggs, and he remained oblivious. His mind, as raw as the scorched earth, flickered with half-formed thoughts and memories, but none of them could take hold, his heart remaining cold and slow and passionless.

He had no idea how long this living death had persisted. But now, abruptly – very faintly – something shifted. The narrowest of cracks appeared in the black walls of his existence. A glimmer of something shone through, seeped into his experience.

Was it physical pain he felt, or fear, or mental anguish? It had been so long since he had felt anything that at first he could not tell what this might be.

The sensation kept growing, like an intense thirst, or hunger, until it filled every fibre of his being. It brought him back to himself, making him aware of his surroundings and his own body – this scrap of skin chained to this dungeon wall.

What was the cause? He began to suspect he knew. A presence was drawing near. A powerful presence he had not sensed in a long time. A presence that once hung over his every thought and deed. A shadow he might almost believe he had cast off, together with all the other trappings of the world.

But no. That shadow clung to him still. It was here. It had a name.

The Sheriff.

And that feeling that first broke into Robin's blank prison – the emotion this man had provoked – it had a name too.

Hatred.

Robin's chains rattled and his limbs spasmed. Rats and cockroaches scattered as he growled low in his throat.

The Sheriff had now reached the bottom of the stone steps. Here he paused, four bodyguards coming to a halt behind him. Finally, leaving the other men where they were, the Sheriff came forward, holding a flaming torch.

As he reached the bars of Robin's cell, and stood looking in, Robin's body spasmed once more – it tried to thrash itself free. But the effort was weak and achieved nothing. He slumped, exhausted.

'Pitiful,' the Sheriff rasped, the fetid air down here rattling in his sick lungs, every detail now coming to Robin clear and sharp. 'I'll tell you a secret,' he said in low tones, leaning closer to the bars. 'I have wanted to come down here for days. But I was afraid. Yes, it is an insidious habit, my fear of you. But now, see what you have become. I have more to fear from my own shadow.'

The Sheriff pressed his ruined face to the bars. 'Nothing to say?' he rasped. 'Do you now lack even words to use against me? When I remember our first meeting – that day I took your eyes. You were ready to fight the entire Sheriff's guard – all for her sake. But now look at you. All you were gifted, yet you lost the will to fight. You never deserved her love,' he spat. 'Had she given it to me, there is *nothing* I would not have done to keep it. I would have burned the forest ten times over – I would have laid waste the world!'

At this, Robin's hatred redoubled, and his rage rattled his chains, while he snarled low in his throat. Startled, the Sheriff retreated. His bodyguard rushed to his side, spears lowered. But once again Robin's surge of vitality was short-lived, and afterwards he slumped more lifeless than ever.

'The power of hatred,' the Sheriff said slowly, waving the rangers away and moving back towards the cell. 'Is there anything to match it on this Earth? Perhaps that is all that has kept you alive – your hatred of me. After all . . . what more do you have to live for?'

He leaned forward, and whispered: 'A messenger returned from the wastes. My son and his force have located the last vestige of Sherwood. They are laying siege to it even as we speak. You will feel it, won't you, when your forest finally dies? I trust you will. I want you to die knowing your entire life was futile – that everything you ever fought for was in vain.'

These words were fresh fuel to Robin's fury. He roared, thrashed, howled. Just for a moment, his strength surged so potently that he believed he might do it – that he could break these bonds and these bars – that he would destroy his nemesis with his bare hands.

But this was mere fallacy. Robin's wasted flesh was like sodden wood – the fire of his rage could find no purchase and soon it fizzled out, leaving him slumped, a blackened shell.

'Truly pitiful,' the Sheriff said. 'Soon, both you and your forest shall be extinct. There will be no one to mourn either of you. No one to even remember you existed. Guards, escort the prisoner to Gallows Field. His pyre is complete. Tomorrow, your final fire shall rise,' he told Robin, as he turned to leave. 'And my own legacy shall be assured.'

So saying, he ascended the steps out of the dungeon,

taking Robin's rage and the last scrap of his vitality with him, the black walls of nothingness closing in once more as the guards unlocked his cell and prepared to bear him to his place of execution.

X. The Last Sacrament

A shocked, exhausted silence had fallen upon Gaia and the surrounding plains. The surviving rebels were gathered in the great glade that lay beneath the Mother Tree. Here they nursed their wounds, and slept, and grieved for fallen friends and comrades.

The Sheriff's troops set up two camps around their remaining war machines, erecting shelters against the sun and posting sentries in the trenches vacated by the outlaws. Not a gust of wind stirred out there in the wastes, and barely a leaf rustled in Gaia.

For two whole days and nights this stunned stalemate persisted. Kit sat alone in The Henge, feeling so depleted he could hardly rouse himself to eat or to find fresh fuel for his meagre fire. He felt as drained as the wildwood, the birds barely stirring in their roosts, all the burrowers gone to ground, no background hum even of insects.

On the third day, he awoke from a fitful sleep to be greeted by another silent dawn. Except, suddenly, it seemed to him the silence was merely a mask. Beneath this hush, the world roared with violence. Wails of rage and war cries and the whip-crack of siege engines letting loose. This violence was of the past but also of the future. The scream of trees as flaming comets explode among their branches. The ravenous roar of fire as an inferno rips through the last remnant of Sherwood Forest.

This dreadful vision overcame Kit's exhaustion, and he dragged himself upright. Staggering out of The Henge, he went to where the other rebels were encamped. He stood on raised ground above the glade, his wolfskin wrapped around him.

'We've nursed our shock long enough,' he told them. 'Perhaps the Earth is already doomed. But unless we take action, we know it to be so.'

'What are we supposed to do?' Jack asked, sitting upright against a tree, his left arm in a sling. 'Look around. We're in pieces.'

'So are they,' Midge said, rising to his feet, grief and rage etched on his face. 'Kit's right. We need to get out there and fight. What else is left?'

'We can't face the heretic hunter in the open,' Ira said, without opening her eyes, her head pillowed on a bed of moss. 'It'll be lambs to the slaughter.'

'If they haven't attacked again, it means they've sent for reinforcements,' Kit told them. 'Now they know where we are, they'll never stop. It will only get worse.'

'He's right,' Midge spat, prowling between the sprawled rebels. 'After all we've fought for – everything we've lost – is that the way you want this to end? Like trapped rats. We need to fight – to the last drop of blood!'

'All right, all right,' Jack groaned, getting to his feet. 'Don't stand over me snarling. I'm up. So, what's the plan?'

'We wait until nightfall, and hope for cloud cover,' Kit said. 'Hit them fast then out again. Where's Marian?'

'She took off alone, as soon as we got back,' Ira said. 'Haven't seen her since.'

'I'll track her down,' Kit said. 'Make sure everyone's ready. I want us armed and on the move as soon as it's dark.'

Marian had been distraught after the battle, clumsy and careless, so her trail was not hard to follow. Kit found her in a secluded dell. She was sitting with her arms wrapped around her knees, cradling her backpack. Her leather armour lay scattered in the grass, together with her bow and arrows.

'We're going back out there,' Kit told her. 'We'll break into three squads. I'll lead one, head on. I need you and Ira to lead the others, try and get round their flanks. Marian, do you hear me? We need you with us. You put fire in the troops.'

Finally, she managed the slightest shake of her head. 'I should never have gone out there the first time. That's . . . not who I am. Not any more.'

'We none of us have any choice.'

'He's here, don't you see. He's out there with them.'

'Rex. Yes. I know.'

'I can't fight against him. I can't. I won't.'

'You've lost him, Marian. You need to accept that. I gave him every chance, but he turned his back. He's the Sheriff's son – now if he never was.'

'Don't you dare say that. You know nothing about him.'

'Perhaps not,' Kit said carefully, 'but I know who you are. You are Marian Delbosque. Queen of Sherwood Forest.'

Again she shook her head. 'I'm telling you, that person no longer exists. None of it . . . none of it makes sense. Not like it did.' She raised her head, and her eyes were red from weeping. 'I need to go to Robin. He needs me. He and Rex . . . They're all I have left.'

'Marian, you need to face facts. By now . . . Robin will be dead.'

'He's alive. I know he is. I can help him.'

'How?'

Reflexively, Marian curled more tightly around her backpack. Kit narrowed his eyes.

'What have you got there?'

'You know what she's got,' came another voice, disembodied. 'She has what you need.'

'Quiet, witch!' Marian hissed, flaring to life, clasping the pack to her chest. 'How dare you! It's mine!'

The goddess laughed, unseen. 'It is a gift of the gods. It cannot be owned – any more than the skin or the shadow. They are merely borrowed.'

'What's she talking about?' Kit said. 'What have you got? Show me!'

He moved closer, reached a hand towards her backpack. Marian's reaction was that of a wildcat protecting her cub – she spat and hissed at Kit, clawed at his face – and when he staggered back she bolted past him out of the dell.

He raced after her, scrabbling across a mossy log and hurdling a stream. There she was – disappearing into that copse of ash trees. The goddess ran with him, scampering through the undergrowth in the shape of a vixen.

'Now the wheel turns,' she laughed, breathless. 'Who shall wield the final piece?'

'The blood of the wolf-god.' Kit gritted his teeth. 'That's what she's got, isn't it?'

'Will it be used to restore life, or to steal lives? Power always flows both ways – that's what my brother used to say. To protect or destroy? To heal or to slay?'

'Marian!' Kit shouted. 'I need the blood – give it to me!'

Ahead of him, a flash of her dark hair as she fled the copse and started down a steep embankment, disappearing into long grass.

'Marian – see sense,' he shouted as he chased after her. 'You know as well as I do, it's the only way we can win. I used the blood before – to hold the heretic hunter at bay. I can use it again, to beat him once and for all.'

'Get away from me!' she shrieked back, darting along a path that snaked through swampland. 'I won't let you have it. I won't let you use it against Rex!'

'He stands against the forest, Marian. He's made his choice.'

'Robin needs it . . . I can save him!'

'You cannot put them before the forest! I won't allow it!'

As he blundered across the swamp, wading through putrid pools, he lashed out with his forest powers, sending a wave of mud and water surging across an islet. Marian wailed, darted out of her hiding place, scrambled for another bolthole.

'You can't escape me here, Marian!' he called. 'I *am* the forest. Wherever you run, I'm already there.'

Lifting both arms, he sent a pair of python vines snaking across the swamp. Their heads snapped at the rotten log in which Marian had taken refuge. As Kit lashed the log, and its soft wood crumbled into fragments, Marian scrabbled free and ran. Kit swept branches across her path, stabbed at her with daggerwood, lashed at her with thorns, but she weaved and ducked and dashed through it all.

'There's nowhere to go,' Kit shouted. 'I'm running out of patience. I need to go out there and face our enemies. The blood . . . Give it to me!'

The longer this game of cat-and-mouse went on, the fiercer Kit's rage blazed. How dare she keep the blood for her own ends, when *everything* stood at stake?

His anger became a white noise, which fuzzed his senses. He knew Marian was dead ahead, crouching in that bed of reeds. He could hear her scrabbling around in there. But what was she doing? Digging? Trying to burrow herself a bolthole? Or – was she stashing the vessel of blood?

'No!' Kit hollered. 'How dare you! Give it to me!'

Planting his feet, raising his arms, he sent six vampire vines slithering across the earth. They converged on the bed of reeds, and Marian shrieked again as they took hold of her limbs. Drawing in his arms, Kit tautened the vines and hauled her from her refuge. She came out kicking and screaming, clinging onto the amphora containing the god's blood.

'I didn't want it to come to this,' Kit snarled as he used the vines to yank her off the ground, dangling her upside down. 'I never saw you as my enemy.'

Stepping close, he reached out for the amphora. Even now she clutched it to her chest and tried to fend him off. But it was futile. He tightened a vine around her wrist, twisted it. She gasped, her fist wrenched open and Kit took the vessel.

'You can't,' she whispered, slumping. 'Please, don't use it against him. I need it. Robin needs it.'

'The forest needs it more,' Kit said evenly, his passion draining away. 'I'm sorry. If there was any other way . . .'

He turned his back on her. 'If you won't fight alongside us, so be it. At least stay out of our way.'

As he left, he released his grip on the vines, which dumped Marian to the ground, where she remained huddled, whimpering and whispering to herself.

From the corner of his eye, Kit spotted the goddess. She was crouched amid the reeds, watching him, smiling, her golden gaze sparkling.

Forget her. You have what you need, he told himself, shaking the amphora, feeling the viscous liquid slosh inside. *A true gift from the gods. Manna from the Earth. Now put it to use. Go out there and finish this once and for all.*

XI. The Betrayer

'To arms! Awake, everyone! To arms! Outlaws!'

Rex lurched to his feet even before he knew he was awake, hauled out of a black and evil dream into this black and evil night, which was ringing with cries of alarm, and with screams.

'Outlaws! They're here! To arms!'

His sword was in his hand and he was staggering towards his horse. The six rangers of his bodyguard rushed to his side, encircling him with weapons drawn.

From the direction of the sentry posts he heard grisly sounds – the wet popping of arrows puncturing flesh, followed by gurgled death-wails.

'Heretic hunter! Where are you?' he hollered. 'To arms!'

But Sir Guy was already on the move. As Rex leaped into his saddle, a giant mounted figure swept across his vision. Sir Guy thundered into battle, flanked by his warrior monks, their robes blood-red against the low moon, their blades raised and glinting.

The outlaws are finished, the thought came to Rex as he brandished his own sword, kicked his horse into motion. This is pure desperation – facing us out here in the open. They'll be slaughtered.

From the east, a piercing cry caught his ear. He swept his gaze along the outlaws' broken barricade – and there, shadowy forms were spilling out of the trenches – demons stealing across the perimeter.

'With me!' he hollered to his bodyguard, kicking at his horse's flanks, the fear and fury of his nightmare still coursing in his veins, merging with the thunder in his heart here and now. 'Ride them down!'

He led the charge eastwards, to where rebels and sentries were locked in hand-to-hand combat. He saw a spray of blood, and a soldier fall, a pair of outlaws clubbing him with their quarterstaffs.

While the night spun around him in fear and fury, Rex charged the marauders, swinging his sword from the saddle. He caught one rebel a glancing blow with the blade. His horse collided with the second man, sending him sprawling.

By the time Rex had turned his mount, his bodyguard had entered the fray and the two rebels were dead, one skewered on a spear, the other pinned to the ground by crossbow bolts.

Outnumbered, facing mounted troops, other rebels were scattering, trying to melt back into the night, or scrabbling for their old foxholes.

'Ride them down! Dig them out!' Rex hollered, in a voice he didn't recognize.

Woken by these demons stealing out of the moonlight, he had become a demon himself, possessed by a fearful rage that worked his tongue and his sword arm, like a puppeteer pulling strings.

'They're here . . . They're escaping! Follow me! Kill them all!'

Perhaps he never did wake from his dark and deadly dream, because this night was unreal, his own words foreign to his ears, his limbs operating of their own accord as he thundered upon a lone rebel and he swung his blade.

The outlaw lifted a spear to defend himself – but the weight of Rex's charge shattered the shaft and threw the man to the ground. Rex wheeled his horse, preparing to dismount and deliver the killing blow.

But then a sight out on the plain stopped him, made him pull up his mount and stare. Out there on the battlefield – a figure came stalking.

It was the outlaw king, dressed in his wolfskin, his bow lowered at his side. Unlike the rest of the rebels, Kit did not come furtively, low to the ground, scuttling from shadow to shadow. Instead, he strode in the full glare of the moon, his cloak silvered where it swirled around him, the eyes of his wolf-head cowl gleaming redly, as if they were still seeing.

As he strode forward, behind his advancing outlaws, he raised his voice to the sky.

'Guy of Gisbourne – come and face me!'

What game was this? Challenging Sir Guy to a duel? As deadly as the outlaw king might be, no one could stand against the heretic hunter one-on-one. Sir Guy would swat him aside like a fly.

'Heretic hunter – I'm here! Let us end this – now!'

To Rex's growing disbelief, as the outlaw king said this, he dropped his bow to the earth. He drew no blade. Did he *want* to throw his life away? Did he intend to make himself a martyr? What else could this achieve?

Well – he would soon get his wish. Because now Sir Guy was galloping along the line of trenches, heading for a gap in the broken barricade. He thundered towards the outlaw king, his blade bared and ready.

Rex spurred his own horse and rode closer. And as he did so, he saw the outlaw chief draw something from beneath his cloak. So – he did come armed, after all. Except this object did not appear to be a sword, or even a dagger. Instead, it looked like . . . a drinking vessel. Or an amphora.

Rex's memory tumbled him back to the Giants' Graveyard. He had watched the outlaw chief sprinkle a mysterious liquid upon the ground. And he had seen the result – a wall of thorns had come bursting up from the lifeless soil . . .

'It's a trick!' Rex hollered, galloping forwards. 'Sir Guy – it's another trap! Halt!'

Thundering towards his nemesis, the heretic hunter gave no indication he had even heard. Rex spurred his horse and rode directly into the giant warrior's path. Sir Guy pulled up at the last moment, his destrier rearing onto its hind legs.

'It's a lie!' Rex yelled. 'He doesn't mean to duel. He . . . he has Earth magic!'

This brought Sir Guy to a dead halt. The whole battle, in fact, now seemed to pause, the clashing of steel and the screams dying away, or drifting to the background. The shadowy figures of the outlaws became still, while rangers stood, weapons poised.

Only the outlaw king remained in motion, sweeping past the dead and the dying, now fixing his glare upon Rex.

'Once again you betray me, brother,' he snarled as he came closer. 'No matter. It won't save you now. I carry the strength of the gods. I bring your reckoning.'

As he spoke, he removed the stopper from the neck of the amphora and he swung the vessel this way and that, dispersing its dark, viscous contents.

Elsewhere, as rangers and rebels alike stood and stared, the stillness and silence intensified until the whole world might be holding its breath. Even Sir Guy seemed mesmerized by this moment, his sword hanging at his side.

Rex watched the outlaw king draw closer, casting the dark liquid like a farmer sowing seeds. The stuff pooled upon the ground, glistening. Rex held his breath, expecting any moment to see the soil split, and tendrils to snake upwards, baring their thorns.

But still he stared, and stared, and nothing shifted. Except now something had happened to the outlaw king. Was he injured? It seemed to Rex he was suddenly having difficulty walking. Yes – again he staggered, almost fell. He clutched at himself – at his chest – and on the stillness of the night air Rex was sure he could hear him muttering a word over and over – it sounded like 'Betrayed! Betrayed!'

'Something's wrong,' Rex murmured. 'His sorcery – it hasn't worked. Unless . . . that's what he wants us to think. Sir Guy, hold your ground. This could yet be a trick.'

The outlaw chief had now stumbled to a halt. As if in a daze, he lifted the amphora in front of his face. Then slowly he tipped it and let its contents dribble past his eyes. Finally, he let the vessel drop, and simultaneously tipped back his head and roared at the moon.

'We are betrayed! She has ruined us all. Run!' he hollered at nearby rebels. 'We are finished! Save yourselves . . . Run!'

While Rex sat stunned, Sir Guy could restrain himself no longer. Brandishing his blade, he roared into battle, his warrior monks in his wake. Rebels scattered, but there was no escape. Rangers were snapping back to life and were targeting them with their crossbows.

The outlaw king himself had slumped to his knees, his neck bared, apparently accepting his doom as Sir Guy thundered towards him, while for the moment Rex could only sit transfixed, the night spinning black and unreal around him, watching the slaughter begin.

XII. True Blood

'Oh my, what have you done?' the goddess whispered at Marian's side.

'I had no choice,' Marian murmured into her bunched fists, her knees pulled up to her chest. 'He would have used it against Rex.'

'You always were my favourite,' the goddess laughed. 'That shard of ice in your heart. But I never imagined even you could be *this* callous.'

'I couldn't let him take it – I couldn't,' Marian said, rocking back and forth. 'Robin needs it. It's his only hope.'

'But now listen,' the goddess said, her voice hushed with awe. 'You've sent them all to their deaths.'

Marian groaned, curled tighter into a ball around her backpack, tried to block her ears. From out there on the plain came the sounds of screaming. Of a massacre.

You've sent them all to their deaths.

Was it true? Was this her doing? She hadn't ordered them to go out there. It was Kit. He was their leader.

But you deceived him, she answered herself. You gave him false hope. And now he will die for it. His rebels too.

She sat upright, trembling, forced herself to fully absorb the noises from out in the wastes. The clashing of steel, and the *zip-thwip* of quarrels, and the crunch of bludgeons. But it was the screams – those gurgled death-wails – they filled the world. And when they ended . . . then would come silence. The rebellion would be finished. And the forest would fall.

'You're having a change of heart,' the goddess said, frowning. 'No matter. It's too late. Listen. Hear the screams.' She grinned. 'And the spaces between the screams.'

Marian opened her backpack and drew out her drinking bladder. When she had hidden from Kit amid the reeds, she had poured the blood into this vessel. Then she had refilled the amphora with muddy swamp water. She had done so in the heat of the moment, desperate to keep the god's blood for Robin. Only now, picturing Kit out there casting useless water upon the ground, did it fully dawn on her what she had done.

'I'm sorry, Robin,' she whispered to him across the years and the leagues of distance. 'I made a mistake. I've made so many mistakes. I so wanted to be with you again. I wanted to keep Rex safe.'

The goddess smiled, then laughed. 'You cannot save them both. Just as Robin had to choose between you and the forest. There will always be choices. Always a sacrifice.'

Marian's mind, until this moment spinning like a whirlpool, and her heart, churning with grief, suddenly came to rest. Straightening her back, she held the gaze of the goddess, and she suddenly felt quite calm.

'Yes – I understand,' she said at last. 'Perhaps I do have role to play here after all.'

The goddess clapped her hands. 'What are you going to do?'

'Come, I'll show you,' Marian said, standing. 'You were right – a sacrifice must be made. And afterwards . . . nothing will ever be the same again.'

*

The end was near. After all the struggle – all the years of battle and pain and loss – it would end here, tonight, Kit's lifeblood draining into the dust. He had no idea how he was still drawing breath, and he barely cared.

He had a vague recollection of kneeling, neck bared, while destruction came roaring down upon him – and then at the last moment being thrown to one side, the heretic hunter's blade slicing the night air, his destrier's hooves thundering past.

Now Kit lay sprawled, while the world around him unfolded like a nightmare, rebels dropping in the dark, wailing their death-cries.

'Come on, Kit, get to your feet!' a voice gabbled in his ear. 'We need to fight!'

It was Midge. So, it was he who had saved Kit, dragging him from the path of the onrushing heretic hunter. Now he was dragging at Kit's arm, trying to haul him upright.

'We fight to the last drop of blood, remember?' Midge snarled. 'On your feet!'

But Kit couldn't stand, could barely understand where he was or what any of this might mean. He was beyond exhausted, as though his blood had already been let from his body and he was nothing but an empty skin.

She betrayed us. Marian Delbosque. The warrior queen of Sherwood. Hers was the last betrayal. And now – what is there left?

'The heretic hunter . . . He's coming back,' Midge barked. 'Are you going to let him cut you down like a dog?'

Vaguely, Kit noted that Guy of Gisbourne had indeed wheeled his mount and was thundering towards Kit in another mad charge. Midge stood his ground, whirling his slingshot. He let fly. The heretic hunter raised the flat of his blade and the rock ricocheted off steel.

Guy of Gisbourne locked his gaze on Midge, raised his blade to strike. Seeing this jolted Kit back to life – he threw himself at

Midge, knocking him aside, the heretic hunter thundering by, his broadsword flashing overhead.

Again, Sir Guy slowed his mount and turned. Standing side by side with Midge, Kit drew his sword. Finally, in spite of everything – despite the hopelessness flooding through him – his survival instinct was rising, bringing the world back into sharp relief.

He saw other outlaws were here – Ira with her throwing daggers, Jack swinging his double sabres, warrior peasants with their makeshift clubs. Between them they were holding off five, six warrior monks. Beyond this Kit could make out little, the rest of the battlefield a dark swirl of chaos.

He focused on the heretic hunter, who was now climbing down from his horse.

'You have run from me long enough,' he growled. 'It is time we finished this.'

Midge launched another rock, which caught the heretic hunter square on the shoulder. He flinched but strode onwards.

'Take care of the other one,' he growled to his henchmen. 'The outlaw king and I must not be interrupted.'

While two warrior monks closed on Midge, and he drew his sword to defend himself, Kit scanned the ground for his bow. There! He leaped upon it, snatched up his quiver – and in the same motion he had nocked and drawn and let loose. Once more, the heretic hunter held his broadsword before him like a shield, and the arrow shattered against its steel.

Kit loosed a second shot, which Sir Guy swatted aside with a gloved fist. Kit's third arrow hit home, penetrating his adversary's horsehide armour and burying itself deep into his left shoulder.

The giant warrior barely broke stride as he powered forward – and with shocking speed he was upon Kit, bringing his blade down in a massive, sweeping arc, causing Kit to throw himself to one side and roll away in the dust.

As he leaped to his feet, he let his bow drop and drew his sword – just in time to deflect another mighty strike, the power of it ringing through the steel and through every sinew of his body, making him stumble, almost fall.

And already the next strike was thundering down, and the next, Kit meeting each attack with just enough force to turn it aside, but even so each one shaking him to the roots, shuddering through his bones like hammer blows.

'This is all I asked,' Sir Guy rumbled from behind his mask, while Kit scrabbled in the dust, breathless. 'To test my mettle against yours. Now finally the moment is here. And I must admit to disappointment. You can barely keep your feet. Without your accursed forest, you are nothing. So be it. Tonight, you both shall meet extinction.'

So saying, with horrendous speed and ferocity, he brought his broadsword sweeping down. Kit dived clear, sprung up again with his own blade raised, just in time to turn a second strike, and a third – and once again he was floundering beneath a barrage of blows, as relentless as hailstones.

While Kit stumbled and struggled for balance, Sir Guy stayed his sword once more – and Kit knew truly then that his opponent was toying with him, drawing out this fight for his own sick satisfaction.

In desperation, he scanned the battlefield for potential advantage – for any possible lifeline. He saw only rangers riding down rebels, hunting survivors deeper into the wastes. Midge was still on his feet, and Ira and Jack, but for how much longer?

'You look in vain for salvation,' the heretic hunter gloated. 'Nothing and no one is coming to your aid. Your forest is as helpless as you are. Your false idol, Robin Hood, stands atop his pyre. You and your kind will soon be gone – and forgotten.' He shook his head, spat in disgust. 'I grow tired of it all. Let us have it finished.'

He came forward with renewed malice, swinging his great broadsword one-handed, the blade humming the air so fast it became a blur of moonbeams – a shard of ice slicing the night to pieces.

Kit reacted on pure instinct, the blows coming so quick he could not be sure he had connected with one before blocking the next. He felt suddenly cold in the right shoulder. A second splinter of ice entered his ribs before running down his right-hand side.

'Is this not part of your creed?' the heretic hunter gloated. 'You talk of watering the soil with your blood. Tonight you shall be good to your word.'

Kit's vision was blurred. More coldness opened up in his midriff and chest – a coldness that burned. He was bleeding now from a dozen cuts, and as the blood seeped out of him it was all he could do to hold his balance. He took a two-handed grip on his sword, and locked eyes with his nemesis. He would never submit. But there was nothing he could do now but await the inevitable.

Guy of Gisbourne raised his blade to deliver the death blow – swept forward – then came to a standstill. He froze, staring at something over Kit's shoulder.

Kit half-turned, blinking sweat and blood from his eyes. And he saw a figure approaching. She was dressed only in a white smock, which shone, spectral, in the moonlight. Bands of black warpaint had run across her face, giving her features a twisted appearance. She was part angel, part demon. Only her eyes were unmistakable – those varicoloured eyes of grey and green.

Guy of Gisbourne remained motionless, looking uncertain. Until finally he forced a guttural laugh. 'Whoever you are, you do not fool me. You are not the forest queen. She lies in an unmarked tomb.'

Marian kept coming forward, her bow at half-draw, the

bodkin aimed at the heretic hunter's heart. Sir Guy lowered his sword, took half a step backwards, before laughing once more.

'I admit, the likeness is uncanny. But you are not Marian Delbosque. She is dead. I killed her with my own hands.'

As he spoke these words, even the moonlight seemed to freeze, as if time had come to a standstill – or the rest of the world had ceased to be. For Kit, all that existed was this charmed circle: him and Marian and the heretic hunter – and one other.

As if he had materialized out of nothing, the boy Rex was suddenly here. He was standing twenty yards away, staring, his sword dropped at his feet.

You are not Marian Delbosque. She is dead. I killed her with my own hands.

Finally, Guy of Gisbourne looked fully at Rex, and he gave another guttural laugh.

'The truth will out,' he spat. 'Well, no matter. I had already decided our sweet prince should not be returning to the city. He is not fit to be the Sheriff's lackey, let alone his heir.'

At this, Marian hissed between her teeth, pulled her bow to full draw. 'Monster. You will not touch a hair on his head – I swear!'

'What is it to you, imposter?' Sir Guy growled. 'Soon you too shall die. The Earth Mage tried to fell me with arrows. You will fare no better. Take your shot. It will be your last.'

The bow trembled in Marian's hands, while behind her Kit spotted more movement. Another figure had entered their charmed circle. Her fox-red hair brushed the cracked earth as she crept into fuller view, moving in a half-crouch, watching them all, her eyes shining bright as the moon.

The heretic hunter fixed his black gaze on the vixen-goddess. 'What is this? Another trick? This is rank desperation.'

'Rex,' Marian called out. 'You need to run.'

Her son merely stood there, his eyes vacant, as if moonstruck.

'Rex! Did you hear me? Something bad is going to happen. You can't be here. I need you to ride for the city.'

Blinking more blood from his eyes, shaking his head, Kit felt some of his vitality returning, his wits beginning to clear. He focused on Marian, and the pack he could see strapped to her back.

'Marian – you still have the blood! That's all that matters. Give it to me!'

She shook her head. 'I told you, I need it. Robin needs it.'

Kit roared. 'It's our only chance! I can save us all . . . I can save the forest. Throw me the blood. Now!'

'See how the wheel turns,' the goddess whispered, while from all across the battlefield came wails of hatred, and screams. 'They said it would end in a storm of fire, and a rain of blood. Now we stand witness!'

'What is this travesty?' Guy of Gisbourne growled, staring at the goddess. 'You will all suffer for bringing it before me.' He turned fully to face Marian, opened his arms away from his chest. 'Take your shot,' he spat, 'then die.'

'Marian – the blood!' Kit howled. 'It's our only hope!'

'It isn't,' Marian said evenly. 'Kit, you need to trust me. Rex, you too. I can't imagine how hard this is for you – but I'm here – it's really me. Time is running out. I need you to get away . . . Now.'

Kit staggered to where his bow had fallen. He snatched it up, together with an arrow. He nocked and drew and took aim at Marian's heart.

'I'll do it,' he snarled. 'The blood – give it to me! It's the last relic. That's all there is left!'

Marian met his eyes, while her bow remained trained on Sir Guy.

'No,' she said. 'It's not.'

'Oh yes, it is,' the goddess said, dancing around them all, her eyes flashing with girlish glee. 'We gave you gifts. The Shadow. The Teeth. You squandered them all. Soon the blood too shall run dry.'

'Soon, but not yet,' Marian said evenly. 'There is more blood. Far more than I carry here.'

'You are mistaken,' the goddess said. 'I collected the blood myself – every last drop.'

'There is more,' Marian insisted. 'It was hidden in plain sight. Its vessel is beyond precious. But we are left no other choice. We must crack it open.'

The goddess became still, and her face changed.

'It was you who helped me see,' Marian told her. 'Death feeds life. Which means there must always be a sacrifice. Rex – ride. Now! Get away!'

So saying, Marian turned her bow, until the bodkin was trained on the goddess's heart. And before Kit could blink, she let loose, and the goddess screamed.

Then the world was in chaos. Guy of Gisbourne roared, raised his sword, lurched towards Marian, then Kit, blind with rage and not knowing who to attack first. Rex finally snapped out of his stupor, uttered a gurgled yell, leaped onto his horse, and was already galloping away.

The goddess, meanwhile, had become a creature from hell, wailing with a pain and rage that trembled the Earth as she fled heedlessly back and forth, Marian's arrow protruding from her chest, her blood spouting high into the air, misting in the moonlight.

Finally, Guy of Gisbourne collected his senses enough to charge at Marian. She rolled clear of his sword thrust, scrabbling away from the blades of two warrior monks, before sprinting towards a riderless horse.

Regaining his own wits, Kit let loose his arrow, which struck the heretic hunter in the lower back, narrowly missing his spine.

The giant warrior stumbled, but didn't fall. He roared, turned on Kit, hefting his broadsword.

From the corner of his eye, Kit glimpsed Marian leaping into the saddle, kicking her heels and galloping away, grabbing the reins of two other horses as she went, dragging them after her. Elsewhere, rangers stood rigid with shock as the dread wail of the goddess shook the Earth – while her fountaining blood washed down upon them like hot rain. Even the warrior monks were stunned, their blades stilled.

Only Guy of Gisbourne remained in motion. Staggering, perhaps from the blow Kit had dealt him, or from the quaking of the ground, he came slowly forwards, fixing Kit with his baleful black stare.

'Whatever witchery this is,' he spat, 'it is too late. Tonight, your rebellion dies. Your kind – your forest – both shall be made extinct. None of your tricks can save you now.'

'This is no trick,' Kit said evenly, opening his palms, which were slick with the rain of blood. 'This is the last sacrifice of the gods. Their final gift.'

'It is devilry and witchcraft,' the heretic hunter snarled. 'It will not stand against my righteous sword. Do you hear me? You will suffer for this sacrilege.'

He lurched towards Kit, but slipped, stumbling to one knee. The burned and rutted topsoil was now greased with blood. The heretic hunter rose to his feet, came forward once more, but unsteadily, his right boot catching on something, causing him to trip.

'Sorcery!' the heretic hunter howled. 'Demon work! Release me, Earth wizard, or you shall suffer!'

With his broadsword, he hacked at the ground near his right boot, which was held fast. Kit looked. He saw suckers had sprouted up through the cracked earth, their heads glistening with god-blood. Two of them had taken hold of Sir Guy's right foot, while more were even now snaking around his left ankle. He hacked and hacked at the suckers, but whenever one was severed, two more sprang up to take its place.

'I warn you, Sorcerer, call it off or my retribution shall be terrible!'

'This is not my doing,' Kit said evenly, standing before him, his bow lowered. 'I couldn't stop this now even if I chose.'

Sir Guy howled once more as the suckers twined around his arms and legs, twisting so tight that he dropped his sword. His warrior monks were similarly restrained – and the rest of the Sheriff's troops. Wherever the rain of blood watered the earth, shoots and tendrils were springing up, seizing the attackers. A few mounted men had been quick enough to gallop away, fleeing into the wastes, but most were struggling on the ground, crying out in fear. Or they were hacking in vain at the vegetation as saplings and thorn bushes grew up all around, trapping them in living cages.

And now those cages were contracting, crushing bones and constricting throats. Meanwhile, the goddess continued her death-dance, whirling through the battlefield like a dervish, shrieking and wailing at the moon, her limbs flailing wildly, a trail of blood glistening in her wake.

Ira came to Kit's side, saying nothing, looking stunned. Jack was here too, and Midge. All three were battered and bloodied, but still alive. They brought with them a scattering of other survivors: rebel peasants who looked dead on their feet, hollow-eyed.

Nearby, two warrior monks had become still, one hoisted off the ground, a noose of vines around his neck; the other encased in a briar bush, impaled by so many fish-hook thorns that he had bled dry, his face white. All across the battlefield it was the same: rangers and warrior monks ceasing their thrashing, giving up their last breath.

Kit stepped towards Guy of Gisbourne, who was still struggling, while tendrils twisted him like a ragdoll, snapping his tendons and wrenching his limbs from their sockets.

Even in the depths of his agony, on the brink of death, he held Kit's gaze, his black eyes burning with hatred. He tried to say something, but his windpipe was crushed. He attempted to raise a fist against Kit, but his twisted limbs would not allow it.

Kit watched him a moment longer, this giant warrior at the last utterly pathetic and impotent against the might of the forest. His suffering only made Kit feel sick. He raised one hand, closed his fingers into a fist; the vines that were wrapped around Sir Guy's bull-like neck gave one last wrench, there was a crunching, snapping sound, and with one final spasm the heretic hunter hung dead.

As the noise of his struggle died away, Kit realized that silence had fallen across the surrounding plain. The last of the rangers and the warrior monks had lost their fight for life. Even the goddess had ceased her wailing. Kit scanned the battlefield, looking for her remains, but could see no sign.

There was only the green life she had left behind. Saplings rustling their leaves. Ferns and bushes shining in the moonlight. The corpses were hidden amid this greenery, and you would never know that this had been a place of such violence. Peace settled, and nightflowers blossomed, opening their white gleaming faces to the moon.

For a long time, nobody spoke or moved. Even the moonlight looked fragile, and the night itself held its breath, not wanting to break this spell.

Finally, Ira stirred and turned to Kit. 'You're a mess,' she said. 'How are you still on your feet?'

'Flesh wounds,' Kit said. 'They'll heal.' He looked around him at his ragged band of survivors. 'Call everyone together. Minister to those who need it. Then we set out.'

Midge looked up, his eyes maddened with hatred and grief. 'We're going for the Sheriff?'

Kit nodded. 'Half his army lies out here in the dust. Ours will grow stronger as we march. The shires are full of folk ready to fight, we've seen that well enough. And now we can promise them victory. Rearm the troops, have them ready to depart. We go to win the war.'

Part Five

Roots of Rebellion

I. Unwanted Truths

As she galloped across the moonlit plain, Marian strained her eyes, desperate for even a glimpse of Rex. But it was no good. She was marshalling three horses, so her progress was slower than his. But his trail was here, clean and clear, she must trust in that. He couldn't maintain this breakneck pace for ever.

He did, however, sustain it for a long time. She judged it was past midnight by the time he appeared as a tiny speck on the horizon. By now her own horse was beginning to flag, its laboured breath clouding in the moonbeams. While still in motion, she cut the beast loose and leaped onto a fresh mount.

Now she ate up the ground between her and Rex. As she got closer and the figure ahead of her became visibly and truly him, her heart yearned to be with him again. Yet at the same time, there was a tightness in her throat. After all that had happened, would this truly be a reunion, or a meeting of strangers? Where did they go from here?

Shaking her head, she told herself this was Rex, her flesh and blood, now and always. She kicked her horse into a gallop and closed the final furlong between them.

His horse was spent and stumbling. She slowed to a walk beside him, suffering as she did so a resurgence of her fears. This was her son, yet wasn't him. His face in the bluish night looked so much older, his features careworn, as if in their time apart he had aged ten years. He stared dead ahead, unblinking, even as she studied him.

'Rex,' she said softly. 'Are you hurt? It's all right, it's just me. I'm here.'

He sat straighter in his saddle, but still didn't turn his head as he spoke.

'Mother, I've not been well. I've always suffered nightmares, haven't I? But now . . . I don't know what's happening to me, but I think . . . my dreams and waking life have switched. Or I can't tell which is which. I *saw* your corpse. Yet now . . .' He turned to look at her at last, and his eyes – that look in his eyes – hollow and haunted, 'now you're here.'

'Please,' Marian murmured past a lump in her throat. 'Please, Rex, don't be afraid of me. I couldn't stand that. I can't . . . I can't explain everything that's happened, not even to myself. There are forces at work we'll never comprehend. You . . . you've been caught up in all this since the day you were born. You didn't ask for any of it, I know you didn't.'

'It's all right, Mother,' he said in a dead tone, his voice even more hollow and heart-wrenching than his eyes. 'It's not your fault. Father was right all along. He told me what the wilderness was like, and the outlaws. He told me about Robin Hood. They made the world like this. But they won't win. Soon they'll be extinct.'

Her heart pounding with sorrow, Marian reached out, took the reins from Rex's hands, brought his horse to a halt.

'Rex, look at me, and listen. You've got it all wrong. You couldn't have known any better. You've been lied to all your life. I lied more than anyone. But now everything is changing, and you need to see. Robin is not the evil in this land. The Sheriff is.'

'You shouldn't say things like that. He's your husband. He's my father.'

'He isn't! How can you still believe that? Except how could you think any different?' Marian sobbed, hardly knowing that she was saying. 'But please – enough! We have to put this right. Start healing these wounds. The Sheriff is not your father . . . Your father is Robin Hood.'

Rex watched her while she said this, and he didn't blink. Finally, he turned his head to look westwards. He lifted a finger.

'I followed the moon here – like you taught me,' he said in that flat haunted tone. 'So long as the sky stays clear, it'll be easy to retrace my steps.'

'Rex – did you hear what I just said?'

'You brought a fresh horse for me. Good. By this time tomorrow, if we keep up an even pace, we'll be out of the wastes. We should reach the city by dawn the next day.'

While he spoke, in that dead monotone, Marian suffered a redoubling of her fears – and a sense of loss, as sharp as grief. Who was this person, riding out here in the wastes, talking this way? Was it truly the same person she had cradled as an infant, cared for as a boy?

She shook her head. These eerie godless wastes twisted everything, made it hard to trust your own perceptions, your own judgement, even your own memories. She should not have tried telling Rex the truth; not here, not now. Once they were back on familiar ground, then he would be ready to hear it.

'We need to leave this place, as soon as we can,' she told him. 'I've got so turned around I barely know east from west. You're sure you can find our way back?'

Rex nodded. He slipped down from his saddle, climbed onto the fresh horse. He made to ride away, but Marian reached out a hand to stop him.

'Is it true? The Sheriff? He means to burn Robin Hood?'

Rex shrugged. 'Means to, or has. It isn't important. But we need to get there fast, to warn him.'

'Warn him?'

'About the outlaws. They won, didn't they? So now they'll be coming for Father. He needs to be ready.'

So saying, he kicked his horse into motion and rode off across the plain.

Biting her tongue, her heart wrenching, all Marian could do was follow in his wake.

II. All That Dies with the Forest

The entire population of Nottingham, every last man, woman and child, turned out to witness the execution of Robin Hood. The merchants, the burghers, the guildsmen came willingly, riding their finely groomed mares, dressed in their gaudiest garments. The craftsmen, the artisans and the rest of the middle rank were likewise enthusiastic, forming great processions on foot, bartering and laying bets as they made their way out through the city gates.

The lowlier citizens, in contrast, had to be dragged from their homes. Soldiers prowled the slum districts, kicking in doors, swinging their clubs, forcing these people to come and bear witness.

Eventually, the slums were cleared, and by mid-afternoon the entire citizenry was gathered on Gallows Field. Here, the pyre stood completed, towering almost as tall as the city walls. Atop the pyre was the tiny bound figure of Robin Hood.

In a wide ring around the pyre stood market stalls serving ale and roasted meats, alongside hawkers' carts selling drums and whistles and flutes. Late into the afternoon, people drank and gossiped and laughed and threw horseshoes and played campball, while children ran around with toy bows and arrows, wearing the leering masks of outlaws.

Bound hand and foot to a stout stake, his weight slumped against the ropes, Robin was only vaguely aware of all this. Since the Sheriff came to taunt him in the dungeons, and that surge of hatred had briefly reanimated him, he had sunk once more into a black sea of nothingness.

Here and there, as the day went on, sense impressions pierced the darkness. A child's shout of excitement. The snarling fury of a dogfight. The clattering creaking of a carriage as another nobleman arrives from a distant estate.

He tries to focus his forest-mind. On the execution field, crows have already gathered. Through their eyes, fuzzily, he sees a change come over the crowd. People are scrambling to make way for a lavish carriage, pulled by six strong sumpters, flanked by armed guardsmen.

The carriage comes to a halt and footmen hurry to open the door and the Sherriff steps down. Robin's awareness, until this moment as soft as eider, now becomes as sharp as thorns. That raw rage is rising once more, burning through his frailty and hopelessness, laying out the world in perfect detail.

A towering spectator scaffold has been constructed against the city walls. Its terraces are lined with benches, which are crowded with elaborately dressed men and women. Dukes and duchesses and barons and baronesses. The Sheriff's most honoured guests, invited here to share in his triumph.

Understanding this, watching through his forest-mind as the Sheriff ascends the scaffold and takes his place on a throne at its peak, Robin's rage redoubles. His senses scream, these perceptions as raw as an open wound. As the sun sets, everything is now drenched in red, as though the whole world is drowning in blood.

And why shouldn't it drown? What use this world? Why shouldn't I tear it apart?

Some part of him believes he can still do it, regardless of his wasted bones and withered limbs. What is flesh and blood to him in any case? Didn't he once cast off this human skin, merge with the forest, in order to battle the firestorm?

Yes – but now the forest is lost to him. He is confined to this cage of flesh. And its lifeforce is almost spent, his heartbeat as weak as a newborn fawn, his strength insufficient even to break these bonds, let alone wield killing power.

His impotent rage spikes as the Sheriff stands to address his subjects, while soldiers prowl through the crowds, brandishing their spears, enforcing silence.

'People of Nottingham,' the Sheriff begins, his voice slow and quiet, yet carrying sharp as spears on the clear air. 'The events of this night will live for ever. My son – my heir – is even now besieging the last vestige of Sherwood – so-called Gaia. As it grows dark, from across the wastes, we shall see the glow of his success. Meanwhile, we shall send him a signal of our own. He shall look back towards his city and see this pyre colouring the night sky. He will know that Robin Hood has been vanquished at last. And with doubled determination he shall slay what remains of the demon forest.'

He pauses while a roar goes up from the crowd, provoked and sustained by the soldiers wielding the butts of their spears, while on the terraces noblemen applaud and duchesses wave their kerchiefs. As the uproar abates, the sun dips below the horizon, the light dying with one last flare of crimson.

'The sun has set. It is time,' the Sheriff continues. 'Tonight, at last, we free ourselves from the wilderness and its shadows. So take up a brand, each and every one of you. Take a hand in crafting your future. This is not my triumph alone. You must all lay claim to it.'

While he says this, soldiers move through the crowds handing out crude torches of sticks and straw, thrusting them into people's hands whether they want them or not. Other rangers are lighting fires in iron braziers.

Vaguely, Robin listens to the people lighting their brands and approaching the pyre. Some are almost rabid to kindle the flames. Others are reluctant, and must be herded by rangers with their clubs. But they all come just the same. Some come in pairs, holding hands, talking quietly. Others in great laughing gangs. A few solitary ones mutter prayers, or are even shedding tears.

But, however they come, they touch their torches to the straw at the base of the pyre. The flames take hold, and already Robin can taste smoke at the back of his throat.

All such sensations now come to him numbly, however, as if he is merely hearing tell of these events. His rage is now utterly extinguished, and with it the last of his vitality. And good riddance to it. What has his rage ever achieved? What has his life been, except so much noise and fury?

His mind is the last of him to go, and dies fitfully. In its death throes, it shows him memories of the forest, and his family of so long ago. And, most of all, memories of her . . . of Marian. But even she is now fading as his mind follows his broken body into oblivion.

Good riddance to that too, he thinks finally, as the flames claw higher, and the Sheriff on his throne watches him with silent hatred. What good are memories? There is no past, no future. All that dies with the forest. The end has come, and nothing shall endure.

III. Spilled Blood

All the way back through the wastes, and on through the scrublands, past deserted market towns and ghost villages, Marian and Rex had ridden without uttering a word. The only sounds were the thudding of hooves on the rutted ground, and the laboured breathing of their now flagging mounts.

Finally, though, as night fell, and they drew close to the city, Marian steeled herself to try again.

'Rex, there are things you need to hear. You think you know what you're riding back into. You don't.'

'You can't talk to me that way, Mother, not now. I'm not a child any more.'

'You were thrust into all this with no chance to get your bearings. We don't know what we're going to find when we reach the city. How the Sheriff will react to your . . . to our return. He has failed to destroy Gaia, remember? We don't know how he'll take the news.'

'The outlaws are coming. We need to warn him. That's all that matters.'

'You don't understand. We need—'

'No! It's you who doesn't understand.' Rex steadied himself in the saddle, stared straight ahead as they went onwards. 'Father always says a man's greatest struggles arise when he refuses to accept his place in life. I've accepted mine, at last. I will be Sheriff of Nottingham. I will protect the city. There's nothing more to talk about.'

With that, he kicked his heels, coaxing a little more speed out of his exhausted steed. Marian went after him, preparing to say more. But then an ominous sight caught her eye, and she faltered, all else forgotten. At first she took it for a cloud, crossing the moon. But no – there were no clouds in this darkening sky. What she saw, twisting towards the heavens . . . was smoke.

'No, no,' she groaned. 'It's started.' She kicked at her mount. 'Rex, quick, we need—'

She broke off, balking at the scene that now lay before her, involuntarily hauling back on the reins and bringing her horse to a halt. They had crested high ground to the west of the city, and suddenly come within sight of the curtain walls. Before the walls lay the great sprawl of Gallows Field. It was dotted with pinpricks of light, like so many stars fallen to Earth. And there at the centre of this starfield was a monstrous shape, reaching as high as the watchtowers atop the wall. It was a gigantic pyre. And it was already alight, tongues of flame licking around its base.

'We can still do it,' Marian murmured to herself, shaking off her shock. 'A pyre that big, it will take time for the flames to climb.' She kicked at her horse, but the exhausted beast resisted. 'Come on!' she shouted. 'Rex, hurry! We can still reach him!'

'Reach him?' Rex said, stepping his horse in front of her. 'Reach who? Robin Hood?'

'What are you doing? Get out of my way! We need to hurry!'

'What is Robin Hood to you?' Rex snarled, glaring, blocking her path. 'Or to me? He's going to die – and good riddance.'

'No, no, this is what I've been trying to tell you. Robin means more than you could ever know – to both of us. We can save him.'

'How?'

Fumbling, desperate, Marian tore open her backpack, pulled out the drinking bladder. 'The last of the god's blood,' she gabbled, beside herself. 'If I can get it to him it will heal him, I know it will. Please, Rex, you should be helping me,' she begged, trying to step her confused mount past him. 'Why are you blocking my way? What – what are you doing with that? Why are you pointing it at me?'

Strapped to Rex's saddle was a crossbow. In one quick motion he had snatched it up, cocked it, and fitted it with a quarrel. Now the bodkin glinted in the moonlight as he held it levelled at Marian.

'Demon stuff,' he spat, his eyes blazing as he glared at the drinking bladder. 'You'd bring it into the city? I won't allow it! Throw it down.'

'What? No! Robin needs it!'

'Do it . . . Now.'

'I won't! Rex – please. Don't!'

She saw the tiny tell-tale signs – the whitening of his shooting hand where he gripped the trigger, the tightening of his jaw – but it was too late to prevent it – too quick to blink let alone move the vessel out of the way.

Marian could only scream as the crossbow bolt impaled the drinking bladder. The force of it, at such close range, tore it from her hands, at the same time bursting it to shreds, the god's blood gushing out and onto the ground in one heavy splatter.

Marian wailed and howled so loud her horse bucked, threatened to bolt.

'No! What have you done?'

'What was necessary.'

'You've killed him!'

'Father told me this, too. Robin Hood, and his forest – they're a plague. They've infected even you. Soon he'll be dead, and you'll be cured.'

So saying, he wheeled his horse and kicked his heels, cantering down off the ridge and continuing towards the city.

Marian sat there, stunned, her hands slick with god's blood, staring at the spot where the last of the precious stuff was seeping into the soil. With it, all her shock and rage were draining away, to be replaced by the deepest sorrow. So then, that was that. Hadn't she done everything in her power? Hadn't she moved heaven and Earth to come this far – to still be on her feet and fighting? If it wasn't enough, so be it. What more did she have to give?

With a resignation almost like relief, knowing already that only one course of action remained, she coaxed her horse into a final exhausted gallop, as she fixed her gaze on Robin's pyre, and she swept headlong towards the flames.

IV. Into the Fire

As Marian rode hard for Gallows Field, and she watched Rex race ahead of her, part of her yearned to chase him down, and to try once more to persuade him of the truth. To turn him away from his dark path, and make him see the dangers he was riding back into. But the greater part of Marian knew it would be futile.

You've lost him, Marian – you need to face up to that.

He's the Sheriff's son – now if he never was.

These were Kit's words, back to haunt her. And now, when she recalled Rex spilling the god's blood that might have saved Robin, and she watched him racing to forewarn the Sheriff of the outlaws' advance, she could no longer deny their awful truth.

For fifteen years, she and the Sheriff had fought a private war – with Rex's soul the spoils. And then the Sheriff had executed his masterstroke, sent her and Rex into the wastes, and opened a chasm between them. A chasm that could now never be closed.

So that's that, she thought numbly, as if she had been hollowed out. *It is complete.*

Over the years, one by one, the Sheriff had robbed Marian of all that she loved: her freedom; her home; the forest; Robin.

And now, finally, he had taken her son.

Everything that she ever was or possessed or cherished, he had stripped it all away until there was *nothing* left.

Nothing? No, that wasn't true. Not yet.

She fixed her gaze once more upon the colossal pyre. The closer she drew, the more demonic it became, towering towards the heavens, crawling with red-black flame. She traced its monstrous shape up and up . . . until her gaze came to rest on the tiny figure at its summit.

Robin.

In the fading light, against the blue-black sky, he was no more than an outline. But it was him. Every inch of her ached to see him so small and isolated. And in that moment, if she still harboured any doubt, it finally and fully dropped away.

'I'm coming, Robin,' she whispered to him. 'You've suffered too much alone. This time . . . I'll be with you.'

As she galloped across the stone bridge, over the river, and she entered Gallows Field, people scattered from her path. Every citizen of Nottingham must be here, many of them holding torches or flaming brands. People cried out in alarm as she charged on through the crowds. Soldiers shouted at her to halt. A crossbow bolt whined above her head.

She didn't falter, and she felt no fear. A calm, clear certainty was on her now, and she knew nothing could stand in her way. Her memory took her back to the day of the Great Fire, when she believed Robin would perish with the forest. That day, the Sheriff and his heretic hunter had snatched her away, denying her even the right to say goodbye, or the chance to die as they had lived, side by side. Now they had been gifted a second chance. No power on this Earth could prevent her from taking it.

More soldiers shouted at her to stop, and two more crossbow bolts zipped narrowly wide. The next shot hit her steed in the flank. The beast screamed and its front legs buckled. Reflexively, Marian leaped clear, tucking her head and landing in a forward roll, tumbling head over heels – then bouncing to her feet and running full tilt towards the pyre.

The heat came at her now, washing across her in waves. Again, her memory yanked her back to the Great Fire – this time so vividly she might be living that day again – fleeing through the forest as Sherwood turned to flames. Perhaps that was her fate, her shocked mind murmured, to enter the fire over and over, for ever and ever. Well then, so be it – nothing and no one could prevent these events unfolding.

As she approached the pyre, head down against the heat and the spitting sparks, she aimed for a section that appeared dark amid the raging yellows and reds. To construct such a colossal blaze, the builders had used every scrap of waste wood they could find. Here and there, amid the rising fire, there were black patches where sodden rotten timbers were resisting the flames. Reaching one such section, no other thought in her maddened mind except reaching Robin, she planted her foot and groped for a handhold and started to climb.

The soldiers who had been in pursuit came no further, held back by the heat and their fear of fire. As she clambered higher, a crossbow bolt missed her by inches, was swallowed up by the pyre.

After this there were no more shots, nor even shouts for her to stop. She was vaguely aware that crowds of people were gathering to watch her, people calling out to one another, and talking in hushed awe.

'It *is* her,' one voice came to her, curiously clear. 'She's returned.'

'She's trying to reach Robin Hood,' another voice murmured on the wind.

'. . . give their lives for each other . . .'

'. . . couldn't keep them apart.'

'. . . die for us . . . for the forest . . .'

These words were getting harder to hear as she climbed, but even so there was something in them that fizzed through her, shivered her skin. There was passion in those voices – anger and a will to resist – so much so that it almost kindled her own fighting spirit. But she knew that was nothing more than force of habit. What could she possibly do now except be with Robin? Whatever might be building down below, it was none of her concern.

She continued up and up, picking her way between timbers that were flickering with fire, the gaps between the flames shrinking by the instant, the black smoke rising thicker and thicker, burning in her lungs. Even wood that was black was scorching to the touch, but she barely felt the blistering of her skin.

A sudden gust of wind tore at her. In its depths, the inferno roared, the noise like some infernal beast. The whole structure lurched. Marian missed a handhold, slipped. The world spun black and red, and she almost fell. She clung to the timbers, blinking through blurred eyes, then one handhold after another she continued her climb.

As she went, she spared one last glance towards the ground. She scanned the crowds, looking for Rex. There he was, nearing the edge of the execution field and the spectator scaffold that stood against the city walls.

With a wrenching effort, she dragged her eyes away from him. There was nothing more she could do for Rex. She had failed him. She would not fail Robin too.

Reaching for the next handhold, and the next, she continued upwards, while flames licked at her heels, knowing truly that nothing remained except being with Robin at the end.

V. Unwelcome Return

As Rex galloped across Gallows Field, heading for the specta-tors' scaffold, citizens and soldiers scattering from his path, he spared one last thought for his mother. Where was she now, and what did she intend? But the thought was short-lived, burned away by his fierce sense of purpose. Following weeks of indecision and doubt and fear, in this moment the world and his place in it was blessedly simple. The outlaws were on the march. His father, the Sheriff's Guard and all the people of Nottingham must be forewarned and forearmed. Only Rex carried the key knowledge and could complete this crucial task. Nothing else mattered.

He reached the west wall, vaulted off his exhausted horse, and without pause began to ascend the scaffold. Recognizing him, guardsman stood aside. Many of the nobles, however, were reluctant to make way for someone they assumed was a lowly messenger, his clothes dusty and wayworn.

'Get out of my way,' he demanded, shoving an earl who looked at him with disdain. 'I'm the Sheriff's son, you idiot – clear the path! I bring urgent news for my father. I said, step aside!'

Eventually, as he climbed, the whisper of his name and status must have run ahead of him, because people began making way respectfully, even fearfully, bowing their heads. He continued to the top of the scaffold, all the while burning with his vital objective.

The confidence left him the instant he reached the uppermost platform and he set eyes on his robed father, sitting upon his throne. The Sheriff greeted him with a cold glare that stopped him in his tracks and left him speechless.

His mind spun with all the things he had come here to say – the warning that had burned on the tip of his tongue all the way across the wastes and the scrublands. The great tangled knot of words lodged in his throat, and he only stood there breathing hard, while his father studied him, the ruined side of his face livid in the rising glow of the pyre.

'I am attempting to fathom the meaning of your being here,' his father said at last, in icy tones, while nearby dukes and duchesses glanced at one another nervously. He stared out towards the wastelands. 'I see no firelight on the horizon. The wildwood is not in flames. Your mission is not complete. Yet you return.'

Rex opened his mouth to speak, but still no words emerged. Moments ago, he had been a warrior prince, armed with tidings that might save the city. Now he was a child, weak and ashamed. He stared at the ground.

'Most unfathomable of all,' his father went on, 'you have apparently returned alone. Must I assume you have left the heretic hunter, and the rest of your host, out in the wilds?'

'They're dead!' Rex managed to blurt at last. 'All of them! The outlaw chief – the Earth mage – he trapped them. The last relic – the god's blood – he used it to summon the forest and he . . .'

He mumbled to silence beneath his father's glare. Even to his own ears, his words sounded unreliable. Those fabulous events belonged to the phantom wastes – they had no reality here beneath the towering walls of the city.

Before either of them could say anything more, two rangers came panting to the highest platform.

'Sire,' one of them blurted, bowing to the Sheriff. 'There's trouble – on Gallows Field.'

The Sheriff didn't blink. 'What kind of trouble?'

The soldier hesitated. 'There's a rumour spreading. It's the slum-folk – they believe they've seen . . .' Again the speaker faltered, meeting the other ranger's gaze. 'Something has stirred them up, sire,' he began again. 'They're forming gangs – a mob.'

'Why?' the Sheriff asked evenly. 'What do they want?'

The soldiers shared another glance. 'We can't be sure, sire. They may . . . they may wish to halt the execution. Impossible, of course. Some of the guildsmen have tried putting them in their place, but the slum-folk outnumber them ten to one. Now they're resisting even us.'

The Sheriff watched the ranger with his cold, dead stare. 'They're *resisting*?' he said quietly. 'Those people are sheep. Do you fear the sheep's bite, lieutenant? Go. Whip them into line. If they fail to obey, put them down. All of them.'

The soldier shook. 'A-all of them, sire? There are scores of—'

'All of them,' the Sheriff repeated. 'I have worked towards this moment my entire life. I will have nothing and no one mar my moment of triumph. Am I understood?'

As he said *no one*, he turned his eyes back to Rex. Then he addressed a member of his bodyguard, a senior lieutenant named Jarrod Farr.

'Select three rangers,' he told the burly guardsman. 'Ride into the wastes. My son has failed me, and returned confused. We must re-establish the truth. Bring back a full report from Sir Guy. How is the siege progressing? When does he expect the wildwood to burn?'

As Jarrod Farr nodded, made to leave, a series of noises rose up from the execution field. Shouts of anger, and cries of pain, and the ringing of wood striking steel.

Rex looked out. Contrasted against the glare of the pyre, the rest of the execution field was a mass of black against black. Vaguely, he made out movement – shadowy figures darting about, while more of those hard sounds drifted up out of the dark.

'As a precaution, sire,' said Jarrod Farr, pausing at the top of the steps, 'it might be wise for you to return to the castle, until this disturbance can be stamped out.'

'I shall not be going anywhere,' the Sheriff told him curtly. 'As I have already made clear, nothing and nobody will rob me of this glory.'

Again, Rex felt these words were directed at him. But in fact his father was no longer looking in his direction, or paying him any heed. He was now sitting as still as stone, staring towards the pyre.

Should Rex try again to convince him of the truth – that the outlaws had defeated his forces? Should he tell him all the rest of it – everything else he had seen and heard out there in the wastes? One recollection above all rang through his mind.

Marian Delbosque is dead. I killed her with my own hands.

But did he, in fact, hear the heretic hunter say that? The Lost Lands were a place of shifting illusions, of deceptive echoes. Could he trust *anything* he had witnessed out there? Were these memories he had carried out of the wastes anything more than phantoms?

With all eyes now turned away from him, an uncanny silence spreading throughout the scaffold, Rex had the ghostly feeling that he wasn't even standing here – that he didn't truly exist – that the rising wind was blowing straight through him.

And in this eerie state, he merely hung there, unacknowledged and unnoticed, while the pyre roared, and the execution field rang with sounds of violence.

VI. Rebellion Rising

Something had changed. The world had lurched into a new and unexpected shape. At first, Robin's muted mind can make little sense of these happenings. Hard sounds fade in and out of his awareness. Furious voices reach him as cracked echoes. All of it drifting up with the smoke from the world below.

As vague as these sensations might be, the changing atmosphere in the air is now unmistakable. A surging of emotion. Waves of anger. Robin feels all this in his guts and in his tightening muscles, as though this fury is his own.

And beneath that anger, or layered on top of it, is something else. An emotion more potent even than rage. It is a tingling in his skin and a dryness in his mouth and a surge of heat that runs through every fibre of his being. It causes his senses to crossbreed, until it becomes the taste of sunbeams, and the smell of woodnotes and the sound of joy. It brings him back into his solid body, while simultaneously making him as light as air . . .

What is happening to him? What is the cause of this passion he can feel coursing through his veins, bringing him back to the world?

It is her. She lives.

She is here.

'Robin – can you hear me? Yes, you can! I can see you can. Thank the gods. I reached you in time.'

Her hand is now touching his face. She presses her body to his. That upwelling of emotion intensifies, swells and swells until Robin's entire life is composed of it – he is nothing and has never been anything other than this radiance coursing through him.

'Marian,' he breathes. 'This . . . is real. You're here. You're alive.'

'Yes, I am,' she whispers, brushing her lips across his ear and against his cheeks. 'Oh, Robin, I never thought I'd feel anything ever again. But now, here with you . . . I feel *everything*.'

'But . . . how . . . I—'

'Shhh,' she presses a finger to his lips. 'The how doesn't matter, not now. I'm here. We're together. That's all that counts.'

Robin groans. 'The fire. You're alive. And now . . . you'll die.'

'It's all right.' She wipes a tear from her cheek. 'It wasn't what I intended, but I see now, it's better this way. I've had to say goodbye to Rex, and I can barely stand it, but I'm no good to him in any case. Maybe I never was. I made such a mess of things, Robin,' she sobs into his chest. 'But I wasn't myself. I stayed alive for his sake, but I wasn't truly living, any more than you were. How could I be? I *am* you, just the same as you're me. We couldn't live separately, either of us, any more than we could die apart.'

Listening to this, Robin's passion, which he already believed to be total, continues to build and build, until it is as fierce as the fire surging within the pyre. The wind strengthens and the inferno roars and he feels Marian tremble.

'Can you move, even a little?' she asks him, drawing a blade. 'I'm going to cut your arms loose. I . . . I want you to hold me.'

Once his arms are free, he strains his wasted muscles, lifts his feeble limbs, and he manages to embrace her. And with this contact – this blessed familiar feeling of holding her close – the bounds of his passion burst. This fierce white light that has been growing within, filling every inch of his being, it can no longer be contained, but floods out to illuminate *everything* – to light the entire world. In that instant, Robin *is* the world, his awareness suffusing every last mote of dust and blade of grass.

After so long trapped in a failing body, a dimming mind, these sudden sensations are dizzying, almost painful in their intensity. Yet at the same time, there is enormous clarity, and peace. Occupying this world-mind, it is hard to say if he is looking down on events, or out at them, or witnessing them from within. But in any case, he observes it all: the flames howling as they devour the pyre; the crowds shouting and jostling on Gallows Field, and down by the river, soldiers fighting to restore order; further off, leagues in the distance, Kit and his outlaws making their slow way across the wastes.

Robin bears witness to it all without fear or fury. Despite the increasing violence below, the soldiers wielding their clubs and cracking heads, the mob pulling a mounted ranger from his horse and bludgeoning him to death, Robin feels no animosity of his own. He is too vast for that. All the horror and hatred of the world passes through him with barely a ripple, like raindrops swallowed into a limitless lake.

Even as his awareness shows him the Sheriff at the top of the scaffold, standing now, his face blotched with rage, Robin knows only the barest tremor of revulsion. A shiver of disdain for this pitiful creature. Look at him there, believing himself master of the universe. From the perspective of the Earth, his lifetime of noise and fury, his catalogue of dark works, they amount to *nothing*, no more significant than the labours of an insect.

'Robin, where have you gone?' Marian's voice pulls him back into his own body. 'I could always tell, when you went. Don't go again, please. There's nowhere left to go in any case. Be with me, here. Promise?'

Pressing two fingers to her lips, she places a kiss on his forehead. 'I love you, Robin. I always have, from the day we met. That's the one thing that has never changed – that he could never take from us.'

These words bring memories flooding through Robin's human mind. He and Marian making home in their tower, before any of the horror began, living that wild and wonderful life, stealing food from the kitchens of her father's estate, raiding apples from the orchards in the village, playing at bandits. Their years living free in Sherwood, standing guard over the forest, and their moments of bliss all alone on their lake isle.

'It shouldn't end like this,' Robin murmurs. 'Not at the whim of one man.'

'It's all right, Robin, really it is,' Marian whispers in return. 'You don't have to fight for me or for anything, not any more. We have what we need.'

'But our work isn't finished. We . . . we can't leave the world like this.'

'That's what I told myself, all the way here. But what can we do? You . . . you're looking stronger, it's true. I almost don't want to believe it, but you're healing, aren't you?' She made a small sound of wonder. 'Yes, of course you are, even without the blood. Because we're together – we're whole. But it's no good, Robin. It's too late. The flames . . . Listen. We couldn't climb down now even if you did have the strength.'

Robin drops his head. 'Maybe . . . we won't have to,' he says quietly. 'The people . . . can't you hear them? They're trying to help us.'

'What? Who? How?'

'I need to look closer. I have to leave you, not for long.'

'No! Not now! Please!'

But Robin is already expanding his awareness, allowing it to occupy that vast bright space that has opened up around and within everything. In an instant he is swimming once more within the world-mind, countless sensations and passions swirling through him, but leaving no mark, like wind through the trees, rippling the leaves and then gone.

And immediately he sees – yes, as he thought. The lowborn folk of the city – the slum-dwellers and the serfs and the refugees – they are attempting to halt the execution. They are trying to extinguish the flames. Some of them have found buckets, others have pots and pans, and they are going to the river, collecting water, running back towards the pyre.

They're still fighting.

Robin's own voice floats to him out of the great white nothingness.

They're still fighting for you and for Marian and for the forest.

But they cannot win. Now that the Sheriff's soldiers understand what is happening, they are hurrying to guard the river, patrolling the banks, brandishing their bludgeons. Robin sees a young woman fall, her head cracked upon, water gushing from her dropped drinking horn. Other soldiers are herding peasants away at spearpoint.

They still have the will to fight. What gives you the right to give in? These people need you.

But what exactly can he do? Marian was right, his vitality might be returning but he is not yet remotely strong enough to climb down through the flames. Let alone wield a bow – even if he could remember how.

Then again . . . why would he need a bow? Why fight bodily, when he could wield his forest powers? This idea was the most daunting of all. The last time he tapped the strength of the Earth, he suffered untold torment, and still the world burned. Dare he walk that path once more, and watch history repeat itself? Besides, he drew those powers from Sherwood Forest, and now the forest is lost to him.

It isn't, his world-mind whispers. *The forest lives in you. It is in your blood, now and for evermore.*

These words themselves cause a shift in the world. All through Gallows Field, particularly alongside the river, Robin senses a stirring beneath the soil. Long-buried seeds swell and sprout; dormant roots wriggle for the surface. Shoots and suckers burst out of the ground; tendrils go snaking through the grass.

A ranger shouts out in alarm as a sucker seizes his ankle. Other men gasp as fibres twine around their boots and hold them fast. Robin feels a tightening in his own tendons as tendrils draw taut and drag soldiers off their feet. A dozen soldiers fall, crying out in shock and fear.

'What's happening down there?' Marian murmurs. 'Robin, what is this? The glare of the fire – I can't see a thing.'

The execution field is now descending into chaos. Freemen and merchants, in their terror and confusion, are running or riding for the safety of the city walls. Soldiers turn around in panic, searching for their unseen attackers, swinging their weapons in vain. Suckers pull taut and more soldiers fall.

The rebel citizens, meanwhile, recovering from their own shock, go back to battling the flames, now doing so unopposed, and with renewed vigour, shouting to one another for more buckets – more pans – bring anything. Some raid wine barrels from the market stalls and are emptying those so they can be filled with water.

Others are falling upon the stricken soldiers, who are writhing in the grass, trying to cut their way free. They steal the rangers' skull-helms, which they begin passing hand to hand, a chain of people running from the river to the pyre. Children steal their cloaks and soak these to use as fire blankets.

By now the inferno has grown huge and hungry. Each bucketful or sodden garment only makes a minuscule difference. But there are hundreds upon hundreds of these people all now working together, with furious urgency, and for the first time Robin allows himself to believe that they will succeed. Little by little the heat and fury of the blaze starts to reduce.

'Robin – what's happening? What's that hissing noise? What are you doing?'

'It isn't me,' Robin tells her, his own voice seeming to come from everywhere and nowhere as he continues to float free within the world-mind. 'It's the people down there. They're putting out the fire.'

Marian sucks a sharp breath. 'Can it be true?' she whispers. 'This isn't one more false dawn?'

'It's true,' Robin's disembodied voice answers. 'It's working. They're going to do it.'

Except, even as he says this he hears his own voice falter. And in the same instant he understands why. These people will never stop fighting; but they are pitting themselves against the Sheriff, and his hatred is boundless.

Dozens, scores of soldiers are now appearing all along the city walls, occupying every parapet and tower. Each one is armed with a crossbow, which they are now winding before fitting with quarrels.

In the darkness, as they go about their firefighting, the people below are unaware that marksmen are massed up there. Only Robin stands witness as the rangers level their weapons, aiming at Gallows Field, preparing to rain death upon the people's heads, and to extinguish the final flame of hope.

VII. Godhood

'**F**ather? You can't truly mean to do this.'

Rex heard himself say these words before he knew he was going to speak. In a daze, in mute disbelief, he had heard his father give the incredible commands. Only now, as he stared at the crossbowmen lining the city walls, their dark shapes just visible in the swirling light of the watchfires, did it all become dreadfully real.

'This is only a threat, isn't it, Father? They won't let loose. Those are citizens down there.'

'They are traitors,' his father said coldly, without looking at him. 'They have betrayed their city, and their Sheriff.'

'How can they even pick their targets?' Rex said, staring into the darkness of Gallows Field, which swirled with shadowy movement. 'It's so dark. There are soldiers down there, and merchantmen. You'll kill them all.'

'Hold your tongue. Do not question me again,' his father rasped. 'By your bleating, you have proved to me only one thing: you are still weak. That you still lack the will to do what is necessary. Today then, will be a lesson to you, as well as to those traitorous dogs. When order and decency are threatened, when the forces of chaos arise, *this* is how a Sheriff must respond.'

He turned to a senior officer, who stood ready with a war

horn. 'Lieutenant, are the last of the marksmen assembled? Yes? Then give the signal. Destroy them all.'

An evil hissing noise – followed by wet thudding sounds. Then screams. So much screaming. As though the night itself has been dealt a deathblow. And there is the stench of fresh-spilled guts, and a welling of shock and terror so thick it is palpable.

'Robin – what's happening now? The firelight – and the smoke – I can't see anything. The screaming! People are dying. What's he done?'

For the moment, Robin has no words. Soldiers atop the city walls have let loose their first volley, and now citizens are writhing upon the ground, or lying still, impaled with quarrels, their bodies torn open by the barbed missiles. Several soldiers were also caught in the death-hail and now lay dying or dead.

Robin expects the remainder of the rebels to flee for cover, but to his amazement the survivors are already shaking off their shock and terror and moving back into action. Some go to help the injured, or comfort the dying. But most return to battling the flames, filling vessels with water before rushing to the pyre.

Meanwhile, all along the walls, the marksmen are winding their weapons, preparing for another barrage.

Observing this from within the vast space of his world-mind, Robin's will to fight, briefly revitalized, slumps beneath a great weight of sorrow and despair. Isn't it always thus – the way things will always be? Human beings slaughtering one another, driven by hatred and greed. What right does he have to intercede? He has already played too big a part, only ever succeeded in fanning the flames. Leave them to their squabbles. Let them tear one another to pieces, turn their world to dust.

'Oh no, listen,' Marian whispers into his chest. 'The war horn. Whatever it is, it's about to happen again. I can't stand it,

403

all this killing! It follows us, even now. When will it stop?'

Never, Robin thinks, as the second rain of death comes down upon the killing field, and the answering wave of terror and agony rises up to the heavens. *It is in their nature. What chance did we ever have, living in a world such as this?*

'They were helping us,' Marian whispers. 'And now they'll die for it. And afterwards . . . who will stand against the Sheriff? He'll destroy the Last Forest. And Rex will live in his world of ashes. Oh, Robin, I thought I'd made peace with it, but I haven't – I never will. I can't stand it. Being here and being powerless to stop him.'

Powerless to stop him.

At these words, Robin's world-mind shifts, almost imperceptibly. And now, at the centre of his vast awareness, stands the Sheriff. His dead gaze is fixed on the massacre. And he does not blink. There is not a twitch of remorse in his heart, nor a shiver of shame upon his skin. He is like a god, crushing mortals underfoot, without hesitation or remorse.

No – he is not a god, Robin corrects himself. *He is a man, nothing more. A man of flesh and blood.*

His power will fade away, like all earthly things. His deeds will be buried beneath the sands of time. Ultimately, all his hatred and fury will count for nothing.

Unless he destroys the forest.

If Marian is right, and he succeeds in annihilating the last vestige of Sherwood – the last of the true wildwood – then the Sheriff's hatred will stamp a permanent scar upon the Earth. A wound that will be worn by every generation yet to come.

Thinking this, Robin's world-mind shows him a shocking vision: a world without wilderness. Robin understands then that his world-mind is still growing – it now exists not only every*where* but every*when*, its great web stretching back to the deepest past, and forward to the furthest future.

The visions that come to him are dizzying, layer upon layer. He doesn't even begin to understand everything he sees: towering edifices with reflective surfaces, sheer as ice; monstrous creatures roaring through the clouds; grey deadlands sprawled beneath poisoned skies. But what he sees is enough.

We are at a crossroads, the unbidden thought comes to him. *The path we take will determine the future, and shape the world for ever . . .*

Atop the city walls, the marksmen are readying their crossbows, preparing another cascade of death.

We must turn away from this dark path. This cannot continue.

As happened before, it is these very words that cause a shift in the world. As they swirl through Robin's world-mind, he feels them stir no less in the vines that grow all across the city walls. These vines twitch and squirm, like snakes awaking from hibernation.

As the crossbowmen raise their weapons, preparing to shoot, the vines whip fully into life. Without Robin lifting his arms, or exerting effort of any sort, they fling themselves upwards, over the parapets, like grappling hooks slung by invading troops.

Soldiers cry out in alarm as vines latch onto their crossbows, tearing them from their grasp. Several men try to cling on to their weapons, and they are dragged off the wall and fall screaming.

The war horn is sounding once more and, even in the midst of chaos, the surviving marksmen, so trained to obedience, squeeze their triggers and let loose.

No – this must stop, the quiet, powerful thought drifts through Robin's awareness, and vines snake up thicker and stronger than ever. They sweep their python heads across the parapets, knocking weapons from hands, brushing men from the wall like so many fingers flicking off ants.

'They're falling,' Marian breathes. 'I see them fall. Robin – this is your doing! Yes, I see the vines. You're doing it . . . You're beating them!'

She gasps through tears, her grip tightening upon him. 'You're getting stronger by the moment. You're growing back into yourself, I can feel it. And the flames – they're dying, I'm sure they are. We're going to live!'

She gasps once more, and when she next speaks her voice has changed, her words cold and sharp as steel. 'You know what this means. We can do better than live. The Sheriff – he's there. This is our chance, here and now. You can put an end to this once and for all.'

As vines hook the last of the crossbowmen, haul them from the wall, Robin's world-mind simultaneously shows him the Sheriff. For the first time, his expression of stone has cracked. His eyes have widened, and his lips twitch.

He is afraid, and trying not to show it. Pitiful creature. He has lived his whole life in fear – terrified of showing his own weakness – loathing his own black heart. To destroy him would be a mercy.

Yes, Marian is right. Tonight, here and now, we must bring the cycle to an end.

So thinking, without rancour, only a cold clear sense of inevitability, Robin extends his fingers, and fresh suckers snake out of the ground, begin twining up the struts of the spectator scaffold, towards the black-robed figure at its crown.

VIII. Beneath the Mask

'Sire – we need to leave – immediately. Something is happening on the battlements. We are under attack from unknown—'

The scaffold suddenly shook, and the guardsman broke off as he caught his balance. Rex's heart lurched. From a lower terrace came a scream as a noblewoman was thrown from the stands and tumbled to the ground.

'Sire,' the bodyguard tried again. 'We're under siege. We need to retreat to the castle!'

Still the Sheriff did not shift an inch, or blink. He just went on staring, dead-eyed, towards the pyre. What was wrong with him? Why wasn't he doing anything?

Again, the platform lurched, and below them people cried out in alarm. Someone nearby was shouting something incoherent, and still Rex's father just sat there, frozen.

And now Rex detected something else: wet, slithering sounds. These noises stabbed needles into his heart. He had heard something like this before.

And suddenly he knew what this was.

Without thinking, or truly believing he was doing it, he took hold of his father bodily, tugging him by the arm.

'Father – come on! Move! I know what's happening. We can't stay here.'

Again, the scaffold shook, this time with a creaking, cracking sound. Finally, Rex's father turned to look at him, and his eyes were glassy and vacant.

'I won't stand for this, do you hear?' the Sheriff said, in a voice Rex barely recognized. 'I won't have disobedience. Tell the men to restore order, at once. Tell the heretic hunter I need him here, by my side.'

'Sir Guy is dead!' Rex cried, hauling at his father's arm. 'Don't you see? This is Earth magic. We need to go!'

'We will wait here for Sir Guy,' the Sheriff insisted. 'He knows how to deal with these heretics.'

The scaffold jerked violently. Rex caught hold of a stanchion to keep his feet. On the lower levels, nobles were fighting one another to escape the groaning structure.

Rex took hold of the Sheriff once more and tried a different tactic. 'Father, quick, we've just heard from Sir Guy. He is at the castle. He awaits us there.'

Finally, his father blinked. Nodding quickly, he said: 'Yes, yes, Sir Guy has never failed me yet. We must join him. Go. Lead the way.'

Darting for the steps, Rex headed down through the shuddering stands, his father in his wake. Bodyguards went ahead of them, swinging their bludgeons, shoving nobles off the scaffold if they were too slow to clear the path.

Those ominous rustling sounds were growing louder – and suddenly Rex saw them – tendrils of green, slithering and twining their way up the stands. They were everywhere! Python vines snaked between the struts and the stanchions, tightening their grip on the timbers and making them groan and creak and crack.

It must be the outlaw king – he must be here! Rex's mind screamed. *How is he doing this so far from the forest?*

His father seemed eerily oblivious to the suckers even now

slithering at their feet. His expression remained hollow as he stumbled after Rex. Why was he like this? Why wasn't he directing his troops, ordering them to find the attackers and strike back?

'Cut these vines!' Rex called out to the bodyguards. 'Keep them away from us!'

The guardsmen reacted as if the Sheriff himself had given the command, drawing their swords and hacking through the tendrils, which writhed like severed snakes, spraying sap like green blood.

Hauling his father behind him, Rex fled down the final two flights of steps and finally reached the ground. No sooner did they get clear than the tortured timbers gave way. The tendrils squeezed inward like the coils of a monstrous python crushing its prey. The skeleton of the scaffold folded in on itself and collapsed with a rumbling crunch, merging with the screams of nobles too slow to escape and the guardsmen who had stayed to battle the vines.

'Father – this way! Hurry!'

Rex's father was standing, glassy-eyed, staring at the collapsed scaffold, which writhed with tendrils, like trapped snakes. Rex ran back to haul him by the arm, and finally, with a puzzled frown, he went with him.

The Sheriff's carriage stood waiting, horses yoked and ready, the driver in place. Footmen rushed to usher Rex and his father aboard, and immediately the vehicle was lurching into motion, bumping across the grass towards the approach road, mounted soldiers flanking them as escort.

Guardsmen atop the carriage hollered to the porters to open West Gate. With a surge of relief, Rex heard the clattering of the horses' hooves and the vehicle's wheels on the cobblestones as they passed through the colossal entranceway, and he knew they were back inside the city.

'Close the gates!' Rex heard himself holler to the guardsmen. 'Give the signal. Close the gates. Every ranger back to the castle. Do it now!'

The carriage guardsmen sounded their war horns, and the hue and cry rippled across the city. The great West Gate rumbled and crunched closed, together with the other major entranceways, while soldiers spilled back into the city through the postern gate and fled for the castle.

'It's all right,' Rex murmured, as much to himself as to his father. 'Whatever that was, we escaped. We'll regroup at the castle, with the castellan and the rest of the guards. They won't touch us there.'

His father said nothing, stared at nothing. For Rex, it was like looking at a stranger. As though his father had worn a mask all these years, and now it had cracked, and his real face was beginning to peer through.

Rex shook his head. *You're not out of danger yet. Get back to the castle, fast. That's all that counts.*

IX. Earth Rising

Little people screaming. Dying like ants crushed beneath a
boot. Robin hears their death-wails all across this slaughter-
field. Some are impaled with crossbow bolts, others beaten by
clubs. Still more have plummeted from the city walls, or lie
broken beneath the collapsed scaffold.

Vaguely, he has the idea that some of this is his doing –
that he raised a hand to swat at these insects. But the thought
is a bare whisper in his vast awareness. From the all-knowing
perspective of his world-mind, none of these deaths is any more
noteworthy than the dropping of a single leaf in the forest.

Except one.

One death will be significant. Is necessary.

And it has not yet been achieved. The Sheriff escaped the
scaffold, and is now racing up through the city in his carriage.
Robin's awareness, at least some tiny part of it, sweeps after him.
It tunnels through the soil that lies beneath the cobbles and the
packed earth of the city streets.

Down here he finds more roots and rootlets and seeds, all
of which have lain in the darkness, patiently awaiting their call
to rise. Now they twitch in the earth, sensing that yes, at last, it
is their time.

With a flick of his world-mind, Robin brings suckers surging to the surface, throwing up soil and cobbles. They rise in the path of the Sheriff's carriage. The horses rear in panic. The driver loses control. The vehicle swerves, cracks a wheel, and is thrown onto one side.

Immediately, the tendrils are upon the carriage, snaking their coils around it, clawing at the Sheriff within.

There . . . he emerges. He is being dragged from the wreckage by someone else – by a young man.

A young man called Rex.

At this recognition, something shivers through Robin's human heart, and he hesitates. In that space, as Robin reins in his powers, Rex hauls the Sheriff away from the vehicle. As he does so, he hollers at two guardsmen to relinquish their mounts, and already Rex is shoving the Sheriff onto one of the horses, before leaping onto the other himself. And now he is kicking at his steed, tugging at the reins of the Sheriff's horse, and the pair of them are once more moving up through the streets, galloping for the castle.

'No – he must not be allowed to live.' Robin hears his human-self speak, his voice heavy to his own ears, carrying out and across the city on the wind. 'He is toxic to the Earth. Rex – you must not help him.'

'What? Rex?' Marian blurts. 'Robin – have you found him? Where is he?'

'He is with the Sheriff.'

'Oh no – this is what I feared. Robin, you need to tell me what's happening. It's as if . . . you're growing. I'm holding you but you're bigger than I can imagine. You're hunting the Sheriff, aren't you? And that's what I wanted, but now I'm scared. Please, if nothing else, you need to think of Rex. Be careful. You mustn't hurt him.'

Why not?

From Robin's vast perspective, he is struggling to understand what difference it would make. He hesitated when Rex stood between him and the Sheriff, but why? What possible consequence whether any of these little people live or die?

Look at them. Rangers in their dozens are pouring up through the city streets, heading for the castle. Citizens, too – the merchants and the guildsmen – have come flooding back in through the postern gate and are fleeing for their homes. How ludicrous their efforts to cling to life. How much harm they wreak with all their fear and fury.

With such thoughts swirling though him, he doesn't need to lift a finger. Instead, he has the sense he is merely an observer as more buried seeds sprout, and dormant roots stir. All across the city, suckers and shoots burst up through cobblestones, tendrils bristling with thorns, while people shout and scream and run and run.

A giant tendril, knotted at one end like a club, sweeps across a trio of rangers. The men are thrown against the wall of an inn, where they lie broken and bleeding. A pair of merchants riding stallions are knocked from their mounts before being ensnared in a briar bush, which constricts and constricts while they scream and scream . . .

'Robin – those noises,' Marian whispers to him. 'What are you doing? Is Rex safe?'

No one is safe. Nor should they be.

These people – the harm they inflict upon their fellow creatures, and upon the Earth. How could Robin have stood aloof, in the face of all that men do? Well – no more. He must suture this wound from which the world bleeds.

Such thoughts are mere murmurs within his world-mind – but they howl through the physical world, burst upon the city like a storm of hailstones, tearing tiles from roofs, turning over carts, sending people scrabbling for boltholes.

At the same time, the green uprising surges across the city

like a tidal wave. Waking roots, quiescent no more, hump their powerful backs through floorboards and flagstones, quaking the foundations of buildings. Vines push at doorways until they splinter beneath the weight. Tendrils pick up people and fling them around like so many ragdolls.

These pitiful creatures. Robin feels nothing for them that might be called anger or hatred. His forest powers rumble through their city as cold and implacable as an earthquake. Walls give way and townhouses collapse and people scream and everything is as it should be, the world returning at last to green, Robin glimpsing a future now devoid of people and all their poisons, the great forests marching once more across Earth.

'Robin – please, speak to me. Y-you're getting further away all the time. But you can still hear me, I know you can. Tell me, where are they – Rex and the Sheriff?'

The Sheriff.

Yes, of course, Robin had set himself a task. One of these little creatures matters more than the rest. He is the one who has wrought the most damage – the one whose very lifeforce is toxic.

There is the Sheriff – he has reached the black heart of the city. Together with Rex and a dozen guardsmen, he is clattering over the drawbridge and into the castle. Perhaps he believes he will be safe there. But there can be no escape. This man has roused the wrath of the Earth, and now he must reap the consequences.

The castle gates thunder shut – as if they could keep Robin at bay. The parapets are lined with marksman – as though they might stand against him. These castle walls are covered in creepers and vines. Robin's Earth powers are already twitching their fibres, filling them with renewed strength. They multiply, growing fresh tendrils, snaking into every arrow-slit and embrasure, worming into every crack and crevice. Then they begin to expand, like water turning to ice, cracking mortar and stone. They twist and squeeze and tighten, creaking like old rope being wound, widening fissures.

There is panic now atop the castle walls, sentries blowing war horns and waving torches. And still the vines grow and squeeze, bulging in every gap, clawing at every stone. The west wall begins to sag and groan, grit raining to the ground. A rupture appears near the foot of the wall and snakes upwards – and suddenly the entire wall caves in, crashing down in a rumbling thunder of rubble, while dust pours skywards and falling sentries scream.

'Robin – what was that? Please . . . What's happening? I'm here. Come back to me.'

But that is no longer in Robin's power. Marian's voice is increasingly distant. He has ceased to be himself and has become a conduit for the Earth's will. And the Earth's will is this: wipe the slate clean. All that mankind has built – it must be torn down brick by brick.

Robin focuses on the Sheriff. He and his guardsmen have dismounted and are hurrying into a large building. The Throne Room.

Rex is with him too. But at this moment, occupying this cold omnipotent space, Robin cares little for that. The Sheriff must be destroyed. This wellspring of hatred must be dammed at the source. Everything else is immaterial.

With this certainty storming through his world-mind, blazing like lightning, Robin tightens his grip on the vines and the tendrils, bringing the full weight of his Earth powers down upon on the castle, preparing to bring this reign of blood to an end.

X. The Face of Fear

'Bolt the doors! Stand guard, all of you! Nothing and no one enters this hall!'

Rex heard himself bark these words as though they were not his own but were merely channelled through him. Regardless, the guardsmen rushed to do his bidding, securing the doors to the Throne Room before standing sentry with weapons drawn.

From outside came a phenomenal rumbling, crunching sound – a thunderous roar that might be the sky itself crashing to the Earth. The ground shook and Rex caught his balance, his pulse pounding in his ears.

'Sire!' called one of the guardsmen, who was standing at an embrasure, looking out in horror. 'The outer wall! It's been breached!'

Rex stood rigid with shock. How in God's name was this happening? Had the outlaw army brought siege engines?

No – you only wish it was that, he answered himself. *You could stand against engines of war – but not this.*

From outside came another roaring, crunching rumble, even more violent than before, while the floor quaked and guardsmen fell.

'The East Tower!' a guardsmen yelled. 'All the dust – it's hard to see, but I— Yes, it's gone! The East Tower has fallen!'

In growing shock and horror, Rex looked around for his father. Unnoticed, he had moved down the hall and climbed onto the dais. He was now sitting on his throne. He kept his hands clasped before him, as if preparing to receive supplicants, and in the weak light of the wall lamps looked very far away and very small.

Rex hurried down the hall. 'Father – what do we do? This is . . . It's Earth magic.'

The Sheriff went on staring at nothing, his eyes taking on a milky sheen. His chest heaved and there was an audible rattling in his lungs.

'I thought it must be Kit, the outlaw king,' Rex tried again. 'But we left him out in the wastes. I think . . . this is Robin Hood. What can we—'

More thunderous sounds arose from outside, and the ground shook, and a guardsman began shouting that the West Tower was gone. And still, through all this, the Sheriff sat upon his throne, mute and immobile.

As before, staring at his deadened expression, Rex had the impression he was looking at an imposter. Or rather – it was that sense again that his father was wearing a mask that had started to crack. Yes, as this feeling intensified suddenly Rex *saw* him. The Sheriff was there – Rex was looking at his true face for the very first time.

'You're afraid,' Rex said slowly, ascending the steps to the dais. 'I thought . . . at first, I thought you were in shock . . . or just thinking. Laying plans. But it's none of that. You're like this because you're terrified. And you can't keep it hidden any longer.'

The Sheriff didn't turn to look at him, but he did blink, just once. And when finally he spoke it was in a small voice, like that of a lost child.

'I always knew the wilderness would come for me in the end.

417

I always knew it would want me back. All my life I've carried that knowing. I told myself I could destroy it, and I'd be safe. But how could I? It's a part of me. And now . . . it's here.'

Rex looked away, listening to more thunderous noises coming from outside and the shouting and screaming beneath.

'Robin Hood . . .' he said slowly, turning back to the Sheriff. 'It's you he wants, isn't it? So then – there's no other way. You need to go out there and face him.'

The Sheriff frowned, as if puzzled. 'No,' he said in that small-child voice. 'I can't. Never.'

'You have to,' Rex said, with growing certainty. 'Listen to it out there. He's tearing everything apart. People are dying. Only you can stop this. Perhaps . . . if you surrender, he will let you live.'

At these words, another change came over the Sheriff. He stopped trembling and sat upright, then slowly shook his head. 'No – he will show me no mercy. Not after all that has passed between us. But you . . .' he paused, looking long and steady at Rex. 'You could go to him without fear.'

Rex frowned. 'What do you mean? What good would it do?'

'You may speak on my behalf. Offer him terms. Yes – yes,' the Sheriff said, his features hardening, reforming into their old familiar mask. 'If Robin Hood will listen to anyone on this Earth, other than Marian, it is you. You must go to him. Promise him riches, land – whatever he desires – in exchange for my life.'

'Why me? I'm the heir to the Sheriffdom. Why would he show me mercy, any more than you?'

The Sheriff paused, held Rex's gaze, seemed to consider, before finally saying: 'Because he would not harm his own flesh and blood. Because you are Robin Hood's son.'

The castle crumbling, swamped with tendril and vine. Thorns clawing at brickwork, suckers wrenching at beams. Roots tunnelling, undermining foundations. A tower quaking at its base, trying to hold its balance like a drunkard, before collapsing in on itself, stones as large as men wheeling across courtyards, dust rising as thick as thunderheads.

Robin observes all this dispassionately. As though he is watching it unfold from untold distance – or through the fathomless depths of time. What did any of this count for in the first place – mankind's petty creations? All must be swallowed back into the Earth.

'Robin, please, you've gone so far away. But just listen! The cheering! The people – they've done it! They've extinguished the pyre. We can live!'

The sound of Marian's voice is something infinitely precious, but not held, only dimly remembered. A single sweet dream amid a lifetime of nightmares. Is that all she ever was: a dream? Is that all any of this has ever been?

As Robin's awareness continues to expand, his world-mind now as infinite as the heavens, he feels himself growing ever more remote from the human world. What has any of it been worth – mankind's vanity and ambition. Does any of it weigh more than a mote of dust?

Indifferently, his awareness sweeps through the city, which is drowning now in a sea of green. The castle chokes beneath shifting layers of undergrowth. Soldiers lie crushed beneath collapsed walls, or are trapped in briars, thrashing at tendrils with their swords.

The Sheriff, meanwhile, cowers in his Throne Room, surrounded by armed guards. Perhaps he still believes he can escape his fate. He cannot. It is time for him to reap what he has sown.

Close to the Throne Room is a walled garden. It is full of roses. Inhabiting the past and the future as fully as the present, Robin knows that this is Marian's garden. He sees her here, season after season, year after year, tending to these flowers, keeping her memories of Robin alive.

A twinge in his human heart. For an instant, he is with her once more, here and now, tasting her tears on his lips, listening to her entreaties to come back to her, body and soul. But already these sensations have passed – what can they matter against the fate of the Earth?

His awareness courses through the walled garden, entering the roots and stems of the roses, filling them with lifeforce as vital as lightning, causing them to fizz and engorge and grow, until with a susurrus, sibilant hiss their barbed tendrils branch up as tall as trees. These tendrils reach out for the Sheriff's Throne Room. They fold like gigantic arms around the walls, and close like colossal fingers upon the roof.

Then they begin to squeeze. The building groans. Its roof tiles splinter. Fissures appear in the walls. The hall begins to sag, and bulge, like a nut being crushed. Soon the whole structure will give way, destroying those inside.

Robin's human mind rails against this, tries to insist that not all these people need to die – that one in particular must be allowed to live.

But that is not his decision to make. He let loose this awesome power – Earth's fury – but it is no longer his to control. He is a conduit, little more than a witness, as the green might continues to squeeze and squeeze, and the forest reaches through him to exact its revenge.

XI. Long Live The Sheriff

*B*ecause *he won't harm his own flesh and blood.*
Because you are Robin Hood's son.

Even as the light in the hall dimmed, and the stonework groaned, and plaster rained from the ceiling, Rex stood frozen, as if mesmerized by the Sheriff's words – or as though the weight of them was crushing him, until he was barely able to breathe.

So – his mother had spoken the truth out in the wastes. But he hadn't wanted to hear it. He had wanted to run from the truth.

But now there was nowhere left to run.

You are Robin Hood's son.

The hall groaned louder and its rafters shrieked like some tortured beast, while guardsmen yelled and the Sheriff closed his eyes and muttered a prayer.

'My mother,' Rex said slowly, 'she thought you didn't know. That's right, isn't it? That's why she lied to me all those years – told me you were my father – so I couldn't give up the secret. Because she thought, if you knew the truth . . . you'd kill me. But all that time, you already knew. You just went along with the lie. Why?'

The Sheriff opened his eyes. 'You must go to him,' he murmured, as the hall groaned once more. 'To . . . to your father. Beg him for clemency. Hurry!'

'First, tell me,' Rex said, tears stabbing behind his eyes. 'If you knew who I was, why *didn't* you kill me?'

'Kill you?' The Sheriff began to gabble. 'No, no – you misunderstand. I *am* a father to you. I always was. Don't you see? You were forest-born – a child of chaos! As . . . as was I. But I was never given the chance to escape its clutches. You would be different,' he said, a glint of madness now in his icy gaze. 'With you I could begin anew. You were my greatest project. Greater even than destroying the wildwood. Think of it. The offspring of the forest queen and the phantom outlaw. Wildness in your blood. Yet raised from birth to become the Sheriff of Nottingham. The champion of order and civility. The *enemy* of the forest. Once and for all, I would prove man's mastery over all that is wild and savage!'

Rex ground his teeth as he fought back tears. 'So that's what I was to you – one more creature to be tamed.'

'I rescued you from the shadows.'

'You made my whole life a lie.' Rex wiped tears from his cheeks. 'I had nightmares. Every night the same. The forest was on fire, and I couldn't find my way out. I was *lost* – do you understand? You didn't rescue me from anything. You just made my whole world frightening. And you did it on purpose.'

As he spoke these last words, and the hall shrieked fit to burst, and the Sheriff closed his eyes once more in prayer, Rex found he had stopped crying. A strange calm had come over him. He turned to watch guardsmen battle in vain to force open the doors, the timbers buckling, and he shared none of their panic. For the first time in his life, he felt . . . fearless. Was that it, then – had he accepted he was going to die here? Did he even welcome death's approach?

No, it wasn't that. This didn't feel like submission, but almost its opposite. He felt . . . resolute. There was cold, clear certainty. As if the fateful decision had already been made for him.

Moving slowly, deliberately, he went to the rear of the Throne Room. Here, in an antechamber, was a small scriptorium. He took a handful of vellum sheets, a quill and ink, and a stick of wax. He went back to the Sheriff.

'I'll do as you suggest – I'll go to Robin Hood in your stead,' he told him. 'But first you need to do this for me.'

He put the quill and vellum into the Sheriff's hands. 'Write what I say, and quickly. Write: "I, the Sheriff of Nottingham, hereby abdicate, with immediate effect. I pass my worldly powers to . . . to my heir, Rex. All those who owe obedience to me, must henceforth pay fealty to him".'

The Sheriff stared at him, the hall for the moment growing quiet and still, his old mask closing over his face, together with a look of suspicion. But then the ground quaked, and the great rafters in the roof screamed as though fit to break, and the Sheriff once more looked terrified, and he took up the quill and dipped it in the ink.

'Yes, yes, I see the wisdom in this,' he murmured, starting to write. 'You need authority, to talk terms with our enemies. But it is temporary. Afterwards, power shall revert to me.'

'Transcribe it word for word. On all twelve sheets.'

The Sheriff blinked. 'Surely one will suffice.'

'All of them. And you'd better be quick,' he said, as more stone-dust rained from the ceiling, 'or we'll both die here.'

Bending his head to the work, trembling, the Sheriff filled parchment after parchment with his spidery scrawl. Rex fetched a candle and used it to heat the wax, and the Sheriff stamped each document with his personal seal: a wolf's head, its teeth bared. As he watched the Sheriff work, Rex's mind churned with all he had heard in this hall.

You were my greatest project.

Raised from birth to become the Sheriff of Nottingham.

I would prove man's mastery over all that is wild and savage.

He was beset too by a dark storm of memories, his entire life seeming to swirl behind his eyes. All those nights he'd awoken drenched in sweat, tortured by night-terrors. Those endless days training in the combat yard until he was dead on his feet, the Sheriff watching on, forever belittling him, or turning away as if he didn't exist. Going into the wastes with his mother and returning alone, half-dead with grief. Standing at the top of the tower, wishing he had the courage to throw himself off and bring his torment to an end.

And all this suffering had been built on what? On nothing. On a lie. For all that the Sheriff had done to him, and failed to do, that was the deepest cut. That none of it was even real. That all this time he had been living somebody else's life.

Even thinking such things, Rex remained eerily calm and still. But something cold and sharp lay beneath the surface. Rage? Hatred? Yes, both of those. But that wasn't all. As he stared at the Sheriff, scribbling frantically, focused only on saving his own skin, while outside his soldiers screamed, Rex also felt . . . contempt.

Yes, more than anything else, as he watched this frail, aging, frightened figure in front of him, and he considered his lifetime of deception and destruction – all of it designed to mask his own fear – Rex felt mostly disdain. And he knew, with perfect certainty, that there was truly no other way.

'This is a means to an end,' the Sheriff was muttering now, as he began on the last transcript. 'Afterwards, you shall cede power back to me. I shall not live without it. I cannot.'

'Yes, I understand,' Rex said quietly. 'The Sheriff of Nottingham. It is not only your title, or your role. It is the skin you live in. Without it, you are nothing,' he said, as the Sheriff sealed the final scroll. 'But you needn't worry about that. Not any more. Nor your war with the outlaws. Nor the wilderness. It's time to let go of all that. Finally . . . you may be free of your fear.'

As he said this, the Sheriff's eyes widened and he sucked a sharp breath. He frowned, peering at Rex, as if puzzled. Trembling, his hands came up, groping like those of a blind man. Finally, his fingers closed around Rex's own, the pair of them now gripping the hilt of Rex's sword.

'What . . . treachery is this?' he murmured, blood bubbling at his lips. 'I . . . I raised you as my own. I . . . I taught you everything.'

'You taught me to do what is necessary,' Rex said, twisting the blade closer to the Sheriff's heart, his own blood pulsing slow and even. 'Even you must see this needed to happen. Listen to it out there. You rail against chaos, but you brought this storm down upon us all. So go – and let it stop.'

He twisted the blade again as he spoke, and the Sheriff shuddered and gripped the hilt of the sword, as if he too was now trying to pull it deeper into his flesh. His eyes flared one final time with a lifetime of rage and hatred and fear, and then he exhaled, like a long sigh of relief, before his head bowed and he was still.

All the passion and strength drained out of Rex then and he fell to his knees, suddenly consumed with sorrow, his hands thick with lifeblood, the hall even now shuddering to pieces around him, guardsmen frantic, but Rex oblivious, indifferent, because it was done, it was done.

As she clung to Robin, and she whispered to him to return to her, and she listened to the dreadful rumbling sounds and the screaming coming from the city and the castle, Marian suddenly became very still, her breath stopped.

Something had changed. The world had shifted shape. What was it that told her so? Had she heard something new, or seen something flicker in the starless sky? She couldn't say. And yet . . . she knew. She knew as clearly as if she had witnessed it with her own eyes.

'Robin,' she murmured, a chill running the length of her spine. 'The Sheriff. He's . . . dead.'

Robin remained as still as stone, but she detected the faintest catch in his breath. Pressing her head to his chest, she heard his heartbeat quicken.

'You sense it too, don't you?' she whispered. 'I don't know how I know, but it's true. He's gone.'

Absurdly, she found she was crying. The crying intensified into heaving sobs. Was this an outpouring of relief? Or something deeper? It felt as though a yawning emptiness had opened inside her, and she was falling into it, plummeting into blackness.

'Oh, Robin, where are you? Come back to me. I need you. What's wrong with me – why can't I stop crying? Robin, you're so far away, I can't stand it. I need you here, more than ever. And I need all this – all the killing – I need it to stop!'

The destruction of the city and the castle continued, regardless. She could hear buildings collapsing; the panic of the citizens and the soldiers. Her grip on Robin tightened.

'You don't need to do this any more,' she whispered. 'It hurts you as much as anyone. I know you, this will cut you to the heart. Lay it down. You've done enough. Our . . . our part in all this, it's almost finished. But others need to go on. Rex needs to live. Please.'

While the green tide continued to swamp the city and the castle, pouring over the walls and the buildings with its creeping susurrus sounds, and the pandemonium of the people continued to ring out, Marian touched two fingers to her lips then placed the kiss on Robin's forehead.

'You're frightened,' she said softly. 'You're more powerful than you've ever been, yet you're afraid. I understand that. I'm frightened too. We've fought for so long. And now . . . What? It would be easier for you to keep your distance. But you never did the easy thing, Robin, not once in your life. So come back to me. We'll face this new world together. We're not quite finished, not yet. But we will be soon. I promise. I don't need to say more, because I know you'll make the right decision. I trust you.'

She raised her lips to his and kissed him. Then she closed her eyes and laid her head against his chest. Letting the sounds of destruction drift to the background, she listened to his heartbeat, focusing on that single sound until it became the world entire – a solitary pulse of sensation in the vast emptiness of existence.

Time passed, and something changed. Other sounds came into her awareness. Birdsong. And beneath that . . . silence. She opened her eyes. Sunrise. And in that soft, golden light, the city was still. The vines and the tendrils were at rest. They lay draped across the roofs and the walls like sleeping serpents, their wet skins glistening in the brightening dawn.

The castle, too, was pacific. Its crumpled walls were thick with foliage, making it look like a ruin from ages past, abandoned by man and reclaimed by the wilderness. The wind had dropped and a shocked silence had fallen across the entire city and the castle and the lands beyond, broken only by the chorus of the blackbirds and the skylarks.

Marian looked at Robin, raised a hand to his cheek.

'You're back with me,' she murmured through tears, 'at last.'

He bowed his head, listening, or sending his forest-mind out across the city.

'I . . . barely remember,' he murmured, his voice raw. 'So much destruction. So many dead. What have I done?'

'You might have done much worse,' Marian said evenly. 'Your power – at the end – it was absolute. You might have put paid to it all. Maybe . . . that's what we deserve. But it isn't our decision to make.'

Drawing her boot knife, Marian cut Robin's remaining bonds. Would he be able to stand unaided? Of course he would

– just look at him. Only now, as the sunrise turned his wolfskin golden, did she appreciate how completely he had healed. In fact, he had never looked more whole, more majestic.

She wasn't the only one who beheld him in this moment. As an awed silence drifted up from Gallows Field, she realized that hundreds, thousands of citizens had remained down there. And now every man, woman and child were standing as one, staring towards the peak of the pyre. As if she were looking through their eyes, Marian saw what they saw – the sun rising behind Robin, casting him in that numinous glow – as if here before them, fresh risen from the Earth, there truly stood a forest god – the last of the forest gods.

'Come on,' she said eventually. 'We need to find Rex. And Kit. We need to face them both. Then . . . we'll be finished. I promise.'

With that, she took his hand and the pair of them clambered down from the pyre, some of the timbers still smouldering and hot, but every last flame extinguished.

As they reached the ground, the sea of people parted to allow them through. Marian met the eyes of men and women and children, all of whom looked back at her in silence, and gazed upon Robin with something like reverence, or bowed their heads, or even knelt to touch the earth where he walked.

So many people, yet so little noise. Barely a rustle of clothing, or a whispered word, or the drawing of breath. It was perhaps the most serene moment Marian had ever known. She felt a great welling of gratitude that she was here to witness this – and gratitude, too, for these people who gave her this gift.

'You look at Robin in awe,' she heard herself call out, stopping on raised ground to send her voice over the crowds. 'But he would have been powerless without you. It was you who stopped the fire. Who saved Gaia. *You* are the guardians now. Never forget it.'

A murmur arose and spread through the crowds, as people relayed what Marian had said to those further back. The noise swelled, became a clamour of voices as if a spell was broken and people were coming fully back to life. There was relief in those voices, and jubilation, and grief, as people cheered and wept and laughed and cursed.

Turning their backs on all this, Robin and Marian walked the approach road towards West Gate, which hung upon its hinges, buckled beneath the weight of greenery.

And then, hand in hand, without so much as a raised voice to oppose them, the streets hushed in their green splendour, Robin and Marian walked into the city of Nottingham.

Part Six

The Deathless

I. Brothers in Arms

As Kit led his rebels towards the city, more peasants joined their cause than he had even dared hope. They left their homes in droves, carrying their scant possessions on their backs, gripping scythes and mattocks, fashioned into crude weapons.

By the time they neared Nottingham, the rebel host was fully two-hundred strong, while in far-flung hamlets and farmsteads many more were even now hearing the call-to-arms and setting out to follow the warpath.

On high ground overlooking the city, they came upon something entirely unexpected. Here, in the Sheriff's otherwise desolate domain, was a large coppice of oak and ash and hornbeam. The ground was coated in thick moss and the boughs warbled with birdsong, as if this miniature forest was age-old.

Kit called a halt amid the trees. And then, for a long while that followed, this great body of people was entirely silent as they stared out and down at something even more astonishing. Kit himself had already heard what had taken place in Nottingham – what Robin Hood had done – but even so, seeing it with his own eyes left him spellbound.

It looked as though the city had returned to forest. Even the highest buildings, the counting houses and the merchants' guild, were hidden beneath towering branch and thick foliage.

Boughs broke through the roof of the cathedral, so now it looked more tree than church. Above this sea of green, a flock of doves wheeled in the evening sun.

'Well – we won't need to breach the walls – Robin has done that for us,' said Jack, finally breaking the silence. 'Shall I run a message to the castle?'

'No – let them come to us,' said Kit. 'Light fires all along this ridge. Share out the wineskins. I want them to hear us in that castle.'

Around their campfires, the rebels ate and drank and sang, all through the dusk and the darkness and the early hours, while Kit sat apart, silent and watchful.

Finally, just after dawn, a lone rider appeared at the city walls. They made their way through a buckled gateway, then crossed the river before winding their way up towards the coppice, and the waiting host. As the rider drew near, Kit was not surprised to see it was Marian herself who came to meet them.

'There's no need for this show of force,' she said, reining in her horse and running her gaze across the great line of rebels crouching in the undergrowth. 'The Sheriff is dead.'

'So we were led to believe,' Kit said. 'The news is spreading like wildfire. Yet now we're here, we find it's a lie.'

'He's dead, trust me,' Marian insisted. 'I buried him myself.'

'In that case,' Kit said, 'what can that be?' He pointed towards the crumbled castle, wrapped in greenery. The Keep stood relatively intact, and above it fluttered a red and black banner. At this distance, its emblem was just visible: a wolf's head, its teeth bared. 'I could swear that was the Sheriff's sigil.'

'I told Rex he should take it down.' Marian shrugged. 'He wouldn't listen. He is his own man. He is not beholden to me, nor the old order.'

'And you,' Midge spat, standing behind Kit, glaring at her.

'Whose side are you on? I never thought I'd see the day. Marian Delbosque, running messages from the castle.'

'More to the point, what about Robin?' said Jack. 'When we march into the city, is he with us, or against us?'

'This is what I'm trying to tell you,' Marian said. 'There doesn't need to be sides. Not any more. Rex is not your enemy.'

Midge snarled. 'That's not how it looked when he came to burn Gaia.'

'If Rex wants peace, let him prove it,' said Kit. 'These are our demands.'

Ira handed him a scroll, which he held out for Marian. She took it, unrolled it, read the script. Then she shook her head.

'I can tell you now, he won't agree to any of this.'

'Either he grants us what we need, or we take it by force,' Kit said. 'Do not regard that as an idle threat. You know better than anyone how long we've fought, and what fighting has cost us. And now, if anyone thinks, even for an instant, that we will willingly put our necks in another man's noose, they are mistaken. Tell your son that. Send me his answer by midday.'

Marian looked tempted to say more, but finally held her tongue. After peering one last time along the rebel ranks, she turned her horse and started back towards the city, while Kit watched her go, deep in thought.

'He must think I'm moon-touched,' Rex said, pacing back and forth across the Great Ward, between lumps of fallen masonry. 'Disband my army? We'd have civil war. We'd have chaos on the streets.'

'Don't let it rile you,' Marian said, watching him pace. 'This is called talking terms. He doesn't expect you to meet every condition. It's just his opening gambit.'

'How dare he come here demanding anything,' Rex said,

increasingly agitated. 'He should be swinging from the gallows! He killed Alpha Johns. He slaughtered my men.'

'You need to keep a calm head. A rash move now could be disastrous. Your defences are broken. He has strength in numbers. Who knows, if he enters the city . . . the lowborn folk may rise up with him.'

He turned on her. 'They wouldn't dare.'

'They rose up against the Sheriff. They fought to save me and Robin. Now . . . things are more complicated. I couldn't say which way it would go.'

Rex dropped his head, then looked at her once more. 'But you'd be with me. You . . . and Robin.'

'No,' Marian said, holding his gaze, 'we wouldn't.'

'So you'd side with the rebels?'

Marian sighed. 'I'll tell you what I told Kit. I'm not taking sides. My fight is finished. So is Robin's. I'm trying to help you and Kit see eye to eye. That's my only part in this.' She held out the scroll. 'Look again at his demands. Not all of them are so unreasonable. He wants you to stay out of the Lost Lands, swear to keep your soldiers away from Gaia.'

'Who is he to tell me where I can and cannot go?'

'He's trying to safeguard the forest, can't you allow him that? In any case, don't you see, you need Gaia as much as he does.'

Footsteps crunched, and they turned to see a ranger entering the ward. He was dishevelled and coated in dust from the road.

'Forgive me, sire,' the messenger said. 'I bring word from the northern shires. Earl Houser is massing his forces. He is ready to pledge fealty but is seeking reassurances.'

Going to one knee in front of Rex, he offered up a scroll. While Rex broke the seal and read the contents, Marian was struck afresh by his bearing. There was no doubt, since the Sheriff's demise, he had grown into himself. Marian had watched him striding around the castle, issuing orders with a conviction that left no scope for disobedience. She had seen seasoned rangers and wily old advisers bow their heads with equal deference, and she could not deny that, yes, this role suited him well. It was almost as if . . . as if this truly had been his destiny all along, to wear the Sheriff's crown.

With a wave of his hand, Rex dismissed the messenger, then stood staring into the distance, looking pensive.

'Earl Houser was ever the sly fox,' she told him. 'He'll whimper while it suits him, but he'll be the first to pounce on any sign of weakness. Send him a clear message by—'

She stopped herself, held up her palms. 'Forgive me. Old habits. You don't need me telling you your business.'

Rex softened then, and slumped, pressing his thumbs to his temples. 'What if I do?' he said quietly. 'What if I can't do it?'

She hesitated, then said: 'We only know one thing for certain: this throne will be occupied. If not by you, then who?'

'Beware, though,' said a voice behind them. Robin had appeared from nowhere and now stood with his head bowed, the eyes of his wolf-head cowl gleaming. 'This power you adopt is not to be worn lightly. It will grow on you like a second skin. It will try to make you its slave.'

Rex glared at him. 'You'd know all about that.'

'Yes.'

'But I'm not you,' Rex said through gritted teeth, regaining his fire, glaring at them both. 'I'm not either of you.'

'You are formed of the same stuff,' Robin said. 'As was the Sheriff.'

'He . . . was a monster.'

'Fear and hatred made him thus.'

'I've heard enough,' Rex spat. 'You were right, Mother, I don't need your advice. And I don't need his.' He stabbed a finger at Robin. 'You had your time. You tried your way. Look where it's left us.'

Marian listened to this exchange with a wrenching of her heart. All those years she had dreamed of seeing Robin and Rex together; father and son united at last. She had imagined a natural affinity between them; a bond that would transcend the time they had lost. But here in front of her was the reality. Three times since the Sheriff died, the pair of them had come face to face, and each time it was the same. Rex met Robin with nothing but hostility – as though he blamed Robin alone for all his personal woes and every ill of the world.

'Go back to the rebel chief,' Rex told Marian, turning his back on Robin. 'Give him *my* demands. Tell him to disband *his* army. The rebels must return to their homes . . . Now. Kit and the other leaders must stand trial as traitors.'

Marian shook her head sadly. 'He won't give himself up, you know that. You'll only fan the flames.'

'I've stated my terms. That's my final word.'

All day long, Marian went back and forth between Rex and the rebels, delivering demands and counter-demands, threats and counter-threats. She did her best to temper the missives, blunting the sharpest language and omitting the most ludicrous ultimatums.

Even so, the standoff continued and became more febrile. The rebels on their wooded hilltop grew restless, endlessly sharpening their blades. The Sheriff's men were increasingly tense, rumours circulating among them that the rebels were preparing to burn the city to the ground; or that foreign invaders were massing at the coasts, intending to join the uprising. Several rangers tried to desert, only to be caught and placed in the stocks. Hour by hour, as the city baked beneath a ceaseless sun, the situation struck Marian more and more like a powder keg, which any moment could explode.

'He is willing to grant you a pardon – every one of you,' Marian said, standing in front of Kit yet again.

'A pardon from what?' Kit scoffed. 'From defending our own lives, and the forest?'

'He has two conditions,' Marian went on. 'The first is this: the shire-folk must return to their homes, and swear never again to take up arms. Secondly . . . he wants all the gold in Robin Hood's cave.'

Jack laughed harshly. 'I bet he does. And he'll use it to rearm against us.'

'He needs funds to rebuild the city,' Marian said, rubbing her eyes, suddenly feeling deathly tired. 'He is trying to see a way forward.'

She paused, head bowed, and when she looked up she allowed herself to speak freely, for the first time since negotiations began.

'He's scared, Kit. That's the truth of it. Not because of your army. Because this is a new world. It's unexplored. For everyone. You need to give him something to work with. In return . . . he'll start to see that you're not so different from him. That fundamentally you want the same thing.'

Kit looked at her steadily. 'Do we? What makes you imagine that?'

'Because you both walk the same Earth. It's like we used to say to the troops back in Sherwood. All those bands – all those different creeds and backgrounds – yet we pulled them all together. We made them see, underneath, that we *are* the forest, each and every one of us.'

She surprised herself and Kit by reaching out on impulse and touching his chest, above his heart. 'There's goodness in you, Kit. Just as there's goodness in Rex. It's been buried deep. How could it not be, with the path you've had to tread. But now that goodness can rise to the surface. And it will. I believe it will. Otherwise . . . what hope is left?'

She fell quiet and everyone looked at her, Kit's expression

a little softer, perhaps, but still difficult to read. Eventually, he said: 'All right, go back to him. Tell him—'

'No,' Marian said, interrupting, a palm raised. 'Tell him yourself.' She dropped her head. 'I'm done,' she said, suddenly knowing it was true. 'Now it's up to you two. It's up to all of you.'

She looked into the eyes of Jack and Ira and Midge – the last survivors of her and Robin's outlaw army, these warriors with whom she had suffered and fought and laughed and lived free all those years – all of that gone, echoes from a world long vanished.

What will take its place? What will come next?

That's for them to decide, she answered herself as she turned away, leaving them for the last time and heading back towards the city, nothing in her mind now except being once again, finally, with Robin.

'Are you sure you want to do this?' Robin said, as the pair of them met in the ruins of the White Tower, a pack strapped across Marian's back.

She nodded. 'I did all I could. Now our being here is only making things worse. You've heard what the soldiers are saying. Half of them think you're going to turn on them, finish what you started. The other half believe you and I are standing against the rebels. The citizens are divided against each other and don't know which way to turn. Once we're out of the way, things will be simpler. For everyone.'

'What about Rex?'

'He won't listen to me, and nor should he. We have to trust him to do what's right. Kit, too. It's their future. They need to shape it together.'

'I meant . . . don't you want to say goodbye?'

Marian peered up at the Keep, which was still standing strong and square. As the gloaming darkened, one window

440

was bright with candlelight. She could just make out a shadowy figure moving around inside. Rex had been in there all day and into the evening, organizing guard details, receiving reports from scouts, talking to the castellan and the craftsmasters about reconstruction of the battlements.

Yes, Marian did want to go to him, desperately. Except, what would she even say? Ever since they had been reunited, he had treated her like a stranger. It was as though, in his deepest heart, he didn't truly believe it was her – that his mother never did return from the wastes.

No, with a lump in her throat she had to admit that Kit was right – what he had said back at Gaia – Rex was lost to her. Their bond was broken, and now he must go on alone.

She reached into her pack, drew out a sealed scroll. 'I've written to him,' she said. 'Tried to explain . . . everything.' She rolled a lump of masonry with her foot, placed the scroll in the cavity beneath, before rolling the stone back into place. 'If he's meant to find it, he will. Perhaps, by then . . . he'll be ready to understand.'

She took a deep breath, wiped a tear from her cheek. 'Ready then?' she said to Robin. 'No point putting it off any longer. Let's get underway.'

Standing on the top floor of the Keep, Rex watched them depart. He had dismissed his advisers and stood alone, and now he allowed the tears to come. Part of him yearned then to run down through the castle and catch up with his mother, beg her not to leave.

But a deeper part knew he was deluding himself. That figure he saw down there, now passing through the city gates, was not his mother at all. Not in the truest sense. The manner in which she negotiated with the outlaw chief was final proof, had he needed it. His mother of old would have set herself on fire to secure terms – to bend the world to her will. Not so this person who had gone patiently back and forth from the castle, delivering demands in dispassionate tones. This being was more like a ghost, a visitation from the past, than someone of flesh and blood.

And that other figure at her side – who was he?

He too was unreal. This phantom figure who trod the Earth without a sound, who came and went without leaving a trace. Who acted as if the whole world was beneath him. How dare he appear in Rex's life as if bestowing a gift, as if gracing him with his mere presence! Good riddance. Rex had asked nothing from him, and needed nothing, and was glad he was gone.

And yet, even as he was thinking these things, that yearning increased – it tugged at him physically, insisting he run after Marian and Robin, to keep them here, at least a while longer. An awful empty feeling was opening inside of him, as if he was forgetting something vital – that he had something crucial to say to them, or they to him.

But no – this was simply more delusion. They had said it all, hadn't they?

There's one thing for certain: this throne will be occupied. If not by you, then who?

Beware . . . this power you adopt . . . it will grow on you like a second skin.

These last words echoed over and over in Rex's mind. Hadn't he said a similar thing to the Sheriff in his last moments . . . ?

The Sheriff of Nottingham . . . it is the skin you live in.

His mind whirled, a maelstrom of ideas and memories. In recent days, he had heard so many words from Marian and Robin, and now they all came rushing back in at once, forming a storm of confusion.

You are formed of the same stuff . . .
Fear and hatred made him thus . . .
You need Gaia as much as he does . . .

Until suddenly, there in the eye of the storm, there was a moment of clarity. Yes, he suddenly knew with certainty, Marian and Robin had said everything they needed to. He had the sense that it would take weeks, years, perhaps a lifetime, to fully absorb all they were trying to impart, and to understand completely what their lives meant.

But he understood, too, in that moment of lucidity, that their lives *did* mean something, and would continue to inform his, from this day to his last. They had lighted a path, and left way-markers, so he need not blunder aimlessly in the dark.

Rubbing at his eyes, collecting himself, he walked out of the chamber to where sentries were standing guard.

'Sergeant, I want you to run a message to the outlaws,' he said. 'Tell their chief . . . this has gone on long enough. I want to meet him, just the two of us, face to face. We need to find a way forward, and we need to start now.'

II. Return to the Forest

They travelled on foot, so the journey took a long time. But the wastes were kind to them the entire way, the air still, the sun softened behind white clouds, so the distance passed with ease, the pair of them talking lightly, or silently content with one another's company.

On the sixth day, at sunset, they came within sight of Gaia. The trees were bathed in a deep red glow, some of the leaves already turning orange and russet and red as the summer came to an end. As they approached, the leaves whispered in the breeze, like children sharing secrets.

When they reached the moat-like ditch and the wall of thorns, they found there was already an archway for them to walk through, and a log-bridge, waiting.

'It remembers us,' Marian said. 'It's welcoming us home.' They crossed the bridge and stepped off into the beechwoods. 'It always felt that way, returning to the forest, when we'd been away. A homecoming. The smell of it! In autumn, most of all. The damp soil, and the moss, and the mist. Oh, Robin, we didn't have a choice. We had to fight for this, didn't we?'

She was crying, sobbing into her palms, and Robin held her.

'I can't help thinking we made a mess of everything – and

now we've left it all to Rex. And Kit and the rest. But what else could we have done?'

'I don't know,' Robin said softly. 'I'm not so sure any of it was up to us.'

'You mean the goddess – and Cernunnos? They're the ones?'

'Yes, except, even them – it's only just coming clear to me, but I think even they were just a tiny part of all this. Like . . . the buds on a single branch. And the tree is vast, and the roots run deeper than we can even imagine.' He shook his head. 'We could never figure it out. I just know . . . somehow, we can trust it.' He took her hand. 'Come on. Not far to go.'

In silence, they went deeper into Gaia, through the glades and across streams and wildflower meadows, until the waste-lands outside began to feel very distant and unreal, so that for Marian this island of wildwood might be the world entire. Or . . . that the great forest might have been reborn, in all its vast, primal splendour. Yes, here they were, surely, in the very depths of Sherwood, far beyond the reach of the human realm, this place alive with sprites and dryads, teeming with songbirds and whistling frogs and all the myriad kinds of insects.

She tugged at Robin's arm. 'Maybe we don't need to do this,' she said quietly. 'We could live here, after all. We won't bother anyone, they won't bother us.'

'We've tried that before. Elysium Glades, remember? How long before they haul us back in? What if they come again, and threaten Gaia? Could we sit back, do nothing?'

Marian dropped her head, rubbed at her eyes. 'It's just so peaceful here. It's hard to believe it won't always be this way.' She looked up, tightened her grip on him. 'But you're right. We agreed. They'll never leave us alone. We've been separated too many times. Never again.'

Once more they went on, clambering now up the mossy slopes that led to the centre of Gaia. And they came at last before the awesome presence of the Mother Tree. Without a word, hand in hand, they stood beneath it, while in its branches and its bole its countless inhabitants scurried and scuttled and chirped, and through its leaves the breeze spoke in greeting.

Finally, at some unspoken signal, they moved forward in tandem and went to hands and knees and crawled together through the wide fissure at the base of the oak. Inside its trunk was a honeycomb of crawlspaces and low chambers. Side by side, they felt their way through this labyrinth. It was very dark in here, and quiet, apart from the sound of the songbirds echoing down through the colossal trunk. Marian's hand brushed against something dry and brittle that in her mind's eye could only be a human skeleton.

'Are you frightened?' Robin asked.

'No,' she replied truthfully. 'This is a good place to be, isn't it? There are nests and burrows – I can hear the creatures. It's quite warm. I know I'm crying, but I shouldn't be. We've very lucky.'

He stopped and held her.

'It's not too late to change your mind.'

She pressed her cheek to his. 'It's all right,' she whispered. 'I'm not afraid, really I'm not. How could I be when I'm with you? Let's stop here. This is perfect.'

She sat and opened her backpack. After groping inside, she drew out two mushrooms. Their caps were so vividly red that they were faintly visible even in this gloom.

'These will help us sleep,' she said, a slight crack in her voice. 'That's all this is. Sleep. With no one to disturb us.'

'Cernunnos told me once . . . that nothing is ever destroyed. It's only transformed.'

'Yes, that's it. How can it be otherwise?' She wiped at her eyes. 'That first day I met you – when you came charging out of your shelter, remember, butting like a boar – you were a force

446

of nature, then and always, and I loved you – I loved you that moment and for ever. Where could that love go? How could it ever stop? It never can! It will go on and on and on, no matter what.'

'Yes,' he said simply, closing one palm around hers, holding with her the mushrooms. 'I will dream of us in the forest. We'll run free. Always.'

'That's all you have to say?' she laughed through tears. 'I always was the talker, but can't you do better than that? Maybe I am a bit afraid, after all, because I'm gabbling, but that's only because it's a big leap, isn't it, and you know what, it's an adventure too – like all those adventures we planned in the tower, remember, to Byzantium and Persia and the rest, but this is the greatest adventure of them all and we're taking it together and we're so blessed, and maybe what I'm afraid of is going first, and you not being there yet, so shall we do it together, on my word? Are you sure there's nothing else you want to say to me first?'

'Thank you for coming back for me. Thank you for everything.'

And he removed his hand from hers, taking one of the mushrooms, and she watched the glimmer of it rise and disappear. And she gasped, and hurriedly stuffed the other one in her own mouth and chewed the sour musty thing and swallowed it and cried.

What now? What should she say? What was there left to say? Or do? She found she was lying on the ground, on her side. Had she meant to move? She sensed Robin shift against her, lying down too, against her back, wrapping his arms and his cloak around her, enfolding her in warmth and a feeling for which she had no name – a feeling that went far beyond love and beyond words.

And then there was only the stillness. The stillness of her own body, and the stillness at her back. At some point, she realized that something had changed. Robin's breathing had changed. It had stopped. And that was all right. That was how it should be.

Marian stayed until she was sure he was gone, and she stayed a moment longer, just long enough to know that nothingness had fallen upon her – long enough, just for an instant, to dwell within it – and to know, with absolutely certainty, that the nothing is everything.

Epilogue

A rora was not surprised when Gaia rose into view. That this place should appear to her now seemed inevitable, in fact. Fated.

The last of her food and water was long gone, and she was painfully hungry and thirsty, yet a deep contentment welled in her as she made her way across the wilderness, and ahead of her the fabled forest grew and grew.

After her brother died, Arora had tried leaving the wastes, wandering aimlessly through half-deserted villages, sometimes staying for a while, helping work the fields and the crofts, receiving food and shelter in return. But always she would get restless, and go on again, treading the old paths with the tinkers and the vagrants, begging for food, sharing the campfires of strangers.

In the end, she returned to the wastes. At first she barely understood why. Was it mere force of habit – because it was all she and Lucas had ever really known? Or was it more than that? Why had their father led them here in the first place? Had they truly come seeking relics and riches?

No – it had never been that. Not truly. As Arora kept on towards Gaia, watched it sparkle in all its spellbinding splendour, she finally understood. It was this place. The forest.

Somewhere in the depths of their souls, this was what they had been searching for all along.

The last furlong was slow going because wherever she walked saplings and bushes were sprouting out of the cracked earth, impeding her progress. The land all around Gaia was sprouting vegetation. Even now it was raining – not one of the harsh downpours of old, but a cool soothing drizzle – and the leaves of the saplings glistened with it while the soil sighed.

Yes, the wastes were changing. If Arora had suspected that before, she now knew it for certain. And here was the heart of that transformation. The last fragment of the great forest was sending out its suckers and its seeds, reclaiming the cursed earth, breathing life into it once more.

She passed through the newborn shrubbery and reached the mother forest. She stood in awe beneath its towering trees, listening to the chattering, wailing cacophony arising from within, gazing into its dark, primal depths.

From further up the treeline, a heavy crack of movement startled her, made her twist her head. What was that? Only now did she recall that this place, Gaia, was the lair and fortress of the rebels. Were they there in the undergrowth, watching her?

No. The outlaws were encamped above the city, in their wooded fastness, everyone knew that. They had been there for weeks, under the leadership of a man they called Robin Hood, facing off against a man who named himself the Sheriff, locked in a brittle stalemate. Perhaps one day peace would reign – or the war would return once more to Gaia.

'But until then, little brother,' she said aloud, 'we have this place all to ourselves.'

A deep ditch encircled the island of wildwood. Briar and blackthorn had colonized this moat. But here and there natural tunnels cut through the undergrowth. Locating one of these, going to her hands and knees, Arora crawled through, crossing a fallen log that served as a bridge.

Reaching the far side, she stood and breathed, taking in these scents she had never experienced, yet somehow were as familiar as her own name, as intimate as her own skin. She stooped at a spring to scoop cool water into her parched mouth, then she went onwards, deeper into the wildwood, its barking, shrieking cacophony enveloping her until she felt she was not walking through air but was swimming through sound.

She stared skywards into the crowns of the beech trees, tall enough to brush the clouds. She gazed in wonder at the giant fern fronds, each as big as a man. Her eyes darted after every flick and flash of movement – every scuttle and jump and flap – until she felt dizzy with it all and heard herself laugh.

'This is it, little brother,' she breathed. 'We've found it at last. This is where we belong.'

At first she had thought she was going mad, when she heard herself talking to her brother like this. But now she thought nothing of it. Often he would answer her back, and even this felt natural and correct.

'We can live here, can't we?' she went on saying to him, as she crossed a burbling brook and entered a wildflower meadow. 'If the outlaws return . . . so be it. We could even go back out to the villages, lead others here. No – don't be like that,' she told him. 'I know those people weren't always kind. But all that is behind us. This is their place, as much as it's ours.'

Talking this way, excited in a way she had not known since her father was alive, she went on wandering through the forest, running her fingertips across the cooling moss and the lichen-quilted boles of trees.

Finally, she came to a small lake, which glistened and glinted in the evening light, a radiant mist drifting across its surface, while fish plopped unseen. Here she stopped and sat back against a tree and just breathed. In the boughs, a pair of squirrel kits scampered. On the far bank, two otters stopped, nose to nose, before diving beneath the waters. Further off a fox and a vixen watched her, motionless.

A bright-coloured bird skimmed the lake before landing on a branch alongside its mate. Arora watched them, preening their blue and orange feathers. Her father had described this type of bird to her – he used to watch them whenever he ventured into the forest, before the Great Fire. Halcyon birds. Yes, that's what he had called them.

A breath of wind rippled the lake, skittered dry leaves. To Arora, in this moment of peace, the noise was exactly like two children running – the breeze whispering through the trees sounded so much like laughter that she found herself turning, scanning the greenery.

'We're not the only ones who've come home,' she said quietly. 'They're here too, aren't they?'

Lucas gave no response. Perhaps he had gone to sleep. If so, it was for the best. It was all right for him. Arora had work to do. It would be dark soon, and she was famished. She needed to collect firewood, and forage for supper.

Pausing only to watch the halcyon birds dart away, vanishing into the dusk, she turned and moved deeper into Gaia, while nightjars sang of the coming dark, and the promised dawn, and all around her the life of the forest went on and on.

ACKNOWLEDGEMENTS

The first and fiercest champion of *The Blind Bowman* has been my agent, James Wills. Even when I got lost in the woods writing the second book, he kept faith in my work and the story I was trying to tell. I couldn't be more grateful for his advice, guidance, and friendship.

My deepest thanks also to all the fine people at David Fickling Books, past and present, for their unwavering support and patience. David Fickling himself has been a wellspring of wisdom and encouragement. Simon, Bella, Meggie, Rosie, Phil, Fraser, Linda and everyone else at DFB have been loyal allies. In particular, Anthony Hinton, my principal editor for *Dark Fire* and *Wildwood Rising*, helped propel this trilogy to the finish line. Anthony understands storytelling at a deeper level than I ever will, and has helped me out of a narrative tangle more times than I can count.

Most importantly, thank you to my wife, Lizzie. My best friend, confidante, soulmate, she has been at my side every step of the way. And to our wonderful daughters, Beatrix and Matilda, who make the journey a joy.

ABOUT THE AUTHOR

As a journalist, Tim Hall has written for various newspapers and magazines. He once worked as a reporter on the island of Bermuda, and has travelled widely in Asia and South America. It was during an adventure into the Amazon Rainforest that he was first inspired to retell the legends of Robin Hood. He now lives in rural Gloucestershire, England, with his wife and two daughters.

To find out more, visit his Substack page, *Wildwood Rising*: tkhallauthor.substack.com

Discover where it all began . . .

A world of gods and monsters, rolling their final dice.
A time of heroes and demons, and the horror that
shadows both.
The world of Robin Hood . . .

Robin Hood is transformed.

Blinded by the Sheriff, he takes refuge in the ancient
heart of Sherwood Forest, where primal powers and
forgotten magicks reach out to him. But the wildwood
itself is under threat, and the old gods face extinction.

Only the blind bowman, Robin Hood, together
with his soulmate, Marian, can stand against the
forces of darkness . . .

DARK FIRE

*'Sherwood knows. It knows something truly terrible
is approaching.'*

Robin and Marian fight on in their quest to save the
forest,and all it stands for: life, beauty, the impossible
made possible. But the Sheriff and his guards advance
ever closer, leaving raw destruction in their wake.

A forest-born boy turned man, whose past links
inextricably with Robin's. A vixen-goddess, whose
presence and power crawls under Marian's skin. Ghosts
of warriors, loved and lost.

All will shadow Robin and Marian at every turn, as they
strive to protect each other, their band of outlaws, and
Sherwood itself. As their relationship reaches breaking
point, they'll be engulfed by passion, hurt and sparks
which become brutal flames . . .